A Portrait of the Arsonist as a Young Man

Published by bluechrome publishing 2009

2 4 6 8 10 9 7 5 3 1

First published in Great Britain in 2009 by
bluechrome publishing
PO Box 109,
Portishead, Bristol. BS20 7ZJ
www.bluechrome.co.uk

A CIP catalogue record for this book is available from the British Library.

ISBN 978-1906061500

Ashes to Ashes c.1980 David Bowie
Reproduced by kind permission of Tintoretto Music/RZO Music Ltd/ EMI Music Publishing Ltd/ Chrysalis Music Ltd.

Heroes c.1977 David Bowie & Brian Eno
Reproduced by kind permission of Tintoretto Music/ RZO Music Ltd/ EMI Music Publishing Ltd/ Chrysalis Music Ltd.

Changes c.1971 David Bowie
Reproduced by kind permission of Tintoretto Music/ RZO Music Ltd/ EMI Music Publishing Ltd/ Chrysalis Music Ltd.

Excerpt from If On a Winter's Night a Traveller by Italo Calvino, published by Secker and Warburg. Reprinted by permission of the Random House Group Ltd.

Excerpt from The Outsider by Albert Camus, translated by Jospeh Laredo (Hamish Hamilton, 1982). Translation copyright Joseph Laredo, 1982.

We have attempted to contact any copyright holders regarding other quotes used within this book and acknowledge these rights accordingly. Please contact the publisher for further details.

Printed and bound in Great Britain by
CPI Antony Rowe, Chippenham and Eastbourne

A Portrait of the Arsonist as a Young Man

Andrew McGuinness

For Janice

The New Religion:

1. Write every day.
2. Read constantly.
3. Be serious, not solemn.
4. Love your characters.
5. Make specificity your King.
6. Show, not tell.
7. Address the human condition.
8. Edit, edit, edit.
9. Edit again.
10. Make every death in a story meaningful.
11. Break the ten commandments whenever necessary.

Imogen Wood, *Metaphorically Speaking* (Write-On Press, University of Pensbury, 2004).

"But the man is, as it were, clapped into jail by his consciousness..."

Ralph Waldo Emerson: (Essays, 1841)

One

In the beginning it was murder.

Until the prosecution commuted to manslaughter that is. They're hoping for a cast-iron conviction. It's laughable. There's no physical evidence, no material witnesses. I don't have any previous; not so much as picked my nose in private. And even if a jury convicts, mitigating circumstances will ride to my rescue. The brain experts think there's something up with me you see, when really it's just that I'm down.

Facts:

1. A building was burnt to the ground last Christmas.

2. A young man died in the blaze.

3. I fit the police profile.

4. The criminologists call me the "average" arsonist i.e. I'm disillusioned, male and twenty-five. I am all these things of course, but I've never believed in the law of averages and as the alleged fire-starter, I am very far from average.

God, what a fix I'm in. What a microscope I am under. Four walls confine and define me. They are my world: north, east, south and west, block upon block upon block upon block, clamped floor-to-ceiling and corner-to-corner. I've been entombed here for twelve weeks waiting for the trial of the century. Come judgement day I could be looking at life. This situation forces you to examine the minutiae. It makes you sit up and question everything you once held dear.

Since the summer my case has become a *cause celebre* and not just in Kent. The whole of England and beyond in fact. A cousin came to see me a fortnight ago - on Halloween - and I don't even have a cousin. He was a tricksy journalist from a foreign newspaper with a hidden camera in his shirt button.

The press want to know all about my life: where I come from, what my childhood was like, how awful my parents were. All that Holden Caulfield crap. That's why I'm putting the record straight, before anyone else does. This is the true story. The story of my family and the curse. But most of all this is about me, Ben Tippet. Like me or loathe me, I speak the truth; my life blighted by so many lies.

Welcome to Ben's world.

Let me say before I begin my cobbled-together story, it's the easiest thing in the world to do in theory yet the hardest to execute in practice. Not killing a man. No, that appears all too easy; even by accident. What I mean is writing about it. If you've ever watched a baby take its first steps, the way he puts one foot in front of another, maintaining a fragile balance between the unknown and familiar, you'll know what I'm talking about. A writer places words in a similar line hoping they won't fall. My own line is taut and precarious; a high-wire without a safety net. I've been tiptoeing along it since the age of sixteen and am still stumbling, still falling, but I always pick myself up and start over.

When I pace my cell (not metaphorical, a real one measuring 12' x 8' with walls so beige and lumpy they resemble vertical porridge), I wonder if my creative juices will dry up; if I will suffer from writer's breezeblock. But my well runs deep, my imagination climbs walls; if it's acceptable to use such a mixed metaphor.

It's ironic. On the outside I struggled to write much. Yet in here, I can't stop. It's as if freedom imprisoned my mind and now I'm locked up, I'm totally free to wander.

Of course, I'll be crucified for writing the way I do, about the things I do. Not least by my defence team who want me to say nothing before the trial opens. I'll be pinned upside-down on a cross for my myopic, wanton self-indulgence; my solipsistic life. Yet I ask the finger-pointers and gory-locks-shakers to consider this: how else can a book be written when it's in the first person? Our lives are lived to expiration in the first person singular. Fact: you come out of a velvet-lined woman alone, go into a velvet-lined box alone and what you do between these two compass points is complete chance. A tiny thought, a short breath, a brief touch; these things are felt so uniquely they may as well be DNA.

In the first person singular then, what I see is what you get, and what I give you ladies and gentlemen is the honest-to-God truth, as far as a 25-year-old can understand it. Alexander Fortune showed me how to write this way. By a million miles he is my favourite author and it is to him I dedicate *Fakers*. Alex being one of the best writers and fakers I've ever had the misfortune to sleep with. Actually, I'm being disingenuous. He is my literary idol, my icon and erstwhile lover. *Erstwhile*. Such a quaint word. Up until this point it means.

Not that long ago, during a BBC radio interview, Alex advised listeners to abandon all thoughts of writing until they were fifty. Why? Because he'd turned fifty and was grumpified about the bright young things outselling him at Waterstone's. The hypocrite! He wrote the finest book of his generation at the age of thirty-four. He often makes controversial statements - probably for free publicity - but one thing I remember him saying at a reading I organised last Spring was: listen to no one, read everybody. Sound advice I think, because I've never listened to anyone and you can never read too much in my opinion.

It's true, navel-gazing is the twenty-first century preoccupation, nonpareil, but you won't find the fluff of my life any more meaningful than yours. I can't claim to understand how the world works any more than the next person, though I can hazard a guess, can pin a tail onto the backside of a donkey in a darkened room. And what I'm guessing is that some people are born shite, some achieve shiteness and others have shiteness thrust upon them, as Shakespeare said. Though he might have said greatness.

So, if you want the meaning of life, you're in the wrong section. You need fantasy. If you desire a dashing hero or damsel in distress, ditto. But if you want to know about reality - why they think I killed a man in hot blood - this is for you. You might not like what you discover, but it's a hell of a journey. Think of yourself as my confidant, my wonder wall. I'll talk to you as if you're my best friend. God knows I could do with one. I might infuriate you, shout at you, sometimes make you sick, but I'll always come back to you, I promise, because you are all I have. Without you I'd not exist. I need you to read me like a book.

What kind? Prison journal? Diary? Memoir? Full-blown fiction? Not so much an autobiographical novel as a novel autobiography? The jury's out on genre so it's whatever you want it to be;

whatever you want *me* to be. Call it a journal if you like. A journal of discovery which I'll keep for company and posterity because I am a writer after all and some day the world will read me, will understand me, will recognise me for doing something decent for a change. Even if it is half made-up. You see, everything one invents is true. Beneath every lie a deeper truth lies buried.

Fiction is my life. I consume it (avid reader), sold it (used to work in Little's Bookshop) and write it (short stories, though there is a novel-in-progress). It's my passion and everybody needs a little passion. It's good for the circulation. I know I shouldn't digress (doing it already) but I'm prone to wander off, metaphorically speaking. After all, my mind is a maze, not a motorway, and I'm the rat in it. It's easy to lose the plot from day-to-day in here, so there's likely to be grammatical errors, time-switches, tense-confusions and jumping all over the place. These things can be moulded into shape with editing. Nothing is written in stone except names and dates on tombstones, isn't that right? If found guilty I'll have all the time in the world to do the editing - time to cover the tracks of my well-trodden path - after I've thrown up my soul. But for now, this is knee-jerk, raw and utterly true. *Ergo* (where does that word even come from?), this version is known in the literary business as "the shitty first draft". That's fine. I know the basic rules of creative writing, so I'm entitled to bend them.

It is only through the confining act of writing that the immensity of the nonwritten becomes legible, that is, through the uncertainties of spelling, the occasional lapses, oversights, unchecked leaps of the word and the pen. Calvino wrote that, in the year of my birth, and he knew his literary onions; although, perhaps, he could have done with a semi-colon.

Advice like this floods back to me in here from the cracked dam of my memory. Neuroscientists say memories are just physical things: electronic impulses and chemical reactions in the brain. They say that one day there'll be a machine who feels; a computer with personal memories all of his own; *Blade Runner* made real. I disagree. A memory is an emotion, a sense, a feeling, not just a thought. Remembering is the act of touching and being touched, like dipping your hand into the cool water of a stream on a hot day. It is watching the clear liquid running through your fingers and knowing there's a lot more water to slip through, and a lot more of you too. If that makes any sense?

I'm used to an ergonomic keyboard in the outside world but it's longhand-only inside. Not that I'm complaining. The handicap is fruitful. The process of writing directly from my brain, physically down my arm onto a page with Bic ink is conducive to "streams-of-consciousness" - a fancy term which means my thoughts willy-nilly as they come out in all directions and not necessarily in the right order; like a vigorously shaken bottle of champagne. I'm just hoping this will not be a case of shitty first draft to highly polished turd. That would play into the hands of the trigger-happy press.

Only time will tell.

You know, I write every day now as if I'm going to die at any moment; drop down dead with an aneurysm or a heart attack, whatever. This prospect acts as a sharp spur to my soul. Honest-to-God, I scribble like a maniac ten hours non-stop, slumping onto my smelly bed unable to release the pen from my crampy hand. Every writer should suffer for his art or his art will suffer for him and I'm no different.

From here on in I'm including inside brackets anything which occurs as I go along. Parentheses should be seen as question marks to myself. The good thing about brackets is that you can ignore what's in them without losing the essential cut-and-thrust of plot (plot, Ben?). They should be treated like DVDs in the box-sets of your favourite films. The Director's Cut. In this case, *Fakers* the metaphorical movie. If you look closely, the out-takes are revealing, mouth-watering, even if they do break the spell of cinematic magic (the illusion of perfection). If you see everything - warts and all - you understand that nobody's perfect. Unlike in real life, inside a fictional space you can change things and redeem yourself time and time again. You can make a hero out of a villain, can lift a phoenix out of the ashes.

To be honest (irony), I'd like to be writing this in my one-bed studio flat which overlooks Pensbury Cathedral. When you're locked in your cell twenty hours a day (I have single occupancy which is a blessing and a curse), writing keeps you sane. It's just about possible to block out the radios, TVs, shouting and banging of doors and echoes of screams. Of course, the testosterone-driven sweat and rotten vegetables can never be wiped from your tongue buds or nostrils. Prison is an overloaded bin. As Morrissey the megapopstar moaner once sang: 'Life is a pigsty'. I don't think he's ever been to prison to know how true that is.

During my first week here, in the full glare of August, the heat was unbearable. The pong from the in-cell lavatory was toe-curling. I paced a track into the concrete like an ape in a zoo. Three long strides to the door, turn, three long strides to the bed and barred window. Twelve weeks on, I stride less. I take a circular route. It makes the journey longer and more interesting.

What's it really like inside? Rise and shine at 6-45 to the sound of the Big Brother bell. Breakfast an hour later. Back to cells, then thirty minutes association time i.e. you get to stand in a queue for the telephone or shower. What's more important you ask yourself: cleanliness or speaking to your loved ones? I pride myself on my appearance. You're allowed your own clobber on remand. All my clothes are top notch. It's not possible to keep clean though. I get five minutes in the shower and I'm thinking: what do the other prisoners get up to in these cubicles? Enough to make you feel dirty no matter how much you soap up.

Back to cells. Let out again at 11-30.

At noon, the "remanders" do lunch, then we are led outside for fresh air. Actually, if the weather's fine this is nice. There's a lovely quad with a quiet lawn dotted with benches and three large palm trees massed in the centre. Their trunks feel like coconut husks. The palms are supposed to symbolise peace, aren't they? Weren't they laid down at Jesus of Nazareth's feet? Then look what happened to him. Or was it olive branches? Or are they the same thing? I don't know much about religion or horticulture. My mother would kill me if she knew my childhood indoctrination has dissolved; if it's possible for a Catholic to forget. My mother's the social secretary at her local church. She's a good Catholic. Her finger is firmly placed on the Papal pulse.

You walk around the quad taking lungfuls of freedom; the same air people breathe on the other side of the wall without knowing how precious it is. You stare at the sky, the clouds framed by high prison walls, regretting things. The prison is only two miles from my flat. During these half-hour walks I imagine growing magic realism wings like those of *The Old Man*...by Gabriel Garcia Marquez. I recommend this story. I read it on Imogen Wood's creative writing course. Like desperate Daedalus, I fly clear of the prison walls, climb high above the city and the chiming cathedral belfry to my front door, closing my wings over as I pass inside. Then I listen to David Bowie on my Bang and Olufsen. The speakers alone cost me a thousand pounds. I really miss my music; Bowie especially. He's always on my mind in here, for reasons I shall go into later.

You get a shout from an officer, then banged up in cells again. At 4pm, it's dinner; way too early and pretty awful. A high-fat, high-carb coronary concoction designed to keep you on the toilet for as long as possible. Congealed pizza, chips and beans. Some things are double-fried. They look and taste like they've been digested already. If you're not careful you can bloat into a real porker before your trial comes up. You can turn into a spotted dick. I've seen it happen to others who've been in longer.

At 5pm you watch a large flat-screen TV; better than the midget one in your cell with a snowstorm picture and only four channels: S, H, I and T. Or you play pool, bar football, do a few weights in the corner, read tabloids, make telephone calls, or stay in your cell. No one goes back to their cell. That would be madness. You watch some freak show TV, have a joke with remanders. You have to be careful though. Got to keep your head down. Stay out of trouble. This isn't Butlins at Bognor. Sometimes it feels like another country altogether. Lots of inmates don't speak English. They are caught at the coast and transferred here to wait for visas, permits, passports, return fares, whatever. They're really quite skinny and huddle together in groups arranged by country of origin, language and religion like something out of *Star Wars* or the United Nations. The English guys are as tough as government-issue toilet paper, off their heads on methadone or doing cold turkey from heroin. They're itching for something to do, like riot. You quickly work out who to avoid. Some innate, animal instinct survival thing. This is a jungle after all. A pigsty jungle.

There's one guy in here called Manston, which is also the name of a local airport, and very close-sounding to the infamous Charles Manson, serial killer. He's from planet Thanet. I like to think he is more Caliban than cannibal. Mid-30s, thick-set, sartorially inelegant in every way; over-faded denims and grotesque football t-shirts, the arms ripped out so he can show off his muscles and tattoos. Around his upper arms are barbed-wire tattoos, and what's that around his neck? A series of dotted lines with a pair of scissors at one end and two words: *Cut here.* Like he's a coupon in a magazine. One forearm is decorated with a pointy blue starburst. His body art is creeping over him like skin cancer. He doesn't need hate on his knuckles, it is stamped in his eyes. You got to avoid his eyes. He's clichéd but he is what he is - a hairy white muscle awaiting trial for armed burglary, and not his first. All the calibanality of someone vastly uneducated. I sometimes wonder if clothes are the only things dividing the homo sapien from the wider animal kingdom. Still, I like to think that even the ugliest person in the world has one admirable physical feature. In Manston's case, perfectly peaked biceps. When he holds the pool cue vertically, waiting for his next shot, the muscles bulge and ripple. A cheapskate's Marlon Brando.

A prison officer told me to steer clear of Manston, as if I needed telling. The officer is called Red but his real name is Rodney Buchanan. People call him Red because of his Celtic colouring: red in the face, red hair, red eyebrows. He speaks with a low, soft, whispery, sometimes whistley Glaswegian accent. This is in complete contrast to his stature. He is so large that when he stands in front of anyone, they disappear. Probably part of the job description: must be six feet tall, stand all day, jangle keys non-stop and have enough physical strength to hold down psychopaths.

'A string of previous,' Red said. 'All involving violence. Steer right clear of Manston.' As if I needed telling twice. I like Red. He is an uncle you run to when you're in trouble. Not my real uncle in the outside world, of course. My Uncle Davina. He's a transsexual and capable of inflicting a different sort of damage on a person.

No later than 7pm you are shuffled back to your cell. Lockdown is at 9pm. The lights go out, your stomach rumbles, your mind turns over noisily. There are no other natural sounds except shouting and murmurs from officers. The only light thrown onto the cell floor is blue, from the moon when it is high on a cloudless night. You think of the room you should be sleeping in. Your home; as the bird flies just a few minutes north-west of here. If all goes according to plan I'll be back there in a few weeks. If all goes bad...don't think about it.

Two

My mother tuts disapprovingly at the state of me.

'Withering away,' she says, shaking her tidy head. She wipes yesterday's coffee cup rings from the visitor's table with a tissue. She's a very hygienic person, which is where I get it from. We are pernickety perfectionists of Howard Hughesian proportions. She comes twice a week, would visit every day, but it's a 150-mile round trip from Bedfordhsire to here. I suspect it upsets her seeing me like this. She doesn't often show her feelings in public. Another gene I've inherited. We are taciturn when it comes to feelings. *Taciturn.* Such a lovely word. It never seems to go out of fashion.

My father is less circumspect, more prone to honesty, though he masks what he really thinks by talking about mundane trivialities during our forty-minute slots. My mother taps my wrist saying, 'Everything will be alright, Benjamin. We've got the best QC in England.' And Dad talks about a) terrorists b) weather c) football results and d) beds. The real world I suppose (a convoluted digression, Ben, and you want to get on with the forward-thrust, the flaming story).

My dad owned and managed a successful bed emporium for thirty years. He was Captain Tippet steering at the happy helm of Bedz 4 Zedzzz. Talk about cheesy! His whole life was governed by frames and mattresses imported from around the globe. He sold side-tables and upholstered boudoir furniture, cheap pine things at £99 a double, all the way up to classic French Bateau Lit worth £2,000. As a teenager, I earned pocket-money in the warehouse. I sold a lot of magic foam in my time. Dad sold the business a few years back because of the accident. Hilarious story if you ever heard it down the pub and weren't involved. A highly-polished sleigh bed (suspended from the ceiling by wires) fell onto his spine, crushing three vertebrae to oblivion. He's in a wheelchair now.

The Tippet Curse. He has it. I have it. My brother, Tom, had it. I was in Brighton doing a BA in Media Studies at the time of the accident. I ran the family business for a few months, never returning to university. There was nothing on the course I couldn't teach myself anyway. I put my father back on his feet (figuratively speaking) and then I moved to Pensbury to work as an estate agent.

Don't hate me already. If anything sends me down in this trial it will be the revelation that I used to sell houses, but someone has to do it. It was only for a few weeks and the commission was good. I'm just brilliant at selling things: ideas, houses, beds, books, myself too. As a reward for keeping the bed business afloat my dad put a deposit down on a flat for me. Somehow - and it's a strong indication of character - he held no one responsible for his personal tragedy. He had accident insurance and received a healthy return, though now he's housebound and unable to feel his toes. Apart from a year's depression following the avalanche he is content with his lot in life. He's brave-faced and never complains (unlike me). He's 55 years old, wearing his thumbs out with boredom. It's my mother's job to keep him happy and she does it like a martyr to the cause.

I don't mean to patronise them if it ever seems like it. Your parents are literally your lifeline. My father is a strong man with an iron will and a quick mind, though from outward appearances he sometimes looks distant in a thick way; but he's not stupid, just lost in thought and space and time. He is a reliable car of a man. He made the Tippet family what it is: reasonably well-off. Not that long ago he bought me a brand new Saab (Turbo) and up until my incarceration in August was depositing money into my account every month. Now, of course, he's lining the pockets of the wily old lawyers.

It's true. I've been abusing their generosity for as long as I can remember. Quite literally, I've been making them pay for their deceit over the years (more of that to come: the heart of the matter, the meat on the bones of this carcass of a story). One of the things I've decided to change when I get out of here is to stop accepting hand-outs; to stand on my own two feet no matter how unsteady. My life will be different when I'm free. I won't lie to feel important. I will learn to trust people and like them for *who* they are, not *what* they do - unless what they do *is* who they are, of course. I'm aspirational to a fault, you see. I wasn't really cut out to be an estate agent. I don't think I'm cut out to be anything at all. I don't hold jobs down. I don't even know if Maurice (owner of Little's Bookshop) will keep my job open. Who in their right mind wants an arsonist working among their paperbacks? Guilty or not, there's no smoke without fire. Isn't that how the cliché goes? Taking me back would be like asking the butcher to look after the barber's shop.

Despite the media circus, Maurice and I remain on good terms, though right from the start our friendship was based on some whopping lies. He gave me the job on the back of a fifteen-minute conversation. This can still happen in the independent sector. No formal interviews or qualifications necessary. The bookshop was handed down to him by his parents when they moved to Majorca for retirement sunshine purposes. Maurice loves people who love books; those whose faces fit. I love books. My face fitted, or I made it fit. We struck up a conversation about J.D. Salinger (Maurice's favourite author) and I made a joke about having to wait a long time for another novel from that old man; although we must all get old at some time or other. Even Dorian Gray.

Maurice is ten years older than me. I told him my mother had been a beat poet and a satirical artist in the 1970s. Not totally false. She once voted Labour and attended part-time painting classes. The most successful lies are based loosely on truths, you see. I think Machiavelli said that. A politician anyway. You only have to believe in the truthful part (as the liar) and the lies fall into place like well-matched dominoes. I told Maurice my father had worked for a government intelligence agency. 'All very hush-hush'. In actual fact, Dad just wishes he'd been a spy and not a bed-seller all his life. 00Kevin or something. Maurice was sucked in. We went for a coffee and then I dropped my atom bomb: 'My parents died in a plane crash when I was six. I was brought up by my uncle.'

You get the shocked expression at first, then the sympathy vote. Actually, if you go in too quickly you can scare the pants off people. They think you're poxed with some sort of bad-luck gene (which I am); they want to run a million miles. But if you choose your victim with care and your timing's right and they're susceptible to hard-luck stories, they'll buy into it because they're humanistically-inclined. Maurice is this sort of man. I told him I had a media degree from Brighton (brilliant half-lie) and the fates kicked in. 'How about that?' he said. 'My wife Louise got a Library degree from Brighton.'

Small worlds...

To cut a potentially sleep-inducing short story shorter, he needed an extra pair of hands. A full-timer had gone walkies, then two part-time students came to the end of their degrees and quit the shop, skipped town and inherited a llama farm in the Australian outback. Who cares about them and their lives? There isn't the time or space anyway.

Everything was old-fashioned when I first arrived at Little's. I unloaded lorries and stacked shelves for a few weeks, then I graduated onto sales. I had to write ISBN numbers onto pieces of paper. The till looked like a giant old typewriter and made a *ping* when it opened. Very dusty and academic. A throwback. Something out of *Little's House on the Prairie* (ha-ha). There was a room dedicated to cartography and archaeology upstairs; the largest room in the rickety Tudor two-storey building. Only about ten people a week ever used it: academics from the cathedral archives and tourists getting lost. A total waste of space. Maurice is into history big time, especially medieval. It formed part of his first-class honours degree. This particular room was crammed with fusty things out of the dark ages: magnifying glasses; drapes at the windows; a pre-historic standard lamp (!); a large oak table in the centre for unfolding maps; woodworm-riddled chairs with maps on; maps of continents on three walls.

Maps, maps, maps.

I made Maurice look closely at the sales figures. 'How much money do you make on maps? This is a bookshop, not a reference library.' He had to agree, difficult though it was to alter anything his father (amateur archaeologist) had established over forty years. He agreed to reorganise the top floor. It took a month. Out went the old books (and maps), in came a raft of textbooks students actually needed. Pensbury is full of students. During term-time they make up 50% of the population. That's a council statistic. They come from every corner of the planet, should planets have corners. If for any reason the government banned students from existing (not so incredible if one remembers Mao's Cultural Revolution), Pensbury would turn into a deserted medieval village.

Anyway, I brought in titles relating to college courses and within a month books were flying off the shelves (very Harry Potter). You have to know your customers, I told Maurice. They are younger than they used to be. I made it my remit to modernise the shop as if I was Tony Blair the Evangelist. 'If you don't evolve, you dissolve, Maurice. We need to do what David Bowie has been doing for decades. Ring the *ch-ch-ch-changes*.'

Pensbury is called a city because it has a cathedral but really it's just a busy market town hemmed inside old flint walls; very pretty on a sunny day. Little's is off the beaten track, down a side street, not close enough to the cathedral where most of the tourists go. There are three huge bargain basement bucket bookstores within a 1-mile radius. We had to adapt or we'd fade from human memory like the duckbilled platypus. The chains were closing in. Maurice is a lousy bookseller. He's in love with the idea of running a bookshop but isn't geared up for it. His head is stuck in the clouds. I think he wants to sell up and do something else, like become a house-husband. He wants to have more children, for sure. If it wasn't for me, Little's wouldn't have been hooked up to the internet; supply and demand would have remained disproportionate etc. I installed a coffee machine and wired the place for sound (eclectic, relaxing jazz, ethnic, classical). We catered for the highbrow and the lowbrow without losing the literary mad-hatters (academics). I stopped drunks staggering in out of the rain smelling the place up. I let customers browse, but every twenty minutes approached them. 'Browsers don't fill the pockets of your trousers, Maurice.' The hard sell. We had to or the business would fold and disintegrate like a forgotten book. A relic.

All of this feels like a long time ago. So much has happened in the meantime.

Three

I love my parents.

There, I've said it. It isn't always easy to say. To the best of my knowledge, I cannot remember telling my parents that I love them; not when they came to see me the night of my arrest nor in the preliminary court hearing at which I pleaded innocent. I love them but have never told them and I wonder if this is their fault or mine. I told the shrink who came in to see me a couple of weeks ago that I didn't love them and she found this hard to believe; and she's not even met them. Her name is Dr Julie Sparkes. I don't give people these names, it's just how it is. She said it was my parents' fault I couldn't show my feelings because they'd been living a lie about my brother, Tom (holy smoke, now we're getting complicated with the plot). Let me explain. It has a strong bearing on matters. Be patient. My head's all over the place in here, just like my story. I can string a few gems together but they might not belong to the same piece of jewellery.

Nine years ago, on my sixteenth birthday, I caught a train to London with some school friends and we went to Soho. We wasted our money in a grubby strip club. It was embarrassing for many reasons. What money we had left we spent in Leicester Square getting drunk on expensive lager. My friends caught the train home and I spent the night at my uncle's flat, not far from Chelsea. I hadn't asked my friends to stay because the flat is too small (a pigeon coop) and anyway, my uncle seems freaky when you've never met him before. He gets nervous with strangers.

He was born David William Burton (my mother's older brother) but for years insisted on being called Davina (way before the famous one made it on TV). He had been uncomfortable with his gender, filled his wardrobe with skirts and dresses, his bathroom cabinet with moisturisers and concealers and lipsticks, his bedroom drawers with tights, knickers and bras. He said he was meant to be a woman and not a man. That's what he felt like on the inside and that's what he wanted to be on the outside. By my sixteenth birthday he had been a woman on the outside for almost six years. But we need to go back a few years, to my tenth birthday, when Uncle D first changed into a woman.

To my parents' dismay, s/he turned up "unexpectedly" on our doorstep, dressed as a woman. He brought me a budgie in a cage. A beautiful multi-coloured bird which died two months later in a vicious cat attack, but that really is another story and not relevant here. The look on my parents' faces when they saw my uncle/aunticle/whatever. He'd had the op! I took the budgie into the kitchen, poking my fingers through the bars. Uncle D was invited into the lounge for tea. My mother was like a lady desperate to leave the room for the toilet. She couldn't sit down or walk or talk normally, even though this was her only sibling. She knew he'd been taking hormones, having body hair removed and taking counselling, but deep down I don't think she ever expected he would have his tackle seen to. It went against everything she believed.

As a man he looked a little queer I suppose; on reflection. But to a boy of ten it made no odds. I'd grown up seeing him as a person not as anything else. He insisted on seeing me on my birthdays, either at his flat or at our home. His visit should not have been a surprise, so why was my mother so nervous that day? And my father, come to think of it. They were trying to shuffle Uncle D out the door and he'd only just arrived.

'I wish you'd said you were coming, David,' my mother said.

David? I was thinking. Davina was his new name. He put a perfumed hand on my shoulder. 'Don't I always see Benjamin on his birthday?'

'Thanks for the bird,' I said.

'What will you call him?' my father asked, trying to speed things up.

'*Her*,' Uncle D said.

'Point taken,' my mother said. She was a cat on a hot tin roof. Couldn't sit down, kept bringing things in and out of the kitchen, leaving them by my father who had similar ants in his pants. Such awkwardness over tea and biscuits. Uncle D soon got the message, brushing crumbs from his dress, saying his goodbyes. Relief flooded my mother's face. It was as if she'd been on the longest ever car journey, holding on to her waters all day and could finally see a service station on the appropriate side of the motorway. Uncle D made his way down our front path.

Then, just as he reached the handle of his car, my mother's eyes popped out of her head. I looked where she was looking. Father O'Rourke was parking his bronze Datsun at the kerb. It was exhilarating. Even at the age of ten I understood. Everything fell into place, especially my mother's misplaced embarrassment. Uncle D didn't rush off. He turned and blew a kiss for me, trilling in his highest voice: 'Look after my budgerigar, Benjamin.'

'He's called Davina!' I shouted back, just for the hell of it.

Father O'Rourke - a priest who looked close to retirement but never seemed to get there - threw a look of wonder at my uncle/aunticle, whatever. 'Hello, Father,' Davina said to him. Mother tottered down the path in her sling-backs, my father held his ground (and breath) at the front door.

'Hell-oh...' O'Rourke said, bemused. He looked my aunticle up and down. Davina had bright red shoes on, sheer tights, a flowing floral dress with a hem just below the knees. Good calves for a man approaching middle age. 'Have we met?' O'Rourke said, extending a funereal hand. He was wearing a musty dark suit, black shirt and dog collar, sporting a 1950s short-back-and-sides. My mother was scuttling (in slow-motion in my mind) to the roadside.

'I'm Lizzie's sister,' Uncle D said proudly. 'Davina. Davina Burton.' They shook hands.

'I didn't know you had a sister, Elizabeth,' the priest called out.

Then the penny dropped, like the expression on his face. I mean, Davina might have been wearing a dress and too-high heels and a very expensive wardrobe, including a red leather handbag over his wrist (all of this is so true it makes me laugh still) but the mannerisms were masculine, the handgrip tight, the jaw smooth but manly, the tits abnormally high. In other words, he was still the transvestite you see on a late-night bus, or tube, or wheeling among women at Marks and Spencer's; the person with too-big ankles and wrists and hands.

Uncle D gave my mother a wry smile as if he was enjoying the moment. If I didn't know he had none, I'd have said he had balls. Dad was looking along the houses, searching out for neighbours, hoping not to find any faces peeking through their nets. Oddballs these Burtons, he was probably thinking. Flaming oddballs. Thank God I'm a Tippet by blood, not a bloody Burton.

Like I say, Davina the bird died in the talonous clutches of a hungry tabby cat, but Uncle Davina lives on. It was my uncle I was going to stay with on my sixteenth birthday, after waving my friends off at Victoria. London got right up my mother's nose. For example: after Father O'Rourke departed the afternoon of my tenth birthday (he had come to discuss my mother's new duties as social secretary at the church), I remember she turned to me and said, 'You see? You see what happens when you spend too much time in London? Don't ever go to London.' As if the metropolitan air turned you into a tranny.

On my sixteenth birthday, I got lost coming out of Sloane Square underground and Davina came to collect me. I'd never been to his flat under my own steam before, and God was I steaming. Four lagers on an empty stomach had done for me. One of my friends had been sick over his shoes and bits had splashed over mine. Uncle D didn't seem bothered. 'Enjoyed your birthday so far?' he said. It was a Saturday and he'd taken the day off work. He'd toned down his wardrobe too. No flowers or high heels. Just understated jeans, grey sweatshirt with a Nike logo, pink pumps, discreet silver earring studs. He'd grown into his femininity. As promised, he took me to a Chinese restaurant. We ate three courses: prawns to start, chicken noodles for mains and fluffy whipped somethings for lasts. We drank a bottle of dry white wine, something I've never lost the taste for since, when really (given the shock of what happened later that night) I should always have hated it.

We talked about all sorts. What did I want to do with the 'O'Levels I hadn't yet got? String them together for a necklace, I said (that was funny). He said he liked my leather jacket. My mother had given me the money for it. 'It suits you,' he said, but after he'd said this he looked out of the window at the passers-by and road traffic. 'London's so busy all the time. No time to stop and stare.' He gazed at me, sullen-eyed. He dabbed at his sockets with a sweet little handkerchief, then blew his nose into the same cloth.

'What's wrong?' I said. 'Is it my parents? They don't mean to be mean.'

He shook his head, smiling weakly. He took an envelope from his bag and handed it across the table. There was a hundred pounds of record tokens and a funny card inside. 'I didn't know what to get you at this age. I was going to get an electric razor.'

'This is great,' I said, and it was. He didn't have much money to throw around. Money didn't stretch far in London. He worked in a big department store (kitchen appliances) but he wasn't a manager or anything. He didn't own his flat even. Nonetheless, at sixteen I admired him. I envied his freedom, his act of rebellion, his ability to be exactly who he wanted to be and fuck the world, fuck his sister, my mother, fuck my father too. I knew he lived alone. No real partners. No one interested enough to stay longer than a week or two. One-night stands, one-week wasters.

I'm not so sure now, behind bars, thinking about everything he said that night in his flat. I don't know whether to like or dislike him for what he told me. I refused to believe it at first (now the plot's moving, though it's still a bloody flashback). We went to his flat, watched some awful film I can't remember. I don't even know what time it was. Late. Everything that night exploded out of focus, after he told me what he told me.

Before he told me, he opened a bottle of Gordon's and we sipped G&Ts with slices of fresh lemon. He lived in a once swanky run-down 1930s building not far from Kings Road. I was feeling quite grown up in his company.

So, we are watching the late news. Bombs going off in Beirut. There's something on Davina's mind. He keeps doing the turn-away thing he did in the restaurant. 'Sixteen,' he says, shaking his head in disbelief. He can still remember me in his arms, at my christening. He studies my face. 'You were a cherub. You have the Burton looks. The cursed Burton bones and eyes. You're your mother's son.' He holds my stare, thinking something momentous.

'What?' I say, putting my glass down on his funky coffee table. 'Something on my face?' I think it's an angry spot which erupted early in the morning and the zit-stick camouflage had sweated off during the afternoon.

'Please, please, don't be angry with me, or your mother, when I tell you.'

I pick up my glass, realising there's only lemon. 'Are you on drugs? Because if you are, no sweat. Half my class smoke cannabis and take Es'

'I'm serious, Benjamin. It's been eating away at me for years.' He downs the rest of his glass, wipes his overly-smooth upper lip. For one awful moment I think he's going to confess undying love for me and the family will be turned upside-down.

I try to lighten the mood. 'Tell me or I'll tickle it out of you. You remember you used to do that when I wouldn't tell you a secret?'

'You once had a brother,' he says, just like that. A gong goes off in my head; the same sort of savage-sounding gong that roused King Kong from deep slumber on Skull Island. A sacrifice in the offing.

'I've told you, and I shouldn't have,' he says, after he's already told me. He takes a long breath, then spits it out like some sort of confession. He tells me I had a half-brother called Tom, from my mother's first marriage. In the year I was born (1980), Tom died in an accident. He was snubbed out in good company. Steve McQueen, John Lennon, Mae West, Alfred Hitchcock and Peter Sellers all came unstuck that year, but they'd lived most of their lives.

Of course, I knew my mother had got divorced and re-married. She said it was very hard for a devout Catholic like her (she'd written to the Pope for an annulment and got a reply with a wax seal on it called a "bull"). There wasn't any mention of children though. Her first husband emigrated to New Zealand. If you lived with my mother long enough you'd do the same probably.

'What you trying to do? Get back at my parents? I haven't got a brother. No brother, full stop.' I pace the lounge but it's too small so I do little circles in the carpet like an ant whose hillock-home has been trampled under clumsy human feet.

'You were a few months old…'

'Lies.'

'It's true. Why would I lie to my only nephew?' He goes on. All this stuff about my so-called brother. Tom had been sixteen, riding his motorcycle to see his girlfriend after a terrible argument. 'It was icy and he came off…Oh, God, it was horrific. Your poor mother. Oh, I shouldn't be telling you.'

'No you shouldn't because I'll tell her you've really lost the plot this time and she'll say, "It's London, Benjamin. They're a queer lot in London."'

'You don't believe me,' he says, 'but I'll show you the box.'

I'm in fake stitches. 'You got my brother in a box?' Uncle D doesn't answer, getting out of his chair, moving towards the bedroom. 'Where's he buried? My mother must go to a graveyard, surely.'

'She does,' he says, out of sight. 'She goes without you knowing.'

'This is really funny, Uncle D. You know that?' I laugh again but the edges of my laughter soon dissolve. The box in his arms is overflowing. Large enough to store a chopped-up body.

He puts it carefully down on the carpet in front of me and sits in the chair opposite, arms folding over his implants. 'It's all I could salvage.'

I refuse to look, just stare at him instead, and Davina looks mournfully at the box. I catch sight of a poster unfurling. I gather my leather jacket, still with a lovely new smell on it, and head for the exit. 'You can't go!' he says.

My head is throbbing, hand on the latch of the front door, vision blurred from booze and traipsing around a strange city all afternoon with a spot the size of a conker. I wait awhile, hang around the hallway, lean against the wall. I feel for money but all I have are record tokens and fifty pence. 'Aren't you even curious?'

I slide back in, instantly sober. 'My mother would've said.'

'You were a baby. She was protecting you, denying it even happened. You were the special one. The only one.'

I peer into the box. 'Okay, I'll look, but for the record I don't believe a word of this crap.'

'Fine,' he says.

There are posters, record sleeves, a few books and odds and sods. I pick through the remains. 'Your mother had a breakdown. Poor Lizzie was sad all of the time. You can understand that.' I pull out a record sleeve: David Bowie's *Scary Monsters (And Supercreeps)*, vinyl still inside. 'I told Lizzie she should tell you when you were old enough. Your father went along with what she wanted, as if silence is a virtue.' I pull out more sleeves: *"Heroes"*, *Low*, *Diamond Dogs*, *Aladdin Sane*, *Hunky Dory* and finally, *Space Oddity*. 'Tom had these posters all over his room and sang Bowie songs all day. He played the guitar too. It's in my wardrobe.'

'Lies.'

'No, Benjamin. The truth.'

'Stop calling me Benjamin! It's BEN! B-E-N!'

'Your mother threw everything out after the funeral. I was staying at your place, taking care of you. I grabbed as much as I could. Tom's things. Some of them. You were only a few months old.'

I dig deeper, picking out school reports for *Thomas Reed*. A real person. 'He had such a lovely spirit, your brother.' There's a religious education exercise book from 1979 and school diaries dated in scratchy ink: 1977-78. On the cover page of the first diary is Tom's home address; my home address! I flick through more album sleeves: The Cure; Sparks; a Brian Eno cassette (*Before and After Science*); some videos, including *Mad Max*, *The Terminator*, *A Clockwork Orange* and *If*. A boy's things and a young man's things. A teenage time capsule.

'I have something else,' Davina says, getting his handbag. He pulls out a red leather purse, takes out a photograph. It is slightly out of focus but has been lovingly looked after. It makes contact with my fingers and my heart flutters. It was taken the day Tom bought his first (and last) motorcycle. He's astride an orange Suzuki 125cc, outside the garden of my home; red leather jacket and dark sunglasses, DM boots. He's smiling at me. My brother. The ghost of my brother.

'Are you alright?'

I shake my head, vision proper blurry. I don't really cry like normal people. What happens is that a rock lodges in my throat, my eyes roll around and soften up. They turn to watery chambers but nothing falls out. I can't see for a while and have to blink hard and the water sinks back down inside. 'They couldn't even tell me?'

'My heart grows cold,' Davina says. Real amateur dramatics. 'You can have Tom's things. I've held them long enough.' He dabs his eyes, sniffs. 'Do you want them? I'll drive you home tomorrow if you like. You can't carry them on the train. God. I'm so guilty. Poor Lizzie. My poor sister. I've betrayed her, and on your birthday. I'm sorry. So sorry.'

Genuinely, he has a look of deep regret, but it is too late for sorry. My family will be 100% turned upside-down. I didn't know how to feel or what to believe. Police might label this box of life an exhibit; historians might call it evidence; lawyers might call it proof. What does a spoilt, half-pissed sixteen-year-old boy call it? An earthquake. A great divide. Would "epiphany'" be too melodramatic? Would "Proustian moment" be too pretentious? I think back on it now and see my younger self as the narrator in Proust's *In Search of Lost Time* (a mixed-up man who tastes lime-tea, bites into a Madeleine biscuit, stirring up memories), though I was more like the Madeleine biscuit floating adrift in a teacup. No man is an island, Donne said, and no man should ever feel like a biscuit either.

It was two in the morning by the time we'd run out of things to say and there was nothing left. I slouched on the sofa in a sleeping bag, unable to close my eyes. I remained awake all night, going through the box, reading the school reports and diaries of my ghostly brother.

He hadn't been the brightest button on the school blazer. Quite poor academically. A late developer for whom there was no time to develop. But I'm no mortarboard myself. There were interesting similarities between us; a remarkably similar trajectory of attitude. *Thomas is sometimes off-putting.* At other times *he is helpful.* Tom, at the tender age of fifteen, *has a tendency to over-inflate his self-worth but tries hard at everything he does.* We were a generation apart, but the same. I read his school diaries, transported back in time to 1977 through the time-machine of an ordinary 13-year-old boy, except he couldn't be ordinary because he was *my* brother.

What I read made me laugh, sadly. His matter-of-factness and naivety. Tom was awful with words. Barely literate. An inky, badly-spelt scrawl. An 8 year old might have done better. Also, there was something immature about his way of thinking. Not slow exactly. More child-like, if that doesn't sound stupid. I wondered if he had been a slow learner rather than just disinterested in pens.

Tuesday 13 Sept
I found a conker in its shell on the floor But When I Went to crack the shell the conker was cracked so I went home (That's life, Tom). *Today a Spider called red Knee escaped and it is poisonous and it can jump to three feet High. And just the length of its body is six inches. it escaped in a Box of bannas and is now on the lose in ESSEX. People are trying to cacth it.* (Did they catch it, Tom?)

Wednesday 14 Sept

Today is my mum's birthday. I bourght her a card and lots of choclate things. She was happy I never forgot. (You're a good boy, Tom)

Friday 16 September

Today mark bolan a popstar died in a car crash I heard it on the news on radio one this morning. people say it is a sad moment but I don't think so there's Plenty more PoPstars. Elvis presly died about A month ago and his record is at number one for about two weeks. I reckon it will stay there for quite a while. (Clever boy, Tom)

Thursday 22 September

I was quite tired and then I fell asleep in minuets. (I know what you mean but this is sweeter, Tom)

Wednesday 2 November

TODAY I saw cops There was a gas leak and There were lots of road blocks and there Were ten Gas vans Five gas cars. And a FUZZ on a motorbike. I Want one. (The beginning of the end, Tom)

Monday 14 November

The firemen go on strike, from now on the people at home put out their OWN fires. I watched the gun fight at the O.K. Coral it had my favourite film Star in it burt Lancaster their was another star in it but I don't like him his name is I have forgotten his name but he had a bad cough in the film. (I can't figure who he is either, Tom)

Friday 25 November

I watched top of the pops last night. there was good music time when one good song was on. I went to a book fair and there was all kinds of books I am no good with books but there was a quick artist drawer and there was a Liverpool book their. We saw a writer called Nicholas fisk and he told us things about writing.

Monday 5 December

The nutrom rocket bomb could cause a World War III. A rocket is having a test flight, but when the time comes, war will start. the lengh of it is about 8 feet. The hight 2 feet. On Saturday Liverpool Played West ham and won 2-0.

Tuesday 13 December
Yesterday three boys blew up some towers in London they said it was great. Today I saw a rover crash into a Ford Zodiac. The rover was coming out the garden and the Ford Was coming down the rover came out and it hit the side of the other car. They had a little argument and they both went back to what they were doing. (That's the way of things in real life, Tom)

Friday 16 December
Yesterday lady Churchill, Winston churchill's Widow died at the age of 92. She was VERY old she was buried at a grave yard and her son cried at the funeral. Me and Vincent got lines for mucking about in class. (I'd like to meet this Vincent, Tom. What's his surname?)

Monday, 19 December
Yesterday we had a xmas party at school and we played records and games and best of all …my pen is runn (ing out, Tom)

Friday 20 JAN 1978
Yesterday I watched a Play on television. the pint has gone up. David steel was been commented.

Monday 23 JAN
A boy who has been missing for a few days has not been found. A thousand people Went looking for him and have not seen him. The boy's name is lester. The Police say that he might be held against his Will in a house.

Monday 27 FEB
Yesterday lester the boy who was missing for weeks has been found dead in a rubbish tip. He was suffocated. Liverpool beat man. utd 3-1.

Tuesday 14 March
In Holland today 72 people are being held as hostages by a scuicide squad. they threaten to kill themselves unless some prisoners are released. A lady Shouted at the Queen today and she threw her handbag at her.

Wednesday 15 March
The hostages are free in Holland it turned out that there was only three in the squad all of them were captured. 2 people were killed.

Friday 28 April
Yesterday I Watched top of the pops. it had a bit of punk in it but there were some slow songs. I went to bed late because I couldn't sleep because of shapes on the Walls. (Don't be frightened, Tom)

Friday 14 May
Yesterday I watched top of the Pops. The Strangler's were on with nice and Squeezy. No. 1 is Boney M with by the rivers of babelon. The new record out by the brotherhood of man. it's making its way to the top 20. David Bowie was on. (Your first mention of him, Tom)

Monday 3 July
Yesterday I watched Burt Lancaster in The Birdman from Alcatraz. Tomorrow it is a day to celebrate in America because it is the Indepent Sate Year of Indepenence. (It's not an easy thing to spell when you're no good at it, Tom)

Tuesday 4 July
Next week it is my dad's birthday I don't know how OLD he is. (Which father, Tom?) *I watched the Two Ronnies last night they made much jokes up. I liked it when they dressed up as Jamacans and started to sing.*

Wednesday 12 July
In Spain there was a tanker carrying gas and it banged into a car and the camp was all blown up. 187 people were killed. When I was in the tent in are garden, my dog jumped on it and had my bisquits and cream crackers. (Bisquits is a funnier word than biscuits, Tom)

The margins were filled with accomplished, intricate doodles: three-dimensional boxes of various sizes interlinked to form futuristic, see-through cities; circles with hairy arrows pointing outwards in all directions. In the bottom right hand corner of every page there was a scrawled matchstick animal (a horse? a dog?). When I flicked through the pages at high velocity the animal came to life, running from left to right like a cartoon creature, an old film; the flicks my grandmother used to call it. I'm pretty sure it was a dog.

I looked at the photograph again; peered into it as if it was a clear, new mirror. Tom's bulky Blues Brother sunglasses masked any facial similarities with me, but it didn't look as if he'd inherited many of my mother's genes. He was a Reed, only half-Burton. No straight, perfectly formed Roman nose, nor high cheekbones, nor full, expressive lips. Bodily too, he was podgy. Puppy fat. He probably aspired to be like his idol, David Bowie, and given a few more years of growing up might have turned into the Thin White Duke of his dreams.

Up all night, not a wink, my brother in my hands, sixteen years of a life I hadn't known to exist; sixteen years of mine lived in complete ignorance, kept in the dark. And my brother (Uncle D told me calmly over toast in the morning) had doted on me, had pushed me around the local park and shopping centre, showing me off to his girlfriend, Amy, tempting her with the notion of children. Tom had hoped to marry her one day. All to no avail.

And how exactly had he died? A broken neck from impact? A ruptured spleen undiagnosed? Punctured lungs from the shaft of shattered ribs? A hideous merging clot in the brain? No. Tom had burned to death in ignited diesel leaking from a tanker, into which the Suzuki had skidded sidelong. Like McQueen snagged on barbed wire in *The Great Escape*, there's no escaping irony; the flames, the hell which awaits a few of us in the end.

It took forever getting out of London. Me and Uncle D upfront, Tom in the boot of the Nissan Micra. Very quiet once we got on to the motorway. Uncle D switched on the radio to block out the silence while I figured out what I'd say to my parents and how to say it, playing the scenes over in my sleep-deprived head.

When we pulled up outside the house, my dad was standing in the front garden, mowing. The air smelled green. He'd changed out of his Sunday best and rolled up his sleeves. He shouted through the open front door, 'Ben's back. He's got David…Davina with him.' Mother appeared in her Sunday frock, apron over, a knife in her hand. They stood together on the doorstep, trying to smile. One extra for lunch, mother was probably thinking. Will the beef stretch?

I left Tom in the boot of the car and bumped past father into the hall. Uncle D stopped to speak to his sister, but she must have sensed something wrong because she rushed inside to me. 'I'm afraid he knows, Lizzie,' Davina said, and I glared.

'Knows what?' mother said, mouth gaping.

'About my dead brother.'

'Well, I'm not having a conversation in the hall of all places. Go into the kitchen. And what's all this nonsense about brothers?' Such an excellent faker. She sat at the table where there was a saucepan filled with peeled, raw potatoes.

'Lizzie…,' Uncle D mumbled, '…it just came out…'

She clicked her tongue. 'A brother of all things.'

'His flaming records are in the boot of the car,' I said, fixing my stare. Father put an arm around her shoulders, squeezing tight. And that's when her head tipped down and her whole body seemed to cave in.

'Why didn't you tell me?'

'Now's not the right time,' Dad answered in his firmest voice.

I glared at him then. 'That's funny, 'cos there was never a right time so it may as well be now. Isn't that right, Davina?'

'I'm sorry, Sis,' Uncle D said. 'I didn't mean for it to -'

'Get out!' Dad roared. 'Get out!'

Uncle D quick-stepped into the hall, out through the front door to his car. A momentous silence descended in his wake. Tyson, our black Labrador, flew out of the back door, jumped onto his old chair and hid his grey muzzle beneath his paws.

'I feel cheated,' I said, taking the chair on the other side of the table. Dad deployed himself behind my mother, sighing, pressing down on her grieving shoulders. He looked at me curiously. I can't explain the look except to say it was pleading. 'When were you going to tell me? This year? Next? The one after? Never?'

'It wasn't like that,' Dad said.

'Tell me what it *was* like then.'

Mother still had the knife locked in her hand. Dad prised it out of her fingers and placed it in the sink. He leaned on the worktop, looking momentarily out of the window towards his tomato plants.

'You're part of this too,' I said.

He turned. 'Part of what?'

'This cover-up, charade, conspiracy. This lie.'

My mother lifted her head, beautiful Burton eyes reddening. 'It wasn't like that, Benjamin.'

'Which room did he sleep in? Do I sleep in his room every night without knowing? Why didn't you move house?' No reply. 'Where's his grave? Do you even go to his sodding grave?'

'Leave it, son.' Dad only ever calls me son when he's being instructive. This is how you sell a mattress with the base, son. You see that woman there, son? See how she's dressed? How rich she is, son? Take her to the expensive four-posters, son. 'Leave your mother, son. She's upset.'

'Leave it? I'll leave it. I'll leave this fucking house for good.'

Dad's face shook. 'Language!'

As I reached the kitchen door my mother caught hold of my wrist and pulled me to a standstill. 'I only ever do anything for you.'

'Pah! You don't even know where he's buried!'

'For Christ's sake,' Dad said. 'Tom's at the cemetery on the other side of town.'

I laughed my head off. 'You say it as if he's visiting. He wasn't even your son, was he?'

Mother started crying then. The first time in my life I'd seen her cry. Great big voluminous salty fat ones rolling down her Burton cheeks. Large enough to drown in. 'I don't know what to say,' I said. 'It's like I'm trapped in a Kafka thing. A stranger turns around and says to me, "You know your family? Well, they're not who you think they are. They're aliens. Spies". Do you get what I'm saying? You're like The KGB. Like Stalin rewriting history, wiping the record clean. The gulags never existed. But they did, didn't they? I'm an insect.' I mocked them with a booming laugh. 'Ha! I mean, are you even my real parents?'

My father's arm came up and out, the flat of his hand smacking my cheek cleanly, making the sound only flesh on flesh makes. I touched my face, then raised a clenched fist and shook it in front of him like a caveman. 'Come on! Come on!' I was as tall as him but this was as close as we ever came to punching each other like common brawlers down the pub. My mother's breath came out in a gasp and I lowered my hand. Dad dashed past me into the hall, mumbling something about 'wringing that Burton bastard's neck.'

'Stop him!' my mother screamed. 'Benjamin!'

I caught up with him at the kerb. Uncle D was locked inside his Nissan and my father was trying to wrench the driver's window down with his fingernails. 'I'll get a rock!' he hollered, feeling around the grass. The neighbours started to appear at their summery windows. He kicked the driver's door then stomped around, pulling at the handles. Mother was tearing at her forehead, screaming, 'Stop him, Benjamin!'

I ran into the road, held his arms in a wrestling lock, but it was no good; too strong, too angry.

'You've done this! To your sister! Why? Why?'

'Leave him,' I said. 'He hasn't done nothing.'

The engine started up, the handbrake creaked loose and we watched Uncle D speed away. His car seemed to take the corner on two wheels. Tom was taken away from me again; what there was left of the brother I hadn't known.

I'm glad that bit's out of the way, and so early on in this story. It's painful to recollect. Sadly, it's all true, right down to the last detail, even though the words read back to me now like a soap opera. Transsexuals? Priests? Domestic violence? Gimme a break. Just imagine how you'd have felt in my shoes? If you want people to stand in your shoes you must learn to stand in theirs. Imagine discovering a whole new life (and death) you never knew existed? Not just Tom's. My mother's and father's. It was as if my own life was being re-written, re-cast, re-moulded right in front of me. I went off the rails (clichéd, must try harder). I locked myself in my room. I went to stay with Uncle D, for longer this time, taking back Tom's things. My parents refused to speak to my uncle on the telephone or eye-to-eye through the letterbox. Every time he tried it was like pouring oil on the fire. Dad told him if he ever showed his face again he'd smash it into the next century, which actually wasn't very far away. I saw a whole new side of my father during this time. He is normally quite placid, even under enormous pressure, quite calm, but he loved my mother so thoroughly that he wanted to kill the man who made her cry.

My mother came to my room and told me things about Tom. It wasn't very different from the version Uncle D had sprung on me. She had photographs. Quite a lot from the top of her wardrobe; baby to boy to young man. The firstborn, the first to die. She took me to his grave. The cemetery was ten miles from our house. The headstone was black marble and north-facing. Sumptuous, deep green moss had gathered in my brother's name and the dates of his life: *Thomas James Reed, Born 10th September 1964, Died December 19th, 1980. A much-loved son.* It was in a nice spot, beside a high laurel hedge, part of the old cemetery, not the new one on the hill where a chimney rises into the sky, where dead people get pyred. Buried or cremated? 'Not cremated,' my mother said. I don't suppose she believed in cremation in 1980, but things have changed a lot since then, even in the Roman Catholic Church.

Sometimes, even now, I can't believe my flesh and blood could have kept my flesh and blood such a secret from me, and for so long. As a result things became strained. Still are, I guess. Like I said, I went off the rails big time and stayed out all night as a form of protest. But maybe teenagers do this sort of thing as part of the familial-separation process (a Darwinian thing?). I didn't eat properly. I asked for food to be left outside my bedroom door and mother dutifully obliged. I had them where I wanted them.

It is true, things changed after my sixteenth birthday; for better and worse. I took advantage. I had the moral high ground. I never thought of them and their pain or what it must have felt like when the police came to the door with the bad news. I put up Tom's yellowed Bowie posters, still with their original grubby blue tack marks in the corners. I played Tom's records to death, loud enough for the whole street to hear.

That's one of the things I'll put straight when I get out. I'll patch things up between my mother and father and my uncle. Nine years is a long time for a brother and sister not to talk. We've all done bad things, sometimes for the right reasons, and they might not be erased from memory but they can be forgiven. I have forgiven my parents (I hope they can forgive me for the hurtful things I said) and they should forgive Davina who only did what he thought was right i.e. telling the truth, even though my parents think I'm sitting in a prison cell because of truth. Truth can hurt, but having your eyes opened is part and parcel of growing up.

About a year after the epiphany I settled back into education and my parents settled back into their routines, but there was always some hurt going on. Trust had been lost in the Bermuda Triangle of our relationship. My parents overcompensated by spoiling me more than ever, if that was possible. It went on for years, maybe still is going on. My 'O' level results were worse than expected but good enough to start 'A' levels, which I was pretty average at. I remember my English teacher, Mrs Harkness, asking me during this time, rather bravely now I think about it: 'Do you love your Mum and Dad?' It was an innocuous question during a quiet lunch break in the library. I answered with a definitive NO. Probably my first big lie after which the lies came thick and streaming; like a cold you can never shake. Because I did love my parents, and I hated them. The two went together. As Johnny Cash famously sang about a good brother and a bad brother: *A man who turns his back on his family, he ain't no good!*

I love them now, more than ever. Now it's me in the doghouse.

My trial is up in a few days, expected to last a couple of weeks, and before then I'd like to lay down a bit more history so you can judge me for yourselves. That seems only fair; democratic in a fictional sense of the word (you're going backwards instead of forwards again, Ben. Gimme a break. We all live in the past; inmates more than most. Believe me, you daren't think too hard about the future. The present is your cell, four walls; the past is your tunnel out of here, the only refuge, though not always).

Where to plonk you down in time? How far back? The origins of my crime? Where might they lie? The first story I wrote as a teenager? The crush I had on my English teacher? The prize I won at school for an essay on how World War Three would start?

A pattern is emerging. Childhood. The tender years of stumbling. But I won't begin there. That would be too predictable, too Freudian to conceive. Although there was a burning, I remember. A hot day in the summer holidays. It burns in my nostrils still. There was a primary school. Not the one I attended. It wasn't good enough for my mother even though it was a short walk from our front door. I was about eleven. Out of knee pants anyway. There were others with me that afternoon. Pete from a few doors down, a year or so older than me, and his sister Claire who must have been nine. Pete could never shake her off. She used to follow him around like a spy.

How did we end up in the dry, brambly bushes beside that school? No matter. We were there, hiding. All three huddled in a den like fox cubs. We ate crushed peanut butter sandwiches, scratches all over our arms and legs from the thorns around us. It was so hot that we lay down side-by-side looking up at the spangled sunlight, making out the blue sky, cloudless. It was windy that day. The warm air whistled. Pete took out a box of matches and lit a half-smoked cigarette he'd stolen from his oldest brother's ashtray. He coughed. Pete the rebel. Claire and I watched in awe as if this was delicious, bad magic. He offered the cigarette around but we shook our heads. Just five or six drags, then he stubbed it out with his trainer on a nest of twigs and dust. We swigged lemonade from a litre bottle, wiping our mouths on our arms, then we crawled out into the bright light again, walking on our way. We re-joined the tarmac that ran beside the school.

We stopped and discussed what we would do next, when Claire shrieked. Smoke was rising from where we'd been. In seconds, I swear, I heard a crackling sound, the tinder going up. We ran back to see. Orange waves were blowing furiously, catching the wind and moving the same way as us.

'Shit!' Pete hissed.

'Phone the fire man!' Claire screamed, as if there was only one in the whole world.

'Leg it back to mine,' I said.

The door was locked and I rapped on the frame. Mother opened and we fell into the hall, jabbering, fingers pointing. 'Fire!' 'Fire!' 'Fire!'

'Where?' she said.

'Pete started it,' said Claire, trembling. 'He dropped a match.'

'I didn't,' he said. 'I didn't drop nothing, Mrs Tippet'. I hope I'm remembering this correctly because on reflection we sound like Dickensian street urchins. Mother scooped us into the kitchen, a room that never got any sun, somewhere cool to think and hide. 'Where is it?' she said.

'By the school.'

'Sit down. Sit down. I'll go and see.'

She hadn't believed us. The crazy imaginings of children. Three minutes later she was tearing through the house for the telephone. She dialled 999, told them where the fire was. She put the phone down and gathered us together again. 'That's the end of it. Do you hear me?' Claire burst into tears and my mother hugged her. 'They'll stop it, honey.' Mother used to call me "honey" and "baby" and "hero" when I was about Claire's age. At eleven she was already calling me her "soldier". 'Say nothing about this.' Mother turned to Pete and me. 'Say nothing to anyone.' Claire's tears exploded all over again. 'They'll put it out darling, but you must promise not tell anyone or you will get into trouble.'

The school didn't catch. The engines went away and the building was surrounded by acres of wet patches. The brambles which had once stretched for a hundred metres had turned to sticky black treacle. People gathered along its length, gossiping. That week the newspapers ran an article about a gang of troublemakers from a nearby council estate. It was easy to blame them. It was never going to be three well-off kids. And we did keep it secret. We told no one. 'You don't see that Peter Klutz again,' my mother told me. 'You understand, Benjamin? You steer clear of that family altogether.'

I don't think I got over what she said. Pete was a friend and now he wasn't. I saw him daily but we barely exchanged a word. When my father's business took off, I attended a different school; a private Catholic boys' school as a day-pupil, and then a boarder from the age of fourteen. Pete became a memory but that fire still haunts me. It was seeing the gnarled up hedgehogs. A family of them. But no human life was lost that day. No building was licked to death in the flames. I've never written about that fire before. Not even in a story. Except once, maybe, about the hedgehogs. And now.

Time inside passes slowly. When you place it next to time outside it goes even slower. It's difficult catching up with the pace of the outside world. I watch the news on my snowy in-cell TV, read tabloids left around the block, listen to the radio stations for news, yet none of it feels real from the inside. They are the mumblings and rumblings you might hear from inside a womb. The outside seems to operate in a different time zone, if not in a different time altogether.

For instance, take my crime and pending trial. They've really become the *cause celebre* in the media. All the channels are talking about it: the dead man, the fire, Alex Fortune and me. They keep showing footage of the blaze from last December. A member of the public videoed it on his mobile phone. They keep showing the photograph of the victim, a Ukrainian undergraduate who moonlighted as a cleaner. He was a good boy. Never hurt anyone in his life. A complete innocent, except he had an illegal permit. Stepan Belonog is dead but he is still a hot potato. The fire has become a political issue but the tabloids are far more interested in me than in a hard-up (in every way) Ukrainian. I am the "dilettante" lover of a novelist. A media milsch cow. Me and Alex both. The story has "bisexual" lovers, "betrayal", an illegal corpse. My face is on TV; the police mug shot taken when I hadn't been ready, hair stuck all over the place. Alex's face is plastered everywhere too but he uses a professional photograph taken in a studio. There's footage of Alex driving through the gates of his country house in Incham, Kent. 'No comment,' he keeps saying. 'No comment,' waving the flashes away. It is trial by TV. A freak show.

Finally, there are the ruins of the fire in Broadstairs and an attractive woman who will be covering the trial for the BBC. I say attractive but actually there is something askew about her eyes, cross-eyed like she's having an orgasm, which is attractive I guess. I say ruins, but building work is ready to begin. The pretty reporter says the jury members have been to look at the scene, which doesn't make any sense as the trial hasn't even started yet! Next thing there's an architect in tortoise-shell glasses saying how extensive the fire was. He's going to build a better building in its place; something modern yet in keeping with the Dickensian seafront. Acorn Publishing House shall be re-born, he says. Nothing stands still outside, but inside you feel like you are standing still forever.

What do I miss inside? Now there's an ambiguous question. I'm not talking about existentialism. I mean physical, concrete things, like my B and O sound system, flat screen plasma HD TV and exploring the worldwide web. I miss the world in my finger. I miss my music: The Divine Comedy, Ash, Afterglow, Placebo, Morrissey, The Killers, Laughing Man, In Media Res, The Kaiser Chiefs, Bitches on Heat, Green Light, and last but not least, David Bowie. I used to stick six of his albums on and listen back-to-back for half a day. I miss strumming Tom's old guitar. When Uncle D gave it to me, the top string was missing. I replaced it and could play a few basic chords. I miss my eyeliner. It's not a crime to use eyeliner. Just a touch and it can make your eyes double in size. I used to experiment with it at Uncle D's. He showed me how to apply it subtly. I miss sex, full stop. Some of the men masturbate in here. I've heard them through the walls. That's why so many have odd socks. I haven't managed to do it and am reaching explosion levels. I'm up to my eyeballs in testosterone. Mine and everyone else's. Maybe I should be the one rioting. I miss the bookshop. It's the only job I've ever enjoyed. I miss Alex Fortune most of all, even though I could happily strangle that Judas.

Eighteen months ago I went to a bookfest with Maurice; or was it a wordfest? Whatever. Lots of famous writers and wannabe writers etc. A supercilious novelist I hadn't heard of was asked what he thought the difference was between a short story and a novel, and he answered: 'A short story is a fragment or two stitched together to make a garment, whereas a novel is a wardrobe full of clothes. Novels are not really experiments with form, they are a hand-stitching process. The more invisible the joins the more invisible the process and the more successful the writing.'

Fuck me. It was as if he'd thrown a brick through my window, jumped in and stuck knitting needles in my eyes. I was gutted, flabbergasted, disappointed (check thesaurus); which is one of the primary reasons I'm writing some things in parentheses. I actually want people to see my mid-thinking-naked-not-hiding process. Then again, I suppose this isn't a novel.

'Surely, novels are not anecdotes dressed up in fancy ribbons?' I spluttered into the roving microphone. He said something about the 'invisibility of the narrator' and I said, 'Don't you mean the author?' and he said, 'No. It's a common mistake to confuse the two,' and I said, 'I'm not confused about the two. You'd have to be a complete idiot to confuse the two. What I'm talking about is the novel in the first person, when the reader will conflate author and narrator. Most of your books are in the first person. Most of your books are about the same thing just set in different centuries, and the voice is the same all the time. There's no process. No experiment. No invisibility cloak. It's just you wearing the Emperor's new clothes.' 'What's your name?' he said. 'Ben Tippet. Writer and bookseller,' I said. That made Maurice laugh. 'And who are you?' I said back. The microphone was wrenched from my mouth so fast I couldn't disrupt the event any further, though that hadn't been my intention. I just wanted to know what the hell he was talking about. I had opinions needed airing.

When you write something in the first person, it doesn't matter how hard you try to be someone else (i.e. a fictional character), what you are doing is pretending to be someone else; persona, mask, acting, faking it. But it's more *you* than you think. That's why I suppose it must be easier writing a novel in the first person than in the third where there's a little more creative distance from self. Isn't there a hell of a lot of J.D. Salinger in Holden Caulfield, and vice versa? Isn't that why he hid the rest of his life, because he revealed too much, had sold his soul?

I hauled the ball and chain of my self-consciousness forward, pawed my way through the crowd and found the novelist at the end of the question time. I told him what I thought, but he was led away for a liquid lunch with a coterie of coat hanger friends. 'The "I" in "I" is insurmountable!' I called out. Maurice was shocked. Then I quoted Rousseau: 'I have nothing but myself to write about, and this self that I have, I hardly know…'

'Oh, get over yourself,' one of the cronies shouted back at me.

I'd gone to the festival because Alexander Fortune was supposed to be giving a reading. In the end, he never showed up. It was a great disappointment. He was, still is, my favourite writer. I tried to get my money back on the ticket but there was no compensation. That's why I laid into the other novelist who stood in his absent shadow, his impromptu replacement. Because there's no substitute for individual genius.

Four

Have I said I love Alex Fortune?

Love and hate him about equally. You have to take some things I say with a mountain of salt. I think I love him. I thought I knew him. It wasn't just because he was my idol. Nor was it because I intended using him to get an agent or publisher, though this was true at the beginning. I love him for many reasons, not least because he brought something out of me I didn't know existed. I couldn't help but be honest with him. I don't think I was ever truly honest with anyone - least of all myself - until I met Alex.

You can sleep with someone (and it is said you don't truly know someone until you have slept with them i.e. sex is a basic leveller, which is rubbish because look at emotionless porn stars). You "know" them and they "know" you. Although I took my honesty too far, showed Alex too much of myself, and so did he, which partly explains why I (we) are in this mess. Take my word for it, honesty is only the best policy if it covers you for all possible outcomes, which it cannot possibly do. My motto in life (up until meeting Alex) was: if in doubt, lie your teeth out. I think it still holds true for most people. And Alex is no exception.

[Enter Alex Fortune]

Out of some sort of guilt (his whole life runs on guilt like plane fuel), Alex visited me last week. I was genuinely shocked, though privately pleased. He's the reason I'm on remand, the rack, the chopping block. Whatever. He was sitting at visitor table 10, in the corner. A striking man from a distance. Younger-looking than his fifty-two years. Close-shaved head, pronounced dome (bullet-like) and grey attentive eyes. Well-dressed. He is a man of the world but the world was getting the better of him, weighing down on his shoulders. More Faustian than Proustian, though sometimes he oscillates between the two.

I sat down opposite him. He put out his hand to shake mine. I was going to tell him to stick it, but shook hands anyway. There came some frosty little chit-chat about life in general.

'What's it like inside?'

I pulled a face. 'Are you doing research? What do you think it's like? What do you want, Alex?' Of course, I was hoping he was going to tell me he'd withdrawn his statement to the police. The whole case would collapse.

No. He had not withdrawn any statement.

I listened with the pretence of not listening. I looked down at my hands on the table, then over the tops of his broad shoulders into the rest of the visitors' room. I watched his lips move; lips I had kissed and teased once upon a time but now wanted to split open, watch his teeth fall out. It must have taken a lot of courage coming in, some might say stupidity, given what he's done and the media interest and the fact that journalists are camped outside his home. 'You must understand my reasons,' he said. 'Whatever I did, I did for you.' (where have I heard that before?).

I had trouble keeping my lid on.

'Even if you are found guilty, the sentence should be lenient. It was an accident. It was hot-headed, reckless, but not premeditated.'

'Alex,' I said. 'Snap out of it. This isn't one of your detective novels. If I go down I'll always blame you and I'll bring you down with me.' I could see he wanted some sort of forgiveness but I wouldn't give him the satisfaction. He cleared his throat, the throat I once sucked dry like a vampire at night. I suddenly felt awful for what I'd said and changed the subject: 'I'm scribbling every day. It's like a writing retreat in here, without the wine.'

'That's good,' he said, without registering the sarcasm. He looked me straight in the eyes. 'So, what are you writing?'

'Not about you if that's what you're worried about.' (A lie inevitably).

To my disappointment, he said: 'Good. There's already enough about us in the tabloids.'

'I'm writing my autobiography if you must know.'

'Oh dear,' he remarked.

'You're never too young or too old to write your life down. Especially if it's interesting.'

'Autobiography's a contagion, Ben.' (Alex is close to finishing his own autobiography; a very beautiful and tragic story).

Something fluttered inside me. A butterfly memory of when he used my name. Only Alex calls me Ben the way he calls me Ben. You'd think there was only one way to say Ben, wouldn't you? I guess it's the way he speaks. Exclusively, authoritatively, reassuringly. Or is it just more important to hear my name on his lips than on anyone else's?

'Evie's publishing her memoirs,' he said.

Evelyn (aka Evie) lives in Edinburgh. She's an abstract artist. By all accounts she milked Alex after their bloody divorce umpteen years ago and poisoned his two daughters against him. He'd played away from home more than once during their marriage and probably deserved it. 'She's using the publicity generated by the trial. My Life of Hell with A Fortune.'

'That could be my own title,' I said, waiting for a reaction.

'That was the header in last weekend's Telegraph. Everybody wants their piece of flesh, Ben.'

My name again, accompanied this time by one of his strained smiles. I've missed the insinuation of his smile. You can tell a lot by someone's smile; whether it's fake for starters. Alex's is genuine because he seems to use it under great sufferance. It's a rare smile gaining value each time it strikes, like a secretive, exotic orchid opening its petals once a year. Just once and you never forget it.

Alex was pretty convincing when he got going. He spoke very much like his prose; concisely, beguilingly, fetchingly. It was his prose that brought me to him in the first place. Then he dumped the bad news on me: 'I won't be attending the trial myself. Apart from giving evidence.' The nail in my otherwise impossible-to-envisage coffin. The real bone of contention between us. He is the chief witness for the prosecution, and he had the gall to be sitting there. Him and his old-fashioned sense of duty. Sitting on his moral highchair.

'You could withdraw your statement?' It bounced clean off.

'It's the media, Ben. Journalists are the proverbial rash. They're all over me, making me ill. I can't sleep at night.'

'You're such a hypochondriac, Alex. What do you think it's like for me in here?'

He did look peaky; dark and puffy around the eyes, skin loosened and lined like the skin on a well-used drum. This despite a facelift when he lived in L.A. I wasn't going to beg him. I only wanted him to be in court to see what he was putting me through. So ironic. Alex used to crave public attention to help sell his books and raise his literary profile. Before moving Stateside that is. It was only upon returning to England after his father's death, after a cluster of terrible migraines and ill-health (most of it imagined), that he became something of the hermit, the paranoid recluse he is today.

'The press are drooling. A photographer snapped me in the prison car park.'

'Did they catch your good or your bad side?' I said, just about hitting the right note of scorn.

'I know this must be difficult for you too.'

Me *too*? I loved and loathed him. 'We all have a good and a bad side, Alex.'

'You'd think they'd already have enough pictures of me.'

The vanity of the man! 'You shouldn't have bothered coming in. *You* at least are free to leave.' I folded my arms for effect.

'I'm sorry it's come to this, Ben. You gave me no option when you tried fleeing the country like a murderous miscreant. I was an accessory to the fact. Don't you understand?'

'I understand you sold me out. You dropped me in the shit, you Judas.'

An officer frowned on the other side of the room. 'Ben,' Alex said, leaning across the table, so close I could smell his French aftershave, *Physiognomie*. 'You say it was an accident and I believe you. But a man did die in the fire.'

'He did,' I said, 'and he dies every fucking night on the six o'clock news and now it's me who's going to get fried, thanks to you!'

The guard who was giving us the eye, cleared his throat. 'Keep it down, folks.'

'Don't you feel any remorse?' Alex whispered. 'Any guilt? I thought you might feel something. You're not the person they say you are. You can take responsibility.'

'What are you here for, Alex? Have you turned into my priest? Are you bugged or something?'

'Of course not. Listen, it's not too late to change your plea. The judge would be more inclined to give a -'

'For the record, Alex...' I leaned into his lapel, peeled it towards me, spoke into it as if there was a microphone: '...testing testing, one, two, three. It - was - not - my -fault. I - have - done - noth - ing - wrong. I - am - inn - oh - cent.'

He pulled away from me. 'I've done what I've come to do, so...'

'What's that? To appease your conscience? Wash your hands of me? Why don't you ever reply to my letters?'

A buzzer sounded and an officer reminded people not to leave anything behind. Alex stood. I was the thing being left behind when all I wanted was to crawl inside his herringbone-patterned jacket, jump into his Aston Martin, speed back to lovely old Smuggler's Cottage and spend the rest of my days there, in Incham with him. Once upon a time, I actually believed that story would come true.

He motioned to hug me but I couldn't bear it, lifting my hands in protest. I was a real wet lettuce. 100% Iceberg. He said he thought about me every day and would wait for me, no matter what. 'I've spoken to BB. He has a legal friend and he says if you take a guilty plea the judge is duty-bound...'

'Duty-bound?'

That was Alex's take on the matter. His father's military genes had rubbed off on him. You see, I was waiting for different words, but he didn't say them. He never once said he loved me during the whole summer we were together. Since my capture, not a single letter. I told him more than once, in letters, in the afterglow of sex, in his plane, arm-in-arm walking along Deal seafront, even in a fucking cinema: 'I love you, Alexander Fortune,' and all he could muster was, 'Me too.' Typical Alex ambiguity. Non-committal. A fake. A cardboard.

The next time I'll see him will be in the courtroom. Me in the dock, Alex on the witness stand; the moralist standing against me. I don't understand why he has done what he has done and he doesn't understand why I have done what I have done. We need our heads knocking together.

Five

I'm quite an early bird.

I wake up before the guards jangle down the corridor. I pick up my notebook and begin with the first thoughts of the day. I'm doing it right now. There's birdsong from the trees in the quad as dawn breaks through the bars. I think I'm the only remander awake.

It's difficult this morning. I slept reasonably well but the second I opened my eyes I thought I was in the bed my father bought for me a few years ago. Top-notch chrome modernist wet dream of a double bed, deluxe mattress (special discount from one of his friends still in the business). I was there in my flat with a view of the cathedral bell tower, listening to the pealing. My heart was as high as Quasimodo. Then I heard the keys jangling and realised where the bed was and I was waking in prison and I could have been sick in the toilet.

There's a word for the moment of awakening. Half an hour after regaining consciousness, the mind is free-floating and more imaginative than usual. Thoughts are unfettered, unchained, susceptible to wander without censorship or control; a passage of time through which one can travel with entire abandonment. It's called hypnopompia. Imogen told me about it in class. It is rather like a hypnotic state: half-awake, half-asleep. A Russian psychologist discovered it (or just gave it a name). Sir Walter Scott swore by this twilight zone saying that he got out of many fictional holes during the wee small hours. George Eliot said it's never too late to be what you could have been. Somebody else said that when a writer is born into a family, that family is doomed (Milosz?). Alice McDermott said that a good writer sells out everyone he knows sooner or later.

I remember all this stuff early in the morning as if I have a photographic memory. I can see the words on a page in my mind just like a song sheet. I know pretty much all of Bowie's lyrics. I've sung them so many times, I could sit on Mastermind and get fifteen out of fifteen, no passes, no problem. The same goes for creative writing. I did a lot of reading during my half-finished diploma at the university. I have a list of quotations as long as my leg, gleaned from books read over three months. How to write this, how not to write that. I used to put them up on the wall in my study at home. I can see them now in my mind's eye. When I was at my pc and the muse had absconded, the quotes made me feel less lonely. They were like advice from close friends. I know it sounds ridiculous, but it's true. I took a peek at them and they made me feel better. I've memorised them and they still comfort me. They are Ben Tippet's bible. My favourite is: *Ever tried? Ever failed? No matter. Try again. Fail again. Fail better.* (Samuel Beckett).

Once upon a time, I caught a train to Paris. I stayed a whole weekend visiting graveyards and museums. Actually, I went to Paris to find Beckett's grave at the Cimetiere du Montparnasse. I'd heard a lot of intellectuals were buried there. It was Spring but quite cold. I was given a map at the main gate and wandered around lost for two hours looking at the gravestones. I stumbled across Jean-Paul Satre, Simone de Beauvoir, Guy de Maupassant, Charles Baudelaire, Serge Gainsbourg and Susan Sontag. A couple were picnicking on her gravestone. When I found Samuel Beckett, I sat at his feet and read his quote back to him about failure and perseverance. There were dead roses on his slab and I was sorry I hadn't thought to bring fresh ones. All I had was a croissant and his words, which I read out in as solemn a voice as possible. I sometimes wonder if anyone will one day read some of my words back to me when I am dead, and if so, whether they will be felt by me? Can words rouse you from the big sleep?

Never in my experience.

It's impossible not to think about life and death in here, and in general. A Zen Buddhist book I once read in Little's said it's important to contemplate death once a day, every day, to make life more worthwhile. Though, thinking about it a hundred times a day is bad karma. In the last twelve months, scores of people have died on remand up and down the UK (time really means something on the suicide watch). You just don't hear about it on the outside.

Why would you even be interested? On average most suicides are male and under twenty-one, but I don't believe in the law of averages. Though, statistically I'm okay. Only last year, Red said, a bipolar kid aged eighteen stuffed his throat with prison toilet paper and choked to death at night, just two cells down from me. Now that must have taken some doing. The paper is so rough. What made it worse was that the kid was a shoplifter and was expected to receive a non-custodial. Try telling that to his parents.

'...the keys go jingle-jangle...'

I know it's Red Buchanan by the low hum of his tune. Some Celtic dirge. He probably played it last night over a whisky and it has stuck to the inside of his skull like Bowie sticks to mine. He probably hummed it in his car on the way into work and now he can't get rid of it. And now some of the inmates will be humming it all day too. It's an old fucking song. '...by the Royal Canal.'

He's on early duty today which is good. I like Red, as far as it's possible to like a screw. See, I've picked up the lingo already! They're not called screws for nothing. Most of them couldn't be arsed talking to you. Some only know you by number. I imagine they share cups of tea in their staff room or mess or whatever, saying things like, 'It would be a great job if it wasn't for the inmates' and stuff like that. Some of the screws yomp around the place like they're in the army. They ball at you to stand by your bed. They stand over you making you clean your toilet. They take things from your cell when you're out having dinner or breakfast or having a shower. You go back to your cell to discover things have moved or are missing. In my case, a book or a sock (I hide my notebooks under my pillow). They must think it's very amusing. Maybe it keeps them from going insane. Sometimes I fantasise about kicking the shit out of the screws but such thoughts are only self-destructive and I've already seen what can happen when you lose control. You only have to look at them the wrong way and the day's written off. You're not given any association time in the quad. Take it from me, when someone wears a uniform and they hold all the keys and the coffee, democracy goes out of the window.

They're not all like that; only most of them. Who'd want their job anyway? On your feet all day, fingers tasting of keys. How would you wipe the prison smell off your clothes? It seeps into your skin, into your bones, into your psyche, into your wife, girlfriend or boyfriend when you make love.

Ironically, the reverse is also true. You can smell home on the guards and it makes you homesick. When Red walks in, checking things over, I can smell his life: the perfume his wife wears, the sickly sweet bile of his babies, his damply-carpeted hall and dusty front room, even his minty car air-freshener. I can envisage them just from the smell. I can smell his washing powder. A clean, nice smell. Unified, normal smells. They remind me of the outside and what I'm missing. Everyone smells differently just as every home is differently-peopled. You don't even know you have a unique smell until you enter someone else's. It's an autograph, a signature of self, embedded in your clothes and hair and skin. Smell is the most effective sense to rekindle memories. Smell and taste. Proust knew that.

Red is commanding but kind on his watch. There's no monkey business. He pops his bright red head around my door again, nodding in approval. 'You just keep writing, lad.'

I salute him. 'Whatever keeps me sane, sir.'

In an entirely different universe, in another time vortex, he'd be my uncle. A reliable uncle. I only have Uncle D and I wouldn't say he's entirely trustworthy. We're not exactly close. But families are not as bonded as they used to be in general. Even the nuclear family has been blown to pieces. Isn't that what they're saying?

Six

I've sent three letters of apology to Alex and have received nothing in return.

All I got in the post was a letter from my brief saying the CPS have requested an extra week to prepare their evidence against me. The letter said this was a good thing i.e. the case against me is weak.

I've never known seven days to stretch so far ahead of me. It's like *Midnight Express*. Walking in never-ending circles. If I'm not writing or reading there is really nothing to do except watch the freak show (TV). I hadn't noticed anything wrong with the goggle box before, but it's an irresistible form of torture. In Victorian times the public paid hard-earned pennies to glimpse the bearded lady, the elephant man, the monkey boy and the double-headed girl. Nowadays you pay a license fee and watch from your armchair. A billion pounds' worth of technical submarine can dive to 10,000 metres below the surface, scouring the deep and dark ocean floors for unspeakable new monsters, but you only have to walk five paces and switch on your TV. Who is the real monster you have to ask yourself: the viewer or the viewee? Stick your hand in the air if you just don't care!

TV masquerades as reality: food and fitness, holidays and hormones, auction houses and car boot sales, jokey-karaoke. It's the magazinification of life. TV is supposed to represent us and what we want. A mirror held up to ourselves. But I can't see myself in it because the glass is too thick and it only goes one way. I can see them but I can't see me. It goes in one eye and out the other. So maybe it's me who's the freak.

Take today for instance. Take today and throw it in the bin. It's a thoroughly drippy Wednesday. There's a before-and-after programme, only with a difference. A man has lost his self-esteem.

He's going to lose his wife if he doesn't sharpen up his wardrobe. She's in tears about their marriage and their love-life. She thinks if he makes an effort for their wedding anniversary (i.e. he changes into a totally different man) there might be hope of a lasting relationship. She volunteered him and he goes along with it for the sake of the marriage and for the sake of their two kids who both think he looks like a tramp from the park. He's an old rocker with a potbelly and thinning, dyed blond hair tied back in a ponytail like someone out of Status Quo. He thinks that wearing a paisley waistcoat with jeans is dressing up. And who cares, if he's happy?

The voyeuristic clothes police/pop psychologists do. That's who. They're on a mission. They parade him around the shopping centre and take vox pops. Ten complete strangers say he's everything from 55-65. Some old grandad. The dental surgeon pulls out his teeth and sticks veneers on those which survived the pliers. When he smiles at the camera he looks like he's got a gobful of piano keys; a second-hand car salesman. He doesn't drink his usual ten pints, only filtered water. He lives on wafer-thin biscuits and celery and cranberry juice. He goes to the gym three times a week, nearly loses his job at a pickling factory in Barnsley because of it. He drops three stone. Even I'm amazed. They cut his locks, shave his nose, pluck his eyebrows to invisibility. They give him new clothes. A too-tight suit. They parade him through the shopping centre again like it's Oberammagau. Vox pops: 33, 37, 45. On average, 42. His wife's ecstatic. She installs ceiling mirrors and a heart-shaped waterbed. They have a future together but now he has a future looking like a rejuvenated Bruce Forsyth. A bad trip. He's not half the man he thought he was and I'm left wondering: how wrong can people be? The experts in this makeover programme; the vox-poppers; the wife; the kids. Is this a conspiracy? Am I delusional? Am I a freak? Can anyone else see what I can see? Fakery, fakery, fakery. Giving someone a new look and identity will not change them fundamentally. This man - I can see it in his bucket-sized eyes - he cannot believe himself in the swivelling mirror. More to the point, neither can I. I'm on his side. If I was a stronger person, I'd cry me a river. TV entertainment is so ordinary and stodgy you couldn't cut through it with a brand new kitchen knife. Desperate Kitchen Knives, there's another god-awful programme. You'd have to cut through the power cable.

Switch over. They're selling someone's junk. The neighbours are buying it. They might be the subject of a future garage sale; just the same old shit going around ad infinitum. What's left goes to the auction rooms. And guess what? The valuers have got the reserve prices wrong and everything sells for pennies, not pounds. We want this to happen. It's funnier. It's sadistic human nature. The punters can't afford their fortnight in Marbella. At the end of the programme they are sitting in their backyard drinking cocktails. A home video. They imagine they're sitting in Spain, not Camden. The world in one city and all that. We're supposed to search our lofts and sheds for fortnights in Marbella.

What was it Einstein said? Make things as simple as possible but not any simpler than that. We've gone too simple. Simple as that.

Switch over. The last programme is nuts. Literally. Affronted consumer rights people are chomping at the bit. A high street supermarket chain has been selling inferior nuts. The bags do not contain the nuts referred to on the packaging. It's nuts. TV is dying of self-consumption. Worse than navel-gazing. At least with navel-gazing you find something fluffy yet mysterious lurking inside you. I stare agog at the presenters. They take turns counting nuts. Using cutting-edge numismatic computer technology they convert the numbers of nuts into percentages and display them on screen. It's high-definition implosion.

There used to be a coffee-table book hidden under the counter at Little's and Maurice often dipped into it. It was called *100,000 Interesting Facts to Amaze Dinner Guests*. The only interesting fact was that every second of every day, 365 days a year, one million people are watching repeat runs of "Friends". I rest my case, mi' lord.

Imogen told me once that TV is dead. 'TV is dead, long live TV,' I'd replied. In here though, I'm not sure. Most of the inmates would like this pap pumped intravenously. At visiting times I've overheard them discussing characters from soaps as if they are real, as if they are friends of the family. What's fictional and what's real anymore? But then, what would I do without the fictional?

Sleazy TV does what it says on the jar of Vaseline. It's after the 9pm watershed and TVs are not allowed after lockdown, but there's a DVD recorder and the officers play the programmes during the day. Programmes about the porn industry, lap dancing clubs and prostitution. Lots of diluted internet stuff, titillating blurred close-ups, crotch-shots, girls leaning on cars, and cosmetic surgery (men and women). Whatever tickles your trousers. At least it's honest. It says: we are all physical beings and screwed up by our bodies and sex. Not that I am, of course. Everything's ticketyboo in that department. In an entirely different world, say if I lived in Shitsville, Arizona or Shangri-L.A. or some place and I was part sex-god/part trailer-trash (you have to stretch your imaginations concerning the latter) I'd probably be a porn star, but I wouldn't get much work because I'd insist on using condoms and the punters like skin on skin.

Rambling now. Angry-young-man-syndrome. It's too easy to rant and rave with eye-ball-level testosterone and a general sense of injustice. I have to do something with the anger I feel about the world (edit out, in the interests of forward narrative flow?).

All the lights come on in the Big Brother house. Red is calling everyone awake, and gradually the men stir. The radios come on. The queues develop for the telephones and the showers. The sounds of mass-produced breakfast surface: *din, clatter, scrape*. The officers on the night shift leave, the new shift take over. They try to keep the queues orderly but there's a brawl beside the phone. Someone's stolen someone else's phone card. Red has to prise them apart like they are clam-halves. Of course, Manston's at the heart of it. He's put on report. A yellow card. A blot on his copybook. More like everyone's landscape. Whatever. This is a very scary school with no lessons, sloppy dinners, sticky cells and no prospect of summer holidays to look forward to.

'Steer clear,' Red reminds me.

Later that afternoon, in the TV room, I'm talking to Rogers over a game of bar football. He's alright. He's in here for alleged theft from a bookmakers. He's about forty-eight but looks closer to sixty in the mornings. His teeth are yellow and his hair has receded, made worse by the fashion *faux pas* of slicking it back with a comb so he looks like an old Jack Nicholson. He doesn't of course, he just looks old. He's got a drink problem too. The problem is that he's not allowed any and he makes up for it by smoking like the proverbial chimney pot. He told me he sleeps sitting up, for chest-drainage. His fag is clinging to the side of the football table, inky smoke coiling upwards in thermals. Are they smoke signals? Warning rings? He twists and turns the arms of his plastic players, to no avail. I'm very good at this game. Lots of practice at university. I beat him 6-0 then let him beat me 4-2 so we can have a rousing final game. Manston's leaning against the far wall, watching. The green-eyed monster can really put the shits up you.

'Woo-woo!' Rogers hammers the table. He's beaten me. I let people win so they feel good, but I come away the real winner because I know better. I pretend to be disappointed and shake Rogers' hand. His hands are pretty shaky anyway to be honest. The poor old alkie sod.

I once slept with a man at university in Brighton who had a similar drinking problem, only he was twenty-two years old. I can't even remember his name. He was a Greek Cypriot. A bear of a man. He had olive skin beneath all the hair. The first man I ever slept with. I was nineteen (same age as the student I'm supposed to have killed last Christmas). What was my lover's name? He was funny and lovely at first. We met in a bar. I hadn't gone there for sex. At the time I'd been flirting with a lot of girls. I'm good-looking. I get attention from both sides of the fence.

Modern man hunts with his eyes not Neanderthal clubs, but the way he looked at me he may as well have clubbed me, dragged me back to his cave and had his way. We had a classic eyes-meet moment. He had a lot of confidence and spoke in sexy, broken English. His pupils were so dilated I could not read the colour until much later (hazelnut?). He speeded through conversations and had a bottle of beer in his hand. As he was telling me his life story (it included what he called "The Nicosia Question", which sounded like the title of a Home Office white paper), he was peeling the label off the front of his bottle of Bud. A sure sign of sexual frustration. It was my first year at University, a whole year before my father's accident. I was lodging on campus and invited this man back to my room. He undressed me. He said I had good "muskles". That's how he said it. He was gorgeous. George! That was his name. Georgi. Gorgeous Georgi. He took his clothes off, the hairy brute, and got on top of me. He sucked me like I was a stick of Brighton rock. His eight o'clock shadow chafed my thighs and I had to apply cream for days. Men's faces can be cheese graters. Up until this point, no man had ever fellated me. A sixth former rubbed me off on the back seat of a school bus once but that doesn't count. Georgi was better than a woman, and a lot of women have gone down on me. I've slept with half a dozen girls, though not at the same time, although that's a stimulating idea. No, this Cypriot was better not because he was experienced, it was because at the time of leading up to my explosion I was thinking, *a man is doing this*, like it's against the law or something, or my father would be sick if he knew and my mother would faint if she thought a man had hold of my cock in his teeth. It heightened the experience. Well, it was my first proper "male" time and it felt like electricity. It wasn't love, it was lust of a carnal nature. How else can lust be, if not carnal?

Georgi would drink all afternoon and then come and see me, or we'd meet in bars along the seafront. We'd go clubbing and he would drink all night. We went to the cinema and he had to have a drink before and after, like he had to before sex. He had to have lots of drinks before doing anything with me. I can't remember a single morning when he didn't wake up with a hangover.

I drink. I like the hum and buzz. I've been legless. I love champagne and orange juice at Christmas. I love Pinot Grigio all year round. It's light and fresh and easy. I love cocktails etc. but there have to be self-imposed limits. A cut-off point, some self-control.

Georgi kissed me this one night. We'd been to his friend's party. He kissed me and he stank to the high heavens of whisky sours. I wouldn't let his mouth near mine. I told him, 'You should drink to live, not live to drink.'

'No platitudes,' he said, pushing me onto my bed. He pinned my arms above my head and forced my legs apart with his knees. 'You want some?' He said he was going to roll me over, pull my pants off and fuck me like a Cyprian goat. Sometimes I like to be dominated but most times I don't like being out of control. He got more abusive, stinking of the gutter. I lay there utterly passive and he couldn't go through with it. His dick was a knob of melting wax and we had an argument so loud someone knocked on my door and we ignored it. 'What are you?' he yelled.

'Very complicated,' I said. 'And I could ask you the same question, you humpback.'

'Are you drinks police or preacher man?'

I ended our affair. No one calls me a preacher. I threw his tacky trousers into the corridor and wouldn't let him back in, despite the hammering. I didn't sleep with him again which is a pity because it wasn't always rough. Beneath the bear-like exterior there was a naive little Greek Orthodox boy; the child he once was who'd lived a joyous existence picking lizards out of rocks with sticks not far from Paphos where he grew up, in a white cottage beside lemon and orange groves; a boy who loved his mother and hated his father for beating a donkey to death because it could not carry him. Very Oedipal. We were both Catholics and took our indoctrinations out on each other in the sack. There was no future with Georgi, only ever the present. He returned to Cyprus a few months later, sent me letters and cards inviting me over for sun and sea and etc. But there was nothing to say. He was history.

What I didn't like about the whole Georgi episode was the "preacher" tag. In psychoanalytical terms I think it's called the Superego. He'd been right to pin it on me. I can be a preacher sometimes and I can't help it (as if you don't know already). I'm a real pontificator. If I was the Pope I'd cripple the world with conscience. I'd be a right Nazi. Georgi had told me what I hadn't wanted to accept. That sometimes I can turn into my father or my mother or my priest; a red-neck rooster full of crowing platitudes. Drink to live, not live to drink? That's something my mother would say. I could have been forty-eight or something. But on reflection, I'd rather have this flaw (call it a safety mechanism) than turn into Georgi or Rogers. Hands and minds all over the shop.

I look at Rogers now with a sense of sorrow and relief it isn't me. His hollowed-out cheeks and shaking hands. Though I guess we all have our foibles and addictions; everyone on remand and everyone in the outside world. We are all doing some sort of daily cold turkey: booze, drugs, sex, violence, gardening, video games, TV. Whatever. Imogen and her cocaine at irregular intervals; Alex Fortune and his painkillers; Maurice and his medieval history; mother and her religion; mother and her appearance; father and his beds; Manston and his heterosexual insecurities. What about Red Buchanan? What drives Red?

He walks the circumference of the TV room passing the occasional comment to inmates, making them smile. Maybe he is the only one who is balanced in the world. Red the Rock. Round the red rock the rugged rock star ran (I told you, you can go crazy in here). Addictions. Yes. We all have these. It's just how you deal with them when you can't satisfy the need.

Short short story, aka "flash-fiction": I say story, but actually it is true. It was in the newspaper only last week. There was once a man (I'm keeping him anonymous out of respect, but we can call him Mr K.West). This man lived alone most of his adult life. Bit of a loner but perfectly polite with work colleagues. Mr West was a creature of habit and time. He caught a bus to work and a bus home at precisely the same times each day and he always took his umbrella. This was what he was known for. No matter what the season or weather he carried his umbrella. Co-workers laughed behind his back. It could be the clearest, hottest day in summer but Mr West had it tucked under his arm or behind his desk. When he took lunch, it was with his trusty umbrella at his side. It was a handy walking stick, a close friend as much as anything else. Sometimes he'd even talk to it, in private. 'Where are you my umbrella?' 'You're all wet, let's give you a good shake'. It was a lovely umbrella. Long and elegant and black with a stitched-in strap for tying; an ornately carved handle and fine metal point to use as a weapon should anyone take him on in the subway to the bus station. It was a very masculine umbrella with a curved oak handle shaped like a question mark. He was more used to the feel of this handle than the hand of a fellow human being. He had held it so often it seemed he could feel the grooves of his own fingers and palm on the wood. People often joked that he must sleep with that bloody umbrella.

Mr West was a sanguine fellow. Bit serious about everything. But when it started raining unexpectedly he was the happiest man alive. He'd flap open the umbrella like a raven's wing, stretch it over himself and dance to the bus stop, almost singing in the rain. Doo-be-doo-doo, doo-be, etc. He'd smile at those who'd not had the foresight to bring an umbrella.

One day, he clocked off at the office as usual, hopped onto a bus and made his way back to an empty house. It was a Friday. The traffic was heavy along the ring road. Real staccato. Stop start, stop start. Mr West was very tired after a gruelling week and momentarily closed his eyes, head sticking to a vibrating window. A sudden jerk stirred him and he opened his eyes to realise he was at his stop already. A stroke of luck not to have missed it. He picked up his briefcase and tore down the gangway. He jumped off just before the double doors closed. The bus stayed stationary a while, its right indicator winking, unable to pull out into the commuter traffic. The man felt a cold splash on his cheek, a spit on his face, and he knew what it meant. He looked at the grey sky as if it was the sea descending. Another splash came, this time landing on his left earlobe. He lifted his hand automatically as if the umbrella was in it, heart slipping to his shoes. He remembered having the umbrella, remembered leaning it against the seat in front of him. His heart banged as if he had left a lover behind. Not that he'd ever had a lover.

'Stop!' he shouted through the closed doors. The driver ignored him, turning the steering wheel, rolling the front out. The man waved both arms, flapped his briefcase. He banged on the doors. Nothing, except funny looks from the passengers. The bus rolled out a bit further, the engine revved, black fumes plumed out of the exhaust. Mr West ran alongside and the passengers pointed at him. Then he jumped in front, got caught under the kerb-side wheel and was instantly killed.

You're thinking, what happened to his umbrella? A passenger liked the look of it, the feel of the handle, took it home, using it against buckets of rain, thinking he was very lucky. But I ask you, the newspaper headline said: "Man killed under bus". That didn't do the story, Mr West or the umbrella any justice. I ask myself: What killed him? The bus driver? Was it falling asleep or the spot of rain? Was it his obsession with the umbrella or was it the umbrella? Or had the man killed himself? Or was it just a fateful combination? I put the newspaper down and thought: the things you think offer you protection can actually kill you; maybe even the things you love the most.

Manston's getting itchy for a kicking. He's been cooped up on remand for longer than anyone else. He moves across to the bar football table and I step aside. 'You're shit, Rogers,' he says, sneering, pushing a ball into the arena. 'But not as shit as Bent Tippet.'

A couple of his cronies titter, hanging on to his words like children grabbing security blankets. A bully needs friends to impress or he becomes useless as a human being. There's only one thing worse than a man who needs to be superior but who feels inferior and that's a man who recognises the nascent superiority of others. The ape-stare he gives me. I give as good as I get. I'll steer clear but I won't tip my head in supplication, subservience, whatever. As my mother used to tell me as a child: 'Walk with your head up. Reach for the clouds. Keep your spine straight. Don't slouch. Stand tall and everyone will look up to you.' Very *Ain't half hot, Mum.*

Manston knuckles down to a fresh game of football, gives me a creepy smile meant to intimidate. 'What you staring at, hard-on?' He has taken to calling me this recently. Failing "hard-on", "Bent Tippet" and "Benny Boy", it's "Ben Dover". How original. I think of him as Manston Pickle which makes us even, and I smile to myself.

'What you got to smile about?' he says, cracking the balls. 'You better get used to going down, faggot.'

Maybe it's what Manston reads about me in the tabloids or sees on TV. He's jealous of my newfound celebrity status or it's the media tag "bisexual". If it's not a man on a woman, you're a bender or a lezza in Manston's warped world. I hate such labels. They inflame me. All it is, is that I like people (men and women) about equally. I am who I am and that is equivocal. I sleep with people for personal reasons. As Oscar Wilde said, humans are sexual creatures, not one thing or another. But people have built pigeon holes and pinned labels and condemned anyone of a different persuasion to themselves. Christ. Byron enjoyed sleeping with his half-sister. Does anyone wag their hoary finger at him?

Manton's probably curious beneath his hyped-up heterosexuality, the page three pictures in his cell, the smutty jokes. He constantly talks about genitalia and fanny farts. Ho, ho, ho. Hold my stitches. He seems to like hard-ons in general. He's taken a keen interest in mine in particular. He's started doing this ugly thing to me: making a tunnel out of his fist, holding it up to his mouth, making a knob-end of his tongue inside his cheek, simulating a blowjob. He does it now. It's childish and hardly original. Somehow he has turned something wonderful into a cathedral grotesque; offensively lunatic and threatening. He could whip me to a creamy pulp if he wanted.

'What's it to be, Rogers?' he says. 'A packet of FAGS?' Rogers is a bit slow on the uptake and Manston looks me up and down for emphasis. 'You're a turf accountant, ain't you, Rogers? What you say? Five FAGS?' Really. How many times can he say FAG like that?

Rogers opens his Superkings, lines a few cigarettes on the side of the table, and Manston puts his Embassy down. 'What you say we play us a man's game?' He thinks he's 100% Spaghetti Western.

Lee Van Cleef or Clint Eastwood. But Manston's more like one of the walk-on meathead parts; some green-arsed Gringo. It's all for my benefit and I pretend not to hear, not to be visibly ruffled.

My mother is a pretty good judge of character. She says idiots are like cow pats; you just have to avoid them. That's fine if you have room, but you can't do much in an enclosed space like this. She once took a good look around the visiting room making judgements about each inmate in seconds. She told me I'm surrounded by idiots and cow pats and the sooner I'm out of here the better. I couldn't have agreed more. 'Him for instance,' she said, giving Manston the evil eye. 'He's a dozy lummox if ever I saw one'. 'Keep it down,' I said. 'No one calls him a lummox.' 'Why?' she said. 'Who is he? King Kong?' And I said, 'How large do you think King Kong's pats are?'

She's right about Manston Pickle though. He is dumb. He's never heard of Sudoku or Keats or ever added up numbers other than on a dartboard, but you don't call him an idiot. He'd half-strangle you, rip out your larynx and play it like a harmonica. I bet his father used to knock him from pillar to post. I bet his teachers used to call him a useless dunce and that accounts for his wasted, violent life ever since. Who knows? Who cares? Sometimes I panic at night thinking prison-proper will be overpopulated with Manstons. You can avoid them for a while, but not forever. They need to be top dogs, kings of the jungle. They've mastered the method: the swagger, the hard stare, the exercise of dominion. They've been in so many scrapes and scraps that their skin has toughened into hide.

Raw hide. Steer clear.

Red mingles close by, ears and eyes wide open. The kind uncle.

Apparently, so Red tells me, going to court is a release (irony). Going for a ride every day is like a holiday, if you don't let the actual trial burden you. Sitting in the dock listening to everyone talking about you is better than counting the number of breezeblocks in your cell. You are the centre of attention, not an anonymous number. You get to see your family and friends in the gallery. You have new faces to stare at too. Good people of the jury etc. Stenographer no doubt. Press people and general public curious. If you don't let the trial actually get to you it can be stimulating, so I'm told. At least you get a few days out.

It's just around the corner. My trial. I should be half way through it already but for the sodding prosecution. I try not to get maudlin. Even so, I go to sleep staring at my toilet roll holder, thinking of the unnamed teenager who choked on sheets of bog paper. The bipolar shoplifter. How low does a young man have to feel to do that? Loneliness and desperation can knock your spirit into touch, that's true. But to end it? To take everything you have been, everything you are, everything you might become, roll them up and throw them away - or swallow yourself whole. You have to be strong, I tell myself. You have to understand that without darkness there'd be no light to cast shadows which you leave behind.

Seven

I don't sleep well.

I have acute hearing which is the problem. Or maybe I'm getting jumpy. It doesn't take much to get the adrenalin pumping: a prison officer's innuendo, a door banging so hard it might come off its hinges, a jangle of keys, a shout, a remander wailing. Last night it was Rogers and his constant coughing. The chain-smoker coughs all night long like that country and western singer Leonard Cohen sang about. Hank Williams. Even though he's five doors down it magnifies in my head as if he's under my pillow. I asked Red for earplugs but he won't let me have any because of fire regulations (ironies abound in this story of mine). 'Pretend you're deaf,' he actually said.

On top of this, the man in the cell next to me has been sent down for rape. He went to court in the morning and never came back. His cell was cleaned out and a new inmate has been installed. He's called Moses Cowper; in for alleged booze and cigarette racketeering, Calais to Dover. Hardly the big-time. You know, a global heroine trail. He's Brixton-African in origin, about twenty years old. Someone said he's an Islamic terrorist using earnings from crime to fund a fundamentalist revolution - just because he prays more than once a day! I don't think he prays. I don't think he's an Islamic terrorist either because his nose would get in the way. He has the worst case of sinusitis you've ever come across. A real disability if you're a terrorist. Always snorting, closing one nose-hole with a knuckle, snorting, then the other hole, same knuckle, snorting. Why can't he use a bloody handkerchief? Moses is worse than Imogen, my creative writing tutor. She's damaged her nostrils with cocaine and should know better.

Moses needs an operation. The sinus headaches are 'fuckin' terrible', he says, which might explain the premature aging and pained expression on his face. He's quite plain-looking over all. His hair is cropped short in tight curls. His eyes are fudge brown. The one admirable physical feature definitely being his eyelashes; long and dark like caterpillar legs when you see them close up. Enviable lashes. Girlish. Liza Minnelli lids. Moses is not biblically-proportioned; not the sort of man to risk life and limb in a desert for forty days and forty nights returning with momentous and informative tablets of stone; not the sort to fly a plane into a building or destroy the underground. The only burning bush he knows is skunk. He says he is innocent, but we all say that until we are found guilty. He swears he bought the booty for personal consumption but he doesn't smoke or drink. Still, he's one of the friendly people in here and there aren't that many. We talk a lot during association time. He swears a lot for someone called Moses. He calls me "The fuckin' Man" because of all the press coverage surrounding my case; at other times, for the fun of it, "The fuckin' BT Man". Moses is really cool.

Bless me reader for I have sinned, it has been quite a few pages since my last narration. Forgive me for jumping all over the place; on the page, in my cell, in my head, from person to person. In attempts to free my mind a randomness has crept in. Sometimes my mind leaps from idea to memory, from memory to idea, from person to person, from time to time, like a randy frog to frogess to frog to frogess hoping not to fall into the murky pond between (lazy simile, try again later. Toad not frog, for starters).

Digression, divurgation, displacement. Where's your plot gone, Ben? It's supposed to be like a deck of cards or dominoes falling into each other, in some sort of order. Think "cause and effect". You've forgotten the basic principles taught in your diploma and the eleven commandments. What did Imogen say? The story is the body, the character is the heart, the viewpoint is the eyes. The narrative framework is the skeleton, the bones, the spine upon which all else hangs.

You need a chiropractor. You need to straighten things out, speak in a straight line, walk the tight rope. Go back to the proper story; the narrative thrust. Onwards and forwards and don't look down. What did Imogen say? Don't load a gun you will not fire; don't start a fire you will not put out (ha ha ha). Pull the trigger, dowse the flames. Quickly, Ben, before you are hung, drawn and quartered. Metaphorically speaking.

[Enter Imogen Wood]

Imogen was my tutor for three months (September to December of last year) but I first met her at a summer school; an inexpensive three-day deal entitled "Writing From Memory". I liked her style straight off. Dressed comfortably in a reasonably tight black shirt and indigo denims with Adidas pumps, she was not one for obvious make-up. I probably had more eyeliner on. She made do with lip-gloss. She was boyish, about 5' 6", with choppy, tousled strawberry-blonde hair and earnest, hard-working ice-blue eyes. Nordic. Her nose was delightfully impish, the tip turning slightly skywards so you could almost see up it. Clear skin for a smoker. The sun had bleached her hair out and huddled freckles across her forehead and nose giving her an innocence she'd not want to recognise. I knew from checking out her blog in advance that she was thirty-five, had published six novels (in the Sci-Fi genre) and had started writing at the age of fifteen. She wasn't married but wore a chunky silver ring on her wedding finger. All of these details have stuck with me. I learnt a great deal from her blog. She was in her e-words, "a rebel without a university clause saying it was okay to be a rebel" and a "friendly feminist freedom-fighter". I fancied her immediately. It wasn't just her body I craved (I'm a sexbloodymaniac if you haven't guessed), it was her critical mind. She was in the writing business. She knew what she was doing, and I wanted an "in".

You see, even though I am a brilliant writer I needed to be told by someone who knew, other than myself. Imogen was my first literary touchstone. I mean, I had trawled through the first pages of so many novels at Little's bookshop to see how easy writing was and I'd written lots of short stories and a few poems (most of which are unfinished). I'd won the Pensbury Gazette short story competition with a story about the Tsunami disaster entitled *Three-Minute Warning* (won £50 of Aveda tokens) so I was feeling good about myself. But you need constant praise when you start out. I'll need it until the day I die; maybe even afterwards.

Imogen put us through our creative paces. The weather was good in mid-July so she broke with tradition and settled us outside, in the shade thrown onto the grass by a bulky oak tree. Her favourite place on earth, she said. Campus was quiet, the full-time students being away for the summer. We wrote things about our pasts, from childhood to the present day. Anything from memory.

The following day, she read some of the pieces out. It was supposed to have been autobiographical but I made a substantial part of mine up for dramatic effect - which is the whole point of creative non-fiction, though most of my co-learners didn't have a clue. Imogen read mine and everyone clapped. It was a 1,000-word piece called *Big Raisins*; something I extended and handed in for my portfolio in the autumn (see appendix).

'Intriguing title,' Imogen said. 'Brave subject-matter. Has anyone else read the subtext? I'm assuming this didn't happen in reality, Ben?'

'Some of it,' I said, and she raised her lovely eyebrows.

Yes. I fancied her straight off. We had a chat at the end of the third day and she suggested I do her part-time course in September, called simply: "Writing Fiction" (all this is so boring, Ben. Jump straight to the sex bits).

I like Pensbury University. It's an expanding 1960s Rubik's cube of redbrick colleges named after famous writers, economists, philosophers and scientists. The buildings are perched on a high-sloped hill overlooking the city and its cathedral. Some of the best views in the city. Imogen called it "A classic English Protestant vista". She's very politicised and controversial when it comes to large organisations such as Church, State, Government, University, business conglomerates, globalisation etc. Some might call her a trouble-maker but really she's just concerned about animals and the planet. For her, the revolution is endless (as a revolution should be), Marxism moves in mysterious ways and feminism is a creed. Her world is governed by isms whereas mine is governed largely by asms: spasms, chasms, orgasms. She's an ism-junkie whereas I'm more of a jism-monkey. We're utterly unsuited, which is why we clicked.

The university is a bustling city-within-a-city having its own bars and cafés, cinema, shops and nightclub; a hive of intellectual and sexual endeavour. Between terms though, it maintains a sad and lonely eeriness as if the souls of its previous hundreds of thousands of students stalk the grounds. Maybe I'm just a romantic at heart. Maybe I'm jealous because I never went there in the first place or even finished my media degree at Brighton. I don't know, I never seem to finish anything.

Cutting a long story short, Imogen convinced me during the Michaelmas term that I was a natural-born writer. Everything I wrote and everything she read was affirmation. I travelled up the hill cheerily in my Saab every Tuesday evening for twelve weeks. Each week her twelve apostles (as she called us) gathered around the table in the English department listening to her pearls of wisdom. Cast before swine if her general aloofness was anything to go by. She was not the friendly tutor of the summer school any more. More teacherly and academic. Sometimes ratty. She gave us punishing esoteric reading lists and insisted we read everything on them. Two people dropped out in the first fortnight, something I think she was pleased about. I could see that teaching starter modules was getting up her impish nose. She revealed as much to me a few weeks later (don't jump ahead too fast, Ben, you're like a yo-yo). Through those Nordic eyes she saw us as hapless wannabees sucking all the honey out of her hive. It was exhausting for her in every way.

"Writing Fiction" was for beginners but she had too-high expectations of us. Some of us anyhow. The average age in our class was fifty (Alex would approve of that statistic) and two-thirds female. I'd categorise them into five attitudinal subgroups: *girly-whirlies, whirly-girlies, burly-girlies, surly-girlies* and *pearly-girlies*. I hope these are self-explanatory. Girly-whirlies are young (18 to 21) or haven't progressed from that stage no matter what age they are. Whirly-girlies are off-the-wall, a bit kooky, a bit mad at times but in a good way (Imogen would fall into this category). Burly-girlies are butch, dealt a lot of testosterone whatever, and can be lesbians, though not necessarily. Surly-girlies are bolshy. They have a gripe, an axe to grind (probably not getting enough sex at home, or anywhere). Pearly-girlies are ladies of leisure, usually married to wealthy husbands, so have a lot of time on their hands. They dress well, sometimes wear pearls, and come from the middle middle-class stratum.

The interesting thing was that the subgroups were not clearly delineated. There was flexibility i.e. women moved from one subgroup to another in a single two-hour class, reverting back to the underlying type by the end of the session. You could have whirly-girly-whirlies, surly-whirly-girlies, surly-pearlies, pearlywhirly-girlies, etc. All sorts of combinations really. What you wouldn't want, for health and safety reasons, is a room full of surly-burly-girlies.

This mutability (great word, Ben) makes women more unpredictable, more complex, more interesting than men who are only of two types: *Blokey-jokey* and *Mr Serious*. In my personal and professional experience, men start off as blokey-jokey blokes but always end up as Mr Serious (me included). It's a genetic jungle survival thing. Men make jokes to mate but they are deadly serious when it comes to marking their territory, finding food, getting drunk, protecting their pack, and making their opinions felt. Alex by the way is Mr Serious, but he does make jokes occasionally. Being Mr Serious does not make him unlovable. All subtypes - male and female - can be lovable in their own individual ways. If you don't believe me, consider those you know: partners, husbands, wives, ex-boyfriends/girlfriends. Determine which subgroup they belong to. You'll find one.

I am too young to be this cynical. It should rub against my youthful grain. But maybe it's the preacher in me. The Superego stamped on my insides. Being nearly twenty-five at that time I brought the average age of the group down. The other men in my class were a 40s and a retired 60s. They were always in the library geeking it to the max. Mr Seriousnesses, you see.

At the first meeting Imogen played an ice-breaker game. We had to discover things about each other in twos, then introduce our 'partner' to the class. I made a b-line for the youngest in the group; an exceptionally pretty girly-whirly called Lea. 'After Princess?' I joked (though she wasn't wearing a diaphanous dress). 'Everybody says that,' she said, real tight-arsed. We didn't hit it off. She was twenty and very shy. She'd only ever written poetry, and only ever for herself, and only ever about herself. She had Plath-angst, playing *The Bell Jar* blues. 'A novel is an open hand,' she explained, 'but a poem is a clenched fist.' Lea was about to have an interview in a beauty salon. I swear she was so attractive and she didn't even know it. A young Elizabeth Taylor. Crystal blue eyes, spotless alabaster skin, glossy jet hair and fairytale lips. 'You would make an excellent advertisement,' I said. Her face. It turned from snow-white to red riding-hood in a millisecond. She really was shy, so lacking in confidence that when I probed she said she shouldn't be doing this fiction course because she was a poet by nature and hadn't lived long enough to write anything meaningful. 'Look at me,' I said. 'You don't have to be a dinosaur to have lived.'

Having said that, most of the class were bony dinosaurs. A giant baby could've picked up the classroom and used it as a rattle. Almost half were teachers or ex-teachers, the rest were university administrators and knew each other well. They formed a clique at coffee-break and said things like: 'Assonance is a very assonant word, n'est ce pas?' and 'I need to use more free indirect discourse, darling,' I kept myself to myself, not always the best thing to do because everyone thinks you're a psychopath or just plain rude. I think Lea cottoned on to my ulterior motives. She was one of the first to leave the course. A great shame, because I really liked the idea of her clenched fist.

Almost without exception, the remaining women in my group wrote about food, babies, motherhood, sisterhood, shopping, abusive or neglectful husbands/partners/fathers/uncles, illicit affairs, holidays and low self-esteem. Whereas the men wrote about only three things: nymphomaniacs, pubs and death. That's okay. You can write what the hell you like. What I don't appreciate is lazy, ineffective writing, especially clichés. Life is not clichéd in reality so why make it so in fiction? (even that's becoming a cliché).

One week, Imogen gave us what she called a "Cliché Class". It was a four-hour workshop and I got into a spot of bother. There was a story from a pearly-girly. Mills and Boon plot. She had written things like: "I arrived in good time for the Aga workshop." GROAN! "As for the knickers, she just hoped today wasn't the day she got run down by a bus" CLANG! "They were so in tune with one another they didn't have to speak" CLANG-CLANG, ALL ABOARD THE GOODSHIP CLICHÉ! "Dark hairs peeked through his crisp white shirt" CLANG-CRASS-STEREOTYPE! "On their anniversary, she opened her husband's coat, lifted out a love letter, and discovered someone else's name on it" CLANG-PREDICTABLE! "He peeled her open with his eyes, like an onion" MIXED-METAPHOR-CLANG-WHOPPER!

I said, 'You don't peel a person - or for that matter an onion - open with your eyes.' The group prickled, one-by-one, like a Mexican wave. A burly-girly jumped to the pearly-girly's defence: 'How about "he undressed her with his eyes"?'

'That's even worse,' I said. 'Why don't you just put in a line-break denoting change of scene or time, then start a new paragraph with "he undressed her with his hands"? Sometimes the literal is better than the figurative.'

The surly-pearly-girly glared across the room, peeling me like an onion, and after that no one in the group got on with me. I was the smart-arse kid who everyone secretly envied. But I was only trying to improve their writing. My suggestions were always practical. I was an outsider; an alien invader of their campus cosiness.

An alien was exactly how I'd felt when I'd read the individual workshop pieces back at home, before the workshop. Without exception, the male writers saw fictional women in black and white: whore or virgin, Magdalene or Mary, lover or mother. The female writers saw their fictional men in a similar two-tone light: sexual predator or poof, Jesus or Judas, lover or father. Or as one disgruntled man put it during the lunch-break: papist or rapist. In reality, men and women are all shades of the rainbow; we just don't see them very often.

Sitting in my flat reading these workshop pieces in advance had me imagining I was an alien sent to Earth on a mission to discover the differences between male and female for a post-apocalyptic breeding programme, but instead of landing in the British Museum (font of all Earthling knowledge), I had landed in Ben Tippet's flat. He went to bed and I scanned all the workshop pieces for knowledge and meaning. I read every word on every page and found myself in a bit of a pickle. The breeding programme was out of the question, unless I could persuade Earthlings to love the differences between themselves, to understand that men are not from Mars and women are not from Venus; they are, depressingly enough, the same species borne of Mother Earth. Knowing what I knew about the future (the Great Earth Wars of 2091 and the end of all Earthlings) I had to make a snap judgement and I chose not to bother saving them. I made an executive decision to let the apes take over again, let evolution run its course, and that was that.

Imogen used to set us tasks each week, sneakily regarding us when our heads were down. Our pens scribbled and splurged in first, second and third person. I caught her out more than once as I looked up from my notebook. She would smile a Mona Lisa smile (cliché, must try harder), a mischievous kink in one corner of her mouth. She tended to look away quickly. I had the same crush on her as I once had on Mrs Harkness, my English teacher from moons ago (get on with it, Ben. Christ!)

It's all about connections. We made a connection every week. At our last one-to-one tutorial in week eight (the first one had been in week one and we'd pussy-footed around the fact we fancied each other), I dropped into the conversation that I'd read some of her novels, copies of which were lined up prominently on her desk. It was true, I had read three of them back-to-back during the night (they were pocket-sized novellas). Imogen seemed to perk up. Every writer worth her salt I have discovered *hates* nothing more than talking about her novel-in-progress, yet *loves* nothing more than talking about her polished, published ones. I told her which ones I'd read and she asked quite bravely, 'What do you think?'

What was I going to say? The narratives seem conjured from fairy tale? The characters so wooden you could smell the shavings on the floor? What I actually said was untrue (Byron said that pure invention is but the talent of a liar). I said I'd been impressed by her handling of complex narratives, themes and wordplay. They are genre books and she successfully breaks the rules in each one. Some important critics like her experimentalism. At least she has a publisher. It isn't pulp. I'd read far worse. I'd read the first page of every novel that came into Little's and the majority were so dire, so wonderfully miresome, that they filled me with enough enthusiasm to write a thousand books of my own.

'Do you think there's too much sex?' she asked, straight-faced. 'In the novels I mean.' Usually, she was very serious in tutorials. Flippant now. A real whirly-girly. She was happy because of a telephone call from her agent; good news regarding her latest novel.

'I really enjoyed the sex bits,' I said, with no embarrassment. 'I read in one of the books you recommended that one can never have too much sex in fiction.'

'Wrong,' she said. 'Just as in real life one can never have too much GOOD SEX, one can always have too much BAD SEX.'

'One doesn't have much sex, good or bad in mine,' I said.

Her eyes flickered and she laughed. 'In fiction or in real life?'

Wow! We'd touched first base. A meeting of minds. Or so I'd thought, because the conversation tailed off then into the banalities of my portfolio when all I wanted there and then was flesh-fiction, not flash-fiction.

At the end of the tutorial, she complained about the weather which was beating at her window. She looked tired all of a sudden. She doesn't drive for ideological reasons. A lot of academics don't drive and I think this is because they have their minds on more exalted missions. This and they drink too much. Imogen hates mechanical things, car pollution, plane pollution. She said in a previous life she must have been a Luddite. I didn't know what she was talking about. I offered her a lift but she turned me down saying she preferred to catch a bus. Besides, she had "work" things to do.

'It's gone eight o'clock,' I said, getting up. 'You need a life outside of this one.'

She looked at me the way someone does when you have hit the nail on the head. A connection. Fingers in the socket moment. Whatever. I walked to the door, was turning the handle and the rain battered her windows again.

'Ben? About that lift...?'

(Excruciating build-up. Why are you taking so long? Because it's worth the wait. If I load a gun, I pull the trigger; start a fire, watch it burn).

She threw on a black trench coat, stuffed her mobile, books and folders inside a backpack and switched off her computer. She hit the lights and we went to my car shoulder-to-shoulder under her black umbrella (not in reality because she's six inches shorter than me, seven inches shorter in her bare feet).

Maybe I had unrealistic expectations. Winning a story competition (local though it was) and making the shortlists of half a dozen small competitions had fuelled my ambition and self-belief. Maybe it was the praise heaped on me by Imogen, getting first class assessments. Maybe it was because writing was the only thing in the world which made me truly happy. Maybes are just maybes like wannabees are just wannabees, but I was very optimistic of the future.

Imogen was in a frivolous mood that November night, and so was I. Two days before I'd received an email from Acorn Publishing telling me that my short story *Me and You* (see appendix) had made that year's long list of 250. The news hatched a rare, uncatchable, beautiful butterfly inside my stomach, fluttering. There had been nearly 5,000 original entries. Flutter, flutter, flutter.

The Acorn Short Story Prize is the most famous prose fiction competition on the planet; not so much a rung on the literary ladder as an express elevator. I'd entered three years running: nowhere first year, long-listed second year, now long-listed again. So, third time lucky? According to the Acorn website, 45 of the anthologised authors had gone on to write collections of short stories, novellas or novels, most of them published. 10 of its outright winners had published novels within two years of winning. The prize money this year had risen to a whopping £5,000. It was only open to "new" writers but you have to take that with a lorry load of salt. "New" is open to interpretation, as I discovered going through the back-catalogue. Half the stories were written by people who'd been published before, some of them well-established names.

That's how blown away I was, getting long-listed I mean. I was a complete unknown. Charlie Nobody in search of his elusive Willy Wonka ticket. The year before, I'd fallen headlong into the longlist hurdle with a story called *Excremental* (not in appendix). That year, I'd told the world and his dog, my work colleagues and bookshop customers, my mother and father and Uncle D, and old school friends, the postman, a girl who works in my local corner shop who I bought champagne from to celebrate my premature success. This, I'm convinced, brought down the terrible curse upon me. The Tippet Curse which follows me like my own shadow. I bragged myself to death that year, looking foolish when my name did not appear on the final shortlist.

So, I would tell no one this time around, not until I'd won or at least had something to show for my efforts. And what efforts they had been, sitting in my flat tapping and scribbling away dreams and visions and working until my fingertips went numb and I could not see my screen, the words floating around like fluff. Efforts and dreams. Everyone should have at least one dream. This was mine. I carried it around like an excitable and rare butterfly trapped in my stomach. It fluttered when I least expected it. The middle of the night when I stirred. Flutter, flutter. Putting a book on a shelf at Little's. Flutter, flutter. Watching some old film. Flutter, flutter.

So paranoid was I this year that I entered the competition under a pseudonym; a female alter-ego called Cassi Hart. An anagram taken from a word which I think is the germ of all powerful writing. Call it cynical. I saw it as pragmatic. 60% of winning stories were written by women. It didn't take a genius. I was thinking about a launch party of the next anthology should Cassi Hart be successful. Would I dress as a woman or ask Uncle D to receive the award pretending to be Cassi Hart? The whole thing being ridiculous. You only had to attend the launch if you were the over all winner and given my story used the word "cunt" at least once I didn't see winning as credible (although I did in my wildest dreams and fantasies).

Now I hope you can see why I was so confidant, so adrenalin-laden, so excited that November night, almost a year ago now, with Imogen in my car, travelling to a restaurant. The restaurant was my suggestion, as we were both starving. The vegetarian place wasn't far from her house. I was itching to spit out my Acorn news but couldn't, fearing the Tippet Curse again.

We shook our coats off and sat down by a window overlooking the river, the gate tower and a little roundabout. It was busy outside and inside. Jazz was playing over the speakers and the whole scene had me thinking of a French movie. It turned out Imogen liked French movies; she once had a crush on a Jean-Paul somebody from a Jean Luc Goddard film called *A Bout de Souffle*.

In keeping with the theme, Imogen ordered a bottle of organic French dry white wine (I decided I would leave my car in the council car park over night). We spoke about Little's Bookshop and then our favourite novels. Imogen had abstract ideas and tastes. Lots of European writers, American hedonists and pill-poppers, Gonzo journalists and psycho-geographers, absurdists and situationists (never underestimate the power of Google - I knew all about these styles, and that Gonzo was not a muppet but a brilliant fool). She insisted I read an existential masterpiece: Albert Camus' *The Outsider*. She could lend me a copy from her collection at home. Why would she do that? I had a whole bookshop full of books to find a copy or order one in. I mentioned Joyce, Carver, Amis, Roth, McEwan, Marquez, Rushdie and Fortune.

'Marquez?' she said. 'Joyce? Roth? Amis? Fortune? Rushdie? Carver? Dirty apologists. You should read younger authors. Or at least those who are still living. And women. Don't forget women writers.'

'Joyce could be dirty but what would he be apologising for?' I said.

So we talked, and the rain battered the windows and headlights flashed around the roundabout. Imogen appeared animated by candlelight, was lively in conversation. She looked at her watch now and then, mumbling about her cat needed feeding and she might have left an upstairs window open. I misread her, thinking she was trying to get away from me and we hadn't even eaten anything. But everything was alright. Her Mediterranean flan with bruchetta side-dish arrived and seemed quite appetising beside my cheese-filled baked potato and coleslaw. Large and hard enough, I suggested, to take ten-pin bowling.

'It's usually very good but I don't eat here that often,' she said. 'It's the only true vegetarian place in Pensbury. All organic.'

Have I mentioned her vegetarianism? I'd discovered this much earlier, on her blog. I've never been one for blogs but I'd read Imogen's with great interest. She'd really put herself out there in cyberspace. Her whole past, not just her professional life. I knew everything there was to know about her without having to speak over dinner. The only thing worth pursuing was her sex. At least sex can be intimate and more revealing about a person. It's a great leveller. It needn't be controlled or contrived. Not like a blog.

Facts: working class council estate, childhood struggle with her father who abandoned her mother when she was very young. Imogen's sole memory of him was a lesson he gave her using his leather boxing gloves (he was a sports columnist for the local newspaper which is not exactly working class and neither is the name Imogen come to that). She swung out a skinny little arm and made his nose bleed, and if she ever met him again she would knock his teeth out with her bare fists.

Personally, reading between the lines, I think she loved and missed him. Absent-father syndrome. Electra complex or something. There was her adolescent struggle (everything is a struggle for a writer) with anorexia nervosa, identity crisis, drug-taking and self-harming; her mother's intermittent depression and finally there was Imogen's reading and writing salvation. Writing had saved her life and now she was on a mission to save others' lives; even if it was through SF. A list of the bands she liked (never heard of them), books she rated highly (not heard of most of them), some "unpublished" short stories (she never had a short story published), titillating extracts from her first three novels (not the sex bits), a few on-line reviews of her work etc.

I've read a lot of blogs and as far it went Imogen's was honest enough. Not too self-reverential. If anything, it embraced the world with open arms. It seemed to say: 'This is me. This is what I believe. Come into my world. I count for something.' Not bad things to live by.

I hadn't believed it. I never believe it all. I believe in hidden agendas, veils and screens, deceits and lies. Probably because I'm so good at them myself. There are always two faces: an outward public one and a private inner one (this isn't actually Freudian rocket-science). The more blogs I read the more misanthropic I become. It's not jealousy; anyone can set up their own blog. If I was a successful writer I'd not have one. It's beyond myopia. A diary saying what you ate for breakfast, what book you were reading when the idea came for your latest novel, your favourite drink, holiday, singer, animal, colour, soup, furniture, film, item of clothing, etc. It's like watching somebody else's paint drying.

Is it just me? Am I a drainpipe-trousered misanthropist or something? Is the world going to end soon so we all have to make our mark quickly? I understand that writers need to raise their profiles (which includes writing reviews for their own books on Amazon) and blogs are effective ways to do it, but what about the mystery of life? What's left of you in the real world? How many pixels of oneself can be passed around in cyberspace? There's only the bones to pick over. I like not knowing everything about a person. That's the fun part.

Alex Fortune comes under that category. He has a website but it is managed by his publishing house and his good friend, BB Crum, no B (wait 'til you meet him, I am still waiting to meet him). It's part of Alex's philosophy that the reader should only know about the writer through his works, no explanation, no confessions. T.S. Eliot believed the same thing. As William Faulkner once said, a book is the writer's secret life, the dark twin of a man. But the truth is the public are human beings. They must know the author behind the words and the wannabe writers must know the secret to publishing success. They take pleasure in unmasking their Gods, their heroes. That's the human predicament; the human condition. The public are hungry. They want to flip you over like an omelette.

(Vegetarianism, Ben?)

On the blog, Imogen spoke out against cruelty to animals. Too right. I love animals. Foxes, bears, monkeys, cats, dogs, dairy cows, cockerels, you name it. I sponsored a gorilla in the local zoo only last year. But sometimes I love animals for dinner too. I was sitting in this fancy restaurant, 100% organic vegan, only it wasn't so fantastic because I was swallowing parts of a bowling ball and Imogen asked if I ate meat.

'No,' I said, because that put me up there in her political estimation. She was a political animal. I was at an advantage because her cyberspace alter ego had already filled me in, but I didn't want to overdo it because she might guess I'd read it and think I was a weirdo stalker. 'I'm not a vegetarian at the moment…' (Not so cool - as if you can be a vegetarian one day and not the next - though ironically this was exactly how I arranged my eating life) '…but I'm thinking about that.'

Very good. The intonation on the word "that" carried just the right amount of gravitas and sincerity for such an innocuous word, often taken for granted by ordinary writers.

She nodded, interested in what I had to say.

'You're obviously vegetarian and you're fit…I mean fit and healthy…' I had paid her a mannish compliment simultaneously coming across as polite. Genius. 'I tend to eat fish…and maybe one day I'll go the whole hog…if you know what I mean?'

The whole hog? Cheesy but workable when used with care.

She laughed and proceeded to tell me what I already knew from her blog. She was planning on turning vegan. She'd been researching horror stories: traces of pus in cows' milk, beakless chickens, bereft cows and calves, cows showing signs of mourning, pigs with high intelligence. Animals were being raped all over the world for personal and economic gain. 'Eating,' she said, 'is a political decision.'

I thought about this for a while. In my head, I saw long lines of people walking into Netto looking for frozen sausages, 50% intestines. 'It is for the middle-classes,' I wanted to say. I wanted to tell her that vegetarianism would make some of my teeth redundant, that I was an omnivore, and omnisexual too. But for a moment I was convinced by her arguments, was about to join her on the vegan crusade, until a waiter appeared with matches to relight our candle and the impetus was lost in the light.

The conversation came full circle, returning to writing. She said I must find a literary agent and that I was a natural talent. Then I blurted it out; the Acorn Short Story Competition! (not this year's notification, last year's. I wasn't going to tempt the Tippet Curse again). She was amazed. She said it was a major achievement getting longlisted because The Acorn was a highly prestigious prize.

'Is it?' I said, feigning.

It turned out that she used to send stories in but had given up with competitions because they were, in her words, 'Layers of subjectivity. A lottery. Forget competitions. Find a publisher. Write a novel. Agents can't sell short stories in the current market anyway. You'd be better off with smaller literary magazines. The Acorn...?' she mumbled over her last sip of wine (we'd finished the first bottle before the main course and settled on individual glasses during it. I had Pinot Grigio). 'You are still hiding your light under a bushel,' she said, rekindling the summer gone. She was beginning to sound merry. I was beginning to feel the effects too.

'Until it goes up in flames,' I said (honestly, I did say that, I remember).

And she said, 'Then you *will* be famous.'

I believed her with every muscle in my body.

(Forget the sex, Ben, this is far more central. No, there is some sex. There will always be sex).

We went Dutch with the bill and stepped outside. The rain was still pouring. I suggested walking her home on account of there being a rapist on the loose, which there probably was, somewhere. I left my Saab in the car park as planned and walked the same way as Imogen.

Ha-ha! I didn't walk exactly the same way as her, as...oh, it doesn't matter. We went back to her terraced house, under her umbrella. Ha-ha! The house wasn't under the umbrella! That's how skittish I was.

It was nearly 11pm and she offered me inside so she could lend me Camus's *The Outsider.* She was going to finish the night off properly with a nightcap and would I like a drink? Turned out she wasn't working the next day but going to London to meet her agent. She fingered the lock with her wayward key. I was heady with wine and great ideas and imminent success, my future as a writer blossoming before my eyes. I nearly asked for her agent's name and number, the question sitting on my lips for a while, at least until we were bumping into each other in the hallway.

It's all about timing. Not kissing her. About asking for her agent's name. She might go cold on me. I know what it's like now. Writers are hypersensitive, paranoid, possessive, jealous, self-obsessed creatures of the night; even when they're pissed. So I held back, waiting for the right time, which didn't come for weeks.

And speaking of creatures of the night, I followed her into the kitchen where she put her drenched umbrella by the back door, the point in an upturned tin lid. She bent down and I clocked (from behind) the elastic edge of her black panties which had risen up her low slung jeans revealing a peachy crack. A story-builder's bum. She flicked open her cat flap and a drowning rat shot inside. Not a real rat. A significant cat. I was still looking at the pale and unctuous crevice of Imogen's bottom (sexbloodymaniac! Any opportunity to ogle. I think most men do it unconsciously all the time and what they can't see they make up. An ex-girlfriend once told me, on the heated moment of our separation, that I treated her and all women as sex objects. I told her this was a damned lie because I treated men just the same).

She stood up again and I diverted my eyes to photographs of people I didn't know on a wall beside the sink which was brimming with dirty dishes. The sodden cat howled up at her and did the strangest thing. It sprang to her chest where Imogen caught her. This cat was a performer, but it turned out to be much more than this. She was all things tragic and literary and Freudian and fucked up.

Imogen waved one of the front paws at me. 'Eadie,' she said. 'This is Ben. Ben, this is Eadie.'

'Pleased to meet you,' I said, talking to a cat now, but the night got weirder than this. She resettled the cat on the floor, semi-dried it with a tea towel, then filled a chrome bowl with vegetarian dried food. It smelled of Brussels Sprouts. The cat tucked in, purring to itself, and Imogen offered me a brandy.

We moved into the sitting room which was swamped with clothes; not dissimilar to a Tracey Emin installation. I don't think there was a single item of furniture which didn't have vestments on it: socks and pants and t-shirts and blouses and jumpers and shorts and bras and towels and all sorts. A totally revealing mess.

My mother had warned me that some people lived like this. She'd turn puce if she saw this place, and I'd had Imogen down as a bit of a control-freak, like me. It is no exaggeration to say her house resembled a student's bed-sit, and it was a pity because it was a nicely-situated Victorian terraced house. I'd sold a few in my estate agent days. The original fireplace was still there, with marble surround and elegant Arts and Craft tiles; cricket bat and guitar propped either side. I didn't tell her I used to be an estate agent. It can generate the wrong sort of impression. I told her instead that she had a lovely house and she returned the compliment by saying I had good taste, which come to think of it was not a compliment at all.

She removed a long brown skirt from the back of a sofa and threw it onto the armchair beside the fireplace, next to an old pair of boxing gloves. I'd never seen her in a skirt and wondered if these were her clothes or someone else's. She invited me to sit down beside her on the sofa. We supped brandy from wine glasses (she'd rinsed a couple straight from the sink and filled them to the brim) and I looked around for a TV set. That's what I used to do when I got in from the bookshop. I'd put on the TV, DVD or a CD.

But there was no TV.

Maybe she was one of these people who hides it in a piece of furniture, but there wasn't much furniture. Everything looked like it had been handed down by various, some might say callous friends and relatives. Not exactly moth-eaten, but in poor taste. In some circles it's called boho-contemporary (I read style magazines) when in fact, it was properly catholic with a small c. Bits of everything from an Edwardian armchair to Habitat door handles and light-fittings. She could've just moved in but she'd said in the restaurant that she'd lived here for more than two years. Stacks of files. Bookshelves bowed in the middle under the weight of literary tomes. Newspapers were scattered on furniture like cushions.

'I don't care for tidiness,' she said, reading me.

I shrugged my shoulders. 'Who does?'

Well I did for starters. My mother's fastidiousness during my early childhood had been so firmly drummed into me that it had become second nature by the time I was ten. Of course, I rebelled in my teens but succumbed to cleanliness in the end. Howard Hughesian proportions by my twenties, especially when I got my own flat in Pensbury. Ever since then I've never got on with domestic dirt, though I don't mind sitting in other people's. I can always leave it behind.

'You don't have a TV,' I said, as if I was saying, 'you haven't got any legs!'

'It's just rubbish,' she said. 'I don't have one. And you shouldn't either. It's bad karma. Why watch TV when you can listen to the radio, play a CD or read a book?'

'What about films?' I said. 'I'm hooked to the silver screen.'

'If I want to see a film, I go to the cinema.' She put her wineglass on the bare floorboards, got up and switched her music system on. A beaten up thing. It had been hiding beneath a plethora of books (plethora? now that's over-written in this context). Mellow trumpets and pianos and guitars and bass came out. Jazz. I won't rant about jazz. It has its place in things; has its place in this story for sure.

'Do you mind if I smoke?' she said, disappearing into the kitchen. The cat slinked out a moment later and for a wicked second I thought Imogen had experienced a transmutation. *Cat People* or something. Natasha Kaplinsky, I mean Natasha Kinksi. I mean Kinski. Whatever. I was feeling heady and frisky to tell you the truth. I couldn't believe I was in this situation.

'It's your house,' I said. 'I didn't even know you smoked.' (lie).

She didn't reply. I heard drawers opening and closing, papers rustling, the click of a Zippo lighter, and her pale face appeared in the doorway. 'Arhh,' she said. 'It's not that sort of smoking?' She held up a very large joint.

'Arhh,' I said, playing it cool.

She sat down beside me and Eadie weaved in and out of her shins, figure of eight. Imogen passed me the joint and I took a small drag, taking it quite shallow. The cat jumped onto my lap, purring and kneading. I took another puff and passed it along the sofa (not the cat, the spliff). Imogen took a huge inhalation, keeping it in for ages before blowing dark blue smoke clouds above her head. I don't know why but I expected to see an Adam's apple bob at her throat.

Ordinarily, dope doesn't do it for me. I was one of the strange people at school and at university for whom cannabis and grass did nothing at all. Georgi said it was my temperament; that I didn't allow the drug to take effect because I was anal. I wasn't being anal now. I liked tasting the wet end. Woozy was my feeling. We took turns sucking on the joint all the way down to the nubble, then she stubbed it out in a terracotta plant pot. 'I can't believe we're here,' I said.

'In the universe?' she said, tousling her hair. A lot of women do this without knowing it's incredibly sexy.

'You're my tutor, Imogen.'

'You're my student, Ben.' She relaxed an arm over the back of the sofa, not far from my neck. 'And *we are* grown up adults.'

'Grown up adults,' I said, laughing, then she laughed at her tautology, if it was tautologous. If tautologous is a word.

That was when I should have leaned across the diminishing divide and kissed her full on. But I delayed, which isn't like me. The restaurant wine? The brandy and dope? Whatever slowing my senses. The window closed. 'I love cats,' I said, pathetically. 'Why Eadie? It's an unusual name.'

She reached out a hand and stroked the cat's fur on my lap. 'Eadie-puss,' she said. 'I know, it's a pretty lame joke but the name kind of stuck. She's a rescue cat. She was Whiskers or George or something weird in a previous life and I changed it.'

'Better than Bagpuss,' I said.

'Do you think I've messed her mind up?' She pressed the cat's belly down into my lap with her persistent stroking. A heavy petting.

'You've given her a complex,' I said. It popped out of my mouth without even thinking. Knee-jerk thing. A gem. Sometimes your luck goes that way.

Imogen wrinkled her nose up. 'You're good.' We held eye contact for a few seconds.

'Not bad for the close of day but you should hear me at the opening.'

My lusty gauntlet was on the table, on the sofa, whatever. She could pick it up if she wanted. I had visions of traipsing home in the rain like a sorry puppy, tail clamped between my legs, as happens to ordinary mortals, because I am not always lucky. I am sometimes ordinary.

Imogen looked at me queerly; sizing me up. 'You have fantastic cheekbones,' she said, leaning in. She slid a finger down the side of my face: temple, cheekbone, chin. We met half way with brandied tongues. Eadie leapt to the floor disapprovingly and Imogen put a hand behind my head pressing my tongue into hers. There was an awkward moment when I thought the plug was going to be pulled. She said she had to go upstairs without an invitation to follow. She came down again a minute later, holding a blanket and a condom.

Imogen Wood, you minx. Where's the romance? It nearly had me wilting. She wanted to do it on the sofa. Odd, but I would have done it pretty much anywhere. It was warm and cosy by the light of the table lamp and the curtains pulled tightly across. She threw the blanket onto the sofa, jeans already off, and I saw her panties in their fullness. It never ceases to do it for me. Knickers/pants/boxers on a woman or a man. It really tickles my trousers. It's the secret. The vulnerability. The half-naked surprise. When I used to flick through my father's copy of the Freeman's Catalogue (he kept it under his bed) I would get just as much of a kick from the women's bulges as the men's. I unzipped, removed my jeans. Nothing dangled. Everything was tight and up for grabs. I don't have a six-pack but I am quite firm all over.

There was a minute without any bodily contact, just glances, as if to say, 'You first.' A doctors and nurses routine going on. We were high, though not so high we'd forget it in the morning. Imogen kept her bra on. Her breasts looked fine to me and perfectly in proportion to her frame, so I don't know why and the few times we did it in the future she unhitched herself without a qualm, and they were wonderful little peaches.

I asked if she wanted to put the condom on and she laughed at me. Something about it not fitting over her head. The ice didn't need breaking but it helped stop a lake of unfamiliarity freezing between us (definitely overwritten, Ben). She slid my pants clean off, flicked them across the room. Her hands were made of electricity and her mouth made a satisfactory O. Nobody could say I was a little finger. More like a one-man army. A sentry on guard.

She leaned back into the sofa and we kissed for longer, slowly and more passionately. She had brushed her teeth since the last time we kissed. A sly move and one which betrayed an attractive self-consciousness. We caressed a while. The juices were up on both sides. I felt them through her silky fabric and tugged the panties down over her ankles to the floor. The late night jazz swooned. I played with the jumble of her pubic hair, then, with my longest finger, stroked her oyster to the rhythm of the chords, the way she had stroked Eadie on my lap.

She moaned greedily. I really like moaning. I'm all for moaning and groaning. It keeps me straightened out. I once slept with a girl called Honey Mills (great name, great hips) who would never moan, even when I was inside her with every ounce of energy and longevity I could muster. Then I was moaning about her not moaning and she was moaning for all the wrong reasons.

We got to the moment of entry. Can I put it more sexily? It was better than that. Pretty fantastic. Does anyone need to know? It's all nature really. There are three basic levellers in the world: birth, sex and death. The first and the last of these only happen once, that's why you should try the middle one as much as possible. We were not virgins per se, only virgins to each other in that normally we just sat around an English department talking about characterisation, beginnings, middles and ends.

The end was inside. Imogen was on top and riding on the middle section of the sofa. I began with her waist, chasing erotic circles with my fingers, then moved on to her buttocks encouraging her to rock to the beat. She had the hardest job, knees fully bent either side of me, thighs taking the strain of the motion. I stroked the hilltops of her thighs which were not quite smooth, squeezed her covered breasts until the nipples sat up like aerial masts. 'Gently,' she whispered. 'They're not knobs on a telly.'

And then, very early into the event, everything tightened and I knew and I hurried along. I wanted to please her, get top marks just like my stories she'd marked, but I also wanted to come if it was at all possible. I once had a friend (not sexually, and he's no longer a friend) who confided in me. He said he had never managed to come and he'd slept with at least a dozen women and why did I think that was? I said, well, do you come when you masturbate? And he said, yes, of course. And when you're with women, do they come? Most times. Then you probably don't want children. Why don't you pleasure your next girlfriend as normal then masturbate as a finale? He never looked back. At least, he never talked to me again.

Imogen slowed right down, almost to a standstill. Her fingernails were pinching my arms, hands gripping my biceps like rollercoaster rails reaching the highest peak. I gyrated beneath her, trying to create some friction. Nothing more embarrassing than the wheels coming off the track at the wrong moment and having to reassemble the parts. We were doing some sort of primeval dance. The okey-cokey. My thighs were sopping, my balls were primed. She was doing something to her lip, not biting it. She was looking straight through me into a pond, concentrating, because she really wanted to explode. Another few seconds and I popped a finger inside her cloister.

In my debased experience it's very much about oysters and cloisters in the sack, on the sofa, wherever. Moving from one to the other at the right moments. These are the things we don't talk about in polite circles. They say there's a tiny spot behind the earlobe which is the most erogenous of zones, but sometimes you don't have the time.

We kissed, I probed and everything moved again to a well-oiled hum. Slow, fast, slow, fast, slow, fast until our skins joined and our bodies sheened and she came with a toss of her boyish strawberry hair. An emphatic, recognisable *Oh-Oh-Oh-Ugh!*

Senses fulfilled, I hurtled into her beautiful, plastic-coated abyss.

(You'd pay good money for this sort of thing in a magazine. Sexbloodymaniac!)

Easy come, easy go (so many clichés). I didn't stay. Imogen pulled on a waffle robe. The sort you find in quality hotels. I got dressed. We kissed at the front door, not saying anything. I walked home in a light drizzle, realizing half way that she'd forgotten to give me *The Outsider*. It didn't matter. I was an insider now. I was sleeping with my tutor.

There was no sense of embarrassment at the next seminar. We didn't avoid eye contact, instead relishing exchanged glances like a private joke. We had sex again a few times at her house and my flat. Sex was good, but we didn't really gel in our heads.

I don't dislike Imogen. Actually, she is quite a good person in this story, not least for being the chief witness for my defence; my alibi on the night of the fire. On the badometer graph of badness, on a scale of 1-10 (with me somewhere at 9), Imogen is a 1 or a 2. A mere blip of badness. She can be a little holier than thou sometimes, stemming from her writing success and craving more. She once issued her apostles with Ten Commandments to follow like a bible:

1. Thou shalt write every day.
2. Thou shalt not bore the reader (this list has that potential).
3. Thou shalt write seriously, not solemnly.
4. Thou shalt love your characters.

5. Thou shalt be specific.
6. Thou shalt show, not tell.
7. Thou shalt read constantly.
8. Thou shalt edit, edit, edit.
9. Thou shalt address the human condition.
10. Thou shalt make every death in a story meaningful.

Contradicting herself immediately, she added the 11th Commandment: Thou shalt break some or all the above commandments whenever and wherever necessary. I quizzed her about this add-on, in bed after love-making, saying the commandments were too dogmatic, and she said if you know the rules then can you break them. She advised her apostles to write about their obsessions; the themes of good writers. 'A good starting point for a novel.'

A retired taxman apostle interjected. 'Most novels seem to be about sex and death.'

Imogen said, 'Aren't they obsessions?' which had some of the class blushing. 'What comes between sex and death?' We didn't have a clue, and she answered herself, 'Love. Love comes between sex and death. Love is everyman's and every woman's psychosis.'

'I suppose my story about a talking cat goes into the bin,' a pharmaceutical secretary apostle said.

'No,' Imogen replied. 'If your talking cat has been loved, great, and has had sex, even better. If she dies, better still.'

Imogen is a drug addict. She said the cocaine she used at weekends was recreational like it was a playground romp. I think proper addicts make this excuse. She confessed to me one time, after snorting a gram and doing it doggy style, that she sometimes snorted before classes, just for the buzz. Her ex-boyfriend (with whom she is still friendly) got her into Charlie going to gigs at the Brixton Academy and The Troubadour. Whenever she goes to London, she still meets him, still buys from him. His name's Brendan; hardly a drug-dealing name. But I don't claim to understand the world, I'm only hazarding a guess at it.

She used to offer me some dust. Was I tempted? No. Drugs scare the hell out of me. I don't want to be out of control. Full stop. To be honest, Imogen frightened me. Sometimes I thought I'd wake up and she would be dead in the morning. But as long as we had good sex and she was giving me top marks for everything,

I was a content and eager pupil. Neither of us wanted anything serious. We were just being grown up adults after all.

'Everyone has their vice,' she told me, 'and yours is definitely sex.' I wouldn't disagree. We'd done it sitting down, standing up, front to back, like a game of Twister. 'You don't smoke, you rarely get drunk, you don't take drugs. Why?'

'Because I don't want to die at fifty,' I said.

She could be snappy too. Capricious. I wouldn't want to share the same space as her for too long. I pointed this out to her once when she chewed me up over tidying her front room. They're my things, she said, leave them where they bloody well are. I wondered if it was her period because she went on about this draggy feeling in the pit of her stomach, but it was actually a big problem at work. Something which had been hanging over her since the summer.

A formal complaint against her was being investigated. A mature student had filed his complaint on the grounds of sexual discrimination! In his final year, he was taking her short story class. An objectionable man in his late forties, divorced with children, and angry about his lot in life. Every story he wrote had hard-done-by men and stereotypical nymphomaniacs panting for sex. He had this aura in class and made subtle innuendoes. A very off-putting manner, Imogen said. His opinions were set in concrete. He was blinkered and immoveable and left a bad taste, she told me. But worse than this, he was demanding, constantly firing off emails from home. Could you look at this? Look at that? Never said please. He took her to task over minor comments and clogged her web space. A jumped-up jerk-off, she said.

Half way through the module she received an email from him with the opening to a short story, and there was a j-peg attachment. She opened the attachment and saw photographs and downloads. Not filthy. Actually, she'd been quite amused thinking the attachment had been a mistake: photos of houses on the market, pictures of boats on the Norfolk Broads, dogs running along beaches etc. Slices of this man's life?

She went through the slides one by one, very amused, until she came across the egg-white ejaculations, buggery, orgies, gynaecological close-ups, woman-on-woman, ebony and ivory, etc. She deleted the file out of disgust and from that moment on made this mature student's life hell.

After receiving distinctly average marks, he complained to the head of department and then to the vice-chancellor. He said Imogen had held his marks down and was different with him in class. She had told him to give up writing fiction and go back to his day job during a one-to-one tutorial. 'And had you?' I asked her. 'Yes. He was a terrible writer.' She denied all of the allegations, naturally, but a tape recording had been made. A hidden tape-recorder in their one-to-one tutorial. The sneaky bastard weasel. And her own "evidence" had already been deleted. 'But still on your hard drive?' I suggested. No. The departmental computers had been sold off and replaced at the end of term so she had no hard evidence. Six months later and still under investigation.

I told her: 'The difference between men and women is that men think they are bigger than they are, whereas women think they are smaller than they are. Men are animals. Apes chasing blondes. Nothing you can do about it.'

'Even if I still had his email it would prove his case. That I had motive.'

'A difficult moral conundrum,' I said. 'It could be argued that both of you were in the wrong.'

'You bastard!' she said. 'What if a woman sent you dirty pictures of men fellating men? Then what would you have done?'

'Jerked off.'

'I don't really know you, do I?'

'And I don't really know you,' I replied. 'So we're even.'

'All we do is fuck.'

'What the fuck's wrong with fucking? It's a basic form of communication. What else do you want to do? Go to the zoo?' Imogen doesn't like basic forms of anything. Basic = unsophisticated.

We lasted about twelve weeks, on and off. She got what she wanted and I got the same. Highest marks in the class come Christmas, but by then we had become gently estranged. The times we made love were automatic like the doors to a department store. When she came into the bookshop looking for me I hid in the storeroom cupboard and asked Maurice to make excuses. A sensible cowardice.

How did it end? Not with the Acorn fire on the 19th of December, though this paled our relationship significantly. Things had withered way before that momentous night. We had an argument from which we never fully recovered.

What happened was this: I was nearly creaming myself because Acorn had sent me another email (all of this fills me with shame now, not the joy of the time itself): *Congratulations, Cassi Hart! Your short story, "Me and You", has made the final shortlist of 50. With nearly 5,000 entries from across the world this is a major achievement. From this short list, 10 winners will be selected by the judges, to be published next year in our annual anthology, volume 21. The overall winner shall receive a £5,000 prize and is obliged to attend the official launch of the anthology in Broadstairs, July of next year. The lucky winners will be announced online at 5pm on 19 December. Watch this space. And the very best of luck!*

Acorn.

From little acorns do mighty oak trees grow.

Flutter, flutter, flutter.

19th December? The anniversary of my brother's death! A good omen, I was sure. My time was coming. Statistically a 1-in-5 chance. I was living on adrenalin for the next three weeks. It was not an omen. It was fate. A rare butterfly inside me.

Maybe it was a mistake to have handed the same story in for my end of term portfolio at the university. I was staying at Imogen's the second week of December. I asked her if she had read my story yet? At first she said it would be wrong for her to discuss my work, and I said, 'Imogen, I'm lying in bed beside you with no clothes on. Surely you can waive a few guidelines?' I was itching to tell her about the Acorn but I didn't want to tempt the Tippet Curse.

She hesitated.

'I'd really value your opinion.'

'I shouldn't discuss it.' She took some serious pressing before she pointed across the bedroom at some drawers. 'The top one. There's some notes on top of the portfolios. Just bring the notes, not the stories.'

I got them and slid under the sheets again. 'What did I get?'

'They have to be second-marked.'

'Did I get a distinction?'

She nodded, going through her notes.

'Why so coy?'

'Here it is,' she said, shifting up the bed, making herself comfortable, folding a pillow in half against the headboard.

'Here what is?'

'You wanted to know what I thought. I've made a list.'

'A list?'

'Don't take this badly,' she said. 'They're only suggestions.'

'I won't,' I said.

'One. There are too many characters.'

I pulled myself up the headboard to her level. 'Aren't you supposed to start with the positives?'

'I knew this was a bad idea,' she said, putting the papers down. 'You know it's good already. Do you want to hear what I really think?'

'Okay, okay, okay.'

'Too many characters. The tramps. You don't need them. They serve no purpose.'

I shrugged my shoulders which were beginning to stiffen. 'They're to reinforce the sense of decay and feelings of loss which make up the theme.'

'Heavy-handed. Slows the pace right down. And the tension dissipates.'

The tension wasn't dissipating. I was prickling all over, going cold.

'Two. Dialogue. There is way too much "I said" "he said" "she said".'

'That's for effect,' I said.

'What effect?' she said.

'Well I don't know. To reinforce the difference in the voices of a schizophrenic as he hears them.'

'Hmm,' she said. 'Too forced. A bit clumsy.' She must have felt my attitude changing because she patted the sheets and I moved my knee away. 'Which leads me onto another point. I don't really like O. Henrys.'

'Imogen. I don't think you've understood my story.'

'It's not the purpose of literature to contrive a surprise at the end. I've given it a seventy. You're not taking this on the chin.'

'I'm taking it on the chin but you haven't read between the lines. The subtext.'

'I have,' she said. 'Besides, you can't criticise a reader for how she reads something. Once written it's not yours anymore. Fictional democracy.'

'Exactly,' I said. 'Fictional. My story's been twisted into something I never intended. There's a mystery but not a sudden twist at the end, Imogen. There are clues in advance and it's revealed two-thirds the way through. It's like you've read a completely different story. Something you've heard on radio ga-ga.'

'I said this would be a bad idea.'

I'm alright,' I said. 'I can take positive criticism.'

'I don't think you are now.'

'Is there anything positive?'

'Four,' she said, and I heard myself sighing. 'The metaphors strain like rusty bedsprings.'

'Where?'

'I think you've overcooked the metaphors to make the reader feel wet because the weather is wet, but it grates on the reader and she doesn't feel wet.'

'I feel wet every time I read it.'

'That's besides the point,' she said.

It was on the tip of my tongue. The Acorn short list clogging my windpipe. Mentioning it would show her; she who'd never been shortlisted for a literary prize. But no, not the Tippet Curse. I would not bring that down upon my head.

'Are you taking this on the chin?'

I stuck it out. 'I'm sure this is all very useful.'

'Five. It's my last point. I don't think your main character should be called Joe Bloggs.'

I was astonished. 'He's not.'

'Isn't he?' She flicked through her notes.

'It's a joke. Anyone he doesn't know he calls Bloggs, including himself, which is the irony of the story. Mr Bloggs. Mrs Bloggs. He thinks of himself as Joe Bloggs. An everyman, but he's no ordinary Joe.'

'I know criticism can be exasperating.'

'You don't know what you're talking about. You don't know the half of it. What was it you said in that restaurant? Subjectivity. That's what you are. A layer of subjectivity.'

She put the notes down and stared at me as if I might be from another planet. 'Welcome to the real world, Ben.' I leapt out of bed, started pulling my Sloggi pants on. I couldn't find my trousers. 'I don't get you,' she said.

'Where are my flaming socks?' She nodded towards the mirror. 'I know you're a good writer and you've had novels published and "How to write" books and that you're a creative writing tutor, but that doesn't mean you know everything, Imogen.' Her mouth fell open. 'You're not God is what I'm saying.' I pulled my t-shirt on and jumper, one sock. I limped onto the landing, odd-socked and out of balance.

'You're being over-sensitive. I won't comment on anything again if that helps. Where are you going?' She folded her arms and laughed. 'I didn't have you down as the melodramatic type!'

'Let's just cool it,' I said, banging down the stairs. I pulled on my boots and looked around for my ankle-length woollen coat which normally hung on the acorn newel post.

'Whatever you want!' she balled down. 'You're going to have to get used to criticism! The best writers in the world have to take it! You're no exception!'

I said nothing. My coat was on the floor and Eadie had slept on it leaving a ring of striped hairs. They wouldn't come off for days. Imogen stayed exactly where she was, Queen Bee in bed, calling down to me as I opened the front door: 'Phone me when you've grown up!' I cut the sentence in half with a slam of the door. What did Imogen know? I should have stuffed it in her face. Given her an Acorn to suck on.

This all feels a long time ago now. In reality, just a few days before the announcement and the fire. I did see her again. We stumbled through the motions in January. Sex at my place. Sex at hers. We were going nowhere. And then came the final two straws. In early February, we were talking on the phone about agents. I simply asked if Imogen might mention me to her agent in London. I might as well have asked if she wanted to be fucked up the arse on Pensbury High Street (which incidentally I had once asked and been refused). She went totally cold, made some excuse about being unhappy with her agent; the agent she'd been praising to the heavens not long before. Why didn't I trawl through the *Writers' and Artists' Yearbook*? Freezing me out. I got the message. She was jealous of my potentiality and newness or something; my talent she had so brutally recognised and simultaneously shredded in bed that time.

I saw her again briefly that February, but it hadn't been arranged. Freezing cold is the right word for the weather and our relationship. Snow hadn't melted in Pensbury. I'd barely exchanged telephone calls with her. Not returned text messages or anything. Neither had I taken another course up at the university; one she had suggested to me. I got drunk with Maurice one night (I was drinking more than usual after the trauma of the fire and the fallout) and had a gilt-edged hangover the next morning. I took it to McDonald's. Something I never usually do, but this horrible morning I needed something fat and factory mass-produced. A Big Mac, fries and a stiff chocolate milkshake. I took a window seat wolfing my meal, watching the world go by, when my mouth dropped open. Someone was staring at me. Imogen stepped out from a pillar at the entrance, walked right up to the window, shaking her politicised, pretty head. All I could do was shrug in her direction. She walked away, back pack over her shoulder. We didn't see each other again until March, and again when the police came knocking at my door. I needed her then and wished I'd kept her a little sweeter. But this is all in hindsight. So painful in hindsight.

(I think you've got convoluted, Ben. Got everything arse to front, leapfrogging over the fire; the conflagrational centrifugal force inside this story. Now's the time to describe the fire. After all, it's why you're in this cell writing about oysters and cloisters and men who can't come unless they masturbate and chocolate milkshakes and all manner of depravities).

Eight

19th December (The Great Fire of Broadstairs: a Dickensian Tale of Fear and Loathing in Las Thanet).

On Acorn announcement day, I decided to drive across to my family. Maurice had given me the day off. Scrub that. I phoned in sick and there was nothing he could do about it. Ever since discovering I had a brother I never missed a trip to Tom's grave on the anniversary of his death. I liked to be on my own when I visited because we used to have conversations. A few private words.

It was Friday. Traffic was nose to tail around the M25 but that didn't put me in a bad mood. Nothing was going to antagonise me that day, for a change. I was so full of optimism, so bursting with anticipation, that even my mother remarked upon my brightness of disposition. 'Do you have a girlfriend you're not telling me about?'

Of course, I'd been itching to make them proud of me in a different way. Dad couldn't understand why I worked in a bookshop anyway, but a writer in the family? Now there's a thing to broadcast. My son, the writer. It had a certain ring, some panache about it. Of course, the proof of the reading is in the writing. I had to win something big to be noticed at all.

After breakfast and a warm chit-chat about my diploma (I told them I was destined for a distinction), I drove out to the grave. It had been lovingly tended to by my mother. Winter pansies were flowering in shocks of deep purples and golds with lovely crumply foliage. She'd planted them in serried, Catholic ranks. She'd pruned the rose bush my father had planted at Tom's feet.

Sometimes, standing there, I'd wonder if the roots reached down to the bones of my brother's toes, making actual contact. From May to October the silky scarlet petals bloomed, then fell at his feet. From what I had learnt about him I think Tom might have preferred black roses, if they come in that colour. Whenever I visited I always took flowers. A bouquet of lilies for their pungency in summer, a wreath of holly and berries for their waxy glow in winter, and to remind him that Christmas was around the corner.

I laid my holly wreath as if at a war memorial, crossing myself appropriately. I even said a prayer for him straight from the Catholic Mass. You don't really ever forget what is learnt in childhood. But half way through my Our Father I forgot the words and mumbled other things into my chest in their place. I'm sure Tom the *rebel rebel* was laughing at me, only I couldn't hear.

'Merry Christmas, Mr Lawrence,' I said. 'I don't suppose that will mean anything to you?'

It was simply bitter. Frost-crunchy. I wrapped my long coat around me, stamped my feet. I took out my card, it being so close to Christmas, one I'd laminated for longevity in bad weather. I'd written a quote inside from TS Eliot's Four Quartets: *Human kind cannot bear very much reality*. For some reason it felt appropriate this December of all Decembers. It was for my mother's sake, for she had really lived the reality and unreality of her son's death and its denial for so many years. It wasn't meant to hurt her, just to remind her that I was human too. That I had feelings.

I asked Tom how he was getting on; if he'd made any friends down there. That sort of thing. I told him I was still playing his guitar and listening to his LPs on my Bang and Olufsen. I asked, 'When are you going to tell me which Bowie song is your favourite?' and 'Are the multiple scratches any indication? Because they might be the songs you hated and wanted to avoid, not the ones you listened to again and again. You didn't even have CDs back then, did you?' I took off my leather gloves and touched his marble gravestone, feeling inside his name. He was perishingly cold, burning my fingers like the touch of a hot stove. I told him about the Acorn Prize. I had to tell someone or I'd go mad. 'Third time lucky, heh?' I said, and he replied, 'Best of luck, Ben.' He doesn't often speak to me, so when he does it makes your heart glow. I told him it was fate for the competition results to be announced today, assuming that telling a dead person could not bring down the Tippet Curse. What harm can come from talking to your brother, dead or alive?

'You can do it,' he said. 'Your time has come.'

I returned to my parents' place. Mother had prepared a lamb roast as if it were a Sunday, saying a prayer over it: 'The Son, the Father and the Holy Roast.' Something like that. I drove home afterwards, almost with a skip in the wheels of my car.

Back in Pensbury it was Christmassy. The council had broken open the coffers and splashed out on tasteful, twinkly lights strewn between the shops and over the roads in and out of the shopping precinct. There was a thrum of activity in the town and around the cathedral where a carol service was in full swing. I could hear it from my flat. Or I might have been imagining that.

It was close to 5pm, and still nothing on the Acorn website; a site I checked every few minutes if the truth be told. I went to the fridge for a beer and when I returned to the screen, my heart skittered. Flutter, flutter, flutter: *Due to a very difficult judging process, the 10 winners will be announced at the later time of midnight, 19th December. Thank you for your patience.*

My teeth grinded. Why the delay? Did I make the final cut?

I put on Tom's *Scary Monsters* album: It's No Game (Part I). *Silhouettes and shadows...put a bullet in my brain and it makes all the papers...Shut up!* During Up The Hill Backwards I telephoned Imogen to see if she wanted to go out; anything to fill the emptiness blind anticipation can fill you with. Not in. My hands were sweaty. I was looking at my pc every minute, willing the winning list, and seeing Cassi Hart on it. The message I left on Imogen's answer machine was gobbledygook: wondered if you were free for a drink or dinner or go to the cinema. That sort of thing. We weren't exactly friendly since the argument about my story (which was going to win the Acorn) which makes it even more ridiculous in hindsight.

Scary Monsters, the title track, blasted: *...blue but nobody home...know what I mean...dangerous mind...jealousies scream...* A neighbour knocked on her ceiling, complaining about the volume. Must have been a broom handle. Mrs Heaton had a baby a few months old and the little cherub darling had been keeping me awake at night for weeks but I wasn't allowed to play my frigging music at five in the afternoon. Not worth the hassle. I put my headphones on, turned it up loud, enough to make my ears whistle. I paced the flat for an hour, switching tracks. More Bowie, for Tom's sake. I always played Tom's albums on his anniversary.

It wasn't meant to be morbid. I think it brought us closer together. When I listened, I could picture him on his motorcycle, Amy clutching his middle as pillion. I saw them going to the cinema. I saw Tom lying in the grass humming tunes in his head. How can you love someone you have no memory of knowing?

'You'll knock 'em dead,' he said, between albums. I think I must have listened to three albums back-to-back, lying on my black leather sofa, gazing out at the cathedral bell tower which is always splendid at night. *Splendid.* Such an English word. The cathedral was a beacon to faith. That tower might stand there splendidly for eternity, like a dead splendid literary giant. If enough people cared, that is.

I looked at my watch. Just gone 7pm. Nothing on the website. I hit the "refresh" icon a few times in case the website had jammed. I imagined all the other finalists doing exactly the same.

Nothing.

I went to my bedroom, pulled out Tom's box of bits and bobs: Watermanship medal, Scouts' badges, a blue Cubs woggle. This Pandora's Box kept my brother alive more than anything else. He was in my thoughts and in my hands. I rummaged around, still with my headphones on, looking for Tom's Religious Education book, written 18 months before his death. There was an exercise he had to do in it called "The real me: What sort of person am I?": *I am a kind-hearted person. I am sometimes stubborn. I'm easily distracted and get angry easily. I am a person who takes chances* (we are not that different really).

Make a list of your strengths and weaknesses:
+
Good at football and athletics
Sometimes helpful
Quite strong.
Good at the guitar

-
bad at words
bad-tempered sometimes.
Great at causing riots
Want too much at times. (Ditto with me, Tom)

People who have helped to form me into the person I am: Choose 5 from this list – parents, God, pals, teachers, television, myself, scouts, government, priests.

Parents, television, teachers, friends, myself.

Why?

My parents help me to form myself by helping me use my ability in different ways. Television helps me by forming myself by violence and sex. Teaching me bad things.

Write a poem about what we can learn about God from the world about us:

A Poem by Tom Reed

We can learn a great deal about what we can see,
the sky, the land, the hills and the sea.
The North, the South, the East and West
Were given to us by the Greatest!
The greatest the greatest I hear you lot cry?
Yes, God is the greatest why do you shout why?
Yes, God made this round chunk of earth
His only thought is for us to live and learn
about his world.

Doggerel. Tom was terrible with words, but he knew that. He was never going to be Seamus Heaney. His strengths lay elsewhere. But his teacher gave him lines for not trying hard enough. Tom had to write two sides, responding to the title: *Why God made the World Round* and it was this that had me chuckling. I don't think Tom took anything too seriously, except maybe his girlfriend, Amy.

Why God Made The World Round
by Tom Reed

The Earth is round and so is the sun. Maltesers are round, but not always. Oranges are round but I don't know why. Eyes are round so we can roll them around to look at people. So maybe everything natural is round so they can move. The Earth, the Sun, the Moon, the Planets, the Maltesers. Orbit means

105

going round, doesn't it? If they didn't move, we wouldn't move, and the sea wouldn't move and the fishes would suffocate. That's why the world is round. Because God wanted everything to move. Things that don't move, stop, dry out, and die.

Wheels are round which proves my point about moving. If a car had square wheels, which might have happened at the early stages of their development, no one would get to work and if nobody got to work the world would be unemployed and there'd be no money to pay for things we live on. And the humanoids would die out.

Apples are round because if they were triangles they would stick in the ground and rot. Maybe oranges are round I've just realized because they are easier to peel for one thing.

Square things are only made by humanoids because it is easier and cheaper to make things in squares, like windows and cardboard boxes. Whoever heard of a round cardboard box?

Footballs. There'd be no football if the ball was a triangle, and it would be dangerous to kick and to head.

Records are round but they are also flat, and it is important they are flat and round so they can turn on the turntable with the stylus and you can hear David Bowie singing.

Babies' heads are round for aerodynamic reasons. If a baby's head had sharp edges it could be painful to pop out. Spock is the exception which proves the rule. Spock is a Vulcan and has dangerously pointy ears. Vulcans have special women who have Vulcan babies.

Fingernails are curved because if they were sharp your nose would bleed when you picked it.

It is harder to draw a perfect circle than it is a perfect square. So I don't know why God made things round. Maybe he was making the point (ha!) that it is harder to make round things, that you have to work hard to get things the way you want them?

God might not be happy about all of the square things the humanoids have built on Earth. He might be looking down on us at this moment and saying, 'What are you doing? Everything should be round. What's with the tower blocks?' But maybe he has more important things to be doing. Maybe he just lets us get on with it. How would we know?

The Romans built a lot of straight things, so they must have got up God's nose. The Saxons were fine, they couldn't do anything straight. The Romans had to straighten the Saxons out, building roads and walls to stop the Barbarians getting in. But the Barbarians built big ladders so the Romans left for good.

You never see clouds with straight sides, do you? Only under a microscope can you see lines in a snowflake.

My conclusion: That's why God made the Earth and the whole world and everything natural in it round. Everything has to move. We would die if things were not round.

God Bless you, Tom Reed. I can see you laughing up your holey jumper.

I put him away and fetched another beer from the fridge. I checked the screen again. No change. My hands were shaking. The rare butterfly was escaping from me. I could feel it going. It was terrible. I don't think I've ever been so nervous, so in need. I wanted that prize more than anything else in the world. I didn't only want it for myself, but for my brother too.

From little acorns do great oak trees grow.

A light was flashing on my answer machine. Imogen had left a message saying she would be out with friends but if I wanted to go around to her house later, I was very welcome; any time after 11pm. I put *Scary Monsters* back on, headset blaring. It was the title track. I looked down at my pc, and there were the ten winners.

The time was an ordinary 9-05pm, etched on my memory now. I shot my eyes down the list, no trumpet fanfares sounding. I raced through the list: names and story titles. Names in alphabetical order. No Cs or Hs. No Cassi Hart. No *Me and You*. My heart turned into a cold stone, dropping into the pit of my stomach, the very soul of me, if there is one. I was looking at the screen but not quite seeing it. My name *must* be there, Cassi's name, it's just I cannot see it. A kind of snow-blindness. A trick of the mind. It can play tricks like that under stress, can't it? I cleared my vision by blinking, then by re-focusing, staring out of the window at the bell tower, but it seemed to have gone, like my nom de plume. Collapsed? Crumbled to nothing? A power cut? There was darkness outside my window but everything was working normally inside my flat: the lights on the small Christmas tree in the corner, music coming from my headset, a haze on my computer screen. The lights had gone out outside the window and a small light had gone out inside me too. More like poured out of me. I read and re-read the winners list. Seven men, three women. I read their ridiculous story titles, huffing. The outright winner, a woman from outer space (the Antipodes) called Bernadette Gambol (her risk had paid off) had won with a story called *Mohammadeus.*

What a fucking title!

The Acorn Prize organiser, Eugene Cutmore, thanked her and everyone for entering the competition; those who had not been successful as much as those who had.

Stick it!

Special praise and congratulations were reserved for Bernadette who the Acorn conspirators had telephoned two days before this public announcement.

Two fucking days before telling the others on the list!

Her story is testament to brilliant new writing on the other side of globe (what goes around, Tom) *and asks searching questions about East and West, culture and politics in the twenty-first century, without preaching. Her story is about the personal loss experienced by a brother and sister after a terrorist explosion, about the encoding of experience within and against a gendered topos.*

What the fuck does that mean?

There was a quote from the victor who was moderately chuffed about winning £5,000 and a future anthology named after her story: *My heartfelt thanks to everyone at Acorn who have helped fulfil my dream, and to the lovelelylovelylovely judges who used an impartial judging process* (been told to say that?) *to choose a wee single mother of four to carry off the most prestigious short story prize known to literarykind. I am honoured to join the universal Acorn family.*

Fuck her! Fuck families! Fuck the world! (The world is undeniably flat, Tom).

If you have ever wanted something so badly you would kill for it, you'll know how I was feeling at that moment. A mixture of excitement: the residue of three months' anticipation and the hollowness of loss, of grieving. Whatever. It was the loneliest I have ever felt, probably lonelier than being here in prison. If you've ever felt like this, you'll not judge me for what I might have done next. It was knee-jerk. The stages of grief accelerating in my veins. Shock, disbelief, anger in a matter of minutes. The whole time Bowie was blasting through my headset: *Ashes to ashes…Oh no, don't say it's true, they got a message from the action man, I'm happy hope you're happy too-oo-oo. I've loved all I needed to love, sordid details following…hitting an all time low…my mother says to get things done, you'd better not mess with Major Tom…I've never done good things, I've never done bad things…never done anything out of the blue…*

I threw the headset across the room, watched it dance along the laminate floor into the far wall shattering in pieces beneath my framed, very collectible King Kong poster. My ears were ringing. Sounds boiling, thoughts tearing around my brain:

1. It's only a competition, a lottery, a layer of subjectivity.
2. No one does this to Ben Tippet.

A pain came at the centre of my chest. I thought at first it was a heart attack but it was only aching, not a sharp pain. I ran to the bathroom with nothing to be sick with. To tell you the truth, I don't remember much of what happened next, like a dream not written down after waking becomes contaminated, corrupted and blurred during the day, through time spent conscious. My dream was dissolving. Butterfly escaping.

I'm no half-way man. It's all or nothing with me. And so it was that night. It is blurry even now, in my prison cell. I do remember thinking, *how does one rise above ordinariness?* I remember an anger so strong it buckled me up, twisted me out of shape so I didn't even recognise myself in the bathroom mirror. A real Jekyll and Hyde show. Tom was wailing in my head. 'What you gonna do now, Ben?' I saw a mental photograph of him on the underside of my lids. Tom on his Suzuki, but it was in the side of a burning lorry. I remember feeling angry about that. I remember feeling angry about my parents. Their deceit. I remember feeling angry about a stupid bed falling onto my father's spine, cracking it in two. The Tippet Curse. My whole life was cursed. I wanted to bury an acorn in Eugene Cutmore's throat and see what'd grow out of it. I wanted to climb up the branches to his eyes and stick my thumbs in them. I wanted to watch him choke on the emerging stems and branches. I don't really remember much else, it happened that quickly. I wasn't drunk. That was true. I drove to Broadstairs legally. And I did so taking my competition entry, *Me and You*. I scrawled obscenities on the pages and my proper name all over it in big black letters. I no longer wanted to remain anonymous. To hell with anagrams and what they mean. I was, am not, ordinary.

It didn't matter in the end.

Didn't I drive for forty minutes to the Acorn offices and park a few streets away, avoiding the town's CCTV? Was that premeditated? I must have known what I was about to do. I had Imogen's Zippo in my back pocket (she'd left it in my flat ages before). Did I stand outside the offices in my ankle-length overcoat in a freezing wind blowing off the sea? No one saw me, even though it was almost Christmas, a Friday night. The offices were tucked away in a quiet residential area. There were lights in some buildings either side but not in the Acorn building itself. Did I check it was the Acorn, examining the polished brass plaque on the main door which was up a few steps? I don't know. Didn't I light the corner of my story and shove it straight through the Acorn letterbox?

Did I really run across the road and watch the flames take hold of dusty old curtains inside the main door? And then, did I panic when it really began to rock and roll up the doorframe and belch out the ground floor windows? Did I look up at the whole building for a moment and see a light come on on the top floor? I must have imagined that. Did I call the firemen on my mobile? Did I call Imogen?

I can't remember.

All I know is that I was at Imogen's next. She was out of her tree on dope and brandy and it was as if time had reversed and I was back at the beginning of our relationship. We had sex, I think. I don't remember. She doesn't remember. It was a Christmas best not remembered.

That is the honest truth. It's an awful thing to say, but I don't remember the vital details, as if picking up the pieces of a dream. A young man died and I don't even remember the sequence of events, or if I was involved in them. Sometimes, I'm convinced it wasn't me. There were thousands of disappointed writers who probably fantasised about setting the offices ablaze. At other times, I have me stoking the flames with a stick because I still have a bellyful of anger with nowhere to go but inwards. It could have been me. Yes, it was me. Or someone very like me.

The following morning, I woke with four legs. Two long hairy ones and two short smooth ones, all sticking out of Imogen's duvet. I had managed to sleep for a couple of hours at least. I went downstairs to get dressed, not wishing to wake her. I scribbled a note on the back of an envelope and tried creeping away unheard, only Imogen was standing right there in the doorway. She came towards me and kissed me on the cheek, standing on tiptoes. 'Are we back on?' she said. 'You and me?'

'Sure,' I said. 'Why not?'

'Good,' she said. 'Because we're great together. But you're not going are you? It's Saturday. You're not supposed to get up this early.' She looked rough and red in the face. She ransacked the drawers of her kitchen dresser in search of paracetomol, found some in their foil and gobbled two down with orange juice from the fridge.

'I have to go to work,' I said, itchy-footed.

'At least have a coffee.' She switched the kettle on. It popped and she re-filled it from the tap.

'I have to go home and change.'

The kettle was slowly boiling.

'What time did you get here last night?' she asked.

'Don't you remember?'

'No. I was at this Mexican place, tequilas, and the rest is history.'

'It was about 10-30.You were still drinking when I got here.' I pointed to the brandy bottle on the table.

'Shit,' she said.

'Look at the ashtray.'

'Shit,' she said. It was overflowing with tiny roach butts like fingernails.

'You were smashed. Stoned, Imogen.'

'I don't even remember getting home. I must've walked.'

'Flew more like.' I was on my way down the hall and she ran to the door, waffle robe falling open, little peaches hanging.

'I'm going to stay with my Mum for Christmas. Remember? Devon? I'm going this afternoon.'

'Happy Christmas in advance,' I said, kissing a flame in her cheek. 'I'll call you, okay?'

She nodded, closed the door behind me and I felt an impending doom; some sort of industrial crusher collapsing my lungs. I walked to the council car park, looking out for CCTV all the way. I slumped into my car seat which was a block of ice through my coat; a lovely cashmere coat I'd later dump for some dumb panicky reason. I switched the radio on, tuned it to the local news channel and waited for the eight o'clock bulletin.

The Great Fire of Broadstairs was top of the list: 'At least one man is known to have died in the blaze.' The crusher crushing. A four-storey publishing house burnt to the ground. Nothing more the fire service could have done under the circumstances. Fire Officer Jason Hunter said a swirling wind had accelerated the devastation. Paper inside the building had acted as a wick burning through the night. *Fahrenheit 451.* Seven teams had fought hard to dampen the flames and were now at the point of exhaustion. Eyewitnesses evacuated from their homes spoke of a living hell. A woman was crying. She had seen a ball of flames falling from the top floor, crashing to the pavement 'like something out of a film.' *The Man Who Fell to Earth.* An OAP said he thought it might have been caused by Christmas lights. Detective Chief Inspector Lennon said he was following lines of enquiry and wasn't ruling out foul play. Forensic investigators were already at the scene but could do nothing until the heat had dissipated. The building was still smouldering.

I drove home. The ring road was busy with eager shoppers. I parked in my designated space beneath the flats. I bumped into Mrs Heaton who was pushing her pram along the corridor. She smiled at me for the first time and I must have grimaced back. For once, her cry-baby was silent. I fumbled with my keys and locked the door behind me. I switched on my TV. The fire was on all the channels. I was already late for work. My hands started to tremble. I nicked my face three times whilst shaving, like Zorro. I nearly broke my neck getting out of the shower. I walked hastily to Little's bookshop; ten minutes through hordes. Whole families on a day out. I told myself all the way: act normal, be ordinary. But I had risen above ordinariness. Maurice checked his watch and made a joke about cutting it fine today. I hung my coat where I always hanged my coat. There was blood on my cheek and I wiped it off with my finger. Jenny, one of the seasonal staff who wears John Lennon glasses and tucks her hair back behind her ears, poked her head around the door of the store room, saying, 'Have you heard about the fire?'

'I saw it on TV.'

'Everyone's talking about it,' she said. 'My mother lives just outside Broadstairs.'

I spent ten minutes with Maurice discussing our window display (he was worried about the lights catching the tinsel at night). We had a coffee, then I went about my business as usual, or as much as I could. I checked the shelves and new stock. It helped that the store thronged all day. There wasn't much time to talk about fires and death. I tried to act normally but when you try you cannot be normal at all. I laughed at Jenny. She said over a lunchtime sausage roll that she'd sold twenty calendars in one hour. I was grateful for the ordinariness. Everything was so ordinary that once or twice I forgot the night before. Then my blood would freeze. Paul the Goth wanted to discuss the fire. He had a morbid fascination with death in general and used to work in Broadstairs. Not far from the Acorn offices in fact.

Every sod seemed to have a connection with Broadstairs that day, when in the past twelve months not a whisper about it. Paul was wearing a retro *Fields of the Nephilim* t-shirt, slicked back greasy hair. His favourite genres are crime and spy thrillers. His acne was flaring. He still gets spots at the age of twenty-eight. He has a stammer which increases the more excited he becomes. I clock-watched all afternoon. Paul had one till, I had the other. He talked over the heads of customers as if they weren't there. 'Re-Rebus would have liked this case,' he said. Maurice overheard, saying it was probably Christmas lights and the tinsel was definitely going. He would drape it around the till. 'Arse-Arson,' Paul said. 'Someone was spotted run-running from the scene.' My legs wobbled under me. 'Didn't you enter the Acorn Competition?'

'Last year,' I said, heart kicking at my chest, ticking more like. I thought it would explode. If I was like that then what would I be like in front of the police later? Maybe I should just hand myself in, throw myself on their mercy while I had the chance.

'I hope you've got your ali-alibi sorted. The police will be knock-knocking on your door.'

'Where were you last night?' Maurice joked, and a customer frowned at me.

'Setting fire to the Acorn offices,' I could have said, as a deft bluff, but it was not what I actually said.

'Imogen's?' Maurice said, perplexed. 'I thought you and Imogen were history?'

'Care-careful,' Paul sniggered. 'Let him get his ali-alibi straight.'

I was bent all out of shape, only just holding myself together, palms frosty. 'We're on and off,' I said, in a blokey-jokey way.

'More on than off, I hope?' Maurice said, and Jenny turned her nose up.

'Whatever or whoever it was,' Paul said, 'a man is lie-lying in the morgue.'

'Happy Christmas to you too,' a customer snarled.

I saw out the day and left the after-work-pre-Christmas drinks at the Bishop's Finger early, making excuses. 'I'm off to see -'

'The Wizard of Oz?' Paul interjected. In all the mess I nearly said, 'my parents', forgetting I had dead parents in their memories. My parents had died in a plane crash, hadn't they? And I'd been brought up by my loving Uncle, hadn't I?

'Because because because because becaaaause...because of the wonderful things he does!' Jenny sang. Christmas can do things to your spirits. Or spirits can do things to your Christmas. Whatever.

'I'm off to see *my uncle*,' I said, and they pulled instantly sympathetic faces.

Lies can get you into holes and tight squeezes, but they can also lever you out of them. You just have to remain calm and considered, and not forget the original lie you have told, and *never vary* the lie. Having no parents from a young age, and losing them under such terrible circumstances, had created in the shop an unspoken admiration for me and my extraordinary courage. I call it the Harry Potter Effect. Jenny wanted to mother me (actually she wanted to do more than that). Maurice wanted to stand shoulder-shoulder with me like blokes do, and Paul was just fascinated with plane crashes but was not allowed to talk about it in front of me.

On the way back to my flat, hungry and exhausted, I imagined what they might be saying about me. How sad it was about my parents. What must it be like to have no parents at Christmas? I bought a Chinese takeaway on the way home but couldn't eat it because I was already thinking what it must feel like to lose a loved one just before Christmas? My parents losing Tom. The Broadstairs ball of flames probably had parents (the mother of all flames).

I called my parents to say I'd be with them on Christmas Day. They didn't mention any fire. I watched TV all night long. The fire was nearly out, they said. Rain had been a blessing. They would know soon if arson was a possibility, if the man who'd been seen running away was involved or not.

There came a critical moment that night when I drove to the police station and parked outside. I watched officers coming and going through the main door and I nearly handed myself in. I had one foot out of my door when a police van arrived, in the nick of time. Three hefty officers got out and led two handcuffed men through a side-entrance. An electric, spiked gate. The drunks were kicking at each other as if continuing an earlier brawl. I put my foot back inside my car and watched the men disappear, and a *tap-tap-tap* came at my window, making me jump.

'You can't park here,' a policewoman said, looking around my empty seats. 'Are you lost?'

'No, no, no. I just didn't want to make a phone call while I-'

'You don't want to park on double yellows either.'

'Sorry,' I said, gunning the engine.

If I were a policeperson I'd suggest setting up CCTVs outside the station and train them along the length of this road and everyone I saw parking up there I'd pull them in and ask them who'd they killed and what bank they'd robbed etc. Because guilt can really lead you to the gates.

I drove on. I didn't look back.

That had been the moment when everything might have been different. But then I would not have met Alex Fortune, and might not have been a better person because of it. In any event, I kept my head down on Sunday, got my hair cut shorter than usual on the Monday and no one suspected anything. I told Maurice that with a New Year just around the corner I was going for a new look. Jenny said she preferred my hair shoulder-length but just above the collar was acceptable, though anything shorter and I'd look like Action Man.

The fire was not in the news for three days following. It seemed to have petered out like the flames themselves. However, there was a smouldering smell I could not ignore. Was that my conscience? All I knew was that I was not going to prison. I had been reckless. Yes, an innocent man had died. Yes, an office block had been destroyed probably worth millions of pounds in insurance claims etc. but I was not going to prison for these things. I hadn't known a cleaner would be working inside so late. I had not intended to burn a whole building down. I had not been in control of my emotions. I only intended to take a stand, make a bold statement which went catastrophically wrong. No. I was not going to make a statement of these things to the police.

Nine

I spent Christmas cocooned in my parents' place, protected from Pensbury and a safe distance from Broadstairs and the police.

Mother had decorated the bungalow tastefully, ruined only by her decision to twist silver tinsel around the arms of my dad's electric wheelchair. He liked my haircut. Manly, he said. My mother thought it was a temporary aberration, which of course its origins were. I hadn't known what to buy them for Christmas and gave them cards with money in. It was just my dad's money going into his own pocket which would wind up back in mine.

We ate turkey with cranberry sauce, pulled crackers and listened to the Regina Monologue wearing paper crowns. The Queen, who looked very good for her age, said how wonderful the Commonwealth was and my mother raised a glass of sherry to that.

'Her nose has grown since last year,' Dad said, raising a laugh.

On Boxing Day we all went to Tom's grave. A solemn time. My mother took a bouquet of fresh flowers and I took some Christmas cake. I broke it into crumbs and threw it to the birds. All done, I pushed Dad back to the car; the gravel being too much for the motorised wheels of his chair.

I returned to Pensbury just after New Year to discover that Maurice and his wife were going to have a baby. Their second child. So that was all anyone in the shop wanted to talk about. I saw Imogen a couple of times, things between us still being a little chilly.

Then the fire surfaced again. It was hot news. Pictures of the burnt-out shell of a building started doing the TV rounds. The man who died in the fire was named as 19-year-old Stepan Belonog. Ukrainian by birth, he studied biochemistry at university by day and worked as an office cleaner by night, on an illegal work permit. He'd been paying his way and sending money home to his parents; something which put me to shame. There was a university photograph of him, a lop-sided smile. A clean-cut, skinny guy. His tutor gave an interview saying how tragic his death was and how Stepan had had a brilliant future ahead of him. His heart went out to Stepan's family who'd flown over from the Ukraine where his body (what was left of it) would soon be returned.

[Enter Elvis Presley]

The police were following a number of leads which pricked my ears. Detective Inspector Vincent Lawless was heading up the investigation now. He had a reputation for dealing with big cases. He came on TV to make an appeal with Stepan's parents and sister, or girlfriend, called Marina (no amount of water in Marina could extinguish the horrible reality of what had happened). They did not speak themselves, even with an interpreter.

This Lawless character was incredible. I mean incredible for two reasons: he was beautiful and iconic. In his early-thirties, eyes clear and grey-blue, face heart-shaped with a firm jaw, brow expansive, lips mischievous and generously fleshed. When he stared through the lens of the camera it was with a ferocious gaze. I swear to you, he was the reincarnation of Elvis Presley - before he got too fat. Same black hair (without 70s sideburns), same wide, almost-boxer's nose and strong teeth. Teeth he'd like to sink into my arse! He wasn't nothing but a hound dog. He even had Elvis in his name (Inspector Lawless), give or take a few letters.

When he spoke, the illusion was shattered. Pure Home Counties, not Memphis Tennessee. Nonetheless, his steady voice sent shockwaves down my spine. He spoke through the camera to me. Into me. Cameras flashed in his face yet he did not blink. Flawless Lawless:

'Following a very thorough enquiry and investigation, I can confirm that the fire in Broadstairs on December the 19th of last year at the Acorn publishing offices on Victoria Road was deliberately set. I can confirm that this is a murder investigation. We are looking for a white male seen fleeing the sea front shortly after the fire took hold. He has been described as aged between sixteen and forty (forty!), approximately 5'10" to 6'2" in height, and of stocky build (I was never stocky), and wearing a dark blue or black overcoat.' (I had thrown my coat into a bin in

Bedfordshire, not far from my parents' house which was very difficult because it was such an expensive, beautiful cashmere coat). 'We are appealing to anyone who has information regarding this terrible crime or was in Broadstairs on the evening of December 19th to contact us on...' blah blah blah.

'That could be a mill-million people,' Paul moaned later in the bookshop. 'They obviously don't have any CC-CCTV footage or they'd have shown it.'

That reassured me a little.

'Hooligans and druggies,' Jenny said. 'My mother's always going on about the trouble on a Friday night in Broadstairs. It's in the papers every weekend.' Maurice was too busy thinking about the future to bother with an old story. 'People get killed every day,' he said. 'I sometimes wonder what kind of a world I'm bringing another child into.'

I didn't join in, kept my nose clean, kept myself busy in the shop. Now and then, in quieter moments (though they could crop up anywhere and at any time like Banquo's ghost) Stepan Belonog haunted me. The photographed Belonog gnawed at me. So much so that I stopped watching the local news and reading the papers which for two solid weeks after the fire I had ravenously ransacked for information. I avoided Elvis too, in every sense. DI Vincent Lawless, I mean. Though he had the look and sound of someone who would not give up easily, like his dead rock doppelganger. Flawless Lawless wouldn't go away until he had achieved what he had set out to achieve; to reach his target audience, which was me, Ben Tippet.

Ten

For a while, I escaped the clutches of the news and Elvis.

In that time I worked out my alibi. It doesn't take a genius. Imogen couldn't remember getting home from her works do let alone when I finally arrived at her house. If called upon, all I needed to do was fill in her blanks, like the easiest crossword in the world.

In time, gradually, I forgot there was a murder-hunt going on. The fire became old news after a derailment at Ashford, killing two Parisians. Yesterday's news is exactly that. I had a one night stand with Jenny (too boring to go into and we remained on reasonably good terms. It was a fruitless frivolous night of gay abandon on her birthday). I let my hair grow back to my shoulders. I worked all hours at Little's, making myself indispensable. I did the stocktaking without complaint. I unloaded full lorries of books by myself without grumble. I worked through the accounts when Maurice was busy with his wife who was having difficulties with her early pregnancy. I threw myself into the bookshop 110%. I pulled it back from the brink once again after an exceptionally quiet month. I instigated a buy-one-get-one-free initiative despite accusations of selling out. I called it the "Back-2-Back" sale: every full-priced hardback customers bought came with a free paperback chosen from a limited range (i.e. remaindered stock).

Finally, come March, to bring the punters in, I converted and promoted the old cartography room on the top floor as a readings venue and I decided upon a big name to establish our new enterprise: Alexander Fortune.

[Enter Alexander Fortune for the first, proper time]

Before sending an invitation to read at Little's, I undertook meticulous research, most of it online, and still didn't know much about the man behind the literary mask. His American publishers, Friedman and Friedman, maintained a website but stuck mainly to his novels and short stories, archived interviews (oral and textual), in which Alex was very guarded. He'd only discuss his fiction. He volunteered no personal information except that he was born in Sussex, the son of an RAF pilot. He was a recluse this side of the Atlantic, yet in America it was a different story. He came out of his shell more in the States. Public appearances two or three times a year, so I knew he did give readings. There were literary reviews from The New York Times, The Guardian, The Times and TLS etc. There was also an email address to which I sent five emails, never receiving a reply, getting a barrage of book-offers instead.

I decided my only chance of getting him was to send mail direct to his home address. I knew from the Pensbury Gazette that he'd bought a house in Incham, a pretty hamlet on the East Kent coast; a thirty or forty-minute drive from Pensbury. It didn't take a genius to discover where exactly. I'd driven my parents there during one of their visits because it was a well-known beauty spot. Original oak-framed houses and thatched-roof cottages etc. Millionaire's row. There was an old pub on the edge of the hamlet called The Duck Inn and that was my first port of call.

On a beautifully crisp Sunday afternoon in early March I went for a warm beer and a ploughman's and got talking to the locals. Actually, I used a bit of charm on the landlord's daughter in good old-fashioned Chaucerian style. She told me the hamlet wasn't what it used to be; information surely passed down from her pot-bellied father because she could not have been more than eighteen. 'DFLs,' she whined.

I'd heard of them naturally. Not a sofa warehouse, but people "Down From London". Second-homers and retiring couples who'd made a mint from London real estate and could afford huge houses beside the sea or in the countryside beyond the London orbital. To be honest, the landlord's daughter sounded part M25 herself. Alex once described the local Kentish accent quite lovingly as "cockney bumpkin", straight out of *The Darling Buds of May*.

Anyhow, we kept chatting and I dropped into our equation a question: 'Hasn't a famous novelist moved into the hamlet recently?'

'Yes,' she said, 'Alexander-'

Her ear-wigging father finished her sentence. 'Fortune and who's asking?' He came across to check me over. 'Are you a journalist?'

'A writer,' I said. His daughter, Frankie she said her name was, seemed impressed. 'I wish to make contact with Mr Fortune.' I don't know why I put on such a ridiculous accent. Maybe it was because the adjoining restaurant was crammed full of fox-hunter toffs. The landlord sniffed. I love Kentish folk. They can be real sniffy about the smallest of things and then they can be as helpful as you like the very next second.

'No one makes contact with him. Keeps himself to himself. Hasn't put a foot in here for a whole year.'

(Get on with it, Ben. You're not actually in the pub right now are you? I can still smell and taste my warm beer and tangy ploughman's pickle though).

Father and daughter pointed me in the right direction, which as it turned out was the wrong direction or I hadn't been listening properly. I took a right at the duck pond, and a beautiful wide pond it was with ducks and lily pads like saucers in it, then a right at a small T-junction, then along another road, passing a white windmill. Yes, that's fine, I'm on the right track, but I was no longer in Incham. I was in the rolling farmland, off the beaten track. Narrow lanes and converted oasthouses and large detached farmhouses. I felt too embarrassed to go back to the pub and ask all over and there was nobody around to ask on this exceptionally sunny spring afternoon. Not even a cyclist. All I had was the name of a house: Smuggler's Cottage. So I returned to my flat and constructed an all-important invitation.

Ben Tippet
Little's Bookshop
11, Butcher's Row
Pensbury
PY6 2LP
Email: Littlebookshop@btopenworld.com
Tel: 01677 461 237
5th March, 2006

Dear Mr Fortune,

Forgive me for sending this to your home but I had no luck with your publisher's email address, having sent ten letters. I think what I have to say is of great importance.

I know you are busy promoting your latest novel, "Dead on Main Street". I am a big fan of your creation Inspector Massey, and was delighted to discover you have brought him back to life. I also know you are a very private writer, so I shall be as brief and as unobtrusive as possible.

I own and manage a small shop in Pensbury called, appositely, Little's. It is in the centre of Pensbury. You may know it? I am also a writer. It is in these capacities that I write; to ask if you would be kind enough to give a reading from your latest novel at Little's? You would of course be paid a modest fee. I have recently converted part of my shop into a live-literature venue with many local poets and short-story writers performing here every other week. We have never had a novelist, and certainly not of your stature.

To be frank, Little's is struggling in the current book-selling climate. Even in Pensbury, the conglomerates are squeezing the life out of small independent sellers such as myself. I need not mention their names. I also know that you treasure small bookshops, that you have given readings before in Boston, New York and Detroit. Is it possible that as a prominent local writer you might consider giving a short reading of your work in support of our bookshop in Pensbury?

I would be unspeakably grateful.

If you would like to do this, we can discuss it over the telephone or you can email me at Little's. Such an evening would be a privilege and a delight, I'm sure. You have a large following here in Kent. I could arrange for a special display of your work and book-signing at the end of your reading? Such an event, I'm sure, would bring a raft of new fans too.

Thank you for your time, and the best of luck with your latest work of art.
Yours most sincerely,
Ben Tippet

At least that's how I remember my letter. It disappears in this story like so much else that's important in the telling of it. Had I overcooked it? A "work of art"? Alex's last six novels were what I'd call "populist" fiction, and not exactly popular in the UK where the market was swamped with better crime novels. He was adored in America but had slipped almost entirely off the UK radar, except for those in the know, those like myself who loved him more for what he had written decades ago, in his younger, more experimental days. The Americans thought he was quaint and clever-clever with his metafictional devices and overblown metaphors and descriptions of an England stuck increasingly in the 1950s and 60s; the time of his childhood and Oxbridge education. Alex comes from a great English tradition of silver spoons and pass the port to the left. All very sinister to me, a suburban son of a bed-seller! Which actually sounds like an insult when you say it quickly. Of course, I loved him for what he had already written, not the most recent work. Alex had once been a literary giant, an experimenter, a real wordsmith, a challenger of literary convention. That could never be taken away from him. Never.

I sent the letter first class on a Monday morning, not expecting to get a reply. I half-believed Smuggler's was a fictitious name and place having driven around the hamlet in search of the elusive cottage and its environs on three separate occasions. Some kind of Kentish Bermuda Triangle. I could do no more now, except wait.

I did not expect a call at the bookshop, or an email. What I got, incredibly, was a short letter within seven days of receipt. I'd caught him (in retrospect) on one of his good days:

Dear Ben,

I read with interest your invitation to give a reading at your bookshop in Pensbury. I'm sorry but I am not familiar with Little's, although I have been into the city for Cathedral choir recitals and business meetings. I understand entirely the modern-day pressures on independent booksellers. Capitalist chains are squeezing everyone from writers, such as ourselves, to agents and small presses too. And this is why I'm accepting your invitation. I agree to give a short reading from my latest novel, as requested, and to sign copies at the end of the evening. There is no need for payment, although it is not unusual to be taken out to dinner, if this is agreeable?

However, you are absolutely right to suggest that I am very busy at the moment. "Dead on Main Street" is doing the UK rounds as we speak. (I'm sorry to say at the same conglomerates which are squeezing you so tightly!) Due to professional commitments I can only make the evening of April 1ˢᵗ, from 6pm onwards. I understand this is short notice but should you wish to proceed, please do make contact with my publicist, Ms Hilary Shears, at the email address attached, where you can make all the necessary arrangements.

Yours,

Alex Fortune

PS: If we are going to dine in Pensbury, may I point out in advance that I have an aversion to cucumbers?

It should have gone down in history, a signed letter like this. Alex was a virtual recluse. An Incommunicado. He'd been forced out of hiding to take a tour of the UK and up until this point only the larger cities. I ran around the shop with my letter. Maurice didn't believe it until he saw the words with his own eyes. '*Your* bookshop?' he said, pointing at the page.

'The only way to get a name like Alexander Fortune is to pretend to be a big-shot owner of a bookshop. It's about respect and deference. I hope you don't mind? It was a one-off.'

'As long as you explain the error when he comes,' Maurice said.

'I can't do that. What will he think? That he can't trust me? He might walk away leaving us with custard on our faces.'

'Egg,' he said, shaking his head. 'You're unbelievable.'

'If you want this shop to survive, if you want the venue to succeed, we have to attract the names. We need to build a reputation, get bums on seats. These things can't be done on the backs of a dozen nobodies, no matter how good they are. We need to stand on the shoulders of giants.'

He could only agree. We'd had three readings in two weeks. All flops. The proverbial one-man-and-his-dog routine. I'm being harsh. I always turned up. But I had to as chief organiser and one of the readers. There had been a handful of keen, local writers, a couple of students from university, but not enough to fill the cartography room. Not enough to get tongues wagging, even with fly-posting which yours truly undertook all by himself.

No. This was the big one. Maurice had originally pooh-poohed the venue idea (for one thing he wanted to spend more time with Louise, his sickening wife. I mean she was pregnant sick). 'If this doesn't succeed,' he said, 'I'm going to pull the plug.'

You see, I thought it would be Alex's reputation on the line at Little's on April Fools Day, but it was mine too. That partly explains the nervousness I had to overcome on the night. I'd done all the prep: hired the seats for upstairs, chilled the Pinot G, allowed the Bordeaux to breathe, got the mineral water, crisps and nibbles – all on the ground floor. There was a buzz about the place and Maurice seemed pleased.

Gradually, the three rooms on the ground floor filled up. Customers browsed the shelves as they chatted. I'd pulled out all the stops, fly-posting illegally and liberally all over the city, including the University. I'd dropped a personal invite into Imogen and she'd been kind enough (despite our relationship ending weeks and weeks before) to circulate information among her cohort of students. Far from being nervous about under-attendance, I was fractious that the old cartography room would collapse under the weight of eighty arses. That and the fact Alex still hadn't showed. I remembered the bookfest the previous July when he hadn't materialized. I had visions of handing back money and lame excuses. The reading was due to kick off at 7-30 and it was already 7-15. Alex's publicist/tour manager, Hilary Shears (an American I discovered on the telephone two weeks before) was not answering her mobile, but the email she'd sent in the morning had said Alex would arrive at 6-30 to mingle and chat.

I couldn't talk to anybody, downed a couple of glasses of Pinot G and avoided Maurice altogether. I shot up the stairs to the top floor, making absolutely sure everything was in place: a small table and two chairs at one end where the floor sloped slightly, a jug of water, rows of seats set out in front of it. A bit of a squeeze but it would do. I'd discussed it all with Maurice. I'd introduce Hilary Shears and she would introduce Alexander Fortune. He would read for about thirty minutes (from a selection of his novels) followed by a Q and A session (I had to really push Hilary for this because Alex hadn't agreed, being so damned paranoid about everything in real life). Everyone would return downstairs for more wine, nibbles, chat, and finally the book signing where Jenny and Paul had established "Fortune Corner". Actually, a very impressive display of books. Jenny had initially suggested bringing in cookies too, which was just plain hammy and ridiculous.

I sat down, panicking, when Paul shouted up the curling staircase. 'They're here!' And I leapt out of my seat.

Downstairs, Maurice was already talking to Hilary; a well-groomed forties, short-ish, mousey-ish woman dressed in a smart business suit. I went over immediately and shook her hand. I looked around for Alex but he was nowhere to be seen. I say looked for him but I only had three mental images to recognise him by: a website mug-shot taken by a professional photographer with no taste (unbelievably cheesy side profile, not playing to Alex's strengths which are definitely his eyes); the promotional sleeve from the novel *Six* where Alex sits po-faced and cross-legged on top of a giant revolver, arms folded across his chest; much more preferable is the photograph from the sleeve of his earlier masterpiece, *Fugue*. Alex had been 34 then. He wears contacts now, but then he wore spectacles and was sitting slumped over an ebony grand piano, po-faced.

Looking back (or is it actually moving forwards in my plot?) this detail fills me with a sudden sadness in my cell, because on closer inspection of this photograph there was an ever-so-slight ironic curve to the left corner of Alex's mouth. A playful, almost missable, upturn of the lip. An insinuation of a kink. When I first noticed it I thought to myself: this piano should not be in a drawing room, it should be beside a lake and there should be a sign in front of this lake next to Alex Fortune, saying "Danger: Deep Water!"

A mid-Atlantic voice swam over my shoulder, smooth and rich in texture. 'I'd like to meet the man who wrote to me,' it said. I was half-turning and felt a gentle hold on the upper arm of my suit.

I've heard that some people become awe-struck when meeting their idols and icons for the first time. I was no exception. I put out my hand and shook his without a single word. He was slightly shorter than expected. An inch or two smaller than me, but I am six feet in my soles. He was naturally-tanned, slim, wearing dark trousers with a brown belt, and a mud-coloured corduroy jacket, the chunky lines of which resembled a furrowed field. His Oxford blue shirt was open two buttons at the throat, a sprout of greying hair showing. He had real presence. The sort of person who doesn't so much light up a room as darken it all around, a spotlight shining only upon himself. His face was muscular, his head fashionably shaven close. It suited him. Everything seemed to suit him that night. The glass of white wine perched in his hand too. He looked fit, in rude health. I couldn't believe I was standing only inches from him.

When I finally spoke, after all the rehearsals in my flat, it came out wrong, as if I was working for the British Secret Service: 'Tippet. Ben Tippet.'

'Shaken, not stirred?' he said, making Maurice and Hilary laugh. 'Well, I'm pleased to meet you. I'm Fortune. Alex Fortune.'

'The same,' I said, 'I mean pleased…'

'I know,' he said, staring suggestively. I am not exaggerating to say I felt a jolt. His eyes were a tempestuous grey, like wintry English clouds. The innuendo of his eyes! He apologised for the delay but didn't explain it. 'Your shop's impressive,' he said. I didn't know what to say and neither did Maurice whose shop it was. 'Genuinely oldie-worldie. It reminds me of my time in Oxford.'

There wasn't much time for small talk. The allotted time had been and gone and I was getting looks. After a few minutes of crippling awkwardness, I said, 'Excuse me, Alex. I should make an announcement, if you're ready?'

'Oh, I'm always ready,' he said, raising an eyebrow to his publicist who clucked at him like a hen at her most wayward chick. I showed Alex the way with a sweep of my arm, the one he had touched. He finished his glass and followed close behind me, then Hilary and Maurice, a lot of eager beavers going up the stairs, Imogen and Paul who strangely seemed to be hitting it off, and more punters I didn't really know. Jenny stayed on the shop floor, it being against the fire regulations to lock customers in for any length of time.

Maurice and I took up our positions in the front row and when everyone seemed settled - squeezed in like a deck of cards, definite fire hazard, I should have known better - I cleared my throat, stood up, and clapped my hands for full attention. I had a crumpled introduction in my hands, though I never looked at it. I spoke loudly and clearly. How pleased I was. No, how grateful I was that Mr Alexander Fortune the well-known novelist could be with us this evening at Little's Bookshop in Pensbury. Maurice folded his arms throughout, giving me the dead-eye. He'd wanted to do the introductions. It was his shop after all. 'Hopefully this will become one of many such evenings hosted here.'

Alex got up suddenly, in the middle of my speech, removing his furrowed field jacket, looking around for somewhere to put it. 'May I hang this in your closet?' he said, handing it across to me. I didn't know what to do. Was he belittling me? Maurice took the jacket, folded it carefully on his lap, grimacing, and Alex re-took his seat.

I mentioned *Dead on Main Street* (great title, shame about the story) and that the reviews were good (actually, very mixed; one reviewer said it was more like Dead on Mainstream) and copies would be available to purchase on the ground floor after the reading, as would most of Mr Fortune's other countless novels which I was sure the author would happily sign. He smiled at me, then looked at his feet.

How I loved you, Alex. Even then, right at the beginning, when you were so rude and unpredictable, playing the eccentric. I know you better than that now. But I wouldn't change any of it. You are you and me is me.

A light drizzle of applause, then Hilary made her pitch. A well-planned, well-oiled probably-done-this-a-hundred-times-on-the-tour spiel. It was funny, but contrived. Too neat, too slick, too inorganic. That's my excuse anyway for having given a comparatively lousy opening. This was her job. This paid for her hair stylist and clothes and pearl earrings. Definitely a pearly-girly. She made sure Alex turned up to things, the audiences were full and enough copies of his novels were available for sale. She orchestrated his flights and trains and taxis. She reported back to her boss (a certain Mr B.B. Crum – no "B") in New York City where she normally lived. Actually, it was in Queens she lived. She was over here for three months, missing her husband who himself was a budding poet (Alex told me all of this in a wine bar later). She sold Alex very well that night. Not giving too much of his mystery away before the Q and A.

The maestro stood to a light ripple of applause.

'And I haven't even said anything yet,' he said. Laughter. He was a natural. So natural I don't know why he'd turned into such a loner in Smuggler's Cottage, in a sleepy hamlet a mile from the sea. I had brought him to the public in Pensbury and he was loving it, as Hilary might say.

He read from three novels, ten minutes each, starting with *Dead on Main Street*. It was alright. Better than when I read it in my head. Norman Mailer-ish. Witty. Pacey. A thriller. It starts with the simplest of opening lines: *I knew by the state of my hands that I'd killed someone, the only mystery was why?* It drifted off and went down hill from there, until he picked up *Six*, a much earlier novel in which his most popular detective, Hugo Massey, was fictionally conceived (his own well-thumbed original edition which Hilary had brought for him in her briefcase). A wonderful book. The book which changed his life, taking him overseas to L.A. then NYC. He was in his early forties then. Truly his breakthrough novel in America. They made a film of it in Hollywood. He could have stopped writing there and then if he'd wanted. You should read it. It's head and shoulders, except maybe *Fugue* which I was dying for him to read.

SPOILER ALERT!

Let me save you the trouble with *Six*. (Skip a couple of pages if you want to read it yourself. I'll mark this with *** so you know where to pick my story up again). Turn away now if you don't wish to know the result, as it were.

***Six is a novella broken into six chapters corresponding to six murders. It starts at six in the evening and ends at six in the morning in the same place a month later; in a redundant salesman's kitchen. The salesman's called Solomon. He is a serial killer. Detective Hugo Massey is the conscience of the novel. The reader if you like.

Originally (so Alex told me over dinner), he wrote the script for television. Granada were interested in prime-time murder in the 1990s. They commissioned it on the back of his reputation as a novelist. But Alex wanted to set it in the 1980s and they said to hell with that, they're over. But Alex persisted. He wanted it set in Bradford and Yorkshire. He wanted Solomon to have contracted AIDS from a prostitute which made the wheels come off his life. But Granada said it was too depressing. They also wanted a female lead, so Alex walked. An American company got wind of the story, then offered cash upfront if he would re-set it in L.A. He did and the rest is literary history.

A middle-aged, divorced insurance salesman called Solomon gets fired from his job. A week later he discovers he has VD from sleeping with hookers. These two things act as the trigger for his rampage. Solomon has a revolver (one his father gave him just before he died). He sits in his kitchen at the beginning of the book, spinning the gun barrel. There's one bullet in the chamber. He is letting fate decide the outcome. Six times he churns the well-greased barrel, pointing the nozzle at his temple and pulling the trigger, having made the decision already that if he survives this game of roulette six times, it will be a sign for him to go and do what he's been secretly fantasising about doing over the past year. Namely, fill this gun, seek out and shoot six people who have made his life a misery.

The first victim is someone he has never forgotten. A school bully who used to pull his hair so hard it came out in clumps and never quite grew back. He tracks this man down. However, in the interest of fairness (as an insurance man, Solomon knows all about calculating odds) he decides to play Russian Roulette in his car which is parked outside his intended victim's mid-state well-to-do condo residence. 'You're not all bad, Solomon,' he tells himself, 'Either you'll die or he will'. One bullet to the brain.

And so the book goes through all the stories and victims. Solomon is blessed (or is it cursed?) because he can't ever blow his own head off. He goes through his victims one-by-one, tracking them down, parking outside their houses, same routine, same outcome. And Massey is the only detective close to catching him, because he's smart. He puts all the pieces together like a good cop should. Solomon has made a fundamental mistake in killing his old boss at the insurance firm, only he's a little lucky because his ex-boss has about twenty enemies who'd happily blow his brains out, death threats from ex-wives included. So Solomon thinks he is in the clear, but he's not counting on sharp-eyed Massey who can think left-of-field. A college professor gets blown away for once making Solomon feel "small" in class. A driving instructor is deadheaded for failing Solomon six times in a row. It sounds ridiculously linear, but it's just fantastic. Part of Solomon wants the rampage to stop, but it is not the important part. He can't figure what to do after each killing. He feels adrenalin-rushes, but no joy. He is still the man he always was: an unremitting failure.

The whole novel builds to the final killing. It is his older brother, Edward. And what has Edward ever done to Solomon? It's the big mystery of the book. The tantalising question mark left behind by very good books. You are led to believe that sexual abuse has occurred, but no, it might just be jealousy. Edward has achieved: big house in Kansas, $300,000 a year + bonuses, happy wife and house full of happy-clappy kids.

Solomon watches from his car and you're thinking: *don't do it. What's he ever done to you?* (except never keep in touch or offer any financial help over the years). Massey is so close he can almost see Solomon over his dash, but he's too late. It's the sixth victim and Solomon returns to his apartment, sits in his kitchen, holds his father's gun to his head. Massey breaks in, his own gun trained on Solomon, but Solomon's already going to shoot. We don't know if there's one, none, or six bullets in the chamber. The scene is played out in slow-motion and we are right back where we started. Massey needs to know why, but he might never know why because the novel ends with a substantial click, the reader none the wiser. Who killed whom?

Six has been reprinted three times. It was renamed *Rampage* in Hollywood and packaged as a schlock horror flick with hard-to-detect political undertones (way before the film *Seven*).

Alex hated *Rampage*, the title and the film. He said as much at the Q and A session at Little's. He told us that he wrote the book as a comment on the state of America at the time. Politically and criminally, he didn't like what he saw in America, where you could be popped for a bag of candy. 'A culture of implosion,' he told us. Solomon was the metaphorical average American, full of high but unmet expectation, someone who had lost faith in the institutions which once held people tightly together: religion, marriage, family, country. Edward was the American dream and Massey was the moral conscience of a country powerless to intercede.

It was true, now that he mentioned it. In the subtext, Solomon's father had dreamed of being a lay preacher. Solomon himself had begged God to fix the chamber of the gun against himself, but God had not seen fit to do so.

Only one thing puzzled me about this brilliant book. No mother. No mention of Solomon's mother. Anyone's mother. Completely mother-free, wiped from the story.***

I was left disappointed by the third reading. No *Fugue*! That's better than *Six* and written years before. I'd bought in a dozen copies of *Fugue* to sell at the reading thinking he'd surely read a section.

Stop me if this gets boring. Well you can, by skipping a page, but I'll keep this short, I promise. It's just another measure of my admiration of his writing. It's not that his recent novels are pulp fiction, more that they are uninspired and uninspiring. Written very well but formulaic and only for effect, not meaning.

Fugue is masterful. (Remember "Danger: Deep Water"?) It is Alex's only truly historical piece of fiction, set in the 1930s. An inter-war novel. Just like the multifaceted word "fugue", the book plays with notions of loss. It is simultaneously a collection of short stories (a polyphonic composition), a dream (state of altered consciousness that may last for hours or days) and at the narrative level, a story about a brilliant pianist/composer in full tuxedo and tails who is discovered wandering along Brighton beach. He does not know who he is, where he has come from or how he has got here (a dissociative disorder in which a person forgets who they are, leave home and create a new life, with no memory of their former life. After recovery, there is no memory of events during the dissociative state).

Five people claim to know who he is and they take temporary possession of him. They provide him with a name and a history he has never known. A whole new identity in fact. He becomes whoever they want and need. They each tell a story about how he came to be here on Brighton beach. Each story is vividly portrayed. There is no obvious moral like the Canterbury Tales. A wife tells him how they got separated during the Great War. A doctor says they are brothers who drifted apart because of a dispute over a rich man's daughter. A young painter says he was the man's lover once upon a time and they had lived in Venice and he has paintings of him to prove it. Each person moulds something out of the anonymous man, making of him whatever they wish. Because each of the people are hurting, their stories move you almost to crying. He is needed and wanted because they are needy and wonting. He plays the pianos in each of their houses, but he is miserable. He can't be truly happy until he knows who he is.

There is a danger in this book of sentimentality, of over-experimentalism, of morbidness, maybe even copycatishness when the man comes out of his fugue, discovers his true past and leaves his recently-invented past behind him like abandoned clothes on Brighton beach (James Mason in *A star is Born*? Reginald Perrin?). Has he walked into the Channel? Is he a figment of vivid and desperate imaginations?

I won't spoil it for you. You have to read it to understand. It's not an easy book to understand, just easy to swoon over. There is mystery. A tantalising question mark remaining to be answered. Never has Alex shown such skill in manipulating the mind with words on a page. Or maybe it is just the way I am. Just the way Alex is. The way we all are.

The final reading. No *Fugue*! Alex read something else from a more popular book of his called *A Local Zero* and it sounded as bad as the title (pure genre). He did it for an "up" at the end and it seemed to work. The spontaneous applause nearly brought the dodgy plaster down from the ceiling. I stood up and thanked him with a lusty handshake and the applause erupted again, my own clapping being the loudest. Alex soaked it up. He'd once been a trail-blazing comet in a galaxy of writing stars. He was a more ordinary star now, a fine and bright star nonetheless. Before re-taking his seat and answering questions from the floor, he took a sip of water and licked his lips.

'Mr Fortune has kindly agreed to answer some questions,' I said, 'but please stick to his works of fiction or to writing in general.' This is what his publicist had advised in her email: *Alex does not answer questions about his own life, only his fictional worlds.*

There came an awkward moment when silence gripped the room; anxious faces waiting for other faces to open their mouths. Then a familiar hand went up. Imogen already knew a thing or two about writing. Her eager beaver students got their pens and pads ready.

'Firstly, thank you for coming to Pensbury,' she said. He nodded, not looking at her directly. 'Hearing an author reading their own words gives them extra meaning and power.' High praise, because in truth she'd told me on the telephone that she didn't like his style or subject matter. 'I teach creative writing up at the university. What advice would you give to anyone starting out as a *new* writer?' It was for the benefit of her coterie of aspirationals, half of whom were drunk.

Alex pondered this, finger tapping his lips as if to stifle the first thought crossing his mind. He cast steady grey eyes around the room, towards the lines of fresh-faced enthusiasts. 'Two things: listen to no one, read everybody.'

I didn't have to see Imogen's irritability, it was in her tone of voice. 'Surely, you would advocate an open mind on literary criticism?'

'No,' he fired back. 'I would not. My only advice to a new writer would be to write from left to right.' I could see why Alex did not normally take part in Q and A sessions. An arrogant flippancy had taken over him.

'Left to right?' Imogen said.

'Yes. Start at the beginning, finish at the end and don't worry about the middle. It should write itself.' (He stole this from Lewis Carroll who said start at the beginning and finish at the end).

'But that's the plot,' she insisted. 'You mean you don't advocate students learning the basics of craft before setting off into the unknown?'

'Did Colombus have a map or did he make the map?' Alex said.

'Colombus wasn't a writer,' Imogen replied, quite astonished.

'Are you referring to creative writing classes?' he said, getting back on track. She nodded, feathers ruffling. 'Courses are for learning how *not* to write rather than how *to* write. Isn't that so? In essence, no one can teach it. Read, read, read. Fiction is its own teacher.'

A murmur spread around Imogen's students. She must have felt as if a redundancy notice had been publicly posted and I jumped to her defence: 'With respect, Mr Fortune, many excellent writers have passed through creative writing courses. Off the top of my head there's Raymond Carver, J.D. Salinger…'

'Great writers,' he said. 'But I suspect they were great despite training not because of it.'

An uncomfortable atmosphere had developed in only a couple of minutes; an unexpected storm brewing. Imogen adopted a combative, self-defensive posture, though still in her seat. 'Then why have so many new writers gathered here tonight,' she said, 'if not to hear about your writing process?' I turned to look at her thunderous face.

'Hopefully, they've come to buy my new book and have me sign it,' he said.

I can see now, looking back in time, that in different circumstances and with better timing this would have raised a few laughs. Still now, I think it was a witty riposte, but it fell awfully flat. Alex hadn't read the room. He looked me straight in the eyes, as if for assistance, and I froze.

'Do something,' Maurice whispered from the corner of his mouth.

I was about to when a mature woman with a steely grey bun on her head called out, 'Your characters are so well-drawn, Mr Fortune. How important would you say it is to get the characters right before the plot?' I could have kissed the old hag!

'Characters are the plot, the root,' he said. 'Everything stems from them.' He laughed to himself. 'There is a writer whose name I won't mention who once told me, "Character is a blob of jam at the epicentre of an ordinary bowl of porridge. It sweetens the otherwise unpalatable."' I felt the audience warming to him again.

'What should a new writer write about?' one of Imogen's pretty students asked and I could have kissed her too for moving things on so smoothly.

'Whatever they want.'

'Should it be topical, political?'

'You should write what you care about. It needn't be either of those.'

'But what if you're not sure what to write about?' she replied.

A gem popped out of his mouth. He said, 'If in doubt, turn yourself inside out. You will find what you will find.' The crowd nodded sagely, the students wrote it down. I have kept it inside me all this time and don't think it will ever leave me. I think about it every day in prison. What you are getting are my insides out.

'You don't know what you're capable of writing until you have written it. That's the beauty and mystery of writing,' Alex continued. 'You can only write what you can write.'

'And what do you say about voice?' someone asked from the back row. 'Is it akin to soul you're talking about?'

'I don't believe in the soul,' Alex retorted. 'Voice is a fingerprint. Unique, like a signature. Maybe more unique even than that. It is personality. All you have to do is express it.'

I put my hand in the air.

'Yes, Ben?' (he did use my name).

'You write literature and you write popular novels, but what do you think differentiates the two?'

'Good question,' he said, stroking his chin, thinking. 'Literature is art, but you can have popular art of course.'

'Are they mutually exclusive? I mean…what makes it "classic"?' I used my fingers as inverted commas.

'I don't like the term "classic"' he said, mimicking my inverted commas, making me blush. 'It makes a book sound old, like a collectible sports car or an old film with Rock Hudson or Montgomery Clift.' (A complete stranger once told me I looked like Clift, before his car accident. Clift's, I mean).

The audience laughed.

'Literature says something fundamental about the human condition and keeps on saying it. Take Marlowe. He's part of our heritage and he died more than 600 years ago, yet he still stirs the juices. We are still discovering him because what he says is fresh and timeless. As Ezra Pound once said: literature is news that stays news.'

There were a few more questions but I could see Alex was getting to the end of what he wanted to say, so I apologised to the audience, said they might continue chatting downstairs at the book-signing. I thanked Alex and Hilary once again. I couldn't thank them enough. More applause.

I'd invited Alex, Hilary, Maurice and Imogen to dinner in advance. An Italian restaurant near the cathedral. Great atmosphere and cosy tables, very good service and an extensive range of home-cooked pasta dishes. Not to mention an excellent Pinot G, robust cherry-laden Chianti and cheeky Puglian reds. I felt like getting loaded.

It was close to 9-40 by the time the books were signed, the wine was drunk and punters had made their way out. Alex signed my dog-eared old copies of *Six* and *Fugue*. I wanted him to know I'd been a fan for some time. 'What would you like me to write?' he'd asked, looking up, pen poised. 'Another *Fugue*?' I said, gazing a gazely stare. He wrote: *To Ben, with love and thanks, Alex.*

With love.

As it turned out, Imogen did not come to dinner. She made excuses of an early start in the morning, and besides, she was 100% vegan now and the restaurant was not on her list of places. I thought it was more likely to have been the contretemps with Alex. She kissed me on the cheek, shook Alex's hand, said it had been very enjoyable and her students had learnt a great deal. That was definitely for Alex's benefit. Maurice locked the shop, leaving the detritus for the morning, and the four of us reached Mamma Mia's just before 10pm.

Mamma Mia wasn't happy in the kitchen agreeing only after a small argument to take our orders. No starters, straight to limited mains with a bottle of red and a bottle of white.

How would I characterise the situation? Alex was jovial. He opened with a joke about cucumbers, saying they were the fascists of the vegetable world, contaminating everything. Hilary was anxious to drag him to London on a train. Maurice wanted to leave before the food arrived and got up, whispering in my ear, 'We sold more than I expected. This could really be the start of something.'

It really was the start of something. For me and Alex.

And then there were three. It was quite stuffy in the restaurant so I removed my jacket and turned to Alex who was right beside me, saying, 'You don't mind if I hang my jacket in your closet?' Then I slung it over the back of his chair. He looked at Hilary who pulled a face, then he burst out laughing. I don't think in the whole summer I later spent with him he laughed that loudly again.

'You learn to plagiarise quickly,' he said.

'I only steal from the best people,' I replied, raising my glass. 'Michael Caine said that.'

He leaned in. I could smell his cologne. 'Copy anyone but never copy yourself. Pablo Picasso.' I laughed but I didn't know what he meant. Picasso, I mean. Unless he meant navel-gazing narcissism and self-destructive vanity.

I can skip all of the preliminaries to the real main course. Hilary was a gooseberry. More like a bodyguard, or Alex's conscience. A nanny. A spoiler. To think I'd planned to lavish all of my attention on her over dinner. Alex was too big a fish, wasn't he? But Hilary Shears? She had a direct line to a huge publisher.

'That's half a dozen,' she said to Alex as he topped up his glass. She'd been monitoring the alcohol all night. She was too busy reminding him of the time of their train to London and generally being a fussy hen to hear about my latest novels-in-progress: *The Whizzkid of Oz* and *Sticky Knickers* (I can't share these with you. They're just too hot).

You know as well as I do, Alex fancied the pants off me and I was playing his not-so-naive apprentice. A tease for wont of a better word. There is nothing unnatural about it. Only fascists and bullies think otherwise (like Manston) and maybe some of these are partial. If the truth be told, very creative men have appreciated the finesse of oysters but retreated now and then into the order of the cloisters. Writers, painters, philosophers and all sorts. Proust, Erasmus, Aristotle, Shakespeare, Herman Melville, Yukio Mishima, Hans Christian Andresen, David Bowie, and it is rumoured, Kurt Cobain are just a few. Closet heterosexuals or wardrobe woofters, no one can argue that these were, or are, bad men. You could actually argue that each is a moral compass, pointing in the direction they must go.

My problem was squashing the gooseberry. As it happened, I think Hilary trod on herself by applying too much pressure. When she wasn't phoning people about this and that, she was nagging Alex. Her biggest concern, as she expressed at the end of the meal, was that he had a book-signing at Foyles in London the next afternoon and she didn't want him "tired". She had a duty to him, to BB and to the publishers.

'BB?' Alex said, smirking. 'BB's a pain in the arse.'

'Who's BB?' I said.

'The legend that is BB Crum, no B,' Alex said. 'My editorial publisher and all-round shit-stick.'

'It's not something we need discuss now, Alex.' Hilary was trying to cut me out. 'You know how upset BB gets if we don't meet appointments. He's been your friend for too long now to -'

'You can say that again,' Alex said dryly.

I'd only asked (both of them, but really only Alex) if anyone fancied going to a wine bar for a night cap.

'What about your headaches?' she said.

I looked at him. 'Have you got a headache, Alex?'

'I feel fine,' he said. He insisted on paying for dinner, Maurice would be pleased to know (Alex had gnocchi and a green salad, I ordered exactly the same and Hilary had a tomato, basil and rocket salad with warm ciabatta, for the record).

Their difference of opinion continued onto the street, with Alex the victor. We walked Hilary to a taxi rank near Southgate Tower and bundled her into a car. She still had time to catch the last train to Victoria. Their original plan had been for both of them to go to London and stay at her apartment. Now Alex was saying he'd just have a couple of drinks and catch a taxi home and he'd meet her at Foyles at the appointed hour. 'It has only just gone eleven after all, Hilary.'

I was thinking, he's not a baby, Hilary pillory. He is a grown-up man. She looked me up and down. 'You'd better be there, Alex.'

He waved her off. 'Fusspot. So…do we have far to walk to this famous wine bar of yours?'

La Galleria is at the heart of Pensbury; a good ten-minute walk. We arrived just before the pub-closing rush. I flashed my card which allowed for one guest, and we were ushered down a spiral staircase into the basement where the walls are lined with local artists' work, of a postmodernist kind. All for sale. La Galleria is owned by two Italian brothers, one of whom I know is gay; the only interesting place to go after midnight. The lighting was subdued.

You can hang around the bar drinking, take a seat, watch the other punters arriving, checking out the talent. I had picked up once here before. The staff knew my name and my tipple of choice: sparkling Prosecco. I asked for a bottle and two glasses. You can move on past, through a narrow tunnel at the side of the bar into the so-called Icon Lounge where the walls are adorned with impressions of classic film stars and rock Gods. It is a smaller, more intimate space. You can sip your cocktail or Peroni in the comfort of sofas and designer armchairs under the gazes of Lou Reed, Iggy Pop, Marilyn Monroe, James Dean, Jimi Hendrix, John Lennon, Betty Boop, Debbie Harry, *et al.* The toilets are down a further passage, or galleria, where Fellini posters watch you pee. I had once taken Maurice to this wine bar. He said it was pretentious and over-priced, preferring old-fashioned pubs. Beyond the toilets there is another room where punters strut their stuff on a discreet dance floor. Chilled out music in the main. Easy beats and jazz mid-week. Techno, Indie and Retro 70s and 80s mixes at weekends.

It sounds like a young place but you'd be surprised just how mixed the clientele is. Gay, professional men in their twenties and thirties, of course, but not exclusively. Well-dressed, well-heeled women too, in their thirties and forties. Some older men and women in their fifties. The Pensbury lushes. I don't think anyone is excluded, except the worst of the riff-raff. Squaddies from the local barracks were never admitted. Hence the membership. There are other bars with late-night licenses, but nothing as relaxed or as inviting as La Galleria.

Alex said he liked the "open" atmosphere. It reminded him of Barcelona. The room was quite full but not so crammed you couldn't find a seat and talk over the music. This Thursday night, low-level jazz was playing in the main bar. Alex and I sat on chrome stools, talking. Hadn't the reading gone well? etc. He asked about my writing, and being drunk I told him about my novels-in-progress (even the titles which he thought very funny) and short stories which had been shortlisted for this and that, including The Acorn Prize. He said he'd heard of it (fire included). I steered the subject away. 'I'm on the lookout for a good agent, if that doesn't sound too clichéd?' 'Never look a cliché in the mouth,' he said. 'Agents are always searching for fresh talent.'

The alcohol had loosened my tongue and I confessed to not owning Little's bookshop, merely being the assistant manager. Only a small lie, and he said he'd guessed as much. I couldn't help but be honest with Alex.

As the night wore on the music got nudged higher and we had to nestle into each other's ears to be heard. I was chilled but strangely warm. The fizz was buzzing in my veins, making the skin stretch across my face. I couldn't help smiling all the time. Alex wasn't smiling much, though he wasn't examining his watch either. I looked at his watch more than he did. It was out of this world. A Jaeger-LeCoultre driving watch with a stopwatch built into a sapphire crystal watch case. A snip at £9,000, I guessed. No. He was about as chilled out as he could be.

'Will you get into trouble?' I said in his ear, almost touching the lobe with my lips. 'You know...with Hilary?' He shook his head, leaned into my ear, actually touching my lobe with his lips.

'In the end, she does what I want.'

I nodded. 'Without me Maurice wouldn't have a bookshop.'

In retrospect, our proximity was predictable. We cupped our hands around each other's ears innocuously, as much to touch as to be heard. We could have been talking about anything if the truth be told. Do you think it will rain later? Nuzzle, nuzzle. The light bulbs keep exploding in my house, why is that? Nuzzle, nuzzle. Will war break out in Iran? Nuzzle, nuzzle. I am a size ten, what size are you? Nuzzle, nuzzle.

When the main bar got busy and we were being jostled, I led him into the more intimate Icon Lounge. A small red sofa was free and I told him to take it quickly. A glitter ball in the ceiling danced flecks of coloured light around our feet. We squeezed beside each other on the sofa, legs pressing. 'Do you come here often?' he said, making me laugh.

'Not as often as I'd like.'

He touched my arm with his right hand. 'I feel like an old man.'

He was fishing for a compliment (looking for a *preferred response* I think Imogen called this sort of dialogue). I couldn't believe I was here with my favourite author, a real flesh and blood icon in the Icon bar, his hand on my hand, this hand which had written so many wonderful things. This brain beside me, so worried about its age. 'You don't look a day over forty.'

'Very kind,' he replied, not smiling. 'How old are you, Ben?' It wasn't rudeness, just probing, and I told him.

'No. I thought you were twenty.'

I laughed. 'Maybe wine makes the world look younger?'

'*In vino veritas*,' he said.

It was true. We were younger than we looked, under the influence of desire. I felt his cupped hand again over my ear and decided just to go for it, turning my head sharply, stopping his mouth with mine. It didn't last long. Soft and made a noise on parting. I pulled away to gauge his response. I couldn't tell the colour of his eyes anymore, so swollen were his pupils, but I knew they were searching. 'Dance?' I said, nodding at the tunnel. He shook his head. Not one for dancing. 'We could watch from the sidelines?'

We took our glasses in, brushing by a couple snogging in the tunnel. I was sleazed up to the nines. Nothing turns me on more than seeing good-looking, underdressed men and women dancing together, or alone come to think of it. Sometimes, I'm in Virgin with the headphones on and a guy or a girl will come next to me and put their headphones on and we will rub up against each other. It's sexy with people you've never met before. It really tickles my trousers. I think it's primeval. All the gyrating. All the meaty parts moving to the beat. I especially like vigorous dancing. Enthusiastic grinding and jiggling. Is it just me or do others feel the same? This tribal rhythm thing. It is simulated sex, isn't it? Designed to stretch your y-fronts.

Six women and two men were dancing to Goldfrapp's "Number 1". They were tipsy and swivelling around each other, bum-to-bum, hands moving in the flecks of light. I could feel their body heat. Alex found a dark corner and watched me watching. I know there are clubs in London and Barcelona where men and/or women just get down to it in darkened rooms. Not in La Galleria. People groped and kissed, nothing more. We watched, and as we watched, kissed and touched each other in intimate places. One of the women on the dance floor saw us and didn't think anything of it. In fact, there was a lot of heavy petting going on in that room, full stop. We were not alone.

Alex said he needed the toilet and I wasn't sure if I was meant to follow. I didn't know his signal. I hadn't known him long enough to catch signals. I'd done it in toilets before of course, with a man and a woman at the same time, but not these toilets. It was on holiday in Spain (get on with it, Ben. Every time there's sex on the cards, the extended foreplay drives me nuts).

Okay. So I waited for him to return, checking the time on my watch. Gone 1am. Way past the bewitching hour when we turn into dirty devils. When he didn't come back, I panicked thinking he'd left, that I'd made a big fool of myself. I waited outside the toilets like a lost child. To my relief, he showed. I think he'd thrown water over his face. It was still wet.

'Long queue,' he said. 'It's been a lot of fun, but I really should get a taxi.'

'Sure,' I said, disappointed. After all, the night was only just getting going.

Outside, we sidestepped a couple who were locked in a wobbly embrace. We slowly weaved a path back to the taxi rank beside Southgate Towers where there is my favourite bench in the world. We didn't say much along the way. Bits of small talk all over again, as if La Galleria had been a mirage in a desert. *Ice cold in Alex* or something; as if he had put me behind him. A worse prick-teaser than I was.

I tried to figure out what I'd say at the rank. 'Well, it was nice snogging your face off and feeling up your crotch, but have a nice life won't you, Alex.' I didn't even know why I was going with him to the rank. I lived on the other side of town. I could just as easily have phoned him a taxi from my mobile.

Half way to the taxi rank, he stopped me dead with an arm across my chest. He looked up and down the cobbled streets, the amber glow from the streetlamps making a river of light under us. 'Do you want to come back with me?'

I could have dropped into the imaginary river. 'To your house?' One of his eyebrows curved into an exaggerated comma.

It was definitely on the tip of my tongue; yes. But my drunken tongue got tied into a knot inside my mouth. I had him though. Alex in the palm of my hand, I mean. I didn't have a game plan. I'd fleetingly thought he might come back to mine and asked if he wanted a coffee then; a sure sign of my intentions. He shook his head. It had to be his place or nowhere.

'I have work early in the morning,' I heard myself say. 'Incham's a long way to get back from in the morning.'

Now who was being the tease? I know. You're thinking, this isn't the Ben we know. The Ben we have come to love and hate, trust and mistrust; the sexbloodymniac and general all-round dirty manipulative fucker we've come to loathe and like all at the same time.

'Are you sure?' he said.

Of course I wasn't sure. You don't get the chance to sleep with your icon every night. He took out a calling card and a pen, scribbled down his private telephone number on the back of the card. 'I don't give this out to just anyone,' he breathed. 'Call me tomorrow. I should be home by eight.'

I wasn't playing hard to get, I promise. For once I was actually being practical. Besides which, I wasn't "just anyone". I was Ben Tippet: 6 GCSEs, 3 A' Levels, two-thirds of a media degree and half a diploma in creative writing. I had won a short story competition. I had a good job in a bookshop and a list of lovers as long as Alex's arm. I had novels up my sleeve which were going to change humankind, as good as if not better than *Dead on Main Street*. I didn't need to be told I was not "just anyone".

(He wasn't saying that, Ben. He was saying exactly the opposite, if you'd only listened.)

I put the renowned novelist's card in my jacket pocket. I said I'd call him, then walked to the rank where a taxi was waiting. Before the driver set off, Alex wound down his window, saying, 'Do call me. We can talk agents. You can bring something for me to read?'

A dangling carrot.

I watched the tail lights disappear through the arch of the tower. I took out his card and felt as if I was blowing up inside. Literally, like a balloon about to burst. I laughed out loud and squeaked like I had helium-filled lungs. I was so light and airy I struggled to keep my toes on the cobbled stones; floating in a mosta peculiar way. Everything was up in the air. My future was full of new possibilities, and who'd have thought it? The son of a bed-seller like me?

This was the beginning. The beginning of the end for me. The first time I'd ever fallen properly in love, I think. And only fools fall in love on April Fools Day.

E*leven*

Incham was quiet on Saturday evening.

I'd telephoned Alex on the Friday night as agreed. Foyles was nothing like Little's, he'd said, buttering me up. There was no place quite like Little's, I'd said. Why not come over after the shop closes? he'd said.

So there I was, dressed casually in a blue denim shirt and off-white chinos, driving past a sign for the Duck Inn, smiling to myself. It felt so long ago. The pub I mean, and the landlord's daughter and DFLs. A lot had changed for me in just a few weeks.

On the telephone, Alex had asked me to bring a handful of my stories and he'd have a look at them. His agent, Todd somebody, might be interested if they showed promise. Dangling carrots. I'd sat up most of Friday night making final editorial choices. Which ones were the best? (*Me and You? Big Raisins? Excremental?*) In the end I selected other, more recent stabs at literature in the dark; three which had never been read by anyone but myself (you don't need to know exactly, except that they were experimental pieces of flash-fiction based loosely on memoir, but immense!)

I got to the white windmill, pulled over and checked Alex's directions. I was lost all over again. I didn't know what it was with this man's house. It didn't want to be found. I was tempted to call him but was too embarrassed. Instead, I struggled on at a snail's pace, doing the rounds in the countryside, stopping at trees which looked familiar. The problem was that the windmill was the only landmark, everything else being high hedgerows, almost as high as prison walls. I said I'd arrive at Smuggler's Cottage at about 6-30pm. I still had plenty of time, but the sun was hovering low above the fields.

I found myself on the right track. Rows of apple trees to my left. Alex said there was a large orchard which had been there for a hundred years, as long as the windmill. Unlike the other tracks I'd already driven down, this one was in better condition. Not so many pot holes. A new surface, and the hedgerows were higher. Proper hedgerows made of yew or something. I don't know much about plants and gardening, being a suburban son of a bed-seller, but they were magisterial. On both sides. I couldn't see many houses, not even through gateways because of the winding drives. Occasionally, I caught a glimpse of a massive detached building. A thatched medieval house, Georgian mansion and the odd modern misfit. I guessed that each one would have at least ten acres attached, stables, a swimming pool etc. As an estate agent I'd never been given the privileged task of selling houses worth millions of pounds. This was what people called "Millionaire's Row". Old and new money. Old as the trees flanking the road. New as the well-maintained country track.

A car came out of a drive and I had to swerve. The driver, an old codger wearing a golfing sweater, shook his head in the way that only millionaires with more money than sense can shake their heads. It was a Rolls Royce, sapphire blue.

End of this track, Alex's instructions said. Turn the corner and stop at the gate with Smuggler's Cottage on it. Press the intercom and he'd open the gates. Follow the drive around, over a bridge...yes, a bridge! And park up outside the main door beside an old green Land Rover.

The gates opened and I did as he'd said. There was a long gravel drive, winding left and right, evergreen trees, firs pressing on either side like Lewisian wardrobe coats. I came to a bridge which crossed over a moat, my wheels knocking over the slats. A proper moat with ducks! And there, on the other side, was Alex's cottage.

Nothing like a cottage. Who called this a cottage in the first place? More like a castle. No. Not a castle. Somewhere between a cottage and a castle. Impressive would be too weak a description.

I pulled up beside an old green Land Rover. Fifteen years old at least, judging by the rust. I stood outside a glorious redbrick porch, smouldering in the setting sun. I looked up at a gabled roof and rakishly leaning chimneys. Ivy stretched across half of the house, cut free from smallish Tudor windows. It was a romantic house. A charming house. An expensive house. Even so, I thought it vulnerable. The chimneys might tumble through the roof any second, as if just pressing the doorbell might usher in a disaster, make it fold in on itself like a house of cards. Left too long, the ivy might creep over the mouth of the house. If not loved and tended, the mature bushes and trees in the garden might overgrow and encroach. And the honeysuckle-draped bridge might, if unprotected, fall into the ducky water. Without stepping a foot inside, I estimated a cool £2million. As it turned out, I was wrong.

Alex opened the main door. He was wearing a crisp white shirt, indigo blue jeans and moccasins. Kind of like a reverse of me, but we complemented each other very well. I'd chosen well.

'You like?' he said, hands on hips.

'I like,' I said, hands on mine.

We kissed. It was an awkward moment because two nights before we'd shared lengthier ones. He walked me inside, past a lovely old grandfather clock which ticked intermittently, unhealthily. Needed a wind up possibly. I was in a hall made entirely of oak, darkened by time. I was walking on foot-wide floorboards looking at panelled walls. Alex was watching me attentively. 'Do you like medieval?' he said, trying to sweep me further into the house.

'I know a man who does,' I said, thinking of Maurice. This being the house of his dreams.

'Come,' he said. 'I've made G&Ts. Unless…you like white wine, don't you?' He led me past a tilting staircase with hand-carved posts, through a small drawing room with a sisal floor, into a spacious kitchen. 'Gin and tonic's fine,' I said, looking around the beamed ceiling and lime-plastered walls. A huge walk-in fireplace was partially filled by a green and cream-coloured Aga, warm to the touch and smelling of casserole. I'd eaten very little all day, in anticipation of dinner. That and I was slightly nervous of the situation.

'This is amazing. I could fit my whole flat inside this kitchen.'

He handed me a tall glass, clinking mine with his. 'You think so? Do you like the floor? It came from Italy.'

I looked down at it.

'Marble's too slippery,' he said. 'This is Tuscan stone.'

I didn't tell him I'd once been an estate agent. I could have told him he was behaving just like one. 'How old is the house?' I said. 'Because from the outside -'

'Tudor.' He took a large sip of gin. 'The porch is Georgian, the upstairs is all Tudor and the ground floor used to be a medieval hall house. A real hotchpotch.'

'Beats pebble-dash,' I said, taking a sip, ice hitting off my teeth. He didn't smile. Wasn't really one for smiles. Privately, he could be a very serious Mr Serious.

Each room on the ground floor was finished, he said, and I should have seen the place eighteen months ago. Pink nylon carpets throughout, Artex walls and ceilings everywhere.

It was Tardisian. One room led onto another and another, a bright oriental rug and original fireplace in every room, walls and ceilings painted off-white. The dining room was floorboarded, buffed to a brilliant shine and matching the heavy English and French furniture. Some of it real Tudor.

However, the main drawing room was the most impressive. Alex was very pleased with the oak bookcases he'd designed and commissioned from a master craftsman. They lined two walls, floor-to-ceiling, and were crammed with brightly bound books. I wondered if this was his study at first, but it was too neat and showy. There was a deep blue three-seater sofa, its back to the books, modern in design, and four plump velvet cushions. Behind this was a long French oak table with a large vase full of purple flowers. Behind this, a black grand piano, set at an angle to the window looking out onto an expansive and lush rear garden. It struck me immediately which piano this was.

'A Beckstein?' I said, moving around the sofa towards it. The music stand was up, sheets open on a Beethoven sonata.

'Do you play?' he said, surprised, his mid-Atlantic lilt loosening, becoming more English, though I doubt he noticed it happening. He was a faker in so many ways, but the accent was natural, having spent so long on the East coast of America. He asked me in such a way that I felt ignorant and talentless beside him.

'I've seen this piano before.'

'Oh?'

'The cover of *Fugue*?'

'It was my mother's,' he said, taking another sip. I knew very little about his family, though in the kitchen I'd noticed photographs of his two daughters at various stages of their lives, from teething toddlers to teenagers. Alex had been the villain of the marriage. More photographs dotted around. Maybe his parents?

'Are you any good?'

'I can play a bit,' he said. 'Otherwise what use would it be? Come. There's the upstairs to show you.' Where we would sleep. Or not, time would tell.

So it went.

In the upstairs hallway he stopped to tell me about the ten layers of wallpaper he'd been forced to remove, discovering original squares of Tudor fabric above some lintels. He ran his hands across the Artex-coated ceiling, tutting. 'It's a beautiful but high-maintenance sort of house. Doesn't get many visitors. The gardener and cleaners see it more than I do.' He explained that up until quite recently he'd spent most weeks in America, and this was his weekend "hidey-hole". Now he was here for good, he was going to sell his Greenwich Village apartment. That life was all past him now.

A claw-footed bath tub was sitting in the centre of a large, double-aspect bathroom at the far end of the hall, a mirrored cabinet four feet tall on the wall. Six bedrooms fed off of the hallway, only two of them habitable. Four were stacked to the ceiling with odds and sods and furniture and decorating equipment. He'd had to rip the guts out, he said, and there was still more to do, as I could see.

The main bedroom was a revelation. A rickety four-poster bed in the centre of a big room with two broad windows. A bed with braided drapes! On closer inspection, moth-eaten and shabby. Until he informed me it was an original Jacobean bed, I'd thought it was ready for the skip. 'Shabby-chique,' he said. If we were going to sleep there, it would be a struggle. It was a little under 5' wide. But I understood from something my father once asked me: what makes a bed, son? Foam? Wood? Coiled springs? Feathers? No, he said. It is people who make the beds. Those who craft them and those who sleep in them.

I'd reformed my opinion of the house price (before even getting to see the swimming pool and stables out the back and the fully-functioning writing studio abutting the orchard. That's where he preferred to do his writing in the mornings, he said. There seemed too much history inside the house. Very few people got to see where the magician cast his spells).

We were back where we started, in the kitchen, sitting down at a farmhouse table with six chairs. I wasn't absolutely sure if more were expected for dinner. It had been rather vague on the telephone. 'Tour over. Do you still like it?'

'I like it even more,' I said.

'Good. I like it too. Shall we eat in the kitchen? The dining room's too formal for two.'

Being honest, I did like Smuggler's Cottage. I'm sure it was worth a cool £2.5 million, but there was something contradictory about it. Outwardly, it appeared confident and reasonably solid. Yet under the surface it was decaying. It was a very English house. It was very Alex. I couldn't imagine anyone else living there but him. For all I knew the Fortune family could have lived there for generations, though as he told me over dinner which his weekend cook had prepared in advance (moules mariniere for starters, roast shank of lamb in red wine sauce with vegetables for mains and crème brule for dessert), he bought the house only two years before.

(Cut Alex's long but fascinating story short, Ben?)

Alex had visited his father two years previously. His father had been fighting advanced prostate cancer and staying in a Sussex nursing home 80 miles away. Whilst staying in the family home (which Alex has since sold), he literally took a trip back in time to his childhood holidays (a story within a story, Ben? This had better be good).

As a child, he used to come to this part of Kent. His father was into engineering and history back then. A real windmill-spotter. Alex was nine or ten. His mother was still alive. His father had explained for the umpteenth time how the windmill worked, his mother laid a blanket on the ground then unloaded the hamper from the car. During lunch, Alex had gone off to explore. He'd whipped the heads off wheat stems and chased rabbits through hedgerows. He kept walking until he stumbled across a hole in a hedge and crawled through, discovering an orchard on the other side. Apples were ripening. Wasps were everywhere and one chased him around the perimeter until he came across a garden with stables. Chestnut horses were munching from nosebags. Alex took a walk around the side of the stables and discovered an old house and another garden. He quickly dropped to his hands and knees because a man and a boy were in the garden, trying to fly a kite. There was no wind so they charged up and down the lawn instead. The kite took flight only briefly before landing in the hedge right beside Alex. He kept quiet. The fair-haired boy came over and bent down to pick the kite out of the brambles. He put his hand so close to Alex's leg he thought he might be touched. There was a skull and crossbones on the kite. The people went indoors and Alex walked further around to a beech hedge and a paddock with jumps. Beyond the paddock he saw a moat and a bridge. There were two swans on the water making a heart together with their necks. At the end of the drive was a five-bar gate and the house's name: Smuggler's Cottage. 'I wanted to live here,' Alex said to me. 'I wanted to be that boy who lived here.'

Alex the boy trudged back, getting lost and feeling disorientated. He reached the windmill, saw the car still there and looked down on his parents. They were asleep on the blanket, arm in sleepy arm. There was an empty bottle of wine at their sides, leaning in the grass beside the hamper. His mother's dress was up around her waist and he could see her petticoat and knickers. His father's hand was resting on her thigh. 'I hated them both,' Alex said. 'At that moment I wished they were not my parents. I don't know why. They knew nothing about me or where I'd been or what I'd seen. I stood over them, my shadow alerting them to my presence. "Your hat," my mother said. I felt for it but it was no longer there. I think it must have come off beside the garden with the boy with the kite. "That's the third hat this summer", my father said, looking from under the sunshield of his hand. "I want a kite," is all I said. They looked at each other and burst out laughing. I don't know why they did. All the way home I was thinking about that house. This house. And the smugglers who might live here.'

(Back to the story outside that story).

On Alex's adult trip back in time to see his sick father, he'd remembered where the house was by the position of the orchards and the white windmill. He parked up on the long lane beside the house, climbed through a hedge (with difficulty), up the drive, over the wooden bridge and knocked on the front door. He introduced himself as Alexander Fortune, the novelist, and asked how much they would be prepared to sell their house for! (Only millionaires can live in such fairytales). As fate would have it, an aged couple whose sons and daughters had flown the nest agreed to sell because of the maintenance and upkeep of such a large house and grounds. He offered them more than they'd ever dreamed, and that's the end of the fairy story.

Alex had stayed in England tending to his father every day for about six months; the old pilot clinging on. But no sooner had Alex bought Smuggler's Cottage and returned briefly to New York for a meeting with his publisher, his father died. 'As if he'd been waiting for me to leave the country,' Alex said.

I couldn't believe he was telling me all of this when he was supposed to be so very private. It was a privilege bestowed upon me. A burden too. He'd been storing it up for a long time.

He went down to his cellar half way through dinner to fetch some claret for the lamb and he took me with him. A cellar more like a cave under the house. A secret passage led from the kitchen. Smugglers used it to hide themselves and their stash in the 18th Century. We were only a mile from the Channel, a mile from "White Cliffs" too; the place where Noel Coward and Ian Fleming had both lived, though never at the same time.

'Listed,' he said. 'House and cave'. Only after some serious wrangling had he been allowed to convert part of the Victorian stable block into a writing studio with vistas of orchards and wheat fields on three sides. He told me over dessert that this would be his very last house. He wasn't planning on moving again; too tired of flying back and forth.

Yes. It was a perfectly-proportioned home with lots of history. I prefer modern homes, like my minimalist flat, but could see the attraction of this wayward house. As a boy, Alex dreamed of living here, hiding in the cave, and climbing the tilting staircase each night to sleep in his Jacobean four-poster with Turneresque views of fat blue and terracotta skies. Now he had it for real. He had his almost-castle and I envied him, and his two daughters who would inherit this beautiful old story-filled house.

We moved into the large drawing room, taking our glasses of wine, and sat on the blue sofa, facing a log fire Alex had lit upon arrival. It was a mild April but quite cool after dark. We kissed and canoodled there. I'll spare you the details. Somehow it still feels private, like the house itself. Something we shared over the summer months. I just remember choral music playing on the speakers, the spit and crackle of seasoned logs and lying down together before the flames, holding and petting. 'What's this?' I said, breaking free from him a moment. 'Sounds like monks.'

'They're Tenebrae.'

'Tenebrae?'

'Yes,' he said. 'Humans who sound like angels.'

'Get thee to a monkery! You're not even religious.'

'It's relaxing,' he said. 'Tenebrae. Latin. Means darkness.'

'You should have lit more candles.'

'That's right,' he said and went to get some.

We moved upstairs without a word. We'd exhausted conversation without once asking what time it was. We undressed by the glow of an ornate bedside lamp and by the candles we'd carried.

Normally, I'd not skip over the sexy stuff. Sufficient to say, for the first time in my life I experienced pre-match nerves. No matter how hard I tried I could not harden. Maybe it was the idea of doing it with Alexander Fortune, novelist and icon. The evening had been something of a dream and something had to go wrong in it. We lay naked together on the bed. I was not frightened of nakedness; his nor mine. As it happened Alex had a good body. Lean, defined. He was a sensitive lover, trying to lift me out of my levitation crisis, trying to resuscitate me, if that's the word. Mouth-to-mouth, mouth-to-south, nothing would happen. It was like snogging a relative. He asked if anything was the matter and I told him I wanted nothing more in the world but couldn't fathom it. I emphasised that it wasn't him of course, but it might have been, indirectly. I fancied him but nothing would come. He told me not to worry, that he'd once spent an entire honeymoon in Venice with a floppy disk. I felt embarrassed, then devastated. As you know already, I'm proud of the Tippetus Erectus (more tipping than erecting at that time).

I pleasured him with my mouth, tracing around his nipples, bellybutton, appendix scar down to his cock. He had an expensive body. Well-moisturised, well-looked after, well-defined muscular arms and legs. He swam almost every day in his heated garden pool, did weights, played tennis, and cycled sometimes. Nonetheless, his stomach was comfortably, reassuringly soft and yielding. The whole time, I could hear choral music lifting from downstairs. We fell asleep to the sound of angels' voices.

I woke early and discovered Alex had gone. The window was open and a cool breeze blew in from the sea, a mile or so away. I heard seagulls and imagined I was at the seafront, in an apartment in Dinard, France (as the seagull flies, not that far from England). Then I noticed the dusty old drapes about the bed and realized where I was, and the embarrassment of the previous night hit hard.

There was a rattle of saucers, a knock on the bedroom door, then Alex entered with a tray: sweet cake, bacon slices, a cafetiere, toast soldiers and two boiled eggs, their heads neatly lopped off. He placed the tray on my lap and sat on the edge of the bed. Still without a word.

Whenever I wake up in the morning (normally it is whenever I'm horizontal for more than sixty seconds), I have a yardarm, and that morning was no exception. Alex plunged the cafetiere and poured me some rich-tasting coffee. I dipped a soldier in a runny yolk, so golden and smooth, the egg-white semi-cooked and wobbly. I ate my soldier, bit into a slice of thick bacon, swallowed some more coffee. We watched each other eating, finishing our eggs. Still without a word.

Alex put the tray on the floor and I unpeeled his paisley robe. I felt his excitement and pulled back the bedclothes, inviting him under. We kissed briefly, the corners of our lips sticky with yolk. We stroked each other gently between the legs, still kissing. Ends meeting. Mouths. Slowly. I licked his fingertips, tasting coffee. I bit into his shoulder, feeling sinews, sucking and tasting last night's sweat, sweet and sour on my tongue. I rolled Alex onto his front. Nothing violent. Only a kind of love. A meeting. A beginning. I entered the cloister softly, not coming. Then he entered me, not coming. We held each other then.

He came in my hand, tears filling his eyes. What he was crying for I didn't know. We forgot there was a real world outside the window. We were the real world for the time being. Alex, Alex, Alex.

It was probably the best sex in my life. I mean, the most meaningful, in a different way. I made a different sort of connection with Alex. Normally, I bounce off people or they bounce off me. But with Alex it was more of an absorption. Maybe that's why I berate him now, from my cell. I gave him all I had, including the truth about myself. Over the coming weeks and months we shared everything. We were so honest with each other it was disgusting. This is what it is like to really know someone. Or to think you know someone.

I don't want to race ahead, but I have to. Memories of our summer of love pour from me now like blood from my veins. I visited him almost every weekend, sometimes staying until Monday morning. Then it became Wednesdays (my usual day off from Little's). By June, I was almost living at Smuggler's full-time. Half of my clothes were hanging in his closet. My toothbrush was in his holder. I stopped using my Fahrenheit aftershave and began using his Physiognomie. Sometimes, I imagined I *was* Alex; sleeping in his bed, cooking in his kitchen, eating from his table. I convinced myself that I lived under his skin. And, in a way, I did. He trusted me with a door key and a gizmo to open the electric gates. We went shopping together. He introduced me to his London writer friends as "writer, bookseller and all-round love-God". They probably thought I was a flash in a pan, but they'd be wrong. I started taking calls for Alex at Smuggler's when he was in America, or on a day trip to London...But now I'm really getting ahead of myself. I need to take you back to that April. Things were really hotting up; the Great Fire of Broadstairs rearing itself once again. DI Elvis was pulling his net in. I said he would be hard to shake off. He wasn't nothing but a hound dog ready to sink those canines into me.

I drove by the orchard that Sunday morning full of the joys of a new relationship. I slowed by the windmill, got out and had a closer look. Its arms were on the grass. There was a notice saying funds had been raised by the people of Incham and the windmill would undergo restoration. I pictured Alex looking down on his sleeping parents. Now they were both dead and he was quite lonely without them. What was he doing all by himself in his house anyway? He really knew no one except me within a thirty-mile radius. By the age of fifty-two, Alex had put himself out to pasture, but it was a most beautiful pasture.

Twelve

Disaster descended the following Wednesday; a knock at the door on my day off.

For once I wished I worked on a Wednesday, though they would have found me at Little's eventually. It had just gone 10am. I was soaking in the bath listening to *"Heroes"* - Bowie's masterful collaboration with Brian Eno. I'd listened to the title track already and reached the darker, more experimental second half of the album; Track 7 called *Sense of Doubt*. Such an ominous, portentous name and sound when I think back. A deep, slow ***de-de-de-der***. A mock Beethoven dirge. I love it nonetheless. The fabricated sound of the wind roaring, a storm about to break (and on my head be it). Moody and ambient, Eno's influence immediately obvious, that album's a journey through murky Berlin, the wall still standing in 1977, three years before my birth and my half-brother's death. Arguably, three years before Bowie's last "great" album: *Scary Monsters (and Supercreeps)* released the year of my birth, the year of Tom's death. 1980. *"Heroes"* was a major influence on the music that followed, everyone knows. We've been looking for other heroes ever since.

I didn't hear the knock at first, and even when I did I thought it was Mrs Heaton hammering on her ceiling with a broom handle. 'Shuddupper ya face,' I said to myself, getting out of the bath. I put my bathrobe on, flung a towel across my shoulders and padded into the sitting room when the knock came again, this time harder, and definitely at my front door.

Even then, I thought it would be something to do with my music and I turned it down. Maybe *Mr* Heaton wanted to discuss it face-to-face? I armed myself with arguments: it's my day off. What about your howling child all night long? Mr Heaton, you're away all the time. You don't know what it's like living here with a balling baby all day, all night. You need to get your own house in order, sunshine.

Opening the front door I probably did a perverse double-take, because I recognised him and I didn't recognise him. What the hell is Elvis doing on my doorstep? Deep down in my soul I'd known he would come and this scene would be played out. I had planned for it. Occasionally, I'd kept myself awake at night worrying about it. But to be honest, not that often. Four months had passed without so much as a whiff of a bobby.

'DI Lawless, DS Kempe,' Elvis said, holding up his ID. 'We're investigating a serious crime and hope you can help with some enquiries.' All basic PC Plod stuff to tell you the truth, though it got very clever later on, I can assure you.

His side-kick was dressed in a natty, navy blue, pinstriped suit, black blouse, large collar. She was not unattractive. Compact, blonde, early thirties. Quite a severe peroxide blonde bob though, and a little bit on the stocky side over all. Blonde Bob is a far more interesting name than DS Kempe, don't you think? In my book anyway.

'May we come in, Mr...?'

'Tippet,' I said. 'Ben.'

'Mr Ben, we'd like to-'

'No. Ben Tippet, not Mr Ben.'

'Sorry,' Elvis said, smiling to himself. 'Mr Toppit, we'd like to ask you some questions about a certain Cassi Hart?'

Well, there was nothing certain about her I was thinking. You got to think fast on your feet, Ben.

'Does she live here?'

'Does she live here?' I said to myself. 'Cassi Hart?' I scratched my head, pulling the most puzzled look I could muster, dripping bathwater onto the doormat. What was it I'd planned to say? Some cock and bull story they'd believe because coppers are not the sharpest needles in the sewing box, are they? He couldn't even get my name right. Only in genre fiction are they clued up and able to read a man in one second flat, like Alex Fortune's Hugo Massey. Even in fiction they do not look like Elvis.

(Have you remembered my pseudonym? Have you guessed what the anagram is? Art is Cash? No, I'll give you a clue. Cassi Hart comes from one word, not two or three. I suspect she is the main reason writers write after all).

'We've called at an inopportune moment,' Blonde Bob said, looking me up and down, trying to get the measure of me.

'What's this about?' I said, barring the door. 'Let me see your IDs again?' They looked at each other as if they'd never received this reaction before. Maybe people normally lie down for the police to walk all over them, like patients at the doctor's surgery. People in power. 'Thank you,' I said, allowing them in. 'Yes. I once knew a Cassi. The little thief.'

There was nothing in my flat to connect me with the fire. I'd changed my email address and wiped my hard-drive. There was no trace of my story, *Me and You*, although I had handed the bloody thing in for my university portfolio if you recall. Even the coat I'd been wearing that December was trashed in a bin north of London.

I sat down in my Keats leather chair, calmly as possible. I asked if they wanted some coffee, then invited them to sit on the sofa, coffeeless. In the light from the window, he didn't half look like Elvis. In another life I'd have fancied him. He was so symmetrical. The proverbial tall dark stranger. 'Have you heard of the Acorn Short Story competition?' he said.

'The what?'

'It's a publisher's, based in Broadstairs,' he said. 'Cassi Hart entered the competition last year and gave this address. Does she live here?' His blue-green eyes took in every detail of my room. He was testing me already, gauging my response. I suspect the police go through training like this. When they knock on a suspect's door they are exactly that to them; a suspect to be manipulated, seen through. I shook my head as honestly as I could.

'I went out with a girl called Cassi. I think she said she was called Cassi. I can't remember. It was a little fling. You know how it is?' I was hoping Elvis would nod in a blokey-jokey way but it couldn't have been further from the truth.

'Tell us how it was,' he said. Blonde Bob got her notepad out, crossing her chunky legs. I cleared my throat and spun the cock and bull story.

I'd gone for a drink after work with a customer who'd wandered into Little's Bookshop. I gave them the address. She was pretty. More sexy than striking. Straight, brown collar-length hair. She spoke with a slight accent. From Denmark or Sweden or Norway or somewhere, though had reasonable English. One thing led to another. 'A very short-term relationship,' I said. Elvis nodded. Blondie noted it down. 'She was a student or something. A foreign student. Total barmcake. A real temper on her. Could switch just like that.' I clicked my fingers for effect. 'She stayed here for a week or so until she got proper digs somewhere.'

'She was attending college? Or was it the University?' Elvis asked.

I shrugged my shoulders.

'When did you go out with her?' Blondie said.

'I suppose it was the beginning of term. Late September? Early October?'

'Do you know where she is now?' Elvis said.

Shrug of shoulders again. 'Good riddance. She ran off with my I-pod. Just cleared out one day when I was at work. And if you ever catch up with her, ask her where my I-pod is.'

'This is very strange,' Elvis said, looking around the room again, making me nervous. 'Why would she give *your* address on her entry form?'

'Maybe she was planning on staying a bit longer? A freeloader? What's this about anyway?' I lunged forward dramatically. 'God. I thought I'd seen you before, Inspector. You were on that TV appeal. Has Cassi done something stupid? Is she alright?' (metaphorically laughing up my sleeve).

'We don't know what she's done,' he said. 'We're following a line of enquiry. When was the last time you saw her?'

'As I said, about early October. This is terrible.' It was terrible, but my performance was pretty special under the circumstances. I got up and paced around the room for effect, but also to calm myself.

'Cutting to the chase,' Elvis said, 'we're tracing everyone who submitted a story to the competition and was longlisted for the prize. You know it was the Acorn building that was destroyed?'

'She never showed me anything. She was very secretive. She was nuts, but I don't think she'd set fire to a building.'

Blondie cut in. 'How can you be so sure…if you only knew her a short time?'

I sat down again, pulling at my chin for effect. 'I guess not. She was a strange one.'

'How old is she?' Blondie said.

'Nineteen? Twenty? She wasn't much of a talker. Tight-lipped sort of person.' It went on like this for a few minutes. I gave them as good a description as I could, given she was complete fiction. Such a blandness that if she had actually been real she would have been difficult to find in a haystack. A montage of girls and women I'd ever slept with or known. I gave her an average height and build. Yes, mousy hair. Sporty clothes. To wrap things up, I recalled a distinguishing birthmark on Cassi's bottom (the devil is in the detail of a brilliant lie). 'If that's any use to you at all? A purple birthmark shaped like a horseshoe.'

Their faces! I'm a genius! It was fibdiclulous! Porkypietastic!

'She was a half-decent writer then?' I said, getting carried away. 'If she got shortlisted?'

Elvis's lip curled. 'Longlisted, sir.'

My heart slipped out of my robe, down my bare ankles onto the carpet, beating Poe-like before their eyes.

'Though you're right, of course. Cassi Hart did make the final shortlist.'

'Sorry, I thought you said shortlist.'

This was turning into really bad TV, which would have been alright if it had been on TV, but it was in my front room, and it was me under the spotlight. I started to sweat. Elvis was a smart one. I was thinking maybe I should tuck out my wrists for cuffing there and then. I might have crumbled if he'd persisted. I might have sung like a lark if he'd pushed. I'm no thick-skinned bonehead-hard criminal.

'Is there anything else you can tell us about her?' said Blondie.

I shook my head (well, there's the fact that she is a he, and he is sitting here right under your hound dog noses).

'Thank you, Mr Tappet,' said Elvis, rising. He wasn't the shaking hands type of guy.

'Tippet,' I said politely. 'And you're most welcome.'

'If she gets in touch...'

'Like a shot,' I said. They reached the door, were about to let themselves out when Elvis turned into Columbo all of a sudden. I told you he was clever.

'One last thing, Mr Tuppit?'

Christ. Get my name right. I only just spelt it out for you. Or was this deliberate? To undermine me? 'Yes, Inspector?' (All very TV show now. If he could do it, so could I in spades).

'Do *you* write?'

'Me?' Don't drop yourself in it now, Ben. That's just what he wants. 'Well…I used to write. That's what got me and Cassi talking in the bookshop. I wrote the kind of rubbish you do as a novice. Teenage angst. I dabbled but I wouldn't say I was a writer. I sell books, I don't write them.' Not such a great answer. Too much information. But not too bad. Vague enough.

Elvis stared me out. 'You don't enter competitions then?' He laughed in an ingratiating way. I knew his game and laughed along.

'No, no, I just sell books.'

'Oh, one last thing. For the record, Mr Tippet..' Hooh-bloody-ray, he finally nailed my name '…Where were you on the evening of December 19th of last year?'

'The night of the fire?' Nice touch. Plead ignorance. Elvis nodded. 'What times are we looking at, Inspector?'

'Between 10pm and midnight, but if you could account for the whole evening. A week before Christmas?'

As if I didn't know when Christmas was or something. I stroked my chin. I was actually trying to think what to say. I didn't want to bring Imogen's name into the frame. Not so early on, not without having spoken to her first. But I had to tell them something. She was my alibi after all. I had been at her house, hadn't I?

Blondie wrote the details down: Imogen's home address, work address, everything. When I finally got to close the door on them, I went straight to the kitchen and threw cold water over my face, heart drumming, hands shaking uncontrollably. I was shocked how shocked I was. The net was closing in. Paranoia setting in. What would they be saying on the way down to their car? 'He's a strange one. Do you think he's lying, guv? That gumpf about Cassi Hart. It's obviously him.' 'Shall we keep tabs on him?' 'If he's telling the truth, he's a bit of a lad. "A young lad in his twenties, Blonde Bob. Footloose and fancy free. It's not a crime, Blonde Bob.' Kempe or whatever your name was.

These were the thoughts racing through my head at the time, before I called Imogen at home, at work, then her mobile.

No answer.

The secretary in the English department said Ms Wood was lecturing, so I got dressed speedily and drove straight up the hill. I was nervous, naturally, clocking my rear-view mirror so much I nearly crashed into a woman with walking sticks at a Pelican crossing. I was going to park in the departmental car park but as I was driving around looking for a space I saw Elvis and Blonde Bob sitting there eating sandwiches in a silver Audi estate!

I drove straight out again. I had to get to Imogen first. I parked behind the library and ran to the lecture theatre I thought she'd be in, taking an emergency side-door entrance. I waited outside, looking nervously about for Elvis and Blonde Bob. What if they got tired of waiting for Imogen to return to her office? They must not see me here. I looked through the glass in the lecture hall door. Imogen was giving her spiel and I waved like a madman.

When she was leaving, I grabbed her by the arm and led her up some steps out of the way. She wasn't happy about being manhandled. I had everything planned. What to say. It was going to be cool. Then it all spilled out in the heat of the situation. 'They think I might have something to do with the fire in Broadstairs last Christmas, Imogen.'

'Fire? That's ridiculous. What have you got to do with it?'

'I entered the Acorn competition.'

'So what? Thousands enter.'

'I entered under a false name. I live forty minutes away from the offices. You can see their point.'

'That's absurd.'

It was obvious she wanted to go and have her meat-free lunch or something. It wasn't as if we'd been keeping in touch. 'Listen. I called myself Cassi Hart to improve my chances in the competition.'

'You wouldn't be the first to adopt a nom de plume.'

'Cassi got shortlisted for the prize.'

'That's great. Congratulations.' She pulled herself out of my grip, started moving away and I got hold again, more firmly.

'It's not great, Imogen. They think she might have set fire to the Acorn building.'

'Your pseudonym?'

'Me. They think *I* did it. Don't you see?'

'Did they actually say that? When did all this happen?'

'This morning. Not in so many words. I panicked. I made all this stuff up about Cassi Hart to cover us.'

'Us?'

'It just came out. I didn't want to implicate you in any way.'

She looked at me funny. 'Implicate *me*?'

165

'You're in this too, Imogen. I had to make it up as I went along. I was at your house that night and you were out of your mind on dope. I could hardly tell them that, could I?'

'No,' she said.

'Not with that other complaint running against you. Has it been resolved?'

'Not yet,' she said, face reddening.

'I need you to put them straight.'

'Ben, this is too weird and totally fictional. Go and tell them you made it all up.'

'Too late. If I change my story now they'll never believe me. I've got to stick to it and you have to too.'

'Well I need time to think about this.'

'No time. They're in the car park.'

'Shit.'

'Yes…and he looks like Elvis bloody Presley.' I stared deep down into her Nordic eyes. 'They're outside. No joke. I need you to tell them where I was on December the 19th.'

She shook her head, irritated. 'Where were you?'

'With you, don't you remember? I arrived at about 10pm. They'll ask you all this. You're my witness. I told them you were ill with the flu.'

'Why? I've not had flu for years. I don't know when you arrived.'

'Don't you believe me or something?'

'Of course, but I don't remember.'

'You didn't have flu, Imogen. You were out of your fucking tree on coke and dope and half a bottle of brandy. Remember? You were so sick I had to carry you to the toilet.'

She looked over my shoulder. Students were still filing out of the theatre. Then she was the one whispering. 'Keep it down.'

'I couldn't say you were off your head on coke. I thought it best to warn you, that's all.'

'Good. Then I'll say I had the flu.'

'That's it. But you'd better sound convincing.'

'I can't believe we're even having this conversation.'

'I'm sorry to put you in it, Imogen.' We walked towards the main door. I took some steps down to the side-entrance. 'Let me know what happens?'

'Promise me, Ben, you had nothing to do with this fire.'

'That's crazy. I wouldn't harm a flea. I used a false name because I thought it would help and it did at first, but now it's come back to haunt me.'

'I won't mention Cassi Hart,' she said. 'It complicates matters. If she was real why would you even tell me about her?'

'Why would I tell you about Cassi Hart? I wouldn't tell you anything about her, would I?'

'Ben, she's fictitious.'

'Yes. Totally made up, Imogen.'

'Okay, I had the flu,' she said. 'I went to the staff drinks party out of a sense of duty and returned early because I felt sick. I did leave early. And then you came over to see me. End of.'

'Thanks, Imogen.' I watched her run up the steps, then I shuffled out of the side door, head down.

Everything was in Imogen's hands. A lot of things had gone against me but I was lucky beyond belief. Lucky she had a coke problem. Lucky she had got so stoned that fateful night she could not remember anything after nine o'clock (certainly not the time). Lucky she had a grievance procedure hanging over her head already which had nothing to do with me but I could use as leverage. She had more reasons to go along with my story than not to. What would it have looked like to her employers (and the police) if they knew she had a Class A drug problem? That she had been sleeping with one of her students? That she was implicated in arson and manslaughter?

Shit. Come to think of it, I don't know why I'd been so anxious that lunchtime at the university (except that Elvis was waiting to pounce). Imogen had as much to lose as I did by telling the truth, the whole truth and nothing but the truth.

The next few days weighed heavily. Imogen told the police exactly what we'd agreed. They asked about Cassi Hart and she said she'd never heard of her. They enquired about my "character" (irony). Did she think I was prone to angry outbursts or rages? Did I ever lose the plot? (So they did think I could have destroyed the Acorn building). She said I was more prone to sulking.

I told Imogen how grateful I was. She imagined the fire had been started by bored teenagers and that the police, like Dennis Potter thick-bricks, were chasing each other up blind alleys.

'Fascists are often stupid,' she said. 'What writer in their own mind would set fire to a building just because they'd not won a prize?'

'I don't know,' I said. 'Didn't someone kidnap Germaine Greer once because of a disagreement over an essay?'

It broke the ice. Imogen laughed. She was in the clear. Ben Tippet was in the clear too. No previous (I'm sure the police ran a check on me on their database whatever), no material witnesses, no CCTV, no forensic connection to the scene (as far as I knew) and now a cast-iron alibi.

I should have been breathing easy, yet I wasn't. The weight of my conscience reared itself and sat leaden on my chest at night. Over the next few weeks it surfaced like a double-decker-sized sperm whale coming up for air, sliding beneath the surface again. Sometimes the whale would plummet the depths so deep I would forget about Stepan Belonog, but then I would see an item on TV, a photo in a paper or overhear a conversation in Little's and up came the whale puffing shoots of water and taking in valuable air that was mine; so much I nearly stopped breathing.

I had taken a life yet I walked about freely, worked normally in the bookshop, carried on my affair with a famous novelist throughout the summer. Under the surface was my whale. In my soul (and I know this is all in hindsight now) I lived with the expectation that Elvis would catch up. He'd exhaust his Acorn list then simply go back to the beginning and come up with me again. Something not quite right about this Ben Tappet, Tuppit, Toppit character, Blonde Bob. Maybe we should bring him into the station for further questioning? Put the squeeze on him, let him crack under pressure...

Thirteen

I cracked of my own accord.

In Alex's hands I was an egg with a damaged shell which might break, the yolk of me pouring out. A bad egg, stinking and corrupted. I don't think I told him a single lie from May to July, other than the small faking maskeries we all conjure to cover basic insecurities as human beings. From the moment I set foot inside his house, maybe from the moment I met him in the flesh at Little's, maybe since before I was born (for that is how I felt at the time), I could not hide things from him.

He led by example, of course. To my utter astonishment, and later gratitude, he told me everything about himself. It was as if I became his confessor, his only true reader. We all need someone to talk to, even novelists with reputations to protect. Maybe it is easier talking to relative strangers? When we were in other people's company, a book-reading or a party (there were not many because he turned most invitations down), Alex would put on an arrogant, over-confident front. A chain-mail. But when we were alone together at Smuggler's, he made himself naked in every way possible. He had less to prove and he'd talk to me about anything, from minutiae to the mountains. He opened up his entire past to me. Not just pillow talk and casual remarks over dinner.

During our summer of love (and self-loathing) he let me into his inner-sanctum, his writing studio; a place no one but himself was allowed to enter. Even his cleaner, Sheryl, a fat woman in tight leggings whose arse moved and looked like scrambled eggs wrapped in muslin, was forbidden to enter the nerve centre. Alex had already given me keys to his house, but not to his studio. That's how important it was to him. But by early June when I asked if I could see inside, he agreed. And I was not disappointed.

The annexe, as he called it, was at the far end of the landscaped garden, close to the orchards. 'It used to be a tacking-out area,' he said. I thought then that I could smell metal and leather and polishing cream, horse hide and dung. He unlocked the door and went in first. He turned the blinds letting in light. Dust motes hung in the air (no writer worth his salt doesn't have dust motes hanging somewhere in their story, and here is as good a place as any). Books lined three sides, floor-to-ceiling. Shabbily bound, well-used books. Not like the beautiful coloured ones for show in the large drawing room. These were the ones he read more than once. This was the engine room, the hallowed space.

He opened a window, letting in the sound of birds, and I brushed a hand along the spines. A small local history section, classic literature, then more contemporary stuff. Everything was alphabetically-arranged. Atwood and Atkinson. Bellow and Bradbury (Malcolm). Hardy and Highsmith. James (PD) and Joyce. Roth and Rushdie, shoulder-to-shoulder.

'The only problems are wasps at harvest time,' he said.

In front of the window was a writing desk. An old mahogany bulk with side draws and a roll top which was up. Twin towers of paper were piled there with notebooks, photographs and documents. "The detritus of my life" he later called it. One tower was in longhand, the other word-processed. The computer was set back away from the window in a dark corner, beside an en-suite bathroom in case he got caught short.

'So this is where you write your masterpieces?' I said, or something wholly predictable like that.

'I haven't written a single piece of fiction since I moved here. *Main Street* was written in Manhattan inside six months.'

'Then what's this?' I said, pointing to the desk.

'Autobiography-in-progress.'

'That's a lot of life. Has it got a title?'

'The Art of Decomposing,' he said, gloomily.

'That will have the punters queuing up.'

Alex can be on such a downer sometimes. Death-obsessed. Mortality-fixated. We once had an hour-long conversation over dinner about famous writers and philosophers and how they'd snuffed it: Plath, gas; Mishima, ritual suicide/seppuku; Woolf, pockets full of stones and lungs full of river; Hemingway and his shotgun; Hunter S Thompson, gun; Jack London, morphine;

Tennessee Williams, swallowing a bottle top or was it drugs?; Sherwood Anderson swallowed a toothpick. 'There is no greatness without a touch of madness,' Alex had said at the end, quoting Seneca. At least we could laugh at Aeschylus, the Greek dramatist who according to legend died when a vulture, mistaking his bald head for a stone, dropped a tortoise from a great height onto it. 'Now that,' said Alex, 'is the way to go.' I asked him why he had so many deaths in his books and he said I'd understand when I'd lived past 30: 'First you reach Jesus' age (33) and you outlive him. That's a landmark,' he said. 'Then you reach the age at which Kafka died (41). A milestone. Then both of your parents; the biggest milestone. But nothing chills human blood more keenly than the dawning certainty of one's own demise; except the unpredictability of its timing.' Such a bundle of laughs sometimes.

'The Art of Decomposing?' I said. 'Really? Is that the title?'

He shook his head. 'It doesn't really have one yet.'

'You're spoilt with a name like Fortune.'

'I thought about that,' he said, sitting on the edge of the desk and folding his arms. 'It would be too obvious. Too corny.'

'I don't know. Making A Fortune? That would be okay. It's multi-layered.'

'It should mean more than *me*.'

'Can I read some?'

He paused a moment. 'Well…it needs editing.'

'I don't mind doing the editing,' I half-joked.

'I'm sure you'd be excellent but BB has someone in mind already.'

The enigmatic, ubiquitous BB again. He was truly a person I could say upon meeting for the first time: 'I've heard so much about you.' In fact, I had spoken to him once before on the telephone, fielding a call for Alex when he was in the bath. 'This is BB Crum, no B,' he'd said, in such a strong New York accent I could taste coffee and bagels in the pauses. 'And you are…?' 'Tippet. Ben Tippet. Two Ps, two Ts,' I'd said. He wanted to speak to Alex about "the book". While Alex patted himself dry, BB and I had a muted conversation. If that's not a contradiction. I heard a helicopter in the background. Alex took the phone off me. 'BB,' he said. 'I forgot to call you back. No, I'm not up to my old tricks. He's a writer from Pensbury.' Long pause and Alex winked at me. 'Since when was it a crime having a writer for brunch?'

'I'm cheap,' I said, in the annexe.

'Well, I know that,' Alex said, lightening in mood. 'Someone's lined up. I suspect they'll be in-house. Someone perfectly objective, perfectly neutral with perfect grammar. I'll come out smelling of somebody else's roses, an erudite-looking mug-shot on the cover. They'll pick out my knots and whitewash me. Polish me up for sale.'

'I wouldn't do that, Alex. Your life shouldn't be objective, not if it's personal.'

'Anyway,' he said, trying to shift the conversation, 'it's incomplete. The final chapter's still to be finished.'

'Please, Alex?'

'Absolutely no one has read it, Ben. I don't know if it's a good idea. It's too long. It's at least 200,000 words.'

'I'll read it in here, in your studio. It won't leave the building.'

'BB says if I can't explain a novel in one line it will never be popular. But I say to him, if you can explain one of my books in less than an hour it's not worth reading.'

'Books explain themselves,' I said quite cleverly (sometimes gems pop out of my mouth too).

'Okay, okay. You can read it. But not right now.'

That was that, that was trust, that was laying your life on the line. His life. Nobody in the world had such treasure. I could hardly wait to dig into it, but had to wait a few days and pick my moment.

The following weekend, Alex was sunbathing wearily beside the pool and I asked for the keys to the annexe. I let myself in and sat at his desk. Beside the typescript was a paperback: *Selected Poems and Letters of Emily Dickinson*. It was a 1950s American publication; $2.50. Inside the front cover was written in blue ink: *ex libris Collette Fortune*. Half-way through, a page was dog-eared. A poem without a title. I'd never heard of Emily Dickinson until then. Never forgotten her since.

I heard a fly buzz when I died;
The stillness round my form
Was like the stillness in the air
Between the heaves of storm

I willed my keepsakes, signed away
What portion of me I
Could make assignable, - and then
There interposed a fly,

With blue, uncertain, stumbling buzz,
Between the light and me;
And then the windows failed, and then
I could not see to see.

I started reading Alex's typescript, and read for hours.

With great difficulty I had to put the work down at dusk; Alex insisting we have dinner, though I would have starved myself to keep reading. I returned to the magnum opus on the Sunday, spending eight uninterrupted hours. Alex was in Brighton seeing an old Oxbridge poet friend. This is what I discovered in his absence.

It was not a conventional autobiography which begins at the beginning and proceeds through chronological time. Alex hopped from event to event in his life, and his parents' and children's' lives, without any sense of order. Everything was connected by memories, and as he said in his brief introduction: *Memory is a child which jumps and flits. It does not walk in a straight line.*

Neither do adults, Alex.

His childhood had been happy. Even the daily trial of mealtimes, when his father (a largely absent flight lieutenant with the RAF) insisted little Alex have something interesting to say or he got no dinner) Alex turned into a beneficial experience: *Singing for my supper was an early lesson in being prepared for an audience and having something important to say. Not least, these were my first forays into fiction. I was telling short stories gleaned from comic books and my father's morning newspapers, at the age of seven.*

However, and I had not known this, the sudden death of his mother Collette in 1976, devastated the Sussex family idyll *more efficiently than a bomb.* She had been a talented, classically-trained pianist. She died aged 47. An aneurysm. A clot in the brain. Alex had been about to leave Oxford. She died, in Alex's words: *Unlike herself, because she was a workaholic, reclining in a deckchair, in the garden of the family home, in the blaze of a hot August.*

Colette had taught him to play the piano when he was a child. The same piano in the drawing room of Smuggler's Cottage and on the cover of *Fugue*. Alex could play melodies at six. His mother enjoyed Erik Satie so he learned the Gymnopedies no.s 1-3, and the Gnossiene 1-6. Alex would sit beside her at the keys and she would place her hands over his at the beginning, and then she would be his audience, applauding what he'd mastered.

When she died part of Alex went with her. He travelled around Europe after finishing at Oxford and when he returned a year later, he found his father shaking on the kitchen floor, drunk. And his father was drunk from that day on. Never sobered, never re-married. No matter what Alex said to him, no matter how he tried, there was no bringing his mother back or his father back from the brink. His father gave up flying. Grounded for good; his plan to become an airline pilot torn in tatters.

This was when Alex wrote his first collection of short stories, aged 22, entitled *All That We Leave Behind* (you can still get it on Amazon). As Proust once said, grief gives painful birth to ideas. And love, love is a vessel into which we pour ourselves. At Oxford, Alex had dabbled with a journal but had not contributed stories, only poems. Now he found his niche, getting noticed in the nationals and TLS for his next collection of prose, published in his mid-twenties. He began his first novel and the rest is history: acclaim and notoriety, moving to the States, living with one foot either side of the Atlantic, getting married to Evelyn, an artist, holding the reception at his father's house. And being the father of two lovely daughters. Blah blah blah.

Alex didn't delve into the messiness of the divorce, didn't mention his various affairs with men and women, merely to say: *People who have amicable divorce settlements should not have married in the first place.* Evelyn also had affairs, more meaningless than his. They had an "open relationship", only it wasn't so open because they started to despise each other. The divorce tore a great hole in the family; the settlement bitter on both sides. It had hurt Alex more than he admitted on the page. He was guilty of doing his own whitewashing. He'd already told me his daughters, Willow and

Summer, blamed him for the separation. Now in their late teens, neither spoke to him. Evelyn took them to Edinburgh and poisoned them against him. Neither daughter showed up for their grandfather's funeral in Sussex. Quite a damning rift.

The sun was getting ready for bed and Alex was still in Brighton. He'd texted to say he'd be late because of traffic. I switched his angle poise lamp on. I was close to the end of what Alex had written; the nub of Alex himself I daresay in retrospect: the passing of his father, John Fortune. I read it with such sadness it nearly opened my wells:

They say you don't become a true adult until you've felt the separating impact of the death of both parents, when you are left paradoxically abandoned like a child. You throw a clod of earth in their faces or watch a wisp of smoke emanate from a cold stack of bricks. They are gone, and you are next in line.

Dementia and cancer are supposed to have taken my father, but actually it was grief. What were his last words? I only have a sweet nurse's word for it. I was in New York. My father had waited for me to leave England so he might die without me, I was thinking. Had he asked for me right at the end? I asked the nurse when I got the news on the telephone. No, she said. Your father asked for Collette, which nearly broke my heart. She told me she had taken father's hand and squeezed gently as if she was herself Collette, and my father slipped away.

I buried him beside my mother at St. James's Church, Sussex. There is a plot for me there too. The burial day sent a remarkable shiver down my spine. A shiver of regret. Old RAF friends gathered around the grave and told stories of a different man called John Fortune; different to the Daddy I had known in my lifetime. Tales of an officer's mess and a practical joker. Howard, a man straight out of Biggles, smiled at me and said he half-expected the bugger to open his coffin lid, and laugh at them all. The last laugh.

Some of my father's female friends (surely some must have been lovers?) attended, dressed in their finest black dresses and suits and scarves and gloves. It was a freezing morning. And tears streamed down the tracks of their lined faces. It's not what you take with you, I was thinking, it is definitely what you leave behind. Good and bad.

And what would I leave behind? A bitterly broken marriage. Disgruntled children. A successful career. That's all. A fictional success. A stack of books which don't add up to a hill of beans. But memories are left too. That's what we leave behind. Imprints in the sand of the minds of all those we have touched in our lifetime. But even these might die out in a generation or two, in a tide of forgetfulness that is living a normal life.

What would I remember about my father? Him putting away his pipe because my mother hated it? His preference for "Army and Navy" boiled sweets which knocked around his teeth like a knucklebone in the jaws of a starving dog? Or swinging from his strong hands on a beach holiday? Or singing for my supper? Or sitting upon the wing of a plane at a military base? (I still carry this photograph in my wallet). Was I so different to him? When I had looked down on him and my mother at the white windmill in Kent that summer in 195? and hated them both, what had I really hated if not myself for not being them? Now I am older than my mother became and I am still a child. I look at myself in the photograph, me on the wing, my father standing beside me, my mother absent as photographer, and I think, you are just like him now. Physically and behaviourally. Across the forehead and nose and chin. The mannerisms too. Why did you want to be so different from him anyway? You even creak in the knees like he used to. And why learn to fly if not the copycat son? Why get your pilot's license if you did not want to fly like he had at air shows?

Yes, another flash-bulb memory to keep. A Hampshire air display. What was my father flying in circles? A Vampire? Hunter? Meteor? MK4? Gnat? Hawk? A Lightning? Everything is hazy but I can look in a book, though it won't be the same thing as being there as a boy in awe of my father, and something I never told him. Whatever it was it was painted red, standing out against a canvas of blue sky. Where was my mother? I do not remember her being there. My father flew low to the ground making the crowds gulp and hold their mouths shut in fear. Anticipating death. 'That's my father,' I turned to them and said. 'My father, the aviator.' I was proud of the word "aviator", but more proud of the word "father". They were synonymous. I watched him do loops and death-defying rolls no more than a hundred feet above the ground. Didn't his plane pass another so close that their wings nearly kissed and burst into flames? Did I fear? My father was an escape artist. And I never told him that.

And that time I flew back from New York first class, only a few years ago, when he was still alive, dimmed with vodka. Hadn't he asked about the landing? Hadn't he been standing in the same garden which took my mother in a deckchair, and looked up towards the sky visoring the sun with his hand, his thoughts cast backwards like the trails from long gone jumbo-jets too high to pinpoint and say...what did he say? He said nothing. Because he didn't have to. It was written in his face for all to see.

These. These are the things my father left behind as memories. Wings almost touching. 'That's my father, the aviator.'

I put the final page down, knowing it was not the final page at all, and as fate would have it a plane buzzed directly overhead like I was in a film. I don't think until that point I'd ever taken notice of little planes. Planes were not my thing. I had offered to be his editor, jokingly, but I had two heads on me at that moment: Ben the intruder, trudging through his house and personal things like a thief, and Ben the giver. I could give, had given something to him. I wanted to help him complete his life story in any way I could. I was giving already. What I knew from living with him, sleeping with him, eating with him, everything with him. The small important things about a person that don't make it into books; the holes in an autobiographical narrative. You see, I had scratched the surface of him, had pulled up the veneer of his cynicism and discovered a softer, more yielding wood beneath; one desperate to be touched, desperate to breathe. There were knots, many knots, but these give a person character.

He had a penchant for pomegranate juice and brazil nuts (think this was to abate any onset of prostate cancer) and vitamin pills he took after breakfast (garlic and a lot of Zinc, for the same reason?). There were the mysterious headaches. God-awful ones which he thought were migraines (which were not, because Uncle D gets them and he's out of commission for days afterwards). His bathroom cabinets overflowed with ibuprofen, paracetomol and Migraleve tablets. The headaches would take over his life, coming at any time and leaving him debilitated in bed. He would lie there without so much as a move of his finger, the curtains drawn. He was terrified he'd be struck down like his mother. The slightest noise would make him groan. Leaves rustling on a tree outside his bedroom window sounded like a death-knell inside his head. That's what he thought, though he never said it. Pure insanity, because he had scans at a private London hospital once a year and they could find nothing out of the ordinary. No lesions, masses, occlusions. At the first sign of a headache he reached for his pills. Aspirin to thin the blood, like a hypochondriac. Even if it was only dehydration. The attacks came twice a week, mainly in the afternoons, and I would put a damp tea towel across his head. Sometimes I would hold his head in my hands, telling him it would be okay, and he would close his lovely eyes, sighing.

If it wasn't his head, it was his troublesome heart. It missed beats, he said, or added them where there shouldn't be any.

Arrhythmia. *Bu-dum, bu-dum, bu-dum, bud-dud-dud-um. Um-Um-bud-um-um-um.* He asked me to listen and I pressed my ear close to his chest, only to hear a regular, strong heart beating. 'There! Did you hear it, Ben? Did you feel it? The miss, the thump? My pump's going to do for me. One day, it will not start up again.'

What else did I know which filled the gaps in his autobiography? That he constantly feared failure? That he didn't want to write fiction anymore? That he was tired measuring his life out in pages? That he had had bouts of depression throughout his life? What can I tell you? That I was woken in the middle of the night at Smuggler's Cottage, hearing music playing, going downstairs to find Alex at the keys of his mother's piano, tears at his fingertips? Only sad people play Erik Satie at three o'clock in the morning, no matter how beautiful it is. Didn't I hold his shaking frame as if he was a child? As if I was his dead mother? Would these things make it into the last chapter of his book?

These are the things you should know in my defence. I was not taking him for a joy ride. At first, maybe, but not after. Not after I knew and loved and cared about him. Everything wrong and everything right with him. If you can fall in love in just a few seconds (so they say), what can't you do in a few months?

Of course, you can fall out of love just as easily. Love is jumping from an airborne plane with a parachute you fear might never open. And when it opens, when it blooms above your head, you are alive, alive, alive. But strangely, the Earth is still thundering upwards. Misty-eyed, you look up, way above your head, and you realise...realise coldly, that your strings have been severed.

Fourteen

I've lost track again.

Apologies all round. One minute I'm onto really important storylines, the next I'm back to square one in my cell. More like back to an oblong in fact. I wake up each day and don't know which Ben Tippet's going to greet me in the mirror. Ben the mover and shaker. Ben the Faker. Ben the morose. Ben the fool. Ben the bender of the rules. Ben the dutiful prodigal son. Ben the mother-fucking one. Ben the writer. Ben the Zen. Ben the then. Ben the now. Ben the coward. Ben the brave. Ben the genius. Ben the idiot. Ben the down. Ben the up. Ben the loner. Ben the boner. I guess he is always me, regardless.

I told you, you can go nuts in here. But as Imogen once said: 'You must try to write every day, even if it's a paragraph of nonsense.'

Virginia Woolf once craved a room to write in, where she could close the door on the interfering real world outside. I certainly have all of those advantages in here. Katherine Mansfield once said: 'Better to write twaddle than nothing at all.' I only hope she was a prophet.

I stand on the foot of my bed and look out through the bars of my window at the cathedral. It's wonderful to see it, although it's a different side of the bell tower and spires to normal. It has become a distant friend.

When I was a boy I had a friend called Frank and he went everywhere with me. We had a special code of speaking that no one else understood. We held hands at times of trouble which only boys of a certain age can do without criticism or adverse curiosity. But no one except me could see Frank, so it didn't matter. He was my imaginary friend and we were friends from as early as I can remember, up until I was about nine or ten. Maybe older. You probably had a Frank or Fanny as your friend.

I spoke to Frank and he spoke to me. An unfathomable puzzle to the grown-ups. Frank felt real. He was not my imagination. He caught the same bus to school, shared my lunch, kicked a football back and forth to me. Frank was older than me, issuing advice about what I should do in tricky situations, and he was usually right (I could do with him now). My parents played along with what they thought was a game and eventually Frank disappeared somewhere in the playground of my pubescence.

At sixteen, when I discovered I once had a real brother, my friend returned to me. This time not as Frank, but as Tom. I wondered if Frank had not been Frank but Tom's spirit all along. Dr Sparkes, the shrink, tells me that Frank was the symbolized reality of the trauma of Tom's death in my unconscious. She says he was "the ghost in the nursery"; that the past cannot be erased; that secrets come back to haunt the next generation if they are not faced up to. My mother once told me that spirits exist. It's a terrible cliché, but if water can change into wine... I mean, if water can change its body from seawater to clouds to mountain streams to lakes and rivers to reservoirs to taps to urine to seawater again, why can't parts of the human body laid to rot or burning at cremation become part of the physical world again in another form? We are just particles, aren't we? Just molecules of water. We're actually made up of a lot of water, like the planet itself. Which reminds me...

The problem with tears:

Dr Julie Sparkes did a preliminary investigation of me as a possible arsonist. The trial hasn't even started! Anyway, she said the "chat" had nothing to do with whether I was guilty or not. She tried to make me cry. At least, she tried digging around my unconscious, my past, trying to get me all emotional. I would have seen her coming if I was blind. She wanted a confession out of me, and if I wasn't going to tell a priest, I sure as hell wasn't going to tell a shrink.

It was all very chatty, in a room on the other side of the prison. I had to laugh when she said she was called Sparkes. 'As in the band?' I said. She hadn't even heard of Sparks, although she was definitely old enough. She was a buttoned-up professional. All in black, skirt ending just below the knee. Petite, trim ankles.

Liquorice strands of shoulder-length hair. She could have been attending a funeral.

She said she was an impartial clinical psychologist or something, not there to judge, only to establish my mental health. 'I don't know about helping you out,' I said, folding my arms. 'I'm not guilty so I don't need a report. That might prejudice my trial. You talk, I'll just listen.'

Well, the prison guard who was leaning up against the wall nearest the door gave me a filthy look. Sparkes asked him to leave which he wasn't supposed to do, but he waited outside anyway.

'We can talk,' she said. 'I'm not taking notes. I have no prejudices.'

'Fair enough,' I said. We did talk, for nearly an hour, and in that time we discussed my medical background, my brother, my parents and myself. She was a wily old shrink. At one stage she asked me when the last time was I cried. Weird. I had to think about it hard. There was that time in Alex's writing studio, though I dismissed it as a "nearly". There were lots of "nearlies" when I came to think of it. And then it just came to me:

'Apes.'

'Apes as in monkeys?'

I nodded.

'Apes as in zoos? Apes you've seen on TV? Tarzan? Planet of the Apes?'

I shook my head. 'I have nothing against Planet of the Apes as a film per se. Charlton Heston was intense. And Johnny Weissmuller, still regarded as the best Tarzan, had fantastic hair and a natural, real man's physique, but I'm talking about special apes, fictional and real.'

I could see I'd lost her.

'Okay, so this ape lives on an island. He's no ordinary ape and it's no ordinary island. It's populated with numbskull cannibals.' The penny wasn't dropping in her eyes. 'He is alone. No other apes to mate with or share bamboo shoots with or anything. He's relatively happy though, because the whole island is scared shitless.' Still no penny dropping. She must have lived in a glove compartment all her life. 'He rules the jungle. He's top dog. He gets humans fed to him. He's God to them. He's something that's crawled out of the primordial sludge but he is God to them. One day, a boat comes along with strangers onboard. These people aren't stupid. They have guns and a beautiful actress. Are you sure you don't know what I'm talking about?'

She shook her head.

'A skinny blonde dame. She doesn't even know the real reason she's on the boat. She's there to ruin the ape. She's bait. The cannibals offer her up to him. She's like a rag doll in his hands. He takes her back to his mountaintop with the best views of the island. Like a view over Manhattan the blonde thinks, instead of: shit, this ape's going to eat me alive! The ape falls in love with her. He smells her all the time. He protects her. He risks life and limb for her. He slings dinosaurs at her pretty toes. Bullets from the white men bounce off his back. Only he's knocked out by chloroform and taken to New York City.

'Stop me if any of this rings a bell? The ape gets chained up and put on stage. It's a great laugh. Some stupid ape this is. Until the chains get snapped and he's on the rampage. He picks women up and throws them aside in his search for the one he loves and needs. He only wants *her*. He tears a city apart searching until he finds Blondie. He takes her up the side of the tallest building in the city, right to the top, like it's his mountain on the island or a big tree in his old jungle. He puts her down and beats bullets away from planes like they are annoying little mosquitoes, but he gets weaker and weaker and weaker. He takes mindless sweeps at the planes, probably thinking what kind of birds are these? These stings, what are these? He's got blood all over his fur, chest, arms and legs. He is falling but he hangs on, looking finally into his whole life's desire: Blondie. And she thinks she loves him then.

'He's done everything for her. His eyes are brown and white half-moons and the saddest things I've ever seen. Seeing them breaks my heart. It's the truth in his eyes, and the truth in hers, but it's all too late. And anyway, what would their children have looked like? He lets go of the mast and falls, falls, falls and is gone, for ever. That. That makes me cry.'

'And *why* do you cry?' Sparkes said.

'It moves me.'

'Because he dies?'

'No, because he fails, and for what? Like the man says at the end of the film: the planes did not kill the ape, it was beauty.'

'Better to have loved and lost than not to have loved at all?'

I'd just laid all my cards on the table and she was throwing (Mark Twainian?) clichés on top of them. 'King Kong's metafictional,' I said. 'It's fiction about fiction. Really clever for its time. Sure, it's about slavery and racism but the real filmmaker is hiding behind the filmmaker in the film itself. He's commenting on the process of filmmaking; what art is; what audience means. Very clever device.'

She didn't have a clue what I was talking about. Alex would have. He used a similar technique in some of his earlier novels. Doesn't use it anymore saying it's too narcissistic and lazy. *Regressus ad infinitum* he says. Literary wank. Write about anything but don't write about writing in your own fucking writing. Write about something that matters in real life, he said, as if life wasn't a matter of writing! In a way, we're all artists painting pictures of ourselves, aren't we? If not on a page, then in our heads. Society was proclaimed dead in the 1980s, wasn't it? So what are we living in now? The renaissance of subjectivity, that's what. Your self, my self, our selves.

I wanted to tell Sparkes about my King Kong poster at home, worth a couple of thousand pounds, sitting on the wall above my TV. But I guess time ran out and she had enough material on me already. Who knows? I'm not sure if she could determine whether I was mentally maladjusted to prison or just generally twisted. I was sorry when she left and I was returned to my cell. It was nice to talk, especially about King Kong.

Later that night, unable to sleep because of Rogers' hacking cough and Moses' rotten sinusitis, I tried remembering things about crying. My problem with tears. I hadn't even cried when Uncle D revealed the family secret, had I? Not when my own mother cried in front of me in the kitchen. I didn't cry when Elvis caught me. Nor when my mother and father came in to the station to see me. Why is that? I don't consider myself unemotional in any way. I hope that's obvious by now. I'm not autistic. I can empathise and sympathise, I think.

Short story quick-fashion:

When I first moved to Pensbury (sharpen your pencil, I told you about renting here before buying a flat with my dad's deposit), I didn't know a soul outside of the estate agent's offices. I realized early on that I didn't like selling properties, despite being good at it. I avoided lunch with colleagues, instead taking my sandwich to

Southgate Gardens. It's a beautiful park in spring and summer, with wooden benches and rows of geraniums, pansies and daffodils. Ivy hugs the remnants of the city walls. The River Sour runs through the middle of the park (that's its name!) and further up river it feeds out of the River Wye. I love those names and am constantly questioning their origins. Wye is the River Sour? (ha-ha). The first time I ever went to Pensbury (I was about twelve, with my parents in the school holidays) we joined the tail-end of a guided tour, hoping to pick up some local history for free. 'Why is the River Sour called sour?' an American in a fedora asked the tour guide. 'Because witches drowned on the ducking stool,' the guide replied. I'd already done my research. 'Excuse me,' I said, tugging her arm, 'but the Sour was called the Sour before medieval times. It's Anglo-Saxon. It has nothing to do with how it tastes.' I was such a smart arse at twelve, and still am.

There was a particular bench I liked to go to at lunchtimes; a bench close enough to see the tower and hear the traffic so you were still in earshot of the world but far enough away for the noise not to be intrusive of your thoughts. This bench backed onto the original medieval wall, facing the Sour with pretty Council flowers between you and the water.

I liked this bench because it was dedicated to *Reginald Cuff, architect, who loved this spot. 1928-2003.* Whenever I see birth and death dates side by side I'm always working out a lifetime; something to measure my own against. So Reginald lived to be seventy-five, but actually, not necessarily, because it depends on the month of his birth and month of death. Anyway, I liked that Reginald had lived for seventy-five years. A good innings. I liked that he was called Cuff which seemed unusual but perfectly fitting for a man I never knew. I liked that he'd been an architect. A noble profession. And I liked to sit on his bench with my lunchtime sandwiches, watching the world go by.

A lovely hint of rose crept over you on this bench from June to September. I'd sit here thinking about Reginald, or was he Reggie to friends, or just plain old Reg for short? Did he ever marry and have children? I didn't know a thing about him except that he was Reginald Cuff, architect, died at seventy-five and loved this spot. And now that I had taken over his bench it might become *Ben Tippet, not quite decided what he wants to be yet, who also loved this spot. 1980-200?*

(Hurry up, Ben. You're losing them! Cut to the tears.)

One day, I took my sandwiches to Southgate Gardens and there was an intruder sitting on my bench. It had never happened before, as if it had always been reserved for my exclusive use. It made my blood boil. I'd have to take the next bench along which was vacant. But I knew this would put my whole day out of whack because I always sat on Reginald's bench and I needed to pay my respects each time, like a touchstone.

As I got closer I could see it was a young woman, a girl of about fifteen. She should have been at school but wasn't wearing a uniform. I got to where she was and heard her crying. Her head was tipped down, sniff, sniff, sniff. Tears were springing from her fingertips in fountains!

I ignored her at first and sat on the inferior, meaningless bench ten yards past. I started eating my cheese and ham pesto panini, peeking at her from the corner of my eyes. She'd never have known I was there, so engrossed was she with the tears. I mean a river running down her nose and chin. Then I noticed that her legs were really something. I wondered who she was crying over. A lost cat? A shoddy boyfriend? Abusive member of her family? It could have been anybody or anything, couldn't it? I stared at the river which was quite full after a lot of rain. It was just me, this girl and the River Sour. I wanted to tell her that today her tears were perfectly suited to the river; that if she kept on crying the way she was, the Sour might burst its banks out of sympathy. Who knows? It might have lifted her load a little.

But I never said any of these things.

Soon, she took out a handkerchief and blew her nose which was clown red, and dabbed her eyes which were tiny slits, and pulled her head up straight. I could see how pretty she was. I watched her walk away, then I got up and sat in her place, my place. It was still warm from her bottom and there were teardrops on the wooden slats. I wanted to know her grief, her story, but now it was too late. I would never know. I'd just have to make it up, maybe use it in a story of my own. I think this was the real birth of me as a writer.

It would turn out to have been the news that her father was leaving again, leaving her mother who had just discovered she had cancer. No, her father had the cancer and it was her mother who was leaving. Somebody had to be leaving in this story. The girl had come here to throw herself in the torrent of the River Sour until a handsome young man came along and sat at the bench next to hers. And in this story, he came across to her and asked why she was crying because he wasn't afraid of crying. This handsome young man shared a panini with her. He told her a story about a boy who humiliated a tour guide and explained the origins of why the River Wye became so Sour which made her actually smile. And she said her name was Rachel. Rachel Cuff. And he said he was a writer, and she said she was studying Macbeth, a wonderfully depressing play. And then he would know her story without having to ask, because she was a Cuff. She had been sitting on her grandfather's bench all along, on the anniversary of his death. And then he'd know that this bench was meant for more than one person. This bench meant more to Rachel Cuff than it ever could to him. But he wouldn't mind, because some things are better shared.

There are benches outside in the prison quad and I like to sit on them during association time. I imagine I'm actually sitting in Southgate Gardens. Last night the humidity was oppressive in the cell. Everyone's talking about the Indian Summer. I lay awake for most of the night, a sticky mess on my bed. A storm was brewing. Distant murmurs of thunder. God moving his furniture about. There was an eerie static-filled sky outside my cell window. Everything was utterly still. The drops of water in the air were tangible on my skin. A soup which needed stirring. Everyone seemed to wake with broken bones the next morning, the way they shuffled into the quad with very little sleep. Somnambulistic recidivists. Like most of the remanders, I opted to go outside for fresh air at morning association time. No one could breathe. It was 10 o'clock but the sky was black. When Red let us out, the heavens opened, the rain so heavy it fell in straight-down sheets and you couldn't see the prison walls. A nice illusion.

I stepped into the rain.

'Tippet!' Red called after me. 'Are you crazy? Get back inside!' He certainly wasn't going to follow me into the centre of the quad and sit down on one of the benches, as I did. I couldn't hear much after that because of the roar of the rain hitting the ground. I was soaked through in seconds. Warm rain, and it was soothing and cleansing. 'You're fuckin' mad, man!' Moses shouted.

'I won't shrink!' I shouted back.

'You *need* your shrink!'

At that moment, a blade of lightning cut the sky in two or three pieces making me jump. I was so wet I could have been in a river. Red shouted again but I ignored his requests. Another rumble in the sky. I was in the park in my mind. The River Sour was filling up and flowing under low-slung bridges on its way to the sea at Sandwich. I always loved electrical storms as a kid.

'I don't want to have to drag you inside!' Red yelled. With the next knife of light and crack of thunder, so loud it took my breath away, I ran back to the others.

'Knob,' Manston said. Everything that comes out of that man's mouth is an obscenity.

'Back to the wing,' Red said. 'Go and change.'

'But I am changed,' I said.

I don't think he understood how important it was to be outside, to feel the elements acting upon me. I squelched up the stairs, got changed again and lay on my bed quite pleased with myself. I listened to the storm passing over. I'd never appreciated a storm's significance in my whole life. This storm smelled, tasted, felt like something new and fresh was happening, which is why I've described it to you. And for another reason. My trial was coming. In a way, the storm was not passing. It was over my head and going nowhere. In fact, I was at its epicentre. In 36 hours or less, I'd be standing trial. This interminable waiting would finally mean something, one way or the other.

I am writing on notebooks that Maurice brings in for me. He believes I'm innocent. He told me as much. 'You can write down your innocence for posterity,' he actually said. 'In black and white. Like Mandela.'

Really, I write to keep sane. It beats the breezeblocks which I find myself counting. Sorry to go on about it but it gives you an idea of what it's like inside. I've started counting things you see. Breezeblocks in my cell, tiles in the shower, bars on my window, number of paces from the wall to the other wall like a caged animal. I catch myself out sometimes. Counting, I mean. And beat myself up about it. This sort of thing must happen to everyone inside sooner or later. God knows what it's like on isolation wing. At least there's the odd person to talk to here, like Moses or Rogers or Red. Isolation must be shocking. Maybe I'm really feeling it now the trial is almost here. Didn't Robinson Crusoe feel it on his island? Didn't the Count of Montecristo feel it in his cell? Did they etch and scratch out the days spent alone? My mother, I know, counts her rosary beads each night for me. She told me as much on her last visit. She was going to take them into court too.

I have to be careful or this cell will begin to feel like home. It has my own smell now and not those of previous inmates. It has already taken on my personality, my identity and I've almost forgotten what my flat smells like. So what would it feel like to have a cell for years? What would happen to me in that time? Would I find a new identity? Would I come out a new man? Would I come out at all?

But I am not going to go to prison for years, am I? I am innocent. There are no material witnesses. I have my alibi intact. 'Based on average and similar cases,' my brief tells me on visits, 'you have an 80% chance of acquittal on grounds of poor evidence.' So why is it then I feel so frightened? Because I don't believe in the law of averages. There is no such thing as average or normal in real life.

I won't be able to write as much in the trial, of course. So I'd better get on with my denouement: confessions and capture.

Fifteen

As I've already said, in the summer of love there were not many lies between Alex and I.

However, not telling the truth is tantamount to deception is tantamount to a lie. And what a whopper! A secret fire burned inside me, lapped over me at times. I was burning alive; so deeply I thought the truth was going to leap out of my mouth at any given moment. Elvis's visit in April had stoked the flames. I had to tell someone. Someone who'd shown me the way of truth so trustingly. Would I tell Alex at Smuggler's Cottage? After sex maybe? When he was relaxed. Over lunch in the Duck Inn? Would it be in the Greek villa Alex took me to in late June? (holiday brochure coming up).

You'd think a millionaire would have his own villa, but Alex leased one just outside the quaint old fishing port of Fiscardo on the island of Kefalonia, famed for the filming of *Captain Correlli's Mandolin*. Whatever. A convertible was waiting for us at the airport. Very pretty drive up the coast. I remember so many goats, clear skies and sheer drops down to the sea, sea, sea, everywhere.

When we got to the villa I was amazed by the location. Isolated, down a hairpin road. The villa itself was hidden by century-old olive trees. A beautiful, whitewashed villa converted from an old farmhouse shell. It belonged to a friend of Hilary Shears. There were private steps down to the water, moorings and a good-sized motor boat. The boat was called "Lucky Us" which I thought was in very poor taste but had a ring of truth about it. We spent most of our time that week in or around a gorgeous infinity pool.

It should have been the most relaxing of holidays and it did have its moments of harmony, I guess. I played at being rich and famous, sitting at expensive restaurant tables eating whole fishes. Alex smoked cigars. 'Holidays are not places for giving up things, they are for beginning them,' he said. I didn't mind. He looked even more distinguished with a fat cigar in his mouth. We took day trips, village to village, went to vineyards and beach to beach in the convertible which he let me drive. We spent each morning lazing around our pool which had views of other islands; Ithaca, or was it actually Greece itself? We browned our bellies and backs. The tiles around the pool burned my soles. We bathed naked, talked, dozed, drank and made love with only crickets for company.

It should have been paradise yet I did not give myself wholly to it. The fire was burning a hole in the pocket of my conscience. We sailed around the island, mooring at isolated spots. A swarm of wasps attacked us like we were in the Iliad or the Odyssey or something. I told him more about my life. No longer embarrassed that I was the son of a bed-seller. I told him about my dead brother, Tom, and he hugged me tight like a brother would, only it was more than that.

The right time never seemed to come. I didn't want to ruin the idyll. Imagine saying out of the blue, 'By the way, Alex. I killed a man in Broadstairs last December but it was an accident. I ran away. What should I do now?' In my dreams he would just raise an eyebrow, saying, 'It was an accident. Forget about it. Don't go to the police, Ben. Let it lie.'

I bottled it each time, playing conversations in my head but never out loud. Even in the convertible I'd be checking the rear-view mirror on the lookout for a silver Audi estate, Elvis and Blonde Bob inside. Elvis maybe in a Hawaiian shirt. I was looking for him in cafes and bars and restaurants. I sensed him.

There were nice times. In one restaurant, a British tourist recognised Alexander Fortune. He came over to our table, red as a lobster, saying he was a big fan and would Alex mind giving an autograph? A bit impromptu. Alex borrowed a pen from the waiter and signed a napkin from the table. Then he handed the napkin to me, saying to his fan, 'This is Ben Tippet. A very good friend of mine and a writer to watch.' I signed the napkin, wrote my scribble just below Alex's. You can only imagine how swelled up I was that afternoon. I wonder now what happened to that napkin. If it ever made it back to Suffolk where the lobster said he lived. I don't suppose it matters now.

The week continued and I began to relish each moment. Simple things like smoothing sun cream onto Alex's shoulders, dropping anchor at isolated beaches and watching eagles circling above our heads. I don't think I've ever talked as much with a person I also slept with. Alex was the happiest I'd ever seen him too, as if getting away from England did him some good. He slept whole nights through which was a first. He only had one headache and it was very minor. I didn't want to disturb his peace of mind, the tranquillity of his disposition. He no longer lived in the past. I guess I didn't want to ruin the future with my past. I did not want to wake from my dream. I did not wish to tear the canvas of the beautiful painting I thought we were becoming (overblown prose, Ben?) We were a work of art.

So I buried the truth, for a little while longer at least.

With tweezers, I pulled small black spines from Alex's foot. He'd stepped on a sea urchin, and as I pulled he mentioned the possibility of a new book. Something he swore he'd never write after his autobiography was completed. He was always going on about "burying the pen". He certainly had enough to live on. His apartment in NYC alone was worth a cool £3 million.

Yes, the fresh air and new environment had re-invigorated him. He'd recently been inspired by a trip to a London exhibition called "The Inner You". A scientific exploration of the human body. With his age-phobia, a terrible place to go voluntarily. He'd long held the view of a devout atheist, a non-believer of the human soul or afterlife. You live, you live, and you die, you die, he said. Nothing before and nothing after, except what you leave behind, which as he discovered at this exhibition was the human carcass, muscle and tendon, nerves and flesh and fat and organs etc. 'The human form preserved in various states of bodily undress' is how he put it. Real dead human bodies coated in preservative plastic. The bodies were posed in ridiculous positions after death, he said. Kicking a football, swinging a baseball bat, hitting a cricket ball with a bat, sitting and contemplating like Rodin's Thinker, skull removed to reveal the workings of the brain. He was telling me this with gusto. Lungs, hearts, prostates and pupils. There was not one thing in the human body not dissected and put on show. Bodies cross-sectioned like cuts of beef at the butcher's. Foetuses too, suspended in fluid-filled bottles. The exhibition was intended to show how intricate and miraculous the human body was, not how disgusting and empty the physical world actually is. Eyes, vulvas and penises turned inside out for all to see.

'That should be fine for an atheist like you,' I said.

No. It was not fine at all. He *had* been disturbed. Everything was too factual, he said. Babies born without kneecaps, 22 bones in the skull, ounce for ounce the femur is stronger than cast steel, breathing 15 times a minute (23,040 times a day), when reading our eyes swing back and forth 100 times a second (100,000 times a day), 1,300 nerve-endings in one square inch of hand, a hand with 54 bones in it, cartilage in the spine absorbing forces of up to 200lb per sq inch (but not a Bateau lit), 10 billion neural pathways in the brain each sending messages at 250mph, nerve endings if stretched in a single line reaching 45 miles, the body is never entirely at rest, UNTIL IT IS DEAD. 'It just showed me how vulnerable we all are.'

But what had upset Alex the most, he said, was not the matter-of-factness but the skin of an entire human displayed from the top of the man's scalp to the points of his piggy-wiggly toes. Nothing but skin in a glass coffin. It lay there like a human shell, an alien chrysalis, a piece of vellum, a human carapace. On closer inspection you could see hairs which had been growing from the crown, around the nipples and navel. A shell. The rest of him (the contents should never be visualised) was pinned and perched somewhere else in the exhibition!

This had sent Alex into a downwards spiral. Downwards and inwards. He could not shake the image from his mind, he said, not even rushing straight to a bar and having a stiff brandy could ease his conscience. He felt like a mad professor in crisis, he said. A philosophical, existential panic set in. He realised that he must have a soul after all. Soul was life, wasn't it? The soul could not be preserved in a jar, so he had to preserve life.

'Being a hypochondriac isn't going to help your soul,' I told him.

'There's more to flesh and bone,' he replied. 'All that you've loved is all you own.'

He'd caught a train from Victoria and on that train made phone calls to Evelyn and his two children. He needed to know that he'd touched their souls or something. But they were not answering. He had his notebook with him and sketched the basic outline of a short story which might have had legs as a novel, about a woman who loved her dead husband so much she paid a fortune privately to have him scientifically preserved just like in the exhibition, keeping him in her house, like a stuffed pet. Guilt, Alex said, had run over his life. He could have been a better husband, a better son, a better father. Now all he had was fictional families. The fickle public were not happy with happy families. They had to have incest and conflict and tragedy and hatred and betrayal. The general public, he said, are rabid dogs foaming at the mouth in anticipation of another tragic morsel.

Just the word "guilt" had me reeling and I changed the subject. It had been the perfect opportunity to tell him, but I let it pass. We flew home first class, brown as chestnuts. I didn't see Alex the following week. He had a literary festival in the Cotswolds (it must be fantastic being such a famous writer). I couldn't take more time off from Little's, so we spoke on the telephone and sent texts. The festival was dreary, he said, getting back to the miserable old depressed Alex again. Could I come over at the weekend? He had a surprise for me.

Of course, I had a bigger one for him. There were a number of surprises on Sunday for both of us.

When I pulled up outside his house that morning, there was an Aston Martin (DB9) parked on the drive beside his Land Rover. A beautiful new car; something James Bond might drive to the Casino Royale. Black as the panthers supposed to roam this part of East Kent. Low to the ground, wide and sleek. Fat wheels sitting on the gravel like paws. My first instinct was that he had another visitor, someone important staying. Maybe BB Crum no B? From what I'd heard about him, he could be flashy like that.

Alex came out with documents in his gloved hands. 'What do you think?'

I ran the tips of my fingers across its side. 'She's gorgeous.'

'I've had her a while,' he said, 'but rarely take her out. D'you want to go for a spin?'

'Does the Pope shit in the woods?'

I don't have to describe the luxurious interior. You can imagine the leather sports seats and trim. He pressed a button to start and she purred like a panther. He took us over the wooden bridge and out through the gates. We speeded along the country lanes. He pressed another button and the top came back slotting behind our ears without even a click. He took her through her paces, gently at first, taking great care at junctions. On the open A-roads, she flew like an arrow. He played Wagner, I remember. The Ring Cycle.

'Where are we going?'

'Isn't this enough?' he said. I couldn't see his eyes through the reflective sunglasses; only myself in them. I guessed his eyes were grinning.

'You're like Alex in *A Clockwork Orange*,' I said. 'A psycho-lunatic.'

'Do you *really* want to fly?' he said, shaven head glinting.

My long hair flapped around my shoulders and into his face. 'Open her up,' I said. Five minutes later, we were running parallel to a small airfield. 'Is this where your father used to fly?'

'It's where *we're* going.' We approached a security gate and he took out his ID.

'Nice to see you again, Mr Fortune,' the security guard said. 'A beautiful day for it.'

'Alex, have you got a freakin' plane?'

We drove through another set of automatic gates and parked the panther behind a large hangar where eight small aircraft were lined up. A few words about engines and weather forecasts with a mechanic dressed in oily overalls. 'How many are up?' Alex asked him. 'Five or six,' the mechanic said. 'Visibility's good.' All that stuff I don't even pretend to understand. Then we walked along the concourse towards one of the planes. I was lost for words, just did what I was told.

Alex got in the pilot's side, threw open the door on my side. 'Don't worry,' he said. 'I've had a licence for years.' I climbed in beside him and strapped myself in. Alex put a headset on, pulled the mouthpiece down across his mouth. He communicated with the fly tower. Wind speeds. Coordinates. Roger this and Roger that. Just like in a film. You don't get to sit in a real cockpit every day. 'I fly two or three times a month in the summer.'

'Is it yours?'

He nodded. 'Not new, but reliable.'

Something about a cricket score on his headpiece and Alex laughed. He signalled to the mechanic who signalled the all clear with waving hands and thumbs. Alex started her up and the propeller spat into motion.

'Shit. I can't believe…'

Before I could finish my sentence we turned onto a wide strip of runway. We straightened up, then stopped. 'You ready?' I was about to reply when the engines roared. The wheels were rolling, the wings were bumping along the scenery and windsocks. My adrenalin peaked as the nose lifted. 20, 60, 100 feet and more. Up, up we went, crosswinds taking us slightly to the left and out over the airfield.

Roger altitude. Copy this. Copy that. Over.

When we were high enough, Alex levelled the nose and let the thermals do the work. We were buzzing along the chalky coastline of Kent. Tankers and smaller boats on the bobbling blue sea. 'Music?' he said, switching on the CD player.

'Are you allowed to play music?' I said, like an ignoramus. 'Won't it interfere with the radio?'

'Angels in the clouds, Ben. Remember Tenebrae? Darkness?'

We maintained a good height, cutting inland over towns and villages, housing estates, A-roads and B-roads, railway lines, oasthouses and orchards. You can imagine how wonderful the views were. How small the people. Over the sea and over the land. We took in most of East Kent in an hour or so. I didn't know what to say except, 'This is fantastic, Alex.' over and over to the point when he asked me to stop saying it. He was in his element, in control of his environment. Free as a bird (cliché's creeping in again, Ben). Fleetingly, I thought he was trying to be closer to his dead father, the RAF pilot and air-show escapologist.

We flew directly over Broadstairs. I recognised the seafront and bandstand at the cliffs and the sandy Viking Bay. I also saw the burnt-out buildings of the Acorn offices, scaffolding still around. Building work going on. 'They're waving,' Alex said, talking about families on the beach but I couldn't take my eyes off of the Acorn building, or where it used to be. Alex took the plane a little higher, turning at a sharp angle out to sea, my right shoulder bumping into his left.

'Our English watering place,' he said, winking. 'I wonder what Dickens would have made of a flight over his hidey-hole. You know he had a mistress out this way?'

We were now heading back towards the south, and Dover. We flew over the impressive Castle and Alex talked about Churchill. We flew over ferries in various stages of departure and arrival, then past the town and further along the coast and the legendary sun-lit White Cliffs. 'Hold onto your helmet,' Alex said. 'We're going for Shakespeare.' He pushed the hand controls forward sharply and we nose-dived, plummeted straight for the biggest cliff.

'Alex!' My stomach was up near my ears. I clung onto the door handle. All I could see was the sea heading for us. 'Alex!' The plane started to pirouette, twisting around, making me dizzy. We were spiralling and the sea was turning. 'Alex!' I gripped his arm, but he was grinning.

'There is a cliff,' he roared, 'whose high and bending head looks fearfully in the confined deep. Bring me to the very brim of it and I'll repair the misery thou dost bear with something rich about me. Gloucester. King Lear.' He drew back, pulled the nose up, engine revving, roaring, the plane rising just above the cliff-top. Once more, we were riding under the low clouds above the countryside, and then the roads. We reached a point of zero gravity, the top of a rollercoaster ride, and the engine seemed to stall as we glided to an endpoint.

'Alex?' The nose flattened out, the wings levelled off and the engine hummed satisfactorily. 'You utter bloody manic!' I said, breathless. I laughed hysterically and he laughed back at me. He was in control, and he wasn't. He was never really out of control, or was he?

'I wanted a grand finale.'

'You did that,' I said. 'I hope you lose your licence.'

We made our way back to the airfield, landed with an easy bump on the tarmac. We got out and my legs were jellified. Alex handed the keys to the mechanic and after a short conflab we were back in the panther, and home to Smuggler's Cottage, safe and sound.

When I think back, carefully, I remember the feeling of being changed after that flight. I don't mean the elation or the danger of imminent death, though that was how I had felt at the time. No, it was the feeling during the safer part of the flight. Alex had taken me on a journey; Alex the novelist, not the pilot. Novelist = pilot, passenger = reader. He had taken me from one place, moved me around and then put me back down on the ground in the same place, but changed. He had gently steered me through an almost-fiction, given me a birds-eye view, then left me suspended unexpectedly in the air, before bringing me to a resolution. My life had been in his hands, and with those hands he'd shown me things about life. If that doesn't sound too ironic, too absurd, too melodramatic? He made me feel special.

That afternoon, sipping gin by the pool in his garden, the proverbial floodgates opened. The flight was a green light for my conscience. I could no longer live with what I had been living with, as if life was too short or something. Maybe I thought I was going to die with him on the flight and did not want any more secrets between us.

We canoodled in the pool, lay drying beside each other on sunloungers, sipping gin and ice. I was watching the clouds thicken, the sunshine getting hazy. I turned to him and said, 'I've done something bad, Alex.'

He shielded his eyes. 'What's Ben Tippet done so bad?' He reached out and touched my fingers with his. I could have stalled, made something up from the top of my head. I really wish I had.

'That building in Broadstairs...'

'Building?'

'The one being re-built. The one burnt to the ground?'

'Oh, yes. What of it?'

'I set fire to it and killed a man who was inside it.'

Alex wiped away a fly which was buzzing around his glass. He laughed. 'And I am Genghis Khan.' I didn't say anything to that. 'What? Don't you think I'd make a handsome Genghis Khan?'

'Alex, I burnt a building down but I didn't know the man, the boy, Stepan was inside. I didn't mean to destroy the whole building.'

It took a while to sink in, then, 'What the devil...?'

'It's the truth.'

I could give you the whole rest of the sorry conversation but it's too painful to recollect. What I'd done brought everything into question, like it should I suppose. Alex turned into a moralist right before my eyes. But what had I expected to happen? He stormed into the kitchen, re-filled his glass, necked it back. I followed quickly after him like a love-sick puppy. A puppy that had crapped all over his finest rug. Everything had changed. I tried to explain why I'd done it, how it all happened and he listened at first, though he was shaking his head in disbelief.

'Now you know.'

'Now I know,' he said sarcastically. 'Though I still don't believe you. Did anyone see you do it?'

'No.'

He wanted facts: when was this? Who was killed? Had I told anyone else? He remembered it then, from the papers and police appeals.

'The police came around to interview me.'

'Christ,' he said, making me feel terrible.

'I've been meaning to tell you, but...'

'...but the time was never right?'

'No,' I said.

He tore into me. 'Well I wish you hadn't told me.' He lit a cigar. 'You'll have to go to the police.'

'Police?'

'And tell them exactly what you've told me.'

'I can't, Alex. It was six months ago. I lied to the police. But the trail's gone cold. I've not heard anything. Can't we just leave it?'

He stared at the kitchen table, thinking, blowing smoke signals. He said, 'This is a very tricky situation.'

'For me more than you, Alex.'

'I wish you hadn't told me.'

'So do I,' I said. 'God.'

'Don't you get it, Ben? I'm an accessory.'

'Pretend I never told you, then you're not.'

He pulled his parental face. 'Too late. I *am* part of it now.'

'What will you do?'

'You burnt a building down, killed a man. I'm sheltering a murderer.'

'Alex? What will we do?'

'*We?* What will *you* do? *You'll* go straight to the police station in Pensbury. *You'll* make a statement. *I* will pay bail. That is if they'll let you out on bail. You say you lied to them?'

'You're worried about the press.'

'Juicy news, isn't it? Novelist's romp with arsonist.'

'I thought you'd understand.'

He rubbed his temple. 'What was I going to say? Ah, forget about it, as if it's a pheasant crushed on the road? You only have one option. Come clean and see what happens.' He got out of his seat and came to me. He stroked my cheek.

'This changes things, doesn't it? That's why I didn't want to tell you.'

'Ben, Ben, Ben, you've lived with this too long. Go to the police. I'll come with you. Whatever you want.'

'And if I don't?'

He pulled back. 'You haven't much choice. It's *your* conscience.'

So much for honesty being the best policy. I didn't stay much longer. I told him I needed time to think it through. I'd call him in the morning, let him know what I'd decided (now we're getting to the nuts and bolts of this whole thing).

I thought very hard about that day of surprises. It was July and heating up. I replayed everything Alex had suggested in my head. It made sense to hand myself in, common sense and moral sense, as he put it on the telephone the next morning. But it made more sense to do nothing. I needed a bit more time. It had been six months since the fire, what difference would another few days make? He knew I was making the correct decision. It might not be so terrible, he said.

He didn't know diddlysquat. He was living in the made-up world of his genre books.

I couldn't function properly at Little's. Three days went by and not during one of them did Alex leave me alone. Had I decided yet? (how I wish I'd never told him). He said he couldn't live with the secret and did I know what he meant by that?

'Sure. You're going to dob me in.'

He said he would have to make the call if I didn't. He couldn't live with the knowledge. Out of fairness he'd give me until the end of the week. Not because he didn't care for me but because he did. He said I couldn't live with a sword of Damocles hanging over my head (him neither, I suspect).

Stalling, I told him I needed to tell my parents first. In actual fact, I had other plans. I phoned in sick at the bookshop and contacted Alex on the Thursday evening. I told him that he had been right all along, that I would hand myself in after we'd spent one last weekend together, and if it was possible at such short notice to take one more flight up in his plane? I wanted to experience the feeling of complete freedom because I didn't know when I'd feel it again. He was hesitant at first, said I was being melodramatic, but after some persuasion agreed. 'The airfield bend over backwards for me,' is what he actually said.

I arrived Friday morning, pumped up. His Aston Martin was in the garage. I was hoping to go in that car to the airfield not his father's hand-me-down Land Rover. I wanted to go out in style.

Before leaving Smuggler's we had a long and intimate chat about what would happen. He hoped the police would see how hot-headed I'd been and not punish excessively. Some utter nonsense like that. I was filled with sadness just listening to him.

Alex needed to use the toilet before setting off, so I took the opportunity to re-check everything in the boot of my Saab: passport, Euros, suitcase full of fresh clothes. I even had my favourite Fortune novels in the zip compartment of my backpack. All I needed for a long trip in Europe. I was going to hop onto Euro Tunnel and drive to Paris, stay there a few days, then move south to Italy and maybe live in a small Sardinian village. I love Italy. I know very little Italian but had a phrasebook. My plan was to tell Alex mid-flight so that he had no time to react or say or do anything to change my mind.

I closed the boot. Alex was coming out of the main door. He threw a set of keys at me. 'We'll go the whole hog on the freedom front, heh? You can drive.'

He went indoors again to fetch his documents and ID. I had half a mind to take what was in my boot and transfer it across to his and make a hell-for-leather dash for the tunnel in Folkestone. But I am not a thief. And anyway, I wanted this last flight to mean something. It was an opportunity to explain myself. And besides, you can hardly "disappear" in a top-of-the-range Aston Martin. It would be like picking grapes in a tuxedo.

It took me a while figuring out the electrical garage doors. I got inside, revved her up and reversed onto the gravel. Alex got in and we were off. I can't explain the mixed-up sense of danger and exhilaration I felt during that half-hour drive to the airfield; the purring panther, me roaring through the gears; the looks people were giving us. How can someone that young own an expensive car like that?

Alex had placed his trust in me. He had given me things as a measure of that trust: keys to his house, first read of his autobiography; more importantly perhaps, he'd sent some of my short stories to his agent in America; a man called Todd Lawrence, though I've still heard nothing back from him and have always been inexplicably uncomfortable with people whose first and last names are interchangeable.

I was betraying Alex now. I was betraying his trust and I was not, because I was going to sever all ties so the police would not investigate him. I knew how much he hated press attention. Only one species of animal got under his skin more than the rabid reader, he once told me, and that was the nosy poke-around journalist.

We said very little. Alex was sombre in mood, seemed lost in thought looking out across the Kentish fields. Early summer had been hot, and by late July the wheat fields were already stripped, dotted now with warehouse-sized stacks and roly-polies. Looking back, I can see a symbolic significance; the promise of late spring/early summer had been delivered and everything that is good must come to an end, even the grass verges had turned from lush green to dusty straw and scrub. Yes, everything that is good must come to an end.

We exchanged short glances as if recognising the fact. We passed through the security gate and I parked up behind the hangar as before, only this time I was extra nervous. No chit-chat with anyone this time, we climbed into Alex's plane and took off without delay.

Alex was going to put on his angel music but I stopped his hand. 'I don't want any more darkness, Alex.' I'd brought a CD of my own. It had been so easy choosing it the night before. I wanted to play a song that meant something to me, and him, equally. Only one song was relevant, so poignant. Before playing it, loudly, I asked him to listen carefully to the words and to feel the music, because that was all I had to say about me, him and our situation:

I, I will be king, and you, you will be queen...though nothing will drive them away, we can beat them just for one day...we can be Heroes just for one day...And you, you can be mean...'cause we're lovers and that is a fact...Yes, we're lovers, and that is that...though nothing, nothing will keep us together, we could steal time, just for one day...we can be Heroes for ever and ever, what d'you say?

He didn't speak for most of the trip afterwards. I tried to lighten the mood as we swung out over the sea. 'Take me to France, Alex. Drop me in a field of poppies and leave the rest to me.' Still nothing out of him. He was tight-lipped, grim-faced, steering the plane along the coast. I decided not to tell him about my plans then. Better he was completely ignorant of my intentions. That way he'd not be implicated in my crimes: the fire, the death, my escape.

We flew from Margate to Dover. I asked if he would cut inland and fly over my flat in Pensbury (I wanted to say goodbye to all that) but he said it wasn't possible. We reached Dover and I was hoping he'd do his daredevil stunt again. At the White Cliffs, just past the ferry point, I said, 'Three o'clock, Alex. England's eroding.' I was talking about the huge grey-white boulders at the foot of the cliffs (if you were making this stuff up you'd have to hold your hands up to accusations of overplaying the symbolism, but it did all happen the way I say. This is all about erosion).

On our return leg, Alex started to open up. Speak I mean. Something was on his mind. He wanted to tell me something important before we landed. He said this summer had been the best he could ever remember and that it was largely down to me. That was about as close as he ever got to telling me he loved me.

The airfield drew closer and the plane started its descent. 'Will you wait for me, Alex? Can you forgive me?'

'I have already forgiven you, yes,' he said, not looking at me.

The plane was buffeted, wheels not far from contact with the tarmac. It never ceases to amaze and draw me in, the air that hovers just above the ground on belting hot days. We bumped in the air and Alex struggled to even the wings out, using both hands, fixing his eyes on the runway. We seemed to leapfrog nothing; wheels hiccupping, down, then up again.

'As you said, Alex. There are mitigating circumstances. It was an accident.' He took her down with a slight bump. 'You might not see me for a while,' I said. 'Will you wait for me?'

He eyeballed me briefly, seemed in some sort of pain. We rolled down the runway, slowing, then we took a left coming to a crawl around the concourse. 'You haven't given me an answer,' I said, feeling ashamed about what I was about to do. The hangar was in sight. Alex removed his headset as he steered. I looked out of the window and everything became crystal clear, black and white: black as the Detective Inspector's raven hair, white as the sergeant's peroxide bob. They were walking out of the hangar, Elvis talking into a mobile phone, Blondie waving a circle of uniformed officers to her side.

As the plane came to a stop, Elvis indicated with a flicked hand towards two cars which drove out of the hangar. They screeched to a halt either side of the plane and the heavies unloaded themselves. My heart skittered. I turned to Alex and said, 'Now's a good time to hand myself in,' or something false-funny like that. I can't remember exactly what I said. Alex switched the engine off, leaned across and kissed my cheek. 'I will wait for you.' He seemed very pale, as if in shock. I kind of laughed, sniggered, a childish scoff. One of the heavies gestured for me to alight from the plane. 'This is the end of the road then,' I said, unclipping my safety harness.

'I'll wait for you,' Alex said again, practically slumped over the steering.

That was all I needed to hear. I opened the door and felt a warm southerly on the place Alex had kissed. A bearded man got hold of my left arm. A younger, fitter man got hold of my right. They span me around and padded me up and down for weapons, which was laughable. They led me towards a marked car. Blonde Bob marched over and read me my rights. 'I am arresting you on suspicion of murder...you don't have to say anything...' blah blah blah.

'Whatever,' I said.

She dragged my hands behind my back and cuffed me. She pressed down on the top of my skull, pushing me into the rear seat. 'In you go, Cassi,' she said. I'm not kidding. That's what she said, with a sense of satisfaction. She got in beside me and told the driver to head for the station. I looked out of the window, craned my neck to get one final look at Alex.

That's when I saw them together - Alex and Elvis - Fortune and Lawless. They were talking like old chums. They seemed to be holding hands. I felt the kiss he'd planted on my cheek sinking through my skin like a penny dropping, my heart breaking. I yelled so loud it hurt my throat, almost burst my own eardrums, and the driver nearly crashed the car into Alex's plane, which would have been some sort of justice: 'Judas!'

There was no justice; no way Alex could have heard me.

The police car took me back to Pensbury. All the way, I was thinking about my Saab stuck outside Smuggler's Cottage waiting for an other me who was not arrested at the airfield; the other Ben Tippet who in a parallel universe was still free and driving full tilt to Incham, then travelling en route to the Channel Tunnel and France and the world beyond, picking grapes and pouring wine, and re-inventing a whole new life.

On the outskirts of the city we got snarled up in holiday getaway traffic. Blonde Bob had a discussion with the driver about the school holidays. She was going to take her son to Paris Disneyworld this year. How about that for irony? I think she was rubbing it in; my imminent incarceration.

They took me through electrical spiked side gates, the gates I'd seen last December, when maybe I should have handed myself in. A Duty Sergeant checked me over, told me my rights again, emptied my pockets, removed my shoes and banged me up in a cell by myself. I was allowed one telephone call and phoned my parents saying a terrible mistake had been made.

It was a full day before I was first interviewed and in that time I had to calm myself down. I was thinking, why? Why grass on me, Alex? Is it your overbearing moral rectitude? Your uprightness? Your incorruptibility? Integrity? Your tender conscience? Your truthfulness? Your ever-so-clean hands now that they were truly wiped of me? You stainless creep! Back-stabbing fucker! I hated you, Alex. I wished you dead. I wished I'd taken the controls of your stupid plane and crashed us both into the eroding White Cliffs of Dover! My reason being - if you love someone, you wouldn't deliver them into the hands of the police. You would want to be with them no matter what. If you loved them enough that is.

Here endeth the lesson, Alex. Though in reality it is yet to be learnt by either of us.

Sixteen

[Enter Judge and Jury]
The court room was not imaginary. In my cell, through my mind's warped and bloodshot eye, I'd envisioned mahogany benches, leather seats (House-of-Commons-green), a highly-decorated ceiling designed by Christopher Wren and walls with Gainsboroughs hanging. Something like that; something quaint and Olde Englishe going back to Magna Carta, 1215. Maybe some high-backed chairs, the faint whiff of snuff and a hint of beeswax lifting from the hand rails (I was never any good at history).

In the cold light of a November morning - there was no natural light but you know what I mean - the room was actually quite small, plain, featureless, ordinary. Two bailiffs led me to my seat; a box railed in to chest height so that when I was seated I had to peer beneath the rail as if it was a fat letterbox. There were rows of seats facing the judge's bench, two rows of six to my right where the jury would sit, and a public gallery slightly behind me, to my left, filled with friends and family of the bereaved, my mother and father and curious strangers. There was a small press gallery to my right, a vapid young man was looking at me and scribbling away at a page. Was he the BBC correspondent or the cartoon artist? My face would appear on TV tonight on the six o'clock news. I turned my head, showing my better side. I was some way back from the QCs' benches.

The bailiffs uncuffed me which was a relief. I was provided with a notepad and a blunt pencil should I wish to comment on proceedings to my lawyers and Dearing QC.

Dearing is a laconic sort of man, or chap, with a David Niven moustache. I'd met him only once; a briefing at which he issued me with advice. To be honest, I think he wanted to get a good look at me, gauge whether I could stand up to court room pressure; whether I was innocent or guilty of the crimes. He advised me to stay silent. Anything I might say may be used against me, he said. I'd convinced him of my innocence just as I'd convinced everybody else, including my parents, Maurice, Imogen *et al.* I'd almost convinced myself of my innocence by this stage.

Dearing was the best my parents could afford; one of the most reputable defence QCs in London, and in his opinion it was better I said plain nothing. 'But I want to tell the jury what happened.'

'I shall endeavour to do precisely that,' Dearing said, an expertly-folded pink handkerchief lolling in his top pocket like a dog's tongue. 'The onus is on the prosecution and they have a very weak case against us. You were not in Broadstairs that night. You were with Ms Wood in Pensbury.'

'What about my confession?'

'To the novelist?' he said. 'Leave him and the so-called confession to me.'

I didn't know what he meant exactly, though I thought he meant Alex would get a pummelling. I'd told Dearing everything about him, from the autobiography to the remand visit.

No. I wouldn't be called upon to defend myself. That was what Dearing and his team were there for. Under no circumstances must I speak directly to Mr Justice Cummings either; the presiding judge who quote unquote: 'Doesn't suffer fools gladly.' These were Dearing's own words. 'Be assured. This is the strongest case I've seen. Do not react to provocation. The jury will stare at you and you must deflect their attention. Don't smile, don't frown. Judgements are made on first impressions. Stare at the back of my wig if you have to but don't curry favour with the judge, the jury or the press. Let the facts speak for themselves.' That's what he'd said and repeated again just before entering the court room on this, the first day of the trial.

The jury were led into the room via a private entrance. I tried not to look at them but it was difficult. Eight women and four men. Some of them hadn't been bothered to dress up for the occasion, looking quite dowdy, as I suppose they should as "twelve ordinary people empanelled from the electoral register". They ranged in age from twenty to seventy, though it was hard to tell because one wore a hajib. She stared at me through her letterbox. There was a middle-aged man with flyaway hair, most of it already flown; an old man with frosty white hair and beard with a look so grave it froze my blood; a young man as black as Moses; and a clutch of others who looked professional in suits.

In keeping with the funereal mood, I was wearing my black suit; the one my mother had collected from my flat. She'd also brought a crisp new white shirt which was problematic as she'd artificially starched the collar and it chafed my Adam's. I wore a conservatively blue tie, 100% Italian silk. I'd shaved as close as was humanly possible. I'd combed my collar-length hair straight back from my face. I looked like an apprentice undertaker. My mother waved from the gallery and Dad smiled. They were at the end of a row because of the wheelchair space. I was their blue-eyed boy. Never so much as picked my nose in private.

The jurors' hungry eyes were upon me, eating me ravenously. I tried to ignore their gaze, imagining they were not twelve ordinary people but a multi-headed animal with too many legs and heads and hands and eyes. I tried to depersonalise them, but as the trial proceeded, I sneaked little looks. Two among them seemed nice; a man in his thirties and a woman in her early forties. Very professional-looking in suits, intelligent faces. I hoped one of these was the foreman - the one who might sway the others in my favour, like Henry Fonda in *Twelve Angry Men*. If Dearing knew what was going on behind his back, he might have told me off, but I did smile at these two now and then. Nothing obvious. Not a cheeky or belligerent smile, just an interested-in-them smile. A winning smile; a subtle come on which worked so well in the outside world.

Mr Justice Cummings entered the room through a separate entrance behind a high chair. An usher said, 'All rise' and everyone stood up like they were in church. Cummings gave the room a cursory glance before taking his throne-proportioned seat.

I'd been wondering what he'd look like. All I can say is that he was an old codger, grumpier than Victor Meldrew, dressed in a scarlet gown with a black sash tied around it, and a dusty wig on top. He was red in the face, and the trial hadn't even started (I call him itchy-wig because whenever he gets irritated, he scratches his scalp like a dog with fleas).

The first day was presentation of the prosecution's evidence: photographs and fire-fighter videos taken on December 19th. The jurors appeared horrified and I fidgeted in my seat. Mr Prosecutor QC (he's called Middle) froze the video and explained how the fire had started. He asked questions of his first witness, an officer in charge of the blaze that night. Perhaps something shoved through the letterbox of the Acorn Offices. No evidence of an accelerant though.

One-by-one, eyewitnesses took the stand, speaking of high winds that fanned the Broadstairs' inferno, the flames ripping through the building on towards town. The firefighters' biggest concern had been to stop the progression of the fire, its spread to shops and residential homes adjoining the building on three sides. 'It was a miracle,' the firefighter said, 'that the mass of flames didn't tear through the neighbourhood and a nursing home right next door.' There'd been a speedy evacuation, Zimmer frames and all.

Middle QC thanked the officer and the seven teams of firefighters, commending them for their bravery, 'without whom many more lives would certainly have been lost.' Nice touch, Mr Prosecutor.

'And the origins of the fire? You are convinced it was arson?'

'The fire was not electrical. It had started at the front door to the premises. Most probably arson.'

Most probably, not definitely.

'Members of the jury…,' Middle said (I've always liked hearing this on TV but not right there and then), '…the next images will be shocking, but we must bear witness to the full horror and tragedy of December the 19th. We must know what happened that night. We must understand the human tragedy, the result of this monstrous act of violence.'

Brilliant touch; monster and human in one sentence. Black and white. Good v Evil. Nosferatu, Vanhelsing, Harker. How I wish Middle would get in a muddle. Instead, he was brimming with confidence. Quite an academic approach. His manipulation of "professional" witnesses was excellent. A forensic expert, a firefighter, but Middle focussed ultimately on the "human" aspects of the case. The jurors leaned forwards in their seats to get a better look at the TV screen. An elderly lady among them, the spit of Miss Marple, put on her glasses.

The images came from a mobile phone camera; a ball of flames leaping from a raging inferno on the third floor of the Acorn building, crashing in a soundless pile onto the pavement below. There was an audible groan in the public gallery. It should have come as no surprise. The images had been touted months before the trial. I remembered watching it on the BBC and ITV and SKY. It had been repeated on a loop for days following the blaze until I could no longer bear to watch it. How could six sheets of story do that?

I caught in the corner of my eye a movement in the gallery at the opposite end to my parents. A slim, dark-haired, olive-skinned woman in a black jacket, holding a hand up to her face and a bulky man beside her, in a suit, putting an arm around her shoulder and squeezing. A young woman beside them glared at me. Was this the Belonog family?

Yes, I remembered them from TV, though they looked older now. I had done this to them. I'd taken their son and aged them. I was alive. My parents still had me. I moved my eyes to them. I had to remain calm. I had to spin this lie further. I had to cloak myself in innocence. I could live with my conscience. After all, I could not have known a cleaner would be working so late at the Acorn offices so close to Christmas.

Middle informed the jury of the victim's name. Stepan Belonog. Nineteen. Born in the Ukraine. A university undergraduate studying biochemistry by day, paying his way as a cleaner by night. This young man had been wiring money to his family each month, at the same time building a life for himself in the UK. He was planning to marry his erstwhile sweetheart (that word again. If I keep using it, it might make a comeback). Was the young woman in the gallery Stepan's fiancée or his sister? All gone to waste in the flames. I heard Stepan's mother crying and resisted looking in her direction.

A forensic pathologist was summoned to the box; a stiff-looking gentleman called Professor Hardcastle. He confirmed death as a cranial haematoma consequent of a fall. 'However,' he said, 'the deceased suffered third-degree burns on his legs and hands, torso and head. About 80% coverage. If he had not died from the fall he would most certainly have died from the burns sustained.'

A horrible death then. Unimaginable pain then. Mumbled groans in the gallery.

A clerk of the court circulated what must have been pathology photographs, judging by the jurors' gruesome facial ticks and expressions. The letterbox-juror was horrified and unblinking, the man with frosty hair stroked his beard which might come off in his hand, Miss Marple held her heaving bosom and Mr Flyaway hair wished he could fly away. The more intelligent-looking ones maintained neutral faces.

I sucked my teeth for moisture.

'These,' said Middle QC, 'show the true and terrible extent of Mr Belonog's injuries.' All eyes now on the jury. Those in the gallery were more horrified than the jurors, their imaginations running riot no doubt, just as mine was. No one needed photographs to see a gnarled up charcoaled body of a man on a slab. Couch potatoes watching too many *Silent Witness* programmes.

The trial had started at 10 a.m. and proceedings so far had taken two and a half hours. Judge Cummings said there was now going to be a break of one hour for lunch. He didn't even say it ironically. Who could say they had an appetite after what they'd just heard and seen? Humankind saddens me.

'All rise,' an usher said. The judge removed himself and the jurors were led out. The public gallery buzzed lightly and I had time to catch my parents' waves. I was taken down to cells beneath the court rooms where I was locked up with a plastic cup of coffee and a snarling, cellophane-wrapped cheese sandwich. Many of the cells were occupied by other defendants, some making horrible whinging in-growing-toenail noises, drunk on desperation and dread. An officer paced along the corridor, keys ajangle, telling the worst offenders to 'put a sock in it'.

These were the bowels of the body of the Law, the labyrinthine intestines of Justice you don't get to see in the real world, even on freak show TV. So, this was where I'd spend my lunchtimes for the next two weeks then. Whenever the trial got adjourned, this hell-hole would be my lot. Sometimes, when the QCs were wrangling over issues and itchy-wig Cummings called for a break, this was where I would be taken. Might be an hour, could be two or three. Up and down the bowels like a peristaltic piece of food. Sometimes I'd not return to the dock until the following day, being driven back to Pensbury each time. Back and forth. Back and forth. My wrists ached with the yoke of the handcuffs. Off and on. Off and on. Off and on again. I had red bands like bangles on my wrists from all of this.

The noise doesn't stop in the bowels. It is a full but empty place. My mother would call it purgatory. I knew she was praying for me, taking her rosary beads each day to court. I'd sit in the bowels wondering about sitting elsewhere: Southgate Gardens bench, having a pub lunch with Maurice in the Bishop's Finger, in the garden of Smuggler's with Alex. This is what you get when you set fire to a building and kill a man: regrets.

But I had to be strong. These were just the facts so far and none of them linked me to the scene; that's what my brief came down to tell me at lunch time. He sat in my cell, told me not to be concerned about Middle QC. Middle was in a hard place, he said. He was a clever prosecutor but Dearing had all of the cards. Once the evidence was laid before the jury, things would swing in my favour. 'In fact,' this lawyer told me, 'if the prosecution doesn't advance their argument faster than they are currently Dearing's going to submit to the judge that the Crown has failed to establish an adequate case for you to answer.'

'You mean I might be let out?' (How naive can I have been?)

'Not today,' he said. 'In a few days. Let's wait for the police evidence. Dearing will know what to do come the right time.'

My nemesis was in the witness box in the afternoon: DI Vincent Lawless, AKA Elvis. Vincent? I was thinking. That's a strong name, though a little arty-farty for a copper. My dead brother's best friend was called Vincent, wasn't he? He got a mention in Tom's diary at least. For a moment I meditated on the possibility that this man might actually be Tom's old school friend; he was roughly the right age, in his thirties. My life might be utterly ironic like that.

His job was to put me in Broadstairs on the night of the fire and give me motive for being there. I'm not kidding you; besides my self, Elvis was the most physically striking individual in the room. A ferocious gaze. A swaggering poise. Tall and straight-backed but loose and relaxed at the same time in his expensive dark blue suit. He put one hand on the rail, the other holding his notes. He had sex appeal is what I'm saying. Women and men of the jury visibly swooned. He was a man's man and a woman's man. He'd had his mop of black hair cut quite neat since we last clapped eyes in Pensbury police station - Interview Room 3. I couldn't shake the image of him hand-in-hand with Alex at the airfield back in July. The novelist and the iconic police detective. Now that would make an interesting love-affair or basic outline for a whole series of crime books. Fortune and Elvis, Elvis and Fortune; something like that.

Alex. Where are you Alex? Will you watch me on the news?

I scanned the room. My stomach growled. I hadn't been able to eat the gnarled up sandwich because my stomach was so gnarled up itself. The Belonogs were in situ, faces bleached with tension; no doubt replaying the ball of flames falling to the pavement, the way I came constantly to see their son fall.

Elvis was good. A real pro. Experienced and well-prepared. A natural. They say on remand that he always gets his man. Everyone knows Elvis. Flawless Lawless. Vincent. Whoever. He is a houndog who knows where the bones are buried. He was on my tail today and the assembled crowd waited with baited breath. First, he provided names and dates and places. He did not look at me for the initial few questions, just answered efficiently. He addressed his replies calmly to the jury and the judge and to Middle QC.

The real Elvis would not have been so methodical. He might have curled his lip for the press in the gallery and swung his hips for the jury. He might whip out his microphone and give us a rendition of *Jailhouse Rock*. No. Too obvious. I know exactly which song he'd sing. I saw him doing exactly that; a Dennis Potter-like performance right before my eyes. I sat there in bemusement and amusement. The music started and Elvis loosened his tie, slipped his hips, jumped over the rail onto the impromptu stage before the QCs, singing and pointing at me:

Elvis: *You look like an angel*

(Jury: *Look like an angel*)

Elvis: *Walk like an angel*

(Jury: *Walk like an angel*)

Elvis: *Talk like an angel, but I got wise...*

...*You're the devil in disguise! Oh, yes you are. The devil in disguise. Ooh-ooh-ooh-ooh.*

You fooled me with your kisses
You cheated and you schemed
Heaven knows you lied to me
You're not the way you seemed
You're the devil in disguise
(Judge, waving his gavel : *Oh yes you are*)
You're the devil in disguise

(Judge: *Oh yes you are)*
The devil in disguise.

No such luck. We were in the real world after all.

Elvis told the jury how he'd trawled through the names salvaged from the Acorn fire in the belief that the arsonist had been an angry loser of the competition, beginning with those on the final short list and living in the UK (just over 150). He had started chasing down the males, arson being predominantly a male crime, and the fact that a man had been seen fleeing the scene on December 19th. Then he'd traced female names, coming to Cassi Hart in Pensbury. Perhaps, he agreed, he could have found this person sooner but the Acorn organisers said they received anonymous threats in the post, year on year, from frustrated writers. One of these had threatened to set fire to the building and had a London postmark. This had thrown Elvis off my scent for a while, but he soon returned to the original list.

'Cassi Hart?' Middle QC said. 'Explain how you came to know the defendant as Cassi Hart?'

So Elvis went on, driving nails into my coffin. That was the name I used as a pseudonym. A pen name. When first visiting me, he told the jury, I had lied about Cassi Hart, giving her a fictional past to cover the fact it was actually me.

To my complete surprise and Dearing's disappointment, Elvis had really done his homework too, revealing three other competitions I had submitted short stories to over the past eighteen months, each with Cassi's name and my Pensbury address on the entry form.

'So for all intents and purposes, the defendant *is* Cassi Hart?'

'Yes,' Elvis said, giving me a look, then turning to the judge. 'Cassi Hart is an anagram, your honour. Coming from the word catharsis. Getting things off of ones' chest. Letting off steam. Relieving oneself of a burden.'

Judge Cummings wrote this down as if it was a game of hangman. Finally, my QC stood up, injecting some common sense: 'Does any of this have any bearing, your honour? I mean…anagrams?'

Itchy-wig waved the complaint away. 'Go on, Inspector.'

Elvis said he'd been put off the scent again when my alibi surfaced; an alibi which turned out to be vague and unreliable. I couldn't help but smile. There was nothing wrong with my alibi. Some of the jurors were looking at me and I straightened my face out. So I was linked to a competition I'd lied about entering. So I lied about Cassi Hart. These didn't tie me to the fire. I couldn't have been there. I was an incorrigible liar (a communal garden weed), but not an arsonist and certainly not a killer. I was just pleased no one mentioned I once worked as an estate agent; that would have nailed me faster than anything else.

'Then there was the defendant's confession,' Elvis said.

I tried to remain calm but the whole time I was waiting for Dearing to say something. 'So-called confession, your Honour,' he said, as if he'd been woken up by my thought waves. 'We only have Mr Fortune's word for it and this can definitely be construed as hearsay.'

'Alleged confession, Inspector,' Cummings reminded Elvis.

Elvis went on: 'Mr Alexander Fortune telephoned the station on a Friday morning, late in July, explaining how the defendant had confessed to him about causing the fire in Broadstairs.'

'Do we have a recording?' Cummings asked, and Middle nodded.

A brief recording was played over the speakers; Alex's unmistakeable mid-Atlantic voice, ever-so-slightly wobbling: *This is the hardest thing I've ever had to do. I know who set the fire. He told me everything.'*

'What is his name again, Mr Fortune?'

'Ben Tippet. He's at my house. Outside right now. Getting in my car. I told him he should hand himself in. The fire was accidental. He didn't mean to hurt anyone.'

It was hard to swallow from the dock. Alex Judas.

'Make sure he doesn't go anywhere, Mr Fortune.'

'We'll be at the Calder airfield within half an hour. You'll find us there.' The phone went dead. A significant nail in my coffin. The Judas.

I shook my head theatrically so the jurors would notice how absurd this all was. I mouthed, 'Lies. Lies. Lies.' I was hotting up in my suit and wanted to loosen my tie but couldn't for fear of seeming guilty.

'And you arrested Ben Tippet at Calder airport?'

'Yes,' Elvis said.

'And later, what did you find in the defendant's car which was parked at Mr Fortune's house?'

'In the boot, we discovered clean clothes packed in a suitcase. We found his passport and £1,000 worth of Euros.'

'Evidence that he planned to flee the country?'

'Definitely.'

'And you interviewed Mr Fortune?'

'That evening at the station.'

So, Alex had been in the same building as me that night. When I had been thinking of killing him, us both, we'd been in the same police station, breathing distance from each other.

'And Mr Fortune told you about the defendant's confession?'

'So-called,' Dearing interjected.

'I believe the confession to be true, your honour,' Elvis replied. 'Everything that Ben Tippet confessed to Mr Fortune matches times and places, the modus operandi. Setting fire to a short story and putting it through the letterbox of the Acorn building. I believe the confession to be true.'

'Opinion, your Honour,' Dearing fired back.

'This is vital evidence,' Middle QC retorted.

Itchy-wig's wig got itchier. He turned to the jury and said, 'Let's just say the prosecution will call it "the confession" and the defence will call it "so-called confession". The jurors seemed perplexed.

'No further questions.' Middle QC re-took his seat and Dearing took to the floor. My daring Dearing do. He wouldn't let me down. Such a clever man. Cleverer than Elvis who was forcing back a smile.

'How many people entered the Acorn story competition last year, Inspector?' Dearing was looking at the jury, not at Elvis. Then, as Elvis was replying, Dearing looked down at the sole of his left brogue, as if he'd suddenly stepped in something unsavoury.

'In total?' Elvis said.

'In total.'

Elvis flicked through his notes, cleared his throat. '4,885.'

Dearing scoffed. 'How many?'

'4,885.'

'And how many of these were winners of prizes in the Acorn competition, Inspector?'

'Very few lived locally, sir.'

'I didn't ask about proximities, Inspector, merely how many won prizes out of...how many did you say? 4,885 entrants?'

'Ten,' Elvis said.

'Ten?' Dearing's moustache twitched with joy. He addressed the jury directly. 'Ten winners. Which leaves how many suspects for setting the fire exactly?'

'I know what you're trying to say...'

'How many?' Dearing repeated firmly. 'For a policeman you are not very good at numbers; just as bad as you seem to be with motives. Let me help you with the arithmetic. 4,885 - 10 = 4,775 possible suspects; people who might be disappointed enough to set fire to the Acorn building. How many of these did you interview?'

Elvis fought back. 'Only Mr Tippet lied about the pseudonym; only he lived close enough to the scene to get there and back within an hour, able to return for his alibi; only *he* has confessed to the crime itself, sir.' What a "sir" that was. An inflammable "SIR". Spitfire-hot.

Dearing wagged an accusing finger. 'Not so fast, Inspector. Precisely how many of these 4,775 people do you surmise set fire to the building?'

Elvis smiled at the judge. 'Everything points to Ben Tippet. His confession to Mr Fortune was confirmation.'

'How so?' Dearing pushed. 'You did not take my client in for questioning after your first meeting him in April. If he was your number one suspect, your prime suspect, Inspector, why not take him in? Why not get the confession yourself if you were so confident of his guilt?'

Elvis hesitated.

'I'll tell you why, Inspector. Because you had - still have – only circumstantial evidence. You discovered that my client had an alibi. He had been with his girlfriend that night in December. You had very little to link my client with the crime and then this confession came along in July, just in the nick of time. The case was growing cold, wasn't it? You had no one else to fit the crime. Why not Ben Tippet?'

'Your Honour,' Middle QC interjected. 'It is now my honourable friend who states opinion.'

'Stick to the facts, the evidence, Mr Dearing,' itchy-wig said.

'I wish others would do the same,' Dearing moaned for the jurors' benefit, a little rattled, but not too perturbed. 'What we have heard thus far in this trial, awful, terrible, tragic though it is, has been largely based on fact: how the victim died; how the fire was *probably* started. But what he have now is a series of suppositions.

'My client, Mr Benjamin Tippet,' (he turned to look at me and I smiled at him which he didn't want me to do) 'my client here has never denied that he wrote under the pseudonym Cassi Hart. He told you, Inspector, at Pensbury police station, that he'd written under that name to improve his chances of winning the competition. Didn't he volunteer this information freely? Didn't he say he was embarrassed to admit writing under this female name? Didn't he also tell you he made up a ridiculous confession to Alexander Fortune because he had felt inferior to his hero? It made him feel more "important". The confession that Alexander Fortune reported to you in his police statement bears little resemblance to my client's. It has been embellished by Mr Fortune for his own purposes.'

Cummings intervened. 'Mr Dearing, shall Inspector Lawless be allowed to answer any of your questions or are you going to run roughshod through the whole cross-examination?'

Dearing conceded. 'Inspector?'

'Once the defendant had no alternative and he was cornered, once he'd confessed to the crime, Ben Tippet manufactured lies to cover his tracks. Up until that point he didn't volunteer any information. If he'd not confessed to his lover, well...'

God. The word lover. My parents were discovering things about me during this trial they'd rather not know; things I'd rather keep from them. Just the word lover had me shrinking into my shoes; the glow of my parents.

'What?' Dearing threw his hands in the air. 'You're saying that in the time it took to drive him from Calder airfield to Pensbury police station my client manufactured these elaborate lies?'

'I'm sure he was prepared for all possible outcomes, sir.'

'No, Inspector. He did not have that level of foresight. He told you the whole truth the day of his arrest because the so-called confession had got him into trouble. But it suited your purposes to believe otherwise.'

'As it suited our purposes to discover the things in the boot of his car in Incham?'

My daring Dearing do said, 'Do you take holidays, Inspector? It is not a crime to pack clothes in a suitcase and take a passport and some money. My client often went to France. Hadn't he been there twice in the previous eight months? No, Inspector. Something smells bad here. Does my client have any previous convictions?'

'No.'

'Not for any violent crime?'

'No.'

'For arson?'

'There's always a first time.'

'No history at all? Stealing a biro from Menzies, perhaps?'

Judge Cummings sighed. He disliked flippancy on this sort of scale, and Dearing reined himself in. 'What I'm suggesting, Inspector, is that in your haste to catch the perpetrator of a fire, you barked up the wrong tree. Indeed, you could have barked up any number of trees in an entire forest.' That was a very funny metaphor, clichéd though it was. Elvis changed his stance, shifting weight from one hip to the other. Not so snaky swivelling now. 'We can dismiss motive because it's not exclusive to my client. There are thousands with this particular motive. We can dismiss opportunity. My client has a legitimate alibi. What? What is it you want to say, Inspector?'

'When interviewed at Pensbury University in April, Ms Imogen Wood stated that the defendant arrived at her house at 10pm but could not be absolutely certain because she was ill.'

Dearing flapped his arms. 'Ms Wood said my client was at her house at 10pm? And the fire is believed to have been started at between 10pm and 11pm?'

'Yes, but after Ben Tippet's confession in July I reinterviewed Ms Wood. This time she said she couldn't be sure of the time he arrived. Quote unquote, "it was probably between 10 and 11, but maybe later."'

'Room for doubt then, Inspector?'

'Well...'

'Certainly room for reasonable doubt, just as there is reasonable doubt surrounding the so-called confession. One man's word against another's.' Dearing flipped through a file on his desk.

'There are huge discrepancies between what my client said and what Mr Fortune heard. There are a gulf of discrepancies in this case, so huge you could call them Grand Canyons.'

(Objection, your Honour. That metaphor is totally awful!)

'Thank you, Inspector,' Dearing said, re-taking his seat. Job done.

I thought he'd done really well, despite a wobble on the alibi. Elvis had been clever slipping it in at that moment. He looked towards Middle QC expecting some sort of counter-response but nothing came. It was approaching 4pm and Cummings had had enough. He raised his voluminous eyebrows, nodding to the clerk.

'All rise.'

Day 1 was dead and buried. I was cuffed, placed in the bowels of the court, then returned to Pensbury prison. I had glanced up at my parents on my way out and they had smiled; grimaced really. I thought this would be the hardest day; hearing and seeing all the evidence against me and facing the true victims of my crime in court, the Belonog family, and facing my nemesis, DI Lawless. But it was only the beginning. The tip of the proverbial ship-sinking iceberg. Tomorrow would be the prosecution's chief witness: Alex Fortune. My erstwhile lover. My Judas.

Seventeen

[Enter Alex]
The court room was abuzz. A great deal hinged on Mr Alexander Fortune's statements, not least a door to freedom, or prison proper. After all, he was a well-known novelist and had been the accused's lover and confessor. *The Arsonist's Confessor.* Now there's a book title to titillate the taste buds, and if not a book then an interesting prospect for the jury and gallery. The jurors, already in situ, were more animated than on the first day. Alex was toppling Vincent aka Elvis in the media stakes, and he wasn't even in the room yet.

I clocked my parents in the gallery, same place as the first day, and the Belonogs at the other end of the same row. My mother was in a dark dress, her raincoat neatly draped over the rail in front of her. She blew me a kiss and I felt it touch the side of my face.

Alex came in, stepped up into the witness box and the gallery murmured. *That's him. That's the writer. He's gay.* Something like that no doubt. He held the handrail for ballast. Poor Alex. He looked like he hadn't slept in weeks, hadn't eaten for days. The summer tan had gone. His cloud-grey eyes were heavy and darkened. He raised his head a little to be sworn in. The atheist being sworn in! He cast his eyes briefly towards me. A strained smile. He was trying to smile for my sake and I was grateful. My lover, idol and nail in my coffin.

Middle QC tried to put him at ease. 'Please tell the jury what you do for a living, Mr Fortune, though I suspect many know already.'

'Novelist,' Alex said, facing the jury.

Middle went on sycophantically about Alex's literary reputation, his good name etc. I noticed then that Alex was wearing the brown corduroy jacket he wore at the reading in Little's bookshop back in April, and wondered if he was wearing it because it would mean something to me. Dearing QC shook his head disparagingly each time Alex answered questions.

Middle was building Alex up in the knowledge that Dearing QC would try to knock him down. Isn't that the way it goes with witnesses? It is the British custom in microcosm. If you are famous in America you are famous forever but in the UK you are made infamous inside six months because the British enjoy hunting and spoiling success. The British enjoy bringing people down a peg or two. Whereas Americans polish their egos, the British scratch them up like keying flashy new cars.

My heart beat faster when Middle moved the line of questioning onto our relationship. 'A sensitive issue, of course, Mr Fortune.' Sensitive for me too. My parents were in the gallery. They knew none of the intimate details of my relationships with men or women. I'd kept them secret, as you do. Just as a child, you can't imagine your parents doing it, they, as parents, can't bear the thought of you doing it either. It's against the laws of human nature to visualise it.

'How did you meet the defendant and how did things develop from there?'

Alex stuck to the facts. My letter to him, then the reading at Little's.

'So, he approached you?'

This was Middle's game plan, just as my brief had expected; to suggest I was a frustrated wannabe, hanger-on, groupie, one of those kiss-and-tell freaks (I am some of these things I guess).

Alex nodded. He told the court about the blooming of our relationship which he described as 'a natural, organic affair that flowed out of mutual interests.' I felt my neck burn. The word "affair" and my mother's glare. I think she despised him. She never mentioned him during prison visits. Alex had corrupted her blue-eyed boy and I'd not told her any differently. Bad enough that Benjamin banged boys as well as girls without them being old enough to be his father; bad enough already that my mother's only brother had turned into her older sister! That had been leaked to the press. Uncle D's neighbour wanting to make a few quid. The TV and newspaper journalists were all over my trial. They smelled a double-killing today. Yet, my mother clung to her faith, the holy beads in her hand.

'Let me clarify, Mr Fortune. You were lovers?'

Another blush in the dock and a glare from the gallery.

'Yes.'

'For how long?'

Alex looked at me again. 'Three months or so.'

'And this was an intimate relationship?'

'We were very close,' he said.

April-to-July flashed by. The months had been slow and easy at the time; a long and glorious summer. Being up in the air with Alex, down in the grass with him, on his four-poster, in the Greek infinity pool, signing a shabby napkin; proof if proof be needed. That napkin might be worth something one day.

As you well know, I'm a sexbloodymaniac. I've had my fill of sexual encounters for someone not quite twenty-six. I've done it in toilets with strangers, swimming pools with familiars, in the sea, in a lift once, standing up and sitting down, done it on a gravestone in Pensbury. I've done it upside-down. But I have only ever done it inside-out with Alex. It mattered is what I mean. Alex had never said he loved me but he is the kind of man who shows you, not tells you, like a good writer should. Why come visit me on remand if I meant nothing? Why, on the day he delivered me into the hands of the police, did he say he would wait for me? Why wear the same clothes today that he wore when we first met, if I meant nothing? (And why then had I judged him for only doing what he considered the best thing for me? His actions were taken out of cool and considered altruism. I had forced his hand.) Yet, deep down, I knew his statements today would nail my sorry arse.

Dearing QC was waiting in the wings, sharpening knives in his mind.

The confession now. No point in going over it again. You know about the flight in Alex's plane, and lying in Smuggler's Cottage garden, and the truth coming out of my mouth. How I wish I'd done things differently.

Alex spoke the truth. Nothing but the truth. My mother looked ready to spit bullets. The novelist perverter of her baby Benjamin. The Belonogs had tears in their eyes. I could see them even from where I was sitting (corner of my eye). They believed every word of the confession. They had to. I don't blame them, but I'm not going down for this crime. Not for an accident. One stupid moment of extraordinary anger. Lies have served me relatively well so far. Too late to turn a new leaf. Not here. Not now. Oh, Alex. What have I done to you? What are you going to do to me?

He looked relieved when Middle QC said, finally, 'No further questions, your Honour.' Alex thought he could go, started stepping down.

Dearing stood and itchy-wig Cummings said, 'Please, Mr Fortune. The advocate will be asking some questions as part of the cross-examination for the defence.'

Alex re-took the stand, long pianist fingers holding onto the handrail once again. So pale his face, so dark his eyes. Poor Alex. I put you in this box from which you cannot escape. The daggers are out and I am helpless to prevent them from sinking into your back.

I needed the daggers if the truth be told. Now I was the Judas, plain and simple. After all, Alex, who knew your secret life better than I? Not your ex-wife certainly; not your estranged daughters definitely; not BB Crum who, as far as I knew, was still on the other side of the Atlantic. None of them had read your autobiography-in-progress; none had shared your intimate spaces as recently as I. Who cradled your addled head at three in the morning when you had one of your "life-threatening" headaches? Who stemmed the weeping for your mother? Who had seen into the soul you said you never had? Who - dressed only in a kitchen apron - danced and sang along to David Bowie in your drawing room to cheer you up when you were really down? I wriggled and jiggled and leg-kicked my way around the drawing room, singing into a wooden spoon: *Rebel, Rebel, your face is a mess....Rebel, Rebel, you've torn your dress...How could they know? Hot tramp, I love you so...* That was you; that was me. Now look at us!

Alex sensed what was coming next, his frame stiffening. Dearing QC was ironic all of a sudden. 'Mr Fortune. Let's be clear about something right from the beginning, shall we? By intimate relationship you mean you were having sex with my client?' My Dearing daring do at full tilt, Niveneqsue moustache doing a dance. He was going to shaft Alex's reputation: sexual predator, has-been novelist.

'Yes,' Alex replied, and I felt my face glow.

'You were having sex with my client.' Dearing paused so that the jury could soak up the imaginary details, then he pressed on with his plan. 'You live in a small hamlet in England, don't you, Mr Fortune?'

'Yes.'

'And in America too?'

'I have a property in the States. I spend time here and there.'

'And do you sell many of your books *here and there?*'

'I don't follow.'

'Neither do I,' said itchy-wig Cummings.

'Let me explain,' said Dearing. 'I have a list of your book sales over the past decade. It shows that you sell rather well in America. Your crime novels are well-received in America. You write crime novels, don't you?'

'My novels have crimes in them but I wouldn't call them crime novels per se.'

'But they sell very well in America, *per se?*'

'Very well,' Alex replied.

Dearing looked down at the piece of paper in his hand. 'Yet you sell hardly anything in the UK.'

'Not as many.'

Dearing sneered, 'A prophet not accepted in his own country perhaps?'

'I wouldn't consider myself a populist author, or Jesus, if that's what you mean.'

The gallery tittered.

'Populist in America, though?'

'The American public are more discerning than the British give them credit for,' Alex replied. I think he was trying to outwit his questioner, play to the gallery, fight back, like he had done at the Little's Q and A session. But this was no oldie worldie bookshop; this was not a cartography room.

Dearing continued to sneer. 'Maybe the British readership have better taste?'

The public gallery tittered again and Cummings scowled. 'This is not a book club and not a literary criticism seminar either, Mr Dearing. Get to your point.'

'Your Honour, I am merely suggesting to the jury that Mr Fortune may well be a shining star in America but the glow has gone out this side of the Atlantic. His literary reputation has been overblown by my learned friend and this has a strong bearing on the so-called confession. Mr Fortune, you had much to gain by going to the police, didn't you? Rekindle public interest in you? Good press? Free publicity?'

'Really!' Middle QC pleaded.

'I'll move on,' said Dearing, having made his point, but it was clever because he was still making it. 'Are you working on a new novel at the moment?'

'No.'

'No? Let me put this another way. You are currently working on a book?' I looked at my feet, feeling the heat from Alex's eyes on the top of my head. 'An autobiography, isn't it? *The Art of Decomposing?*'

'It has no title as yet,' Alex said.

'Is it nearly complete?'

'I wouldn't say so.'

'You have a final chapter to write?'

Eyes burning into me again. 'Possibly.'

'This would make an excellent final chapter, wouldn't you say? A crime novelist taking the stand in a serious trial?'

Judge Cummings waved Middle QC back to his seat, mildly interested himself. 'Answer please, Mr Fortune, but I'm warning you, Mr Advocate, not to base your arguments on suggestion or opinion.'

Dearing nodded, almost bowed. 'Mr Fortune, I put it to you quite bluntly; with flagging sales there would be pressure to deliver a successful book this time. Your relationship with my client and his trial would make excellent copy as fiction, wouldn't it? I mean your autobiography? Come on, this makes meaty prose no matter which way you cut it. I've never known a case to be covered so meticulously before and during a trial, and no doubt afterwards. But onto other matters. I can see this is difficult for you.' Point made, Dearing QC asked Alex about his past marriage. 'You divorced from your first wife in 1993?'

'You make it sound like I've had more than one.'

Sniggers in the gallery.

'Your wife divorced you on the grounds of adultery?'

'The symptom of a failing marriage.'

'You are famed for your affairs, Mr Fortune. You never remarried?'

'No.'

'Was it a homosexual affair?' (My mother's and father's eyes!) Alex looked pleadingly at the judge who shrugged his shoulders. 'In the past dozen years you have had a string of affairs, Mr Fortune. I put it to you that my client was the last in a long line of short-lived relationships. He was good fun, no doubt. A good-looking, naïve conquest. My client was attracted to you by your reputation as a novelist; the trappings of writing success. He was young, attractive, impressionable. He wanted to be a writer just like you. You used him, Mr Fortune.'

'Your Honour!' Middle barked.

'Your Honour, it's in my client's statement to the police. To be seen as more interesting in the eyes of his literary idol, he lied about setting the fire in Broadstairs. He lied to feel important. It was not physically possible for him to have been in Broadstairs at the time of its setting. My client felt inadequate beside the Colossus that was Alexander Fortune. He concocted what can only be described in layman's terms as a complete cock and bull story.'

Middle was out of his seat gesticulating. 'Your Honour?'

I was out of my seat about to blow everything. 'No. No. It was me! He's telling the truth. It was me!' But I was pushed squarely down by a bailiff.

'Isn't it true that you visited my client on remand less than two weeks ago?' The look on the prosecutors' faces. They hadn't seen that coming, but there was nothing they could do about it. Middle got in a muddle, all tongue-tied.

'Yes,' Alex said.

'It's most unusual for a chief prosecution witness to go and see a defendant awaiting trial, Mr Fortune.' He was addressing the jury and judge as much as the witness. 'Why did you visit him?'

'Because I felt guilty for-'

'Guilty?' Dearing almost leapt with joy, his trap springing. 'Guilty for what exactly?'

'For forcing Ben's hand.'

'For forcing my client's hand. I see. You believed this naive 25-year-old man, a bookseller by trade, and now - how did you describe him in your police statement?' My ears pricked. Dearing took a file from a side-kick lawyer. 'You described him as "foolish, with delusions of grandeur".' The words struck like arrows between my shoulder blades. 'You believed this boy's story about the fire? A story he has never denied making up? You believed this fiction? That he destroyed a building and killed a man because he had not made a shortlist?'

'Unfortunately, yes,' Alex said, unable to look at me.

Dearing scoffed. 'Couldn't you see it was laughable? Naive? Foolish? Deluded? I put it to you, Mr Fortune, that you wanted to believe the cock and bull story because it suited you to believe it. You are an opportunist. Struggling to be popular in this country, struggling to sell your books, an autobiography due out within a few months, you seized this opportunity as if handed to you on a gilt-edged platter. You had everything to gain by going to the police.'

'It wasn't like that.'

'How else could it have been? You are the older, wiser, far more experienced man. What had my client to gain? No, in a moment of madness, a fit of envious pique, my client spun a yarn and you reeled him in. You had the power in this relationship and you abused that power abominably.'

I leapt to my feet. 'It wasn't like that!' The bailiffs struggled to push me down.

'Mr Dearing, advise your client to remain silent during proceedings or he'll be taken down to the cells.' I hated being talked about in the third person as if I was invisible or in another room or dead. 'Alex! Alex, I didn't mean for this!'

'Bailiffs?' Cummings said, and they got hold of my arms.

'I'll be quiet,' I said, sitting down again, and Cummings nodded.

Dearing frowned at me. I was stinking his pitch, or whatever you call it. 'I have nearly finished with the witness, your Honour,' he said, turning again to his prey. 'You visited my client before this trial began in order to assuage your guilt, Mr Fortune. Not because you had forced his hand but to advance your own. And once done, like Macbeth, you became a prisoner of your own conscience. That's what you have to live with. No more questions, your Honour.'

Dearing had stitched him up. Ashen-faced, the weary novelist stepped down, looking fleetingly in my direction, never catching my eyes, stumbling backwards. He was caught at the elbow by a male usher. Alex had never seemed so old and frail. He was becoming all the things he most feared.

For the press it was the highlight of the show. For my mother it was probably a blessing from God. God had finally answered her well-fingered rosary bead prayers. For my dad it was nearly too much. For the Belonogs it was a never-ending circle of bad news. For me it was a half-open door to freedom. I should have been grateful to Dearing, but his smug, self-satisfied face turned my stomach. I watched Alex leave through the side entrance, held ajar by an usher. I wanted to cradle my lover's head. I wanted to smell *Physiognomie* on his pulse points. I wanted to stretch my fingers through the pianist's and say how sorry I was it had come to this. If I could have turned the clock back (and I've thought about little else since capture) I would have done it then.

The door closed over the back of him. The brown corduroy jacket he'd worn for me to remember, the lines of which were wide furrows in a freshly turned-over field. I would write to him. I would explain everything. I would not just let him go. Maybe he wouldn't want to know me, after such a de-trousering in the witness box. We were equals now. Both Judases.

Itchy-wig Cummings whacked his gavel down to silence the gallery. I was taken down to the bowels of the court, then transported back to Pensbury. Cummings adjourned proceedings for two days pending discussions with the QCs. Who knows, maybe a deal was being struck.

Eighteen

I can't tell you how mixed up I was or how miserable.

Alex once said that happiness is not something you can possess, it is a state of mind, a *feeling* of contentment. 'If you're not content with what you have and strive for more things, you will never be happy, because happiness is not a thing you consume. It consumes you.' (He could say that with collateral worth millions). 'I have everything,' he said, 'yet I don't have everything.'

The flipside of happiness, of course, is misery. Like happiness, misery is a thing which can consume you.

I was delivered back to jail at about 5pm, returning in time for lumpy lasagne and rubbery green beans. I ate nothing, having developed a keen dyspepsia, once described by a French writer as "the remorse of a guilty stomach". Manston prowled around the TV room but I couldn't face the news anyway. I returned to my cell and sunk my face into my pillow.

Everyone cries in here, they just do it when no one is looking. It is worse on remand because you are in a conscious and unconscious state of anticipation all the time. What will be my fate? Will the scales of justice tip in my favour? Will the double-headed coin of happiness/misery land this way or that? It is the same theory as a pint half-full or half-empty. Which one am I? Which one is Alex? Did I deserve to be happy? In the old days the poets called it melancholia; a fancy word for Churchill's Black Dog.

God knows how miserable I am. And it was God I next turned to. I had demons to exorcise. All of my life I think this has been coming. Payback for all the wrongdoings committed in twenty-five years. You can accumulate a lot of bad karma in that amount of time.

My mother visited me the next day. She came alone. Dad was feeling under the weather, she said, which is something he never usually feels. Maybe the homosexual revelations turned his stomach. I don't know. Mother was full of positivity. She fairly prickled. She mentioned Alex only once and only in the context of his corruptibility. We did not talk about the affair. Brushed under the carpet. She couldn't countenance that I was an arsonist, or in his arse. Not her blue-eyed boy.

'God sees everything,' she said.

Even through my thick skin and countless veils? She is so devout, so faithful, so confident. I wish I had her conviction. Never misses a Sunday service, even does the Stations of the Cross. She arranges flowers for weddings in church, appropriates the church kitchen at social functions making sure everything is in good order. She is close to the priest, Father Mackie, an Irishman in his late thirties, though I've never met him. He's quite new to the parish, replacing our old priest, O'Rourke, who was taken ill with old-age. What happens to old, retiring priests? Are they put on an island and forgotten about? That would make an excellent documentary. It's already a sitcom.

'Is there a chaplain on remand?' my mother said.

'All sorts commit crimes these days, mother.'

She didn't approve of the joke. There is one, of course. A Church of England chaplain who is available for chit-chats on a Monday and a Thursday afternoon. He sits in a little room on the other side of segregation block twiddling his thumbs, waiting for a flock to form. What he doesn't realize is that religion is largely dead in the hearts and minds of remanders. If any of them see him it is only to pass the time or break the monotonous prison routine.

So when mother asked me if I'd like to see Father Mackie, I was stunned. What had God ever done for me? What had I ever done for him? God hates liars. I could see it was important to her though. She pressed me some more until I caved in. 'Send him in, mother.' She squeezed my hand reassuringly.

Father Mackie showed the next day. No need to book his visiting appointment days in advance like everyone else. Priests still get privileges, well after the Lutheran Reformation. I haven't been to church since the age of 16 and even then under great parental duress. After the Tom epiphany, God was over for me. So I wasn't sure how to go about this visit. I was pleasing my mother. I could pass forty minutes for her sake. I had put her through plenty already.

Mackie wasn't in regalia. No gown, just ordinary shirt and slacks and pullover and jacket. The dog collar, like a slipped halo, was the only sign that he was a man of the cloth. I'd expected swinging silver balls of incense.

He smiled a serious smile. A bit put on. We talked about my mother for a while. Mackie looked good for his age, if you're bothered with such things. Since knowing Alex, I've developed similar obsessions as him. Rosy is how I'd describe Mackie. Vital. Short but well spread out. Maybe the casual clothes made him look closer to thirty than forty. The holy robes can transform a child into a man. As an altar boy, I thought the costume made me look older and more important, when actually it made me look like a girl.

He spoke in an engaging, rural, soft, west coast of Ireland tone, and to be frank I quite enjoyed our slot together. The visitor's room wasn't so busy because a lot of the remanders were in court. A lot of small-talk, but I find that without the small-talk there is nothing to build on; like foundations for much bigger things. Small-talk, I know from being with Alex, is the benchmark of a relationship, no matter how short. You can only screw for so long before you have to go shopping. If you can't talk about the small things, what's left to talk about? You're never going to solve the Arab-Israeli conflict but you can comment on each other's clothes until the cows come home.

So it was with Father Mackie. I called him "Father" more than once and he came on all informal. 'Call me Alan,' he said. "Alan" didn't seem right somehow. You know how some faces do not look like their names or some names don't sound like their faces? Father Alan Mackie was like that. He should have been a Kieran or a Patrick or a Colm or something.

'Ben,' I said, shaking hands again as if starting over on a more equal footing.

We didn't discuss my alleged crime. Taboo. We talked about music. He ran a church social club and allowed bands to play. He couldn't understand why I liked Bowie, me being twenty-five and Bowie just turned sixty. I didn't tell him why. I kept telling myself, you're just doing this for your mother.

But within fifteen minutes I was telling Alan all about my anxiety dreams. I told him about waking up in the dead hours of two and three in the morning, the times when you think you've slept like the dead only you've slept for just an hour or two. I told him I'd half-woken and discovered a shadow lurking in the darkest corner of my cell. This man would not identify himself, though I thought he was Tom, my dead brother. Was it a dream, a spirit, the devil or my tired imagination?

Alan didn't know. I told Alan that I spoke to this man in the corner of my cell for three nights running and it was always about being a good or a bad person.

'Did this man say anything?'

'He was non-committal. Infact, Father, I mean Alan. He never even turned his body around, so I couldn't see him. He murmured things like, "The jury's out on the soul". Do I have the devil in me, Father?'

'Just like anyone else, cat o licks can be good and bad, even at the same time.'

Cat o licks. That's how he spoke, and it was lovely.

Then I changed the subject, asking him if he disliked Protestants for vandalizing and ransacking the Catholic churches in England? Henry VIII and all that. The dissolution of the monasteries which Maurice had told me about. Pensbury Cathedral is C of E, but it didn't used to be. Without Catholic pilgrims visiting the Catholic saints inside, the C of E cathedral couldn't afford to keep the building waterproof.

Alan laughed. 'What goes around comes around. The Protestants will be the saving of the cat o lick faith.'

'How?'

'They're flocking to our church.'

'I see people on a badometer, a scale of badness from one to ten,' I said, 'with me at an eight or a nine. So will I go to hell?'

'It's God's barometer. He knows your mind and your soul.'

'I'd like to make a confession,' I said, freaking him out.

'I could come back at a pre-arranged time?' he replied, looking around the room.

'For years I have been living with guilt.'

Alan got in close. 'Guilt you say? Let it out then. Let it out.'

'There was a girl in junior school. She had a name that sounded like "Mildew". She was bullied because she spoke with a terrible lisp, wore shabby hand-me-down clothes and had this amazing pong. I swear there used to be crusty snot on her cuffs. But she was a human being nonetheless. I didn't stop the bullying. In fact, I was a fundamental element of her torture because I wouldn't dance with her in country dancing classes. I refused to hold her hand and wouldn't do the dosey-do. Ever since, I have thought about her. I regret the way I was but all I can do is reach out to her with the hand in my mind.'

'We all have regrets, Ben. We don't have to stay the person we were. We can change. We can be contrite.'

'There was another boy. In big school. I hate violence but I lashed out at him once because he took a piece of paper from my desk and wouldn't give it back.' I sniggered. 'A piece of sodding paper, Alan, with nothing on it. I rapped my knuckles on his cheek and he cried his glassy pebbles out. That's the only time I've ever hit anyone.'

'Then it was an effective lesson,' Father Mackie said.

'But when we were in a science lesson later that day, I continued to torment him, Alan. He was looking in a text book at a photograph of a group of piglets sucking at their mother's teats. It was a reproduction lesson. I pointed at the photograph and said, "That's your family". What about that?'

'Nothing you can say will shock me, Ben.' (A scene from *The Exorcist*, I was thinking. I could puke streams of mushy peas over his shoulder, swivel my head 360 degrees, stick the holy cruciform up my jacksie and this priest would still hold out hope).

'Father, I used to masturbate into my pillowcase three times a night.'

'These things happen in life.'

'When I was twelve, Father, Alan.'

'Children say and do things without the benefit of experience or self-control. It is who we turn into that counts. The grown-ups we become.'

'What if someone doesn't grow up? What if they still have no self-control? What if they never learn? Will they burn in hell?' I couldn't believe what was coming out of my mouth.

'You mustn't be so hard on yourself, Ben. We all do bad things. Cat o licks are no exception.'

'My mother believes that 100%.'

'Your mother is a good woman, a true believer.'

'She says the rosary every day for me like I am dead, Father.'

'She is praying for your soul every day and every night, Ben.'

My mother wanted me to join the priesthood, you know. Can you believe that? On the day of my Confirmation, she asked me if I'd like to live in a Jesuit college. How little can a mother know her own son, and vice versa? It's funny. I think about the Keys to the Kingdom a lot. You know? Peter at the gates. Only my Peter has a mobile phone, and each time someone approaches, he stops them like a bouncer might at a nightclub. He ticks their name off on a clipboard and makes a quick call to God (owner of the nightclub), and God - magician that he is - beams down lever-arch badness files on the sinner. From these, Peter makes his judgement. Are the squeaky gates opening or is it "on your bike"? When I approach, Peter checks me off on his clipboard, makes his call and a hundred lorries pull up on the drive, queuing around the block, each one full of my misdemeanours carved in blocks of stone. There are as many blocks of stone as there are pages in Tolstoy's *War and Peace* or Marcel Proust's *In Search of Lost Time* . St. Peter looks me up and down and says, 'What do *you* think, Tippet?'

'We have to look hard at ourselves, Ben. No one can change the past, we can only have an effect on the now and the future.'

Towards the end of the session we returned to the subject of my parents. How strong they were being; how the whole church was praying for us. Complete strangers! I asked if my dad attended the church and Alan nodded.

'Yeah? But Dad stopped going when I did.'

'We are all praying for you and for the soul of Stepan Belonog. You see, good things come out of bad. When God closes a door he opens a window. A window of opportunity.'

I was beginning to think the opposite inside my prison cell; that bad things come out of good things. I had come out of my parents, hadn't I?

'Do you pray?' Father Mackie asked; his final question before going. I shook my head. 'It needn't be to any particular god. It could act as a meditation. Bring you peace of mind.'

'I'll try that then,' I said, shaking his hand goodbye.

After he'd gone and I was back in my cell, I wondered what he'd made of me. Did he think I was guilty? Obviously I had a conscience. I had owned up to bad things. And I asked myself, is Stepan Belonog a cat o lick? Alex would have choked on his pistachios and G&T if he'd heard my thoughts. He'd probably keel over if he saw me get on my knees and pray the way I did in my cell. I faced the barred window, hands pressed together, mumbling to myself. 'If you are out there, God. If you exist, you will hear me now. I want you to take good care of Stepan Belonog's soul. I don't give a flying fig for myself, but he didn't deserve what happened to him. But while I'm at it, if you could find it in your heart to forgive me all the bad things I've done in the past, like at school, like in my pillowcase, that would be very much appreciated. I know I haven't been to church for years, and that even when I used to go I spent most of my time looking at people's clothes rather than reflecting on your omniscient and benevolent presence, and for these things I would ask your forgiveness.'

I waited. Didn't know what for. A thunderbolt? Rainbow? Dove? The Holy Spirit to enter me? I didn't see or feel anything. It was as if I'd cast an arrow out of the window into the sky and it had landed in the trunk of a very earthly tree. Or I had cast a pebble into a deep well, had cocked my head like a dog to listen for the splash, only the pebble never sounded, falling out the other side onto rocky ground at the feet of a bemused llama in the Australian outback, and the beast dumped straight over my pebble. Yes, Alex you'd keel over if you could see and hear my thoughts.

Alex, Alex, Alex. I'm missing you. Really missing you, especially after your appearance in court. Whenever I close my eyes I see myself sitting in your side-garden which you allowed to overgrow into a meadow with dandelions and daisies. I am sitting down in the middle of it, pulling up daisies; pulling off a tiny purple-tinged petal, saying to myself: 'He loves me,' letting it fall and picking off another petal, 'he loves me lots,' then another petal, 'he loves me,' and another, 'he loves me lots,' until there are no more petals left. I can never lose you that way.

Nineteen

Red passes by my cell carrying over his shoulder a sack of letters.

They are not all for me. We get post once a week and this week Red has drawn the short straw on postman duty. All letters are opened before being given to inmates just in case there are drugs or weapons lurking inside. Believe it or not, people have sent letters impregnated with Ecstasy and LSD and all sorts. Talk about eating the evidence! Apparently, one parcel recently arrived weighing something equivalent to a monkey wrench; staff opened it and found a monkey wrench!

Red does the others first and returns to my cell with a half-full sack. The letters have been growing in number since my arrest and the press coverage has broadened. It's slightly disconcerting to read the dates on some of the letters. They are always a few days old, getting caught in the system.

'Hate mail,' he says, tipping the sack's guts out onto my bed. I know he's joking by the creases around his eyes. He's not a very good liar.

There is hate mail, of course. One person hopes I burn in hell, another can't wait for Judgement Day to come. But why? It's not as if I walked into a shopping mall with a machine-gun, or travelled on the London underground with a ticking rucksack, or threw a grenade at the Queen. The English in these letters is pretty dire. I guess they are from the Ukraine. I wonder if any are written by a Belonog hand? Maybe Stepan's bride-to-be? Or his sister? I don't spend too much time on the hate mail. What's the point?

Fortunately, most letters are supportive. They start with *Dear Mr Tippet* or *Dear Ben. Dear Benjamin*, whatever. *Wishing you the best of luck with the forthcoming trial* (told you there is a delay with post). *I know you are innocent* etc etc. *My sister thinks you are good-looking* etc etc. To date, I've received five marriage proposals and three civil marriage proposals. Lots of mail from gay guys. They say they have rocks for me; not real rocks, oh you know what I mean. They enclose photographs but all photographs are removed and stored or kept by the prison staff because they are pornographic. There are supposed to be knickers enclosed, but ditto with them.

One letter says that I am all over the internet; photographs of me from when I was young up to the present day. How the hell did they get those? One letter tells me I am very handsome. Another says it is true, I do look like Montgomery Clift. You get the picture? I am being touted around the globe, on blogs, chat rooms etc. Everyone seems to be talking about me, grabbing a piece of my arse. A bisexual society in Illinois is inviting me to give a lecture when I am set free, all expenses paid and honorary membership etc.

I never reply to any of these letters. I've always detested labels of any sort, unless they are designer. I hate pigeon-holes, club badges, affiliations, societies, political parties, organisations etc. Maybe I'm a nihilist. I only represent myself. In court, I cannot represent myself. I can't speak without being spoken about in the third person like I died recently. The QC who defends me cannot truly represent me because he is an Oxbridge graduate. The QC who wants to nail me is the same. I am not like them. I am me, and only me, no matter what the outcome.

Dear Ben, you should own up to it – you are queer, not bisexual... (bin).

Dear Ben, I am bisexual (straight in the bin).

Dear Ben, I am like you (ditto).

Dear Ben, the press are slaughtering you in the name of censure, but it is because nobody understands we are coming from the same sexual... (bin).

Dear Ben, Alexander Fortune is a phoney... (bin).

Dear Mr Benn... (bin).

Dear Ben, I want to have your children... (bin).

I can't believe this stuff, in such large quantities it takes half the evening reading and binning. I need a shredder. They make me feel more like a freak than a celebrity. As mother said, the world is peopled with idiots and freaks and numbskulls. However, post day is the highlight of the week and I take pleasure and solace from well-wishers. They tell me I am photogenic, a handsome young Englishman with film-star looks, gorgeous and beautiful. But most of all, I am innocent. What do they know?

A more recent letter states that my name has been mentioned on the Richard and Judy show. They chaired a discussion on "wannabe culture" and my name got mentioned. More than this, one of my teachers appeared on the show saying I used to perform in school plays, that I always wanted the leading role, even if it was Miranda in *The Tempest!* (for the record, I played Caliban).

A ridiculous notion is wannabe culture. I mean, if no one ever wanted to be anybody or do anything the human race would run its course. If I'd appeared on the R&J show in person, I'd have said, 'From so-called wannabes icons come and from icons come wannabes. It's the cycle of artistic endeavour. All wannabes are equal but some are more equal than others. Though icons don't necessarily make good role models.' Something like that.

I'm being turned into a self-parody, a faker, a cardboard cut-out I always hated seeing in others. The media are dissecting my life. My neighbour, Mrs Heaton (The Sun called her a *buxom brunette!*), said she knew I was crazy, just by my eyes! The Guardian ran a feature saying I was the tip of a self-seeking psychotic iceberg, a symptom of what's wrong in our modern world. My childhood friend, Peter Klutz, sold his story: how *I* set fire to a school! Wormy ex-lovers, male and female, are coming out of the woodwork with their rotten stories too. I thought there was supposed to be a blanket press embargo during a trial? Prejudicial or something.

One letter informs me that Alex has gone into retreat at Smuggler's Cottage. Press photographers are climbing over his gates and walls and hiding in the bushes. There's not much left of me to strip bare at the age of twenty-five but there is an endless goldmine of Alexander Fortune. He has accumulated a lot of precious rock in fifty-two years. And seams and seams of bad stuff.

I'll never know how, or why, my parents still love me. The Tippets have been ransacked. Journalists go through the bins and hang around their bungalow asking lewd and leading questions. They chase my dad's wheelchair around Tesco's and snap my mother paying at the till. She's very photogenic which makes good copy. My mother and father have become as much celebrities and prisoners as I have. Less than a year ago I was a swell guy living in a modest flat, working in an ordinary bookshop in Pensbury. Now I am on the lips of TV hosts, in the gossip pages of shit-lit magazines, on the front pages of tabloids, in the editorials of broadsheets; not to mention being fired around the globe from the internet cannon. *You are around the world in eighty ways*, one person writes.

Why? Because I might have killed a man? No. If I looked like Marti Feldman instead of Montgomery Clift and hadn't slept with a famous novelist, do you think anyone would be interested? It would just be an immigrant dying in an office blaze; someone who shouldn't have been paid so little to do the work of a WASP who didn't want to do that kind of work.

I understand now what natural beauty can do. It can light up a room. It can turn heads and pages. It can fill your bed with strangers. But in the end it destroys everyone who looks at or touches it; anyone you touch, anyone who touches you. The Minus Touch. None less than poor Alex. As he would say if he were with me now in my cell, 'Every death is beautiful and ugly, because life is.' Such a cheery sod, but I love him regardless; miss him beyond belief.

[Anecdotal interlude about looking too good]

I used to go out with a woman who lived in Brighton. She was attractive in a conventional blonde, slim, athletic, obvious way. Her name was Megan Lake, which sounds like a place. She was studying leisure and tourism. We went out for half a year and in that time people I loosely term friends (they were all *her* friends) called us an "item". The beautiful, model couple. All friends have them, and envy them.

Megan had an interesting back story, coming from Adelaide and having been a lingerie model in her teens. She was a couple of years older than me. A street-wise girl. No one would say she was born with a silver spoon or anything. They were her own bootstraps she was pulling herself up by. She confessed to me that she would love to stay in England. Adelaide was history for her, she said, and she would marry an eligible Englishman and have dual passports. She was having a love-affair with England. She loved unpredictable weather. She loved football and cricket and tennis. Christmas in sunshine and bikinis was no fun. How she loved the rain. It was different rain in Adelaide, she said. She was always saying I 'luurve' your this and I 'luurve' your that and everything was 'kinda quaint' (move it on, Ben. Make your point. It's starting to sound like she's from America).

We got invited to these grown-up soirees. Dinner parties for couples etc. I went along out of interest. There was an after-dinner game doing the rounds back then, maybe it has always done the rounds? called "The Truth Game". It's like the *Mr and Mrs* TV game show, only in more relaxed surroundings. The rules: In turn, each person sits on a designated piece of furniture which is called the "truth sofa" or "truth chair" or "truth pouf", whatever. The other persons present sit together like a committee of interrogation (it helps if you are drunk). Each committee member asks a single question to the occupant of the truth furniture and he or she has to answer it 100% truthfully. After the final question is answered, the committee decide whether he or she has been honest or not. It sounds pretty dull, there are no dares attached, but believe me, it can get pretty heated and emotional. I mean, I saw fireworks more than once. It depends on the questions and the levels of inebriation.

This one time, there were a lot of Truth Game virgins. In particular, a couple who'd been seeing each other for a couple of years and had just got married. Under the auspices of a parlour game - which I'm sure even the fuddy-duddy whale-bone-corseted Victorians once played - I watched this couple dissolve right before my eyes. The husband was slumped drunk in the truth sofa and his new wife asked him: 'What, if anything, would you change about me?'

Whoa! Hold the honesty brigade! The key to the dissolution (if her husband had been properly listening) was the "if anything". This should easily have been translated as "We are in company now" or "There isn't anything to change, is there?" or "Did we make a mistake getting married?".

What did he say? What he should have said was a pack of lies. A simple "nothing". What he actually said, because he was soaked to the eyeballs with tequila slammers, was a list of things he'd like to change. You could tell by his body language that he was telling the truth before the words even came out. 'I wish you'd show me the same respect as I show you.' Talk about an open-air marriage counselling service. We were stunned into silence. I almost laughed it was so honest. 'I wish you cared for me the way I care for you,' he went on. The look on his wife's face. And then the killer blow.

243

'I wish we could turn the clock back two years.' His wife burst into tears and couldn't be consoled.

You see where honesty gets you?

Somehow - and this is the amazing British thing about that evening - the hosts settled her down in the kitchen with a slug of malt whisky– and the Truth Game continued! I was on the truth sofa and Megan Lake asked me the potentially dangerous question: 'Who in the whole world would you most like to make love to?'

'Me,' I said, making them fall off their chairs with laughter, but it was quite true.

Megan turned tight-lipped, but she'd asked the question. Then the wounded wife asked me: 'If you could change anything about yourself, what would it be?' A much safer question you might think. But I was sitting on the sofa, mulling it over, wracking my brains for something to criticise myself for. I asked for clarification. Did she mean intellectually or physically? Not allowed. One of the rules. If it had been now and I'd been on remand, I'd probably have said I'd change just about everything, but there and then, I said: 'Nothing.'

'You smug bastard,' Megan said, not having got over my previous answer.

'No, no,' another committee member said, 'I think he's telling the truth.'

I *was* telling the truth, as I perceived it. Probably for the first time. You see, the same question had been asked of everyone else and you wouldn't believe it. A girl wanted a turned-up nose, a bloke wanted to flatten his ears. A twenty-first century catalogue ensued: six-pack, longer legs, bee-stung lips, larger hands, longer neck, thicker hair, bigger breasts, smaller breasts, tighter bum, a wider girth around the penis! You name it, the men and women wanted to change just about everything. I was the only one who didn't care. They were the fakers.

Or were they? I'm blessed with physical wealth. Naturally tall and rangy, with good skin and thick hair. There's a fine line between self-assuredness and conceitedness, confidence and vanity.

That evening saw the closing down of two relationships because Megan and I drifted apart (unmelodramatically) soon after.

I'd like to see the Truth Game philosophy applied to BBC's *Question Time*. I think if government ministers were put on the truth sofa and plied with drink, the results would be interesting. Problem is, we'd think too many people were lying and there'd be a revolution and the British aren't very good with revolutions. Every Government that comes along is like washing powder. New and improved but still the same old whitewash.

[End of unmusical interlude]

Alex has not written. I don't expect he will now, given the cross-examination. I don't blame him. I've betrayed him and he'll never trust me again. Maybe he doesn't get my letters. Maybe he's gone back to New York. What is there to keep him here? I phone him every day and leave messages. He must have changed his number this week because there's an awful voice saying 'number unrecognised'. Might be that he's avoiding the press and not me. I hold onto the glimmer of hope from what he said at the airfield: 'I'll wait for you.'

To cut a long letter I wrote to him quite short, I told Alex I was sorry for the way Dearing QC undermined his literary reputation and for revealing the contents of his work-in-progress; that it had never been my wish or intention; that what I had told my brief had been twisted; that I still believed Alex was the most underrated writer in England and that one day the public would come to realise this fact. I told him I loved him and thought of him every day and night (all of this is true). I told him how being on remand was filling me with despair. *Please come and see me, Alex.* I made a vain attempt at humour with *PS: I am busy Monday to Friday but always free at weekends*, Monday-Friday being trial days (usually).

I gave this letter to Red the next morning. We're allowed to send letters twice a week. Alex is always at the top of my list.

Twenty

On the last day of the first week of my trial, a Friday, Middle QC focused his whole attention on me.

He was hoping to plant something indelible in the minds of the jurors over the weekend before Dearing QC built the case for my defence the following Monday (all this is perilously close to boring, Ben. Move it on).

So far in the trial there'd been no real exhibits. A trial is not a trial without exhibits. The pickaxe which bevelled Trotsky's brain. The syringes found beside Sid Vicious in the Chelsea Hotel. Body parts in drains. I could go on. You know what I mean.

Dearing had objected, saying that my stories were inadmissible as evidence because they were works of fiction; figments of a lively imagination. But Mr Justice Cummings thought otherwise. He said if Mr Fortune could be cross-examined for his writing intentions, in the interests of parity so should I be. It thrilled me to tell you the truth. To be compared to Alex in that way.

'Exhibit A, your Honour,' Middle said, asking the clerk to pass pieces of paper around the jurors. 'This is a story written by the defendant in July of last year as part of a creative writing summer school.'

Big Raisins! That got my juices going.

'This aptly shows us the mindset of the defendant.'

Dearing intervened again, saying this was a semi-fictional piece of writing, not a diary. And secondly, how could it be connected with any crime? Waved away by itchy-wig Cummings, and the jurors were given a few minutes to digest the opening of my story. Each juror would be expected to read the whole thing during final deliberations at the end of the trial, or during recesses. My God, there were enough recesses to read a hundred novels. Still, it was rather nice this Friday to have an audience, although by the looks of them only a handful might get my story and what it is supposed to be about.

Middle started to explain: 'It's an amateur, sordid little tale of sexual abuse…' I could have jumped to my feet but Dearing was already doing it for me.

'Your Honour, really!'

'Matter of opinion, Mr Middle. Re-phrase that.'

(Read the story. Do you think it is about abuse?)

'…Sexual awakening. A fixation on a teacher. A homoerotic relationship with a boy…'

I had to bite my lip or I'd call him a moron. My parents were in the gallery.

'…but I draw your attention, bearing in mind that this was written just a few weeks before the fire in Broadstairs, to a passage about fire and burning. Page 5. It has been underlined. Schoolchildren have been evacuated from a building and are now lined up on a tennis court.'

I like this paragraph. It's my favourite bit. He read aloud in quite a strong, slow, impressive voice: '*Above our heads, pouring from the roof, is a pall of grey-black smoke which smells of spoiled gravy. "Humans cooking," Oates says. "The staff barbecue." The thought makes my spine tingle. A week ago, at the council bonfire, I saw a family of hedgehogs burning. There were four of them. Two big ones and two small ones. They hadn't even tried to escape. They hadn't run or crawled or whatever hedgehogs do. They just huddled together as if ignoring the flames would make them disappear, and I remember thinking, do hedgehogs make wishes?*'

'This,' he said to the jury, 'is a piece of autobiographical writing. It is not fiction.' The jurors were still reading the passage, some nodding sagely. I wanted to know what they thought about the writing, not the fire.

'Exhibit B, your Honour.' Middle handed a second story across to Cummings and the clerk handed the rest around the jurors. 'This is the important story. The story the defendant submitted to the Acorn Short Story competition in August of last year. It is entitled, *Me and You*. Shortlisted by the organisers, it did not win a prize and was not published.' Again, he explained the story, getting the rudiments wrong: 'A schizophrenic boy contemplates setting fire to a residential care home.'

'Your Honour!' Dearing bleated. 'I've read this story a hundred times and nowhere have I come to that conclusion. My learned friend is reading a different story altogether. The story suggests many things but not what has been suggested maliciously here.'

'I apologise for being subjective,' Middle said sarcastically, 'but let me draw your attention to page 6 and you may make your own minds up.' The jurors turned the pages, as did itchy-wig in his highchair. I braced myself because I knew what was coming.

[Spoiler alert: if you haven't read it yet, skip the next paragraph]

'The narrator has gone to a public park with his so-called friend, Joe. We discover later in the story that Joe is infact the narrator's alter ego. *We sat on a slippery bench. Joe lit a cigarette and looked up at the monument to burnt Protestants. Then we looked down at the dog shit and the broken glass scattered at its foot. "What do you think it's like to burn?" he said. I took a drag from the cigarette and handed it back. "Hot." "Yeah hot, but what kind of hot?" "The kind of hot you can only imagine." He shook his head, spraying rain onto my shoulder. "Like a fagburn?" "A hundred times worse, Joe. All over your skin. Your hair would crackle. Your eyes would melt like balls of wax." Joe stroked his eyelids. I got up from the bench and walked around the cold, grey monolith. There was enough light to read the names of Bland, Sole, Waterer, Fishcock, Albright and Final. Lest we Forget, it said."*'

'Lest we forget,' Middle repeated in a grave tone. Then he drew attention to a violent confrontation on page 8: *'Bash, strangle, cut, burn him, Joe was saying. My heart was pumping and I lunged.'*

'Your Honour,' Dearing remarked quite coolly, taking the heat out of the situation. 'This is a work of fiction. An invention. None of it actually happened. This is not admissible. How many authors would we drag into this courtroom because of violence portrayed in their stories? You have said this court is not a book club, nor is it a literary criticism seminar.'

'I am merely indicating the state of mind of the writer at the time, your Honour,' said Middle. 'This is the story the defendant submitted to the competition whose offices were burned to the ground the night the winners were announced. This story did not make the final cut. I'm contending that this failure led to extreme rage and ultimately to the fire itself.'

'But these excerpts have been read out of context and misinterpreted.'

Here, here, I wanted to cheer.

'I'll allow it,' Cummings said. Dearing returned to his seat blowing hot air from his nostrils.

'Ladies and gentlemen of the jury,' said itchy-wig Cummings. 'You will have time to place the excerpts in their proper contexts and make your minds up for yourselves in due course.'

It wasn't looking good. The trial had a terrible Poe-like pendulous quality, swinging backwards and forwards so I never knew how the axe would fall (mixing metaphors once again).

[Enter Raymond Carver]

The American short story writer, Raymond Carver, has driven his car to the beach. The beach is long and horseshoe–shaped, curving away from the car and out to sea like the curvature of the earth. The sea is blue and bobbly. I'm on the beach; a spirit watching. I'm here, but not here. I can see Ray, but he can't see me. He's a giant of a man, getting out of his car, its wheels at the join of the sand and stones and bits and bobs tossed up by the tide. He's tall and wears plaid trousers and a lumberjack shirt, the sleeves rolled up to the elbows, like he means business. Gonna get his hands dirty. He's got clumps of boots. In his big old hands is a Smith and Wesson; an old-fashioned gun with a big clickety barrel. The gun chamber is empty (I can see inside the barrel for some reason).

Ray has been shot (or has shot himself) twice; once in the stomach because the blood is streaming out of the exit wound low down his back, out through the lumberjack shirt. The important wound though, the one which will ultimately kill him (and possibly me as his spirit) is the one in his chest. The bullet he took there is lodged visibly half-in, half-out like a plug. If he moves too much it will come out of his heart and he will die from blood loss (I'm thinking this is figurative, symbolic, because it is the heart. Is this love? Is this what he talked about when he talked about love?).

Ray staggers from his car, apparently calm, making strides towards a ridge, like a sandbank close to the water's edge. He's such a lovely big man with big boots and big hands. The one with the gun in has black smudges on it which I guess is from firing a gun (at himself?). I know everything (almost) that is going on inside his head. I've been waiting a while on the beach because I know he's come looking for me. He's come here to die. Writing has sent him mad. He's had enough of trying to find the right words.

Reading his jumbled thoughts, I can't determine if he's killed Tess, his second wife, and his kids who have grown up to misunderstand him. Is that why the barrel is empty? A bullet for Tess, one for each of his two kids, two for himself? Would that mean there's one bullet left in the barrel? Is it not empty after all? (such a tasteless dream).

He'd told Tess he was off going fishing and she'd watched him pull out of the drive of the condo car park. He hadn't put the rods in the back. He hadn't taken a right turn but a left which would have meant he wasn't going to the usual place to fish at all. He was going to the coast and it had nothing whatsoever to do with fishes.

You see, in actual fact, he's here to catch something else: words; words which have eluded him his whole life; the ones he has been meaning to write for so long but has never managed to put down. Words have crazied his mind. Moving commas and full stops (he calls them "periods" which never ceases to amuse me because I once thought it was an American word but in fact was used by Shakespeare in one of his plays) has driven him mad. He's come here because he can't stand it no longer, and it's a privilege to be in his company; even more so to share his last thoughts, last words before going to the writers' club in the sky.

Tippetian Health Warning: Raymond Carver did not die from a smoking gun but from smoking-related diseases but for the purposes of this dream (do dreams have a real purpose?), that's irrelevant. Everyone dies from something. It is compulsory.

He's wobbly on his feet, setting them apart to balance himself up straight, blood coming out of his back, the slug still perched half-in, half-out of his heart, and he's looking about for someone or something.

Is it me? He can't see me but he's aware of my presence. I can think his thoughts, can feel his feelings. He's here out of fascination and madness. He wants to know what his final words will be. It's important. It's final. He's shot himself in such a way that he is conscious of what his last words might be. He needs to know what they will be. He is hastening invention. He's impatient like any good writer, and saying sentences, wondering if they'll be the final words after all. They got to be good words. Mean something profound.

'Cortege of silence?' he asks.

A beautiful metaphor, but a bit of a cheek given it's lifted directly from Albert Camus's *The Outsider*. Obviously he doesn't want to end on that, though there are far worse things to end on, like: 'Help! The pain!' Or 'It's been a nice life.' Or 'Beans on toast!' Or 'It's getting dark in here.' Or 'I may be gone some time.' Or 'Kiss me, hard-on.' Or 'I'm dying!' Or 'I don't want to go!' as if it's the dentist you're talking about. Or 'I fancy Dover sole.' Or 'Wish me well...' Or 'I should have used fewer semicolons in my work.' Or 'Who put out the light?' Or 'Say that again?' Or 'I think I might leave you now.'

'Cortege of silence' is pretty damn good when you put it next to these morsels of mortality.

Ray shakes his head in frustration. He's thinking of Kafka, Chekhov, Turgenev, Kees, Hemingway and his dead friend, John Gardner (his writing mentor who died on a motorcycle). It isn't right at all. He staggers a little further to the water, stares at the deepening blue, almost to the ocean floor. Have the words sunk to the seabed? There is a full-scale cathedral under the water. It goes up in flames then turns into a peacock, then into a bottle of scotch. What's that doing there? He has thick, greying brown hair. He has a strong face. Lined. Etched. A brave big noble face with big, honest, troubled eyes. What words are you looking for, Ray?

He turns suddenly, sees a black man strolling along the beach; a man in overalls as blue as the sea, and an all-American baseball cap. He carries a Hessian sack into which he puts things; rubbish tossed up by the sea? Seashells? It doesn't really matter. Ray is perplexed. He's standing right in front of this man, blood is pouring from his back, blood's draining from his face, a bullet is lodged in his chest, a gun is in his hand. You'd think if another man saw these things he'd react or something, run away and call the police. It's as if Ray is thin air to the collector, like I am thin air to Ray. Ray watches him with incredulity. Can't you see me? Can't you see what I've done? What I've become? Aren't you even a little bit intrigued? Frightened even?

No to all five, obviously. The beachcomber bends down, picks an object up, puts it in his sack and carries on. Ray watches him until he's just a speck on the shoreline, like a pebble at his feet, and I watch Ray watching.

Ray is a giant of a man, not the pebble he thinks he is. Still, he is all washed up. Behind him is a row of mature palm trees, their branches and leaves clapping in a freshening breeze, but Ray can't hear the applause; he's too busy looking down the curvature of the earth at a whole bunch of people gathering in the distance like more pebbles. The beachcomber has joined them, a pebble among pebbles. No one else is coming. No one else will see Ray again. Though - as he knows - they have stopped seeing him already.

He's struggling for words. What will the final words be? Sometimes there are no words for what you feel, but a writer must search, regardless of feeling. Ray is weak, readjusting his stance, shifting his weight to a different foot. He nearly falls over in the wind which is stiffening, turning him into a piece of paper. The sky had been 100% blue, but now it is 50% grey and 50% white and Ray's shirt ripples perfectly.

The words. The words. The words. What will my final words be? It's as if the world is waiting with baited breath for these words (you too, I guess). He has to be sure. He won't be hurried or harangued by a stray seagull. He doesn't have long to make up his mind. Surely any words will do, Ray, because they will be inadequate for your purpose, which is longevity. Whatever you choose will be hopeless in this respect, but words there must be; not a groan, not a moan; words. He has to get them right, and up until that point he will stand here pressing the bullet in so it doesn't pop out and he'll drown in blood from his heart. He isn't ready to die, not just yet.

I'm waiting (you are waiting). I can feel the bullet move each time Ray presses it, as if it is into my heart. My finger presses, pushing the point of the bullet back into my hole. I'm keeping my blood in. It's my chest, my car, my life. They will be Ray's words yet they will be mine simultaneously. I'm scrambling around like Ray, like a lost thought in his mind. The words. The words. What shall my last words be?

And then they come; the ridiculousness of them. They don't make any sense, and we laugh at them together. Yet they are the right ones somehow. They mean something. As a boy we held them, many of them in our sweaty little hands at the funfair when we were at our happiest and most secure and most excited; only not so secure because we let go of them, like words, and they flew up and away in the wind and we never got them back.

'Barrage of balloons,' he says.

'Barrage of balloons,' we say, finally dropping to our knees. All these years we had wondered what the words would be; we wondered whatever happened to those balloons, and now, finally, they've come back, and the thought is special, peaceful, holdable and calming, and comforting, making us rise up slowly from the earth, smiling.

This was the dream and if I'd told Sparkes (the shrink who has seen me twice on remand), she'd have said something meaningful about it. Freudian Dreamscape analysis or Jungian communal reconstitution. Whatever. She'd say everyone in my dreams - everything in my dreams - is actually symbolised wish-fulfilment etc. *I* was Ray, the beachcomber, the cathedral, the peacock, the bottle, the weather, the pebbles, the sack, the palm trees. They all came out of my unconscious world, based on my anxiety about the commonplace real one.

'Do you have suicidal thoughts?' she'd ask.

'Well, only in my dreams,' I'd say, 'and I don't believe in psychoanalytical mumbo-jumbo anyway' (to be honest, I have thought of suicide more than once. It goes with the territory in here). I'd tell her how *real* Ray was, how *solid*. I had touched him and he had touched me, like a memory. I'd say the beach was the backdrop, there just for decoration.

'No,' she'd say, 'everything's symbolic. Colours, language, everything. I'm especially interested in the bullet and your heart.'

'Wouldn't anybody be interested in that?' I'd say.

I never told Dr Sparkes about the dream. Who really gives a fig for other people's dreams anyway? Except shrinks who are paid to be interested. Dreaming is like surfing the internet for your past life: only virtual realities. In a far realer sense, dreaming is just putting your dirty cups and saucers in the dishwasher overnight so that when you wake up in the morning everything has been cleaned. And each new day, more dirty dishes piling up.

I never told anyone about suicidal thoughts. Don't even like the word suicide. I'm not really looking to die here, or anywhere else if I can help it. I'm a bit of a coward when it comes to death. Wouldn't want to speed it up.

If you had the opportunity for last words though, would they make sense only to you, or to everybody? Whoever heard of a barrage of balloons? A barrage, yes. A balloon, yes. A barrage balloon, yes. But a barrage of balloons? It's bizarre but no one said dreams have to make sense. Maybe that was Ray's genius. He could (even at the very end, even in my dreams) make something interesting out of something quite ordinary. He was a brilliant mystery. And I'm sorry he died in a hospital and not on a beach.

I'm sure in real life he said things much funnier and much more meaningful on his real-life deathbed.

I can write anything in this book, can't I? Even insights into my crazy dreams. No one gets to read it if I don't want them to. Anything that occurs at the time. I might decide never to send it to a publisher. If it all gets too soul-bearing. Too confessional. We'll see.

[Enter Imogen Wood]

Saturday. A prison visit. Imogen's getting nervous about her appearance in the witness box next week. She looks terrible. Her strawberry blonde hair is lank on the shoulders of her trench coat. She's lost a lot of weight and her Nordic eyes are wide, dark and watery; more like the Baltic sea than a Norwegian fjord.

Manston and one or two of the other inmates give her the once and twice over. Animals. They do the same thing whenever my mother comes, checking out her ankles, legs, bottom, breasts, storing the images up for their odd socks later. You know what I mean. Men are like this. I am one but have never managed to …well, maybe once. Once only have I given sacrifice at the temple of Onan in here.

Imogen twiddles her fingers, twists the marriage-less ring on her finger. She tells me guilt-inducing news. She no longer works at Pensbury University; left by mutual agreement. She had no option, she says. The complaint against her was withdrawn but the mud stuck, and besides, she's had quite enough of students. Had enough of their hunger; 'the neediness of neurotics'. They've been transferring their hang-ups onto her for too long, she says. They just write the same old mumbo-jumbo month after month, year after year. 'The Pensbury rumourville is working overtime too,' she says. She hasn't come out of our relationship unscathed. Now she's taking a year off to complete her next novel. She's sold her house and has moved back in with her ex-boyfriend, Brendan, in London. All inside six months. She's thinking about having a baby. A lot can change in six months, I know. She might look for work in the big smoky, but hopefully not teaching. She's had enough of that. She hasn't written anything of quality for ages. *Teaching* creative writing and actually *writing* creatively are incompatible monsters, she says, like siblings at each other's throats, or simultaneously patting your head and rubbing your belly 24 7.

255

I apologise profusely for my role in any of this.

'I know you didn't do it, Ben' she says. 'The police are fascists, just like the petty-minded bureaucrats at the University. It's a jumped up charge, everyone knows.'

Still, there is some confusion in her mind about the evening of December 19th. The night of the fire. She thinks she's made a mess of it. She's told the police different things at different times because they wouldn't leave her alone. She can't remember that night. She knows how important it is for the trial, but she can't remember.

I calm her hands, tell her the witness box isn't as bad as it seems (though how would I know? I've never been in it and the people who have, have been politely torn to shreds). She's not bothered. She can handle bullies. It's the times she can't remember.

'Thanks for coming all this way,' I say. She apologises for banging on about her life when it's me in the dock. 'No sweat,' I say. 'The defence team do all the hard work. They're quite good. Have they spoken to you?'

I know they have. Imogen's the prime witness. My only alibi. They've advised her in meetings. So my brief tells me. But will she hold up?

'I'm sticking to the flu story.'

'Ssshhh, Imogen.'

She whispers across the table. 'Well, I can hardly mention the you know what?'

'There's nothing to worry about. Stick to the time of ten o'clock.'

'I've given different times to different people.'

'You were tired and ill, Imogen.'

'That's what I'll say.'

'You know I'm innocent. Just tell them how innocent I am.'

'Of course I will. I've been following the trial in the newspapers. Fortune's obviously hiding something.'

'Him?' I huff. 'Look, I know we've never spoken about me and Alex. I mean about our relationship…'

'You don't have to explain,' she says. 'I don't have anything against you or him. I'm surprised that's all. You know, after …You seemed to enjoy it…'

'I did, but with Alex it was…Well, I tend to bounce off people, but with Alex I kind of got absorbed.'

'Thanks a bunch,' she says. 'You were just bouncing off me?'
'That's not what I meant. Yes. Oh, I don't know.'
'I'm not judgemental. It's a free country, or so I used to think.'
She leans back in her chair, thinking.
'Have you heard anything? About Alex?'
She shrugs her shoulders. 'Keeping a low profile. Working on his autobiography.'
'I know you don't like him, Imogen, but he's not so bad.'
'I have nothing against him. I just don't like the way he writes, what he writes about.'
'Me neither,' I lie. 'Too populist. Too traditional.'
'Not that,' she says. 'He's completely narcissistic.'
'That too,' I say, but maybe it's not him she's talking about.

[Enter Maurice Little]
I'm compressing time now and to be honest I can't really remember which days people visit, especially Maurice, because he likes to come and see me that often, sometimes dropping off books. Maurice is a mobile library. He is a reminder that the world still spins on its axis outside these walls. What would his newborn daughter know about the static world her father was entering?
He is so crushingly normal. Louise is his normal wife and they live in a normal terraced house together in a normal part of Pensbury. Maurice has a normal 39-year-old man's beer gut and receding hair. He's a really nice man and I wish I'd never told him the lie about my parents dying in a plane crash. He's mentioned it and forgiven me. He thinks I'm very insecure but not capable of violence. I'm innocent because he wants to believe I am. There isn't a shadow of doubt in his mind. Booksellers are too soft to hurt anyone deliberately. Charlotte, his newborn, is the centre of his planet now. She was a difficult breech birth and Louise had only just been allowed home.
'I was breech,' I say.
'Was you?'
'Yes, and I turned out alright, didn't I?'
The look of horror on his face. 'Louise said it was like passing an inflated umbrella.'
Maurice has not slept for a whole week. Bags and circles. Pleasurable marks. He shows me a photograph taken at the hospital. Mr Little, Mrs Little, little Little, and the littlest Little.

257

Family of four. I once lived in a family of four without knowing it. Do I envy him his normality? This family scene? No, I do not. I look at this baby in pink swaddling clothes (she has the same bobble nose as Maurice) and wonder what she'll look like in five years, ten years, fifteen years. The time I might spend behind bars if things don't go my way. For some people, the Littles might be a barometer of personal and professional achievement. They are happy and comfortable. They are normal. But not all families are happy or normal, as Tolstoy once said.

Maurice is a kind man. The kind of kind man anyone would want as a friend and a colleague. He drinks too much, eats junk food, swears too often and sometimes smokes, but he is true to himself and is faithful to his family. Even his belly is reassuring, like ballast.

He's taken in the books I asked for: a biography of E.E.Cummings and Albert Camus' *The Outsider*, though the guards have taken them, which means I'll get them in a few days. If you can smuggle things inside an envelope, what can't you smuggle inside a book?

It's nice hearing about the bookshop. The day-to-day dramas I've been missing. How a thief stole a Jamie Oliver cookery book but the fool locked the wheel of his bicycle to a drainpipe and pulled half of it along the street during his escape. He was rugby-tackled in a subway by Paul.

'How are Paul and Jenny?'

'The same,' he says. 'Paul thinks it's a conspiracy. The immigrant was pushed out of the window. He wasn't an immigrant at all, but a spy, and the Acorn Building was a front for MI6. Messages were being sent around the world disguised as fiction.'

'Good old Paul,' I say. 'He reads too much John Le Carre.' There isn't really much good or old about Paul. We weren't exactly friends or anything. To be frank, I haven't thought about him once since my arrest. Although that can't be true because looking back, he is in my story.

Maurice tells me that takings are well up on last month's. Little's is the hottest ticket in town. He has been holding readings in the cartography room every week, all well-attended. He's thinking of re-naming it "Tippet's" in my honour because he thinks people are coming to look at the shop where everything happened. 'A literary car crash,' he says. 'We've started a petition on your behalf. Free Ben Tippet! Free Ben Tippet! It's right by the door.'

'Great. How many signatures have you got?'

A long pause follows. 'Fifty-seven.'

'Fifty-seven? You could've lied. Could've said a thousand and fifty-seven.'

'We've only just started it.'

'Thanks, anyway,' I say. 'Really. I appreciate the thought.'

All of this is to humour me, though I suspect he is right. It is the human condition to be interested in death and murder and love and all that stuff. The Pensbury papers have been running articles since my arrest. Maurice, Paul and Jenny have had their faces in the paper too. Takings are up because curiosity sells books. Good things come out of bad, as Father Alan Mackie would say.

'But how is the trial going?' he asks. 'I watch the news. I'd take time off but you know how it is with the baby and work and that?'

'How's it going? It's a boxing match and I'm winning on points, just.'

'Everything's crossed for you,' he says. 'You'll come out of this alright and there'll be a job for you when you do. If you still want to work in a bookshop?'

The bell rings, my rest is over before the next round begins. Maurice gives me one of his legendary bear hugs. A nice man through and through. I go back to my cell thinking he would make a wonderful older brother.

Twenty-one

[Enter Imogen, again]

Second week of my trial and things speeded up. How did Imogen look in the witness box? Anxious? Definitely. Terrified? Not quite. She confirmed her name, address (new), occupation (novelist, not writing tutor), and relationship with the defendant (friend). The jury were probably thinking, two novelists in ten days? Ben Tippet slept with both of them? (never at the same time I can assure you ladies and gentlemen of the jury. Strange bedfellows they would make).

The defence QC's turn to shine, but Dearing daring do was playing it calm this week. Witnesses had been hand-picked, beginning two days before with Maurice Little, bookshop colleague and friend. He provided the initial character reference from which the defence would build an unassailable case. Maurice had not let me down. In his opinion I was an enthusiastic and committed bookseller, never showing anger, not capable of violence. I was liked by all the staff and was bursting with ideas for Little's Bookshop. He would go as far as to say that without me the shop would have gone under. 'Not the type to set fire to a publisher's then?' Dearing had asked.

'Not in a million years.'

Maurice had worn his best suit. I think it was from Debenhams and looked quite smart. I could see he was very nervous. He used over-enunciated words. He'd never seen me lose my temper, he said. I was totally reliable. So much so that he asked me to baby-sit more than once. I managed the shop single-handedly whenever he was absent. 'Not a loner?' Middle had asked in the cross-examination. 'A private person. Yes. Mysterious sometimes. But not a loner, sir.' Self-obsessed? 'No more than anyone else.' A liar? Maurice had looked at me and then back at Middle QC. 'No.'

Maurice had lied for me! He had not mentioned the supposed plane crash, and he could see my parents in the gallery for himself. *Brick* is too light a word for Maurice that day.

Imogen painted a bright picture for the jury too. I'd been one of her most promising students, she said. Our relationship had been professional and personal as we'd become friends during the course. No mention of an up-and-down, on-off affair. She did not milk our differences, just said confidently (encouraged expertly by Dearing) that we had both been single, free agents. And what did she think of me as a person? She looked me straight in the eyes. 'I'd say he was sensitive and intelligent.' I wouldn't have said the same about myself. It was as if she was talking about a stranger. 'Is he capable of violent outbursts, Ms Wood?' She shook her head. 'He has a tendency to sulk, but nothing more.'

I didn't mind her saying that. It was perfect. She wasn't painting too rosy a picture of me. The jury would have seen through perfection. 'He is a human being with faults just like anyone else,' she said.

Then onto the real business of the examination. The night of the alibi.

Imogen was flying. The well-rehearsed influenza story. I'd been kind enough to come around and look after her, she said. She'd gone out with colleagues, had drunk a little out of politeness but felt ill. She'd taken too much flu remedy and was dizzy. She said I was at her house from about 10 o'clock that night but could not be more precise because of the state she was in, but it was definitely not much later than 10pm. 'And when he arrived, was my client acting strangely? Agitated? Was there anything unusual or different about his behaviour that night?'

'He was the same as usual,' she answered. 'He looked after me and stayed all night.'

I remembered the night differently. A different time and space altogether. I had looked after her, but it had not been because of flu or remedies. More a cocktail of drugs and alcohol. Holding her head straight over a toilet bowl. Not sleeping a wink. Maybe an hour or two. 'Thank you, Ms Wood,' Dearing said, giving Middle a satisfied eye.

And this was when everything fell to pieces.

Middle QC hitched up his trousers and pulled up his sleeves (metaphorically) and went straight for the jugular like Sweeny

Todd. 'Do you make a habit of sleeping with your students, Ms Wood?'

'Objection, your Honour.'

'Mr Middle,' itchy-wig Cummings said. 'Ms Wood is not the one on trial here. Neither is it a crime.' He had visibly taken a shine to Imogen. Maybe she reminded him of his daughter, or niece, or grandaughter, or maybe he just liked pretty, feisty women.

'The trial hinges on the alibi she has provided, your Honour,' Middle said. 'Ms Wood was sleeping with the defendant during this time. Surely their relationship needs exploration?'

'Continue,' Cummings said and Middle turned to his witness again. Imogen would just have to dig in and be strong. Middle repeated the question.

'No,' she said.

'No you don't make a habit of sleeping with your students or no you don't sleep with your students?'

Dearing jumped up, flapping his arms about. 'Your Honour, this is nit-picking.'

'Answer the question please, Ms Wood,' Cummings said.

'I don't make a habit of it.'

'You were sleeping with the defendant at the time you were teaching him creative writing, and marking his work? That must have been a conflict of interests? Seems awfully unprofessional.'

'In retrospect, yes, but-'

'So you were unprofessional retrospectively. I see.'

Imogen visibly prickled. I'd seen it happen once before in one of her classes at university when someone challenged her over the meaning of "authorial voice". This was just what Middle intended. He had her going, dangling.

'*Men* have been having affairs with students for millennia but a *woman* has one and the world drops its jaw.' Her voice was high and slightly tremulous.

'That is your considered opinion is it, Ms Wood? Let's stick to the facts shall we? Are there codes of conduct regarding relationships with students?'

'That would be reactionary,' she replied. 'This is not *1984*. We are not children. We are grown-ups.'

'Grown-ups who have childish outbursts and burn down buildings with people inside them, Ms Wood.'

Dearing was apoplectic. 'Leading the witness and the jury. Opinion and supposition, your Honour.' Cummings itched his wig, a sure sign of irritability. He called the QCs over to the bench, said something which had them shaking their heads in exasperation.

'I'm suggesting, Ms Wood, that you had a leaning towards the defendant and this coloured your opinion of him. That you were blind to his machinations. Blind to the real Benjamin Tippet. The man who was capable of violent outbursts and vengeful attacks. You cannot stand in this court room heaping praise on the character of a man you were sleeping with but knew very little about in the ten or so weeks you were seeing him. Were you grading him on imaginary flair in the classroom, or in the bedroom?'

'Mr Middle!' itchy-wig said, raising his voice to new levels. 'I should remind *you* of the codes of conduct.' The gallery tittered to itself and I caught my mother's eye, making my neck burn again. This was no joke after all. 'Stick to the evidence, Mr Middle.'

Dearing leaned back in his chair, an alligator smile for his adversary.

'Certainly, your Honour. The facts then. Not long ago, Ms Wood, a grievance procedure was taken out against you by one of your students, wasn't it?'

She nodded. 'It has since been retracted.'

'But it is on record?'

She nodded again.

'The complainant recorded favouritism as the cause of the grievance, didn't he?'

'Unfounded and retracted.'

Middle waved a sheet of paper in front of her, reading: '*Ms Imogen Wood discriminated against me. Her marking was unfair and inconsistent as a result.* I wonder why this was retracted? Either way, as you say, we are human beings and we all make mistakes.' Very unsubtle but it stained her character when taken out of context like that. Much more was to come. The night of the alibi.

Middle got her to explain her account. Where she was and who she was with and when she got home and when I was supposed to have arrived. 'One minute you're telling the police the defendant arrived at "some point during the night" and in a later statement, made after the arrest of the defendant, that he arrived "about 10 or 11". Then "midnight". This is the worst case of memory loss due to influenza I've ever heard. How is it that at first you cannot remember and a few months later can remember the exact hour?'

'It came back to me.'

'It came back to you?' Middle was cranking up the pace and the volume, not allowing her the space to answer. 'I suggest it was "brought back" to you by the defendant in the meantime. I suggest you were drunk, Ms Wood. So drunk that you could hardly stand. I have plenty of witness statements saying exactly that. It was the week before Christmas, the end of term, and you were letting your hair down, pushing the boat out. The landlord said you had six or seven glasses of wine, and some spirits.'

'I had taken some flu remedy and shouldn't have been drinking.'

'Not a single witness says you had signs of a cold, let alone flu, Ms Wood. Didn't you drive to Devon the very next day? This is all fabrication, made up between you and the defendant to protect him. I put it to you that you staggered home at about 10 pm and could not remember much thereafter. You cannot remember much about the evening of December the 19th. Isn't that so?'

'No,' she said. 'That's a lie.'

'Do you remember a phone call, Ms Wood?'

'Phone call?' she said, blinking rapidly.

Phone call? I was thinking. Dearing looked over his shoulder at me.

'Yes,' said Middle. He held up another sheet of paper, waving it before her. 'A telephone call received by you on the night of December the 19th.'

Dearing leapt to his feet. 'Your Honour, evidence has to be seen by both sides of Counsel before admittance.'

'This has just come to light, your Honour,' Middle said. 'It has taken the police some time getting access to the records. It being Christmas at the time of the call and some records have been lost, but this has been recovered painstakingly.'

Cummings frowned. 'Let me see this evidence.'

Then I remembered the call.

'I see,' Cummings mumbled to Middle who was pointing at the paper. Dearing was handed his own copy. He looked at it and his face dropped. He whispered something to the judge, maybe something about a recess in proceedings? The judge waved him away. It was horrible watching Dearing re-take his seat so angrily. All his faith in me destroyed.

Middle approached the witness box again. 'Ms Wood, the call was answered at your house at 11-32pm. Do you remember it?' She shook her head. 'The call came from a mobile phone and the phone was registered to a Mr Ben Tippet.' I could see Imogen trying to recall it, but she couldn't remember. 'If the defendant was caring for you inside your house, why would he be calling you inside your house?'

The jurors' faces. My alibi blown to pieces. 'Maybe Ben didn't lock his phone properly and pressed redial? I don't know. It's easily done.' She looked across to me and I tried to remain calm but I remembered making the call. In my fit of panic that night I had made a call, making sure she was at home. If only I'd called her mobile.

No,' Middle said gravely. 'This was no accident. He was on line to you for nearly six minutes, but still you cannot remember?'

'Maybe we did speak. It's possible, I guess.'

'But he was in your house, wasn't he? According to your statements?'

'It could have been later,' she said, the fatal cut finally inflicted, just as Middle had planned. How long he had this information, only he, his team and the police would know.

'It could have been later,' he repeated for the jury's sake. 'Thank you, Ms Wood.' He sat down to a post-hammering silence, the longest nail I have ever heard being drummed into a coffin. Imogen stepped down and I watched her slip through the same door Alex had disappeared through. As with Alex, she did not look back at me and I turned my gaze from the jury to the gallery where my mother seemed frozen stiff, my father with an arm to warm life into her.

Where are you, Alex? I was thinking. Will you come for the verdict? Will you wait for me? Because I am well and truly stuffed.

Twenty-two

[Enter Uncle Davina]

Uncle D hasn't visited me the whole three months I've been inside and I have mixed feelings about it. Despite my circumstances, Uncle D and my parents are still not communicating, by letter, phone, or in person. That's how close this family is. A crisis is supposed to draw members tighter, bury the axes, whatever. It all dates back to the epiphany on my 16th birthday in London when I suddenly had a dead brother on my hands. How could anyone ever forget it? I'm sure my parents still blame Uncle D for my situation. If he hadn't told me about their secret I wouldn't have become the mixed up person I am today sort of thing. Uncle D had betrayed my mother's trust and she could never forgive him and Dad was always fighting the need to punch his lights out, even from his wheelchair.

Uncle D was an easy target, but I didn't fire anything in his direction. I think he had been right in telling me. I've had time to dwell on the matter in here, and he was absolutely spot on in telling me. But in my letters to him (I've written two or three), I've suggested he steer clear for my parents' sake and he has been courteous and understanding in his replies. In reality, I've been terrified that the other inmates would humiliate me if they saw my uncle/aunticle D in the flesh. In his letters, he had been frank about my trial. What he gleaned from TV and radio reports. Rather non-committal on whether I was guilty or innocent.

So I was surprised this week to be sitting across the table from him. The trial had been adjourned for a day so the QCs could put the finishing touches to their closing speeches. Whatever. I was in the visitor's room again, only this time with my aunticle to deal with. He had dressed down in a beige Mac, white blouse and black jeans. Quite a tight shirt and sticky-up bra to exaggerate his dumplings. The jeans were also tight, emphasising his shapely bottom.

What he didn't realise was that he still looked like a gender curiosity. His upper-lip and chin were way too smooth and there was nothing he could do about the manly hands and narrow hips. He'd grown his hair to shoulder-length, dyed a rich auburn, fluffed up at the hairdresser's. Lipstick pale pink. Earrings, small silver studs. If you saw him from the back or the side, and if he didn't speak or look you in the eye, at a glance you would say he was a smart business woman.

He'd turned up fashionably late, so when he came around the occupied tables and chairs, the guards and inmates clocked him two, three and four times. A strange kettle of fish. Something not right about her. They watched him put his handbag on my table. I felt their necks craning, their ears bending to hear this curiosity speak, to confirm their suspicions. Unfortunately, I'd sat with my back to Manston (can no longer bear to look at that oaf) and this meant Uncle D was in Manston's sightline.

I spoke quietly. 'What happened to your eyebrows?' They had gone and he had painted some new ones on.

'What happened to your manners?' he fired back. 'You could do with a waxing yourself.'

Good old Uncle D. I used to love sparring with him. You can turn into a right bitch in his company. Midway through our slot he leaned forward and said, 'I know you did it, Benjamin.' It was a relief to tell you the truth. Coming from family like that. 'But what I don't understand is why?'

'I wanted recognition. Most writers are fakers and cardboards. I wanted to be real. A real writer. I wrote an important story.'

'You judge a man by his actions not by his words,' he said. Something platitudinous like that.

Without thinking, I said too loudly, 'Well, not anymore they don't, *Uncle* D.' I heard Manston laugh. A dirty snigger. I looked over my shoulder and saw him release a broad, animalistic grin.

'He looks like a real monster. Will he make it difficult for you?'

I shrugged my shoulders. 'I don't care. But they're not all bad in here.' He reached for my hand and I involuntarily withdrew mine.

'I understand,' he said.

'It's not like that. It's just the way things are around here. Just the way things are.'

Then he went all sermoniser on me (a Burton trait). 'What will you be remembered for, Benjamin? For a story or for killing a man?' I had to hand it to him. He never holds his punches. 'You've made your bed, so you can lie in it.'

'You mustn't tell my mother and father.'

'I'm not going to,' he said. 'I've split the family in two before, remember?'

'Do you really miss them that much?'

I watched it wound him. 'You're cold, so cold, Benjamin. You get that from your mother. It's not just the looks you inherited.'

'I'm sorry...but you know what I mean?'

'The truth hurts, Benjamin, and you should face up to it.' He put out his right hand, placed the palm at the centre of my chest, saying, 'If you don't use it, you'll lose it.' There was a pause, time to think about what he had said. I felt Manston's eyes digging into my back. 'Your family love you. I love you. We will forgive you anything in the end. But you must be true to yourself.'

What else can I say about that meeting? After that everything kind of faded into insignificance. The bell went. We stood and embraced and I felt his dumplings at my chest. He kissed me on the cheek, leaving a mark. I squeezed his hairless arm, saying, 'I'll talk to them about you. About making things better again. Back to the way things were.'

He picked up his handbag. 'Best of luck,' he said. I still don't know if he meant best of luck with Manston, with what I'd just said, with the rest of my trial, or the rest of my life.

With the trial close to closure I've been keeping my head down and my nose clean, just as Red suggested way back in August. I've been avoiding Manston (as much as you can in a rat cage). His trial is being held at the same court as mine so he's even less avoidable. He shouted once through the almost transparent van cubicle wall, 'You're going down, hard-on. You may as well go down on me.' Disgusting. I won't even tell you what he wanted to do with my mothers ears. In any other institution this would be stamped on as bullying, but in prison you just don't say anything because of the repercussions in the big boy's playground when the teachers are absent.

After Uncle D's visit I knew there'd be some flack so I remained in my cell a good part of the afternoon. Actually, I prayed again.

On my knees, to the window. 'I might not have taken you seriously enough, God. And for that I am truly sorry. All I need is a sign that you are there.'

Nothing.

By the evening - with or without God's backing - I decided to face the music. By that I mean Manston. You can't live your life afraid. I wasn't going to let Manston dominate me. I wasn't frightened of him. I was frightened of him, but didn't want to let him know I was.

There was a numbskull programme on in the TV room. A fashion-guru thing. Two voyeuristic clothes police/amateur psychologists ripping into the wardrobes of two other women who had low self-esteem. "Tranny and Godzilla" I call it; each presenter probably having more personal issues than the general public in the whole of Kent and Sussex put together.

Manston was lumped right in front of the screen waiting for the bottom and boob shots. He saw me come in and made his customary blow-job gesture which I ignored for about the millionth time. Back to the dark ages. Moses was playing pool with Rogers so I stood by the table exchanging a few words. Strength in numbers. But it didn't take long to kick off.

Manston laughed across the room. 'You got a nice uncle, *Benjamin.*'

Ignored it.

'Where you been hiding him...or is it a her?'

Ignored it.

'Ah, come on. I'm only pulling your plonker. I live in the modern world, don't I?' He winked at his lackies. 'There's room for everyone. What she called?' He turned to one of his lackies. 'Good-looking, like his old girl.'

Ignored it with increasing difficulty. 'I'll play the winner,' I said to Moses.

'Heh! Leave him alone!' said Moses, directing it at Manston, stirring the ape up, making my pulse race.

'Oooh! Leave him alone! Leave him alone! What's it got to do with you, sambo? You know the Tippets come from planet faggot? You from the same place?'

I saw Moses' grip tighten on the cue, watched Manston stand up.

'The Manstons come from planet gannet,' I said. Really childish stuff; like I was ten or something. You see, I could no longer do what I had successfully done for months. It was not a red-mist moment. That's all melodramatic baloney. What it was at first was eyeballing. I stared at him, he stared at me, then Moses tapped my arm and handed me the cue. 'Game on,' he whispered, but in a nervous way. His exact words. One of the few things I remember of the events. Moses filled me in on the details much later, at the prison hospital.

'You have a peculiar interest in faggots,' I said, bringing it on, though none of what followed was actually premeditated. Not on my part anyway. I bent down to rack the balls and felt something come up behind me. He didn't touch me, just stood there, about six inches away. I felt his ugly breath on my neck. He must have been making a rude motional gesture or something because there were sniggers along the walls. That's when I noticed there were no guards. I looked to my right, saw one of Manston's lackies standing by the door peering through the reinforced window. When he turned and nodded, Rogers backed off, and Moses didn't know what to do. Seeing his eyes was like watching a spaghetti western. That's about as close to the feeling as I can describe. What were they going to do? Rape me? Kill me? Both?

I turned to face Manston, pleased to be a good eight inches taller than him, though he was as wide as he was tall when he squared up like that. 'What did you just say?' he said. 'You grease pole.'

If I hadn't been so pumped I would have laughed at grease pole. What a vocabulary. Monkeys can count to a hundred, paint pictures and pour tea into cups and they have an advantage over Manston.

'I'm playing pool,' I said. 'So you'll have to wait your turn.' However, I'd have to play pool by myself because there'd been a complete exodus from the table. Moses moved away, parting a sea of inmates. It was just me and the ape. He span me around by my shoulders. 'I've been waiting for this,' he said, and in a flash his forehead came into my face.

I heard a crack inside my skull, felt blood firing from both nostrils. Jet-propelled. Everything's quite slow in films but in real life so much faster. I fell backwards onto the carpet at the foot of the table and couldn't hear anything except ringing, which I thought was a riot alarm. A school friend once told me it's the *flight, fright or shite your pants hormone*. Everything but the essentials shut down. There was nothing in the seat of my trousers though. I wasn't running anywhere. I was strangely unafraid. No red mist. No baloney. If anything, it was quite crystal clear like seeing France from Dover with your naked eye.

I was in the crouched position holding the bridge of my nose which moved slightly in my fingers. I thought I was going to pass out at first because of dizziness; a feeling of strange displacement. Moses told me the story of what happened next, from beside the hospital bed: 'You struggle to your feet, feeling your nose, man; swelling like a yam. Blood streaming down your mouth. All over it. You pull your T-shirt up to stem the flow. You look like you were in the zone, man. Gonna kill someone. Ding-ding, round two. You bend down and pick up the cue. "Watch it, Manston!" his mate shouts. Manston's back by the TV. He turns and clocks the cue, man, and you hold it up in front of you, and he says, "Let's be having you, hand-job," something like that.'

'What did I do, Moses?'

'You can't remember nothing at all?'

'Nothing.'

'Well...you weren't knocked out.'

'What did I do, Moses?'

'You charge at him, swinging the fuckin' cue, man. You swing right at him and he puts an arm up to protect himself and the sound the cue made, man. Like a bat on a ball. Crack! You broke his arm, and the cue! Fuck. Hee. Cracked it clean. Fuckin' did it. You don't remember nothing? You better watch that temper, man.'

'Then what?'

'Manston ain't no slouch potato, right. Straight back up again, seething. Cradling his arm like it's a baby. A man who don't make a noise when his arm cracks in two is some sort of lunatic. "Go get' im, Manston," his mate said.'

'And what were you doing?'

'I was keeping well out of your way. You were like a helicopter blade with that cue. Then it gets real tasty. You're in the zone. Ding-ding, round three! Manston roars that he's gonna to stick the cue where the sun don't shine. Rogers tears out looking for a guard. It was like a Kung-fu film. Manston came at you with his legs, man.'

'His legs?'

'Fuckin' legs! One, then the other, off the ground! And you're sweeping the cue left to right, blood running over your chin. Then it happened, man. The connection. You land the killer, plum centre of his mouth. I ain't ever seen anything like it! You sock him right in the tunnel. He's out cold, man. His mouth's a ribbon of blood. His teeth are lying around the room. I get hold of you…and Manston's lying in a coma…'

'Dead?'

'I get hold of your cue, the remaining bit, but you won't let go. Your eyes, man.'

'Is he dead, Moses?'

'He ain't dead. Pensbury A&E getting fixed up. He won't look pretty in the mirror, but he's no looker anyway. Don't worry about charges. Self-defence. Me and Rogers told them already. We should throw a party. You did everyone a favour, but I'm sorry about your nose. Respect, man. Fuckin' BT Man. You stood tall for your family.'

What he said next frightened me the most: 'You jump onto the pool table with half a cue, raise it above your head, roaring. You roar like the Incredible Hulk. The guards had to pull you down. Red slapped the cuffs on. Next thing you're sedated and carried off. It was your nirvana moment. Smells Like Teen Spirit. You know when the song fuckin' explodes?'

Now I'm on segregation block, my nose taped, my eyes bulging and purple and beginning to yellow. I'm slammed up for 21 hours a day. I've phoned my parents and explained. Mother wants an investigation. So do the prison service. You shouldn't have been left unattended, Benjamin. But I tell her, 'I did something I had to do but the worst part is not remembering.' My poor Benjamin. We have to get you out of there.

That's right. Poor Benjamin. Seg block is miserable. Manston's been transferred to another prison and I can't even take advantage of the clean air I created on the remand wing. There are some real mean bastards either side of me. I miss Moses, and it's only been a day or so. It's not for long I tell myself. The closing speeches, the summing up, the verdict, and hopefully I'll be gone and Manston will be a distant memory.

Nagging doubts: What if I *am* sent down? What if this is what it's going to be like for years? What if prison proper is full of Manstons? I'll have a reputation and everything will be hopeless.

When you're locked up for so long each day, you get to looking at yourself closely in the mirror. I can't bear to look at myself but have to now my face has been smashed up. I am changing, have changed, have been changed. It's as if the purple bruises are on the inside as well as the outside. The purple is the same purple I once made in primary school. I remember it quite well. I thought I'd forgotten it forever, until now. Maybe it's my first proper memory in life.

All the kids have a small tray in front of them, circles in the bottom like empty eggcups, except three are filled with red, blue and yellow. 'These are the primary colours,' Miss Stone says. 'From these you can make every other colour but any other colour cannot make them. They are special.'

'What about black and white?' somebody says.

'Black and white are not colours,' she answers.

'If I can see them, aren't they colours, Miss?' I ask.

'They aren't on the spectrum of colour. If they're not in the rainbow they're not colours. Remember, it's not what colours *are* but what colours *do* that counts.'

Do? I screw up my face. I look at a poster on the wall beside the blackboard where there's a big rainbow surrounded by big black letters: MONDAY. Two jam jars are standing on my desk, one filled with clear tap water, the other with black water from dirty brushes. I can't understand how black can be every colour mixed together yet you can't single each colour out again. I call out, 'Miss, how do you make purple again?'

Miss Stone comes up behind me and reaches over my shoulder. She takes the brush from my hand, dips it in the clear water making it dirty, dries it on a cloth. She dabs the brush in the red colour, drags it across a clean sheet of paper like a line of blood. She cleans the brush in the dirty water, dips the brush in the blue, drags the blue across the red line. 'This is a secondary colour,' she says. I watch it happen right in front of me; the colour purple magically appearing. It's as magic as 2+2=4 for the first time. It is purple like the bruise you get from a kick on your shin or a punch in your eye.

Miss Stone's body presses warmly at my back like she is my mother. She hands me my brush, smiling, and then I make purple. Purple everythings. We're supposed to be making a picture using all of the primary colours and some secondary colours. In five minutes, I know what grass is made of, and oranges. I have an orange tree with dark green leaves in a big field of grass with a blue sky, white clouds and a bruised aeroplane.

It is only when I get home and stick my picture on the kitchen wall that I realise I've forgotten the sun, and something else occurs. 'I know about purple and orange and everything, but what makes red red, blue blue and yellow yellow?'

My mother says, 'The sun makes yellow, the sea makes blue which makes the sky blue, and blood makes red red.'

'Paint isn't blood,' I say back. My dad shrugs his shoulders at me. He doesn't know either.

'God made all the colours in the rainbow,' she says, 'and he probably had his reasons.'

None of this makes sense. I'm restless at night thinking about colours and God. Questions unanswered: Why is it that at a distance the sea is blue but when it's in a bucket it is no colour except the bucket? Black is all the colours mixed because I saw it happen in a jam jar, but what is white made of? What does white do? Where does white come from? It's a very important colour yet no one knows. Most of my school shirts are white. Every colour is explained except white which has nothing in it. So when people say they have seen something clearly "in black and white" do they even know what they're talking about?

Twenty-three

[Enter Judge and jury]
The court room is buzzing. It's my blackened rainbow eyes and white patched-up nose. A clean break, the doctor said, but there's nothing he can do for a broken nose except stick hard wadding up inside each nostril so I can hardly breathe and mumble like Moses. I might have a small bump to remember Manston by. I am in serious danger of looking like Tony Bennett for the rest of my days.

Dearing wants to adjourn, tells the judge I've been attacked on remand but I want no more adjournments and neither does the judge. Dearing comes over and says, 'This looks very bad, today of all days. What the hell happened?'

'Airports are bad luck for me.'

He thinks I've totally cracked, definitely wants to postpone the closing statements, but it's all systems go when the jury trail in. They take one look at me and either think I'm *The Elephant Man* or an alien. Maybe *The Man Who Fell To Earth*. I'm hoping for sympathy, hoping not to be treated the way the two freaks had been on celluloid and real life. Now would be a good time to grow wings and fly away. I scribble on my notepad:

magic realism is dead,
long live magic realism
Is dead,
long live realism
is dead,
long live magic

I should stick to prose.

Middle QC is up first, super-confident. He goes through the rigmarole again. Heard it already. He's literally holding court, holding everyone hostage with his legal acumen. He is a small, weighty man. Is he bald under that judicial horsehair toupee or whatever they're called? Probably wears it in the bath, in bed. His wife says to him, 'Why don't you take it off when we make love for a change?' But he can't. He hides under this wig. This and his gown give him power and status, just like the monks and subject masters at my old school. The whole courtroom suddenly feels like the headmaster's office and I am a schoolboy in heaps of trouble.

Middle grips his gown, thumbs up and out. He asks each and every juror to examine their conscience. Think about the overwhelming evidence against me. He reminds them of the crimes, takes them back to the fire, the forensic photographs of Stepan Belonog. He milks the victim's innocence and misfortune and some of the jurors look to the bereaved family in the gallery. 'A devoted son, a groom-to-be, but no longer.'

I write Stepan's surname on my notepad. *Belonog.* I make anagrams from it:

o belong
on globe
Ben gloo
everything sticks to you

Middle asks the jurors to put two and two together and come up with me in Broadstairs on December 19th. He reminds them of my motive and opportunity afforded by close proximity to the Acorn Offices. *From small acorns do great oak trees grow.* He reminds them of the stream of lies I used to cover my guilt. The fictional Cassi Hart. How the police rumbled me but their hands were tied because of the alibi, an alibi which has been proven in this court to be at best vague, at worst unsafe. 'Remember the telephone call to Ms Wood?' he says. 'The defendant could not be in two places at once.'

A pity though, I'm thinking. Where would I prefer to be, if not here at this moment?

Middle tells them I am clever and ambitious, that I have fooled a lot of people since the fire. I am a very average writer with an above-average envious streak. I am deluded and live in a fantasy world. 'Irony of ironies,' he says, 'the defendant finds a conscience. In a fit of unusual honesty, he tries to appease his guilt by confessing to his then lover, Mr Fortune, so chillingly accurate to the actual crime that Mr Fortune could not have made the confession up. Mr Alexander Fortune is a highly respected novelist. He's an honest man. He does what is best for the defendant and for society. Out of an admirable sense of moral duty, he informs the police.

'Remember what the defendant shouted while being arrested by DS Kempe at the airfield. "Judas! Judas!" to the man who gave him up. We know the defendant was going to flee the country. Remember what was in the boot of his car. For a holiday? It was a final bid for freedom, a chance to escape. Because Mr Fortune had said he was going to telephone the police. The police had caught up with Mr Tippet's lies.

'Ironically,' he says, 'it was one moment of truth, his confession to Mr Fortune, which has brought him to trial today, and this truth is damning. The evidence is overwhelming.'

Close to his conclusion, he draws their minds back to my writing (Exhibit A and Exhibit B). They no longer have their original titles. He asks them to consider the chilling words; prose which shows an unhealthy obsession with sex and fire and violence. He reads aloud: '*Humans cooking... the staff barbecue... the thought makes my spine tingle.* And Exhibit B, a story which burned in the fire that December night: *What's it like to burn? Hot but what kind of hot? Your hair would crackle. Your eyes would melt like balls of wax. Lest we forget.*'

A terrible moan comes out of the gallery right on cue. It's Mrs Belonog and I wish I could melt into the wood-panelled background.

'Lest we forget. Lest we forget the memory of poor Stepan Belonog,' Middle says, 'I urge you, urge you, to examine this evidence. To search your consciences and find the defendant guilty of arson, and guilty also of manslaughter.'

The proverbial pin-drop. A silence so full of doom I can only stare at the jurors with a resigned, fixed gaze. Everything Middle suggests is true. He's on the money. But hearing it sends a chill right down my spine to my toes; so what can it be doing to the twelve ordinary members of the jury?

Dearing QC steps up to the plate, takes centre stage. My Dearing daring do. Just the sight of him makes my heart pitter-patter. It's now or never, Dearing. I'm sorry about forgetting the telephone but I can't be blamed for Manston's temper.

He parades himself before the jury for a minute at least - a proud peacock - allowing them time to shake off the prosecution's lingering speech. I don't know. The suspense is killing me. My palms are ice-cubes in my lap. Cases are won and lost in the closing speeches. Isn't that what Rogers said only this morning, in my cell?

'Evidence is evidence,' Dearing starts. A very relaxed approach. I admire his professional poise, but when is he going to say I didn't do it? 'I'm not going to waste time on circumstantial evidence.' Okay. A slow build-up. My mother's actually holding her mouth open. My father's transfixed by Dearing's walking motion. He should stand still or the jurors will get sea-sickness.

He lays it on the line suddenly: 'Ladies and gentlemen of the jury, all of the evidence against my client is flawed. My client's motive is meaningless when you place it beside the thousands of competition entrants who also failed to win the prize. How many court rooms would we need to try each and every one of *them*? Since when has proximity to a crime denoted intention? And means? There is not one physical shred of evidence linking my client to the scene of the crime. Not on his clothes, nor in his car, nor in his flat. His car is not on any CCTV. No witnesses saw him in Broadstairs that night. How did he set the fire? What with? We don't know.

'Why is this? you have to ask yourself. Because Benjamin Tippet was not in Broadstairs that night. He was watching TV at home and then he went to see his girlfriend. It was a week before Christmas. His girlfriend was intending to leave Pensbury for a winter vacation and he wouldn't see her again until the New Year. Ms Wood noted no change in his behaviour that night. Someone who had set a building alight would, I suggest, be acting rather differently. Not caring for someone with flu.'

So far so good. Then he picks up speed.

'The *so-called* confession. We have heard a great deal about this from my learned friend. I only ask you this: if a man is so scrupulous, so clever, so manipulative and such a brilliant liar, so desperate to protect his secret, his crime, why would he drop the whole pretence and tell someone he had only known for a few months? Why sacrifice his freedom so easily? It doesn't make sense. And Mr Fortune, the novelist. We only have his word for the confession *as he remembers it*. My client has never denied the invention of his *so-called* confession. In his own words, "I was trying to make myself feel more important". He felt "too ordinary" in the company of Mr Fortune. He was "eager to make a splash in the literary world". Whereas, and this is the important distinction, Mr Fortune was a waning star. His time had almost been and gone.

'Why did Mr Fortune exaggerate and embellish my client's *so-called* confession? Perhaps he genuinely believed it. Perhaps he wanted to believe it. He is supposed to be a private man, something of a hermit. Yet he drives a James Bond-type car, flies a private plane every week. These things get you noticed.

'He calls the police about this *so-called* confession bringing full media attention on himself. Are these the actions of a hermit? A recluse? A private man? No. They are the actions of an opportunist, a manipulator. It emerges in the press that he is writing his long-awaited autobiography. A coincidence? I don't think so. I suspect there is a whole press and publication machine at work. No...' he turns to face me and opens up a parental palm, '...my client is the innocent party here. Out of his depth in a world he knows very little about, an insecure young man hoping to make it as a writer suffers one moment of misplaced exhilaration and makes a ludicrous confession, *so-called*. It is used against him without a second thought. Benjamin Tippet has a blemish-free past. He has never committed a crime in his life. He has a job he enjoys, a flat of his own, and loving parents. Why would a man wish to jeopardise such things?

'And finally, the irony, as pointed out by my learned friend, is not that the truth has brought Mr Tippet here, but that a brilliant fiction has. A ludicrous lie beautifully crafted by the novelist, Mr Fortune, into a masterful, almost credible fiction. Something he is renowned for. It is a story which stands in stark contrast to the tragic reality of Stepan Belonog's death. With every piece of evidence, reasonable doubt runs through this case like a stick of Blackpool rock.

'So, concurring with my learned friend, I too ask that you question the evidence, search your consciences and find that Benjamin Tippet is completely innocent of arson and entirely innocent therefore of manslaughter.'

I have to hand it to him. Mr Dearing QC is a genius. I'm breathless, can hardly breathe through my blocked up nose. If you were on the jury, how would you swing, if you did not have this record in your hands? I can imagine a juror shaking her fuzzled head each time a piece of evidence is laid on the deliberation table. Reasonable doubt running through it like a stick of Blackpool rock. Hopefully Dearing has planted a seed which will grow in the jurors' minds.

Judge Cummings takes up the slack, reminding the jury of their duties and the gravity of the charges. Then he gets into the technicalities of law, the central aspect of his summing up: '*Actus reas* means...to find the defendant guilty of arson you must be sure the physical act of setting the fire is down to him. If you believe the victim would not have died *but for* the defendant's setting the fire, you must find him guilty as charged. On the principal count of involuntary manslaughter - this means unlawful killing or reckless killing - you must decide or be sure of *mens rea*. By *mens rea* I mean that the defendant must have *foreseen* and therefore *intended* death or serious bodily harm. It does not necessarily mean that if you find the defendant guilty on the first count of arson that you also find him guilty of the principal one of manslaughter. You must be certain in your own minds that he intended death or bodily harm or that his actions made either of these most probable or likely.'

Some of the jurors look terrified and lost, as if they are going to be tested on this later. If this wasn't my trial, I'd be asleep in the stalls.

'However, to find the defendant guilty of involuntary manslaughter, you must be absolutely sure that the prosecution have proved *mens rea*. In other words, that his foresight equals intention. If you are not certain or if you consider there to be reasonable doubt as to guilt, then you must find the defendant not guilty.'

He takes a short pause, straightens his itchy wig, then says, 'This is my last trial and I can say with all honesty that it has been a complex one. I urge you to consider the facts very carefully and, as far as it is possible, to come to a unanimous decision. But should this not be possible, it is within my power to accept a majority verdict.'

Dearing shifts uncomfortably in his seat, looks exasperated, writes furiously on his notepad.

'What this means is that I will accept a verdict of ten or more jurors. If ten or more of you *cannot* decide upon the same verdict, I am bound to dismiss this case and find the defendant not guilty as required by the law. Do you understand what I'm saying?'

Perfectly, I'm thinking. This is your last ever trial and you want to go out on a rocket; a guilty verdict. The jurors nod. Cummings thanks them in advance for their hard work. He stands, the QCs stand, I stand, the whole room is standing, except my dad in his wheelchair. He smiles at me through gritted teeth as the jurors leave the room.

This is the worst time for a defendant, yet I suspect it is the most exhilarating for the press and the public. If I had better hearing I'd have heard the nattering in the halls and corridors and canteens and chambers above my purgatory cell. 'What do you think?' 'Guilty as hell.' 'I'm not sure.' etc. But only twelve people's opinions matter now.

I drink a cup of stagnant coffee, half-swallow a sausage roll. There's a man in the cell opposite. He hammers on his door, calls out: 'What did you get?'

'Still out,' I say. 'You?'

Well, it's extraordinary, maybe even fate, or just coincidence, because this faceless man starts singing *Five Years*, loud as you like: 'Five years, what a surprise. I got five years, stuck on my eyes, five years, my brain hurts a lot...' as if Tom, my brother, or Bowie himself has come to court. He is the faceless man and I listen to him sing his song, singing along with him. He gets to the end, the wailing bit, and then it's just the drum beats of my heart and the guards' boots coming to take him down to hell.

Three hours later, still no decision. What do I expect? The jury are not deciding what to buy each other for Christmas. Each time I hear keys jangle or a voice echoing down the corridor or a door banging, my heart springs into my throat and the adrenalin strips moisture from my mouth. I turn cold. Fingers deep-frozen. 'Tippet?' A bailiff opens the flap on the door. 'Jury's reconvening in the morning. You've been in the wars, haven't you?' He cuffs me. 'Back to Pensbury.'

Segregation = isolation. A kind of limbo. I am locked up now sometimes for 22 out of 24 hours and unlike my other cell, there isn't a window. The only good thing, in theory, is that it is actually quieter here than on remand. It is a smaller block and no one's allowed a radio. Every now and then a nutter is brought in, there's a lot of commotion and noise, then it's back to relative quiet, and speaking of which...relatives I mean...

[Enter Mother and Father]
My parents are allowed to see me. Special dispensation because they haven't seen me since the Manston debacle. My mother has been kicking up a stink, making threatening complaints. She should be careful or she'll end up in the cell next to me, vacated today by a murderer.

We have the visitors' room to ourselves. It's quiet and eerie in here, like a parents' evening at school. Mother and Father are very quiet too. Like me, the waiting time has been the hardest thing and now we are so close to knowing what we are waiting for.

As ever, my mother is the first to speak. Silences make her nervous. She wants to know all about the fight and I tell her I can't remember much of it. She's been to my flat and had my navy blue suit dry-cleaned. 'I've given it to a prison officer, Benjamin, and you should have it in the morning, with a clean shirt and I bought you a new tie.' She thinks my black suit is looking tired, that it drains all the colour out of my face and the blue one is much better. 'Blue sets off the Burton eyes.'

I have to laugh. She has beautiful eyes but I actually look like a panda because of the bruising. She tries touching my nose and I rear back. 'It's amazing how many times you touch your nose in one day without even thinking,' I say. 'Even when you're not lying.' I tell her a lie then, saying it is tender, when actually it is very painful; painful enough to make my Burton eyes water.

'Dearing's done a good job,' Dad says, and I nod in agreement.

'That other man's a weasel,' Mother adds.

'I'm grateful to you for getting Dearing.'

'Only the best for our son,' he says.

We are stuck then, an awful tension or sense of anticipation hanging in the air between us like static (as a point of information, "Benjamin" means "beloved youngest son". I discovered this in Little's Bookshop. A book of baby names we stocked at the time. "Thomas" or "Tom" means "the twin" or "devoted brother").

'What are the beds like on segregation? I bet they're foam.'

Mother rattles his ribs with her elbow. 'Benjamin doesn't want to hear about beds right at this moment.'

284

'They're foam on segregation, Dad, but not on remand,' I say to please him. He is a strong man but has his weaknesses. Bedz for Zedzzz was some years ago and his physical life has been affected badly by the falling bed; yet mentally he's the same, still in working order, still interested in things, even if it is mainly beds. I have seen him at his lowest point before and no one talks about it. It was when he was told he'd never walk again. He was given a wheelchair to take home. I was managing the bed warehouse. It was unusually quiet for a bank holiday so I shut up shop and went back to see how he was. I walked into the kitchen and thought my mother was murdering him. She was standing over his body.

'Get off me!' the body shouted. I tried to help him back into the wheelchair but he flew at me with his arms, 'I can do it! Get off me!' We watched him drag his dead legs like slugs along the tiled floor. He pushed himself up, grabbed the wheel of the chair and the chair rolled backwards, away from him banging against the kitchen cupboards. He slumped back down with his living, feeling hands on these fucking dead legs. He wept into his chest. Wailed. He couldn't look at me. 'Go away,' he roared. But we couldn't leave him. I put one arm around his waist, the other under his arm, lifting. My mother helped hoist him back into the chair. I remember thinking later that night, it's bad karma, bed karma! The Tippet Curse! And there is nothing right with this family of mine; except that we love each other in our individual ways.

Dad reminds me again about ordinary stuffed mattresses gaining weight over the years from human sweat and the droppings from dust mites. '70% of the bed! Foam is better. Rubberised. Italian.'

'Do you want the contract?' my mother says to him, pulling a face.

He shakes his head. 'You don't want real criminals getting a good night's sleep, do you?'

It makes me laugh but mother rolls her eyes to the ceiling and I can see it is not because of any embarrassment with my father, it is because she is about to cry. After years and years of drought she's been crying rivers these past few months. Tropical, straight down rain. She rubs a patch of skin at the side of her eye. It's the size of a postage stamp; angry and pink. I ask her what the mark is and she deflects the question with a question of her own, but I know what the mark is. It's where she cries. It's where the tears come out running and she's always wiping them away; so much now that the skin doesn't have time to heal before the next load of salt comes, causing the skin to dry and crack.

'I'm sorry,' I say. 'I'm really sorry I've dragged you down with me.' I close my hands over hers on the table. My father puts his over mine and hers so we have made a Tippet hand sandwich. Somehow, this whole sorry business has brought the three of us closer together. As Father Mackie said, good can come of bad. When one door closes, a window opens. Whatever. 'Thank you for being here,' I say, and it is enough to open the Burton sluice gates.

'I'm not going to lose my only son,' she pours into her hankie.

'You're not going to lose your only son,' Dad says, opening his well too.

I want to tell them the truth; tell them that the Belonogs have lost *their* only son and it's because of me; the whole kit and caboodle of my confession. But trapped between them the way I am, the tears the way they are, including mine in my throat, I can't. I show them with my eyes, but they don't want to read the truth in them.

'Be strong,' Mother says.

'The final hurdle,' Father adds.

We are in this room as a family, still with secrets undisclosed, but we are a family nonetheless. I used to look at them half in spite, half in disbelief that they were actually my flesh and blood. For six months after the Tom epiphany, I convinced myself they had adopted me, that my real parents lived elsewhere. But I look into my parents' eyes now and know I belong to them. One glance in my mother's eyes to see I have the same marbles, one glance at my dad to recognise the mannerisms I too possess. Once upon a time - when stories started with once upon a time - my parents hid the truth from me (protected me from the truth) and now I do the same. I have chosen my path and must stick to it. I must make my journey, whatever the consequences, wherever the endpoint.

After we have hugged and kissed, I am led back to my cell. The lights go out at 9pm. I look up to the place where the window used to be in my other cell, wondering if the moon is out. If it is blue. It is very dark and I imagine all sorts: Tom in one corner strumming Bowie riffs on his guitar; Stepan Belonog working on scientific equations in the opposite corner; Alex sitting at the desk writing me a letter. No sooner have they appeared than they have gone into the grainy darkness once more.

Twenty-four

Back in the bowels of the court cell in the morning, wearing my blue suit which smells of dry-cleaning fluid, and the crisp blue shirt stapled around my throat, I wait.

I wait upon the fate to be decided by twelve ordinary men and women. Why twelve? Why not thirteen? Because there were twelve apostles? Because thirteen is unlucky? Because of history? Because you have to draw a line in the sand somewhere I suppose. How long is a piece of string? Or rope, come to think of it. Fifty years ago, or less, I might have been looking at the scaffold.

There is a feint whiff of white spirits. Part of the cell has recently been painted. It's best not to think about it. Ghosts of the past. There are dents in the metal door and scratches on the walls and drops of dried beige paint on the concrete floor which leads under the door. Best not think of anything at all.

It is almost lunchtime when news filters down and my door is unlocked. 'Jury's back,' the bailiff says. It's as if he's talking about the November rain.

Nothing blots out the team of majorettes drumming in my chest and ears. My legs are custard. The waiting is over. Maurice once told me that King Charles I wanted to wear a coat on his way to the axe-man because he didn't want his subjects to think him a cowardly king for shaking; the day he lost his head for all posterity. To be remembered for that one thing!

The court room is a hive of excitement. I'm not uncuffed which isn't a good sign. I see my parents but don't wave because of the metal bracelets. The Belonogs are here, of course, and sitting close beside them are DI Lawless and DS Kempe in their best suits. Elvis is firm-jawed, in defiant mood. The jurors are in place. Some of them steal a glance at me and I try to read their expressions. A man looks away. The QCs are talking to each other like friendly competitors.

Mr Justice Cummings, chief itchy-wig himself, enters the room. Cummings and goings. I imagine he is actually E.E. Cummings (I've been reading the biography. "Hee-hee Cummings" Maurice calls him). You have to break the tension somehow. My legs are not working properly when I stand for him. He sits in his highchair, then I sit.

If I am found guilty it will be up to him to determine my sentence. This grizzly-faced man with pin-prick eyes; a real puffed-up piece of work. He probably enjoys sending people down. Probably jumps on their coffins. I don't know, I could be wrong. I don't claim to understand how the world works; I'm only hazarding a guess at it. Some people are born shite, others acquire shiteness and others have shiteness thrust upon them. Remember?

When everything settles down, Cummings begins. There is not much preamble. He asks a clerk to go to the jury, then asks me to stand up again. My heart drums so loudly I think I won't hear the verdict and my legs will give way. The court is silent except for the clerk who is talking slowly and clearly, reading from a sheet of paper.

The foreman is asked to stand, though she is actually a forewoman. An irony. She is the very woman I'd fancied at the beginning of the trial and had occasionally flashed a winning smile at during the proceedings hoping she would be my saviour. My Henrietta Fonda. She is stiff and formal now. The clerk reminds her of the two charges against me: 'On the first count of arson against the defendant, Benjamin Tippet, have you reached a verdict?'

The forewoman nods. 'We have.'

Blackpool rock, I'm thinking. Reasonable doubt. Blackpool rock. Blackpool rock. Like a mantra.

'And is this the verdict of you all?'

Huh? What *is* the verdict?

'Yes,' she says, clearing her throat. My heart is hammering. There's an awful pause, a fraction of a second, but it feels like a lifetime. Have I missed the verdict?

'And on the principal count of manslaughter against the defendant, Benjamin Tippet, have you also reached a unanimous decision?'

'No, your Honour,' the forewoman says to the judge. My heart nearly pops. Dearing fidgets in his seat. My mouth is utterly dry, like swallowing ash. Blackpool rock, Blackpool rock, Blackpool rock cracks invisibly on my lips. I've been found guilty of arson, haven't I? But there's reasonable doubt, reasonable doubt over manslaughter, isn't there?

The judge leans forward, disappointed. 'I see. Well, in that case I must now ask you to return for further deliberation, in the hope that you will all be agreed, or at least a majority of you be of similar mind. For there to be a conclusion to this trial ten or more of you must be agreed.' He nods to the clerk who nods to the ushers and the jurors leave the room to an orchestral murmur.

Below, down in the purgatory cells again, sitting here frozen on the edge of the bed like a doodle in the margins of a diary; frozen in time. You've come a long way, I'm thinking, only it doesn't look like it. I shake uncontrollably, as if a ghost has poured liquified ice-cubes down the collar of my shirt. I cannot stop this shaking, not with my hands in my pockets, not with pacing, not with mind-control. The forces at play are too strong and too many. Three hours pass like this. Intermittent bursts of adrenalin. I cannot take it for much longer, but I have to take it.

'Tippet,' a guard says, stiffening me with his voice. He unlocks the door and I'm led up the stairs and fed into the court room where I'm told to stay standing. I can't look at my parents, only at the jurors.

The clerk asks again if they have come to a verdict upon which they are all agreed. Once again, the forewoman answers, 'No.'

'Have you come to a majority verdict upon which you are all agreed?' An oxymoron if ever I heard it.

'Yes,' she responds, not looking at me, only at the judge.

'And how many of you are in favour of this verdict?'

I'm going to have a heart attack.

'Ten,' the forewoman says.

The clerk turns to the judge who indicates with a wave of his hand to progress as quickly as possible. 'On the count of manslaughter, how do you find the defendant? Guilty or not guilty?'

Christ, God. I'm holding onto the rail in front of me, praying.

'Guilty,' she says, and there's a single gasp from the gallery, then a hoot, a mumble, a light ripple of hands. I do not turn around to look. I think I'm falling backwards and down. I focus on the back of Dearing's head. The scrolls of his wig. He has folded his arms. A gun goes off in my head, but actually it's more like a bark from the gallery. Mr Belonog is on his feet shouting something in Ukrainian. Then his daughter, in English: 'Justice! Go to hell! You burn in hell!'

My heart stops for a millisecond, the blood freezes then surges again. I do not exaggerate when I say the roof nearly comes off the courthouse. Most of the gallery are up on their feet now. I turn to my mother and father, mouthing sorry. I could be sick. At the other side of the gallery there is a commotion. A woman has collapsed, her legs stuck fast under the seats. She is pulled free by Mr Belonog and carried from the room by ushers. In the meantime, Cummings is banging his gavel down like he's pounding nails in a plank. Middle is dragged to his feet by his team of lawyers. He's not exactly jubilant, more like shocked. 'We did it,' his mouth seems to say.

'In accordance with the law,' Mr Justice Cummings says loudly, 'it is my duty to tell you, Benjamin Tippet, that you have been found guilty as charged. Your sentence shall be decided upon in due course, with the relevant social and psychological reports considered as appropriate. However, you should be advised in advance of my sentence that crimes such as these can carry a heavy penalty. You are to remain in custody until sentence is due. Take him down.' He bangs his hammer on its block once more and I am led away.

So, there you have it. My fate. But the coffin lid is not completely sealed. The nails must be driven home. How I wish I could be driven home.

There's a debriefing session in the cells below. A hopeless puzzle to unravel. Dearing QC is at a loss. The decision is a slight against his professional good name. He cannot fathom it; how the jury had not swung in his favour. He's amazed and angered by the judge. One of his team suggests I should have taken the witness stand. 'Don't be a fool,' Dearing snaps. 'We should try not to speculate. That way lies disappointment.'

'How disappointed do you think I feel?' I say to him.

'I'm sorry,' he says, putting a hand on my right shoulder. 'We shall appeal, naturally. Too many reasons not to.'

'He led the jury,' one of the team says.

'The telephone evidence was inadmissible,' another lawyer says.

'He's a tough old cookie that Cummings.'

'Cookies should crumble.'

'Maybe he wants to go out with a bang.'

It's as if I'm not in the cell with them. Invisible. Dearing is incredulous. He rubs his chin, looks at me curiously, thinking. And what is he thinking? That the telephone nailed me? That I had garrotted myself with my own cheese wire, or phone line? That I was an arsonist and murderer anyway, so what the hell? Look at the bruises, the broken nose. Who gets involved in prison fights unless they invite them? Something not right about you, Ben Tippet. How come he had been so blind to my guilt in the first place? Now it is so obvious to him. The guilt is stretched across my face like a bruise.

'The idiot jury,' his sidekick suggests. 'It's as if the electoral register threw up a dozen duds.'

Dearing replies, 'We shall definitely appeal. But we will wait for the sentence.'

'How long will I wait?' I say.

'Knowing Mr Justice Cummings,' Dearing says, grimacing, 'not too long.'

The following is what I discovered back at prison. I got talking to an experienced con during a rare moment of association time. He tells me Cummings is a pure bastard. Thirty years a judge and as predictable as piles. A cousin of this con got top whack for stealing a carrot from a market stall. They don't come more hard-nosed than old Cummings. He might look like Mr Bumble in *Oliver Twist* the musical but he's a rod of iron. Equanimity is not in Cummings's dictionary (the con didn't actually put it that way; I did). If this is his last trial, I can kiss goodbye to the bookshop forever. Rumour has it he's going to the House of Lords after retirement from the bench. He's in with the government. He toasts the Queen every night before tucking into his roast pheasant pie. And now he's going to roast and toast me, good and proper.

What did I tell you about The Tippet Curse?

Twenty-five

I feel strangely calm three days after the verdict, as if the life-force has been sucked out of me and I don't care anymore.

I've nearly accepted my fate, the consequence of my guilt. I barely eat my dinner, my stomach growls all night long. I can easily count my ribs. Sometimes I play with the odd one out. The one left behind by Eve. Or is that a myth? My ribs press through the bed sheets like the bones of an emaciated cadaver in the morgue, but I quite like being the Thin White Duke. The bruising is turning a yucky, greenish yellow across my cheekbones; blood vessels breaking up to be reabsorbed. I've seen the prison GP three times for headaches and nosebleeds. I'm getting worse than Alex for aches and pains.

Alex again. I can't escape him. He's always there or thereabouts with me. I didn't think it was possible to become so obsessed by a man, or the idea of a man. I think I must have been obsessed by the idea of him before I was even born, it's that bad. I see him in my mind: flying his plane around the coast, free as a phoenix, listening to "Heroes"; floating on the surface of an infinity pool; at the wheel of his Aston Martin like the oldest ever Bond; standing in the cartography room reading aloud; sitting at the keys of his mother's piano (Satie is to him what Bowie is to me if that doesn't sound too crass?); in my arms, I'm cradling that tired old head so full of sadness it makes me sad just thinking about it. So much genius and trussed up anguish inside that eggshell head. The migraines are not migraines, merely manifestations of painful memories. Nothing can bring dead people back to life. Music is just a conjuring trick. Blink and you might miss it.

I wrote to him: *Our names are together on a stranger's napkin.*

Ice cold in Alex. Nothing back. I have written to him twice this week (not to mention countless other letters) and none have been answered. I feel sorry for him. I once envied his life, his work, his home, his cars and planes and Greek villas and yachts etc. They still have a basic attraction but they are nothing without the man, and I'm starting to believe he is nothing like a man.

I wrote asking why he had deserted me when I needed him most: *Where were you at the verdict? Whatever happened to 'I'll wait for you?' The first sign of trouble and you fly away like a frightened sparrow. I thought better of you, Alex. I still love you and hope you can love me?*

Fat lot of good. Not a dickybird. Probably thousands of miles away sipping a G&T on a Greek island or has his feet up in his Greenwich village apartment. Whatever. I'm finally seeing Alex for what he is. To see someone in their true colours you have to take off your rose-tinted glasses.

When I look in the mirror, I see a slightly different Ben Tippet. A rearranged one. Bruised and battered but not a total coward. I told my brief yesterday that I wanted to tell the judge at sentencing that I was guilty after all, but my brief was having nothing of it. Horse already bolted. 'Let the judge do what he wants and then we will appeal no matter what he throws at you.' I think they are just looking for more work. 'There's the possibility Cummings will be lenient,' he said, but he wasn't very convincing. That is why they have suggested I see the forensic psychologist again. See what comes out of it.

Two days later, I'm on the opposite side of prison, in a room with a wonky handle and a screw standing outside (a prison screw that is, not a handle screw). Dr Julie Sparkes explains at the beginning that she is putting a psychological report together. Ben Tippet's profile. The judge is obliged to assess it, though not obliged to follow any recommendations. I shrug my shoulders.

'This will be a highly structured interview which makes DSM4 diagnoses of particular psychological dysfunctions and disorders including major depressive disorder as well as borderline personality disorder. It also enquires about positive symptoms of schizophrenia, extrasensory experiences, substance abuse and dissociative disorders.'

'That's a lot of disorders,' I say. 'I don't believe in aliens and I don't do drugs if that saves you any time?'

She laughs, crosses her shapely legs, making a lovely static noise. 'We can talk a little first, if you like?'

'Trying to soften me up?'

'To put you at ease it says here in my guidelines.'

Double-bluff. A clever woman. She had me fooled that first time, way back when I told her about King Kong and crying and all that stuff. She claimed back then never to have heard of the film. I ask her about that now and she says she'd been pretending, just to get me talking. 'No way!' I say. 'You're a better liar than I am!'

Confident smile. She is a smoker, not that she has stained teeth, it's just coming over from her clothes. A quick one in the car park before coming into the prison nut house. We all have our foibles. She's a cool concombre, for sure.

We chat a bit about life on remand and life on isolation ward. 'To find out what it's really like in here,' I say, 'open a tin of sardines. We are treated the same and smell just the same after a while.'

She looks at me curiously, asking, 'If you had to choose between fame and fortune which would you rather have? Fame or fortune?'

It makes me laugh because I've already tasted both. 'Fame, of course. Fame can bring you a fortune, but a fortune cannot bring you fame.'

She asks me about my writing then. What do I write about? Where does the inspiration come from? What's the best time of day to write? Who is my favourite author? It's great. Just like I'm on a book-reading tour. I answer all the above but never mention Alex who is actually the answer to two of these questions. Then she asks a much more complex question which catches me off-guard. 'How does writing make you *feel?*'

I have to think about that one. 'Do you mean *why* do I write?'

'Okay. Yes. *Why* do you write?'

'I turned to writing as therapy, catharsis, but what do you know, Julie? I'm more neurotic now than I ever was.' She writes this down. Then a gem pops out of my mouth. An impromptu pearl of wisdom. They come out of me when I don't think too hard. Sometimes the thing you are desperately seeking is right under your nose. 'Oxygen,' I say (it sounds trite, but it's true). 'Writing is how I breathe. There are probably as many reasons to write as there are blood cells in my body.'

Dr Sparkes writes it down.

'I write fiction because one life isn't enough. I write because I have to. I write because I don't want to be forgotten. I write because I'm angry at everyone and want to understand why I'm so angry at everyone. Sometimes I'm so angry I want to punch a hole in the sky. I write to be happy, I guess.'

She nods, scribbling. Then we're onto the major stuff. She takes some papers out of a well-used briefcase, holdall, whatever. 'Most of the questions I will ask can be answered "Yes", "No" or "Unsure". A few of the questions have difficult answers and I will explain these as we go along. Okay?'

'Okay,' I say, 'and how long will it take? Because you know I have a hair appointment in an hour.'

'Let's say you'll make your hairdresser's appointment.' She's getting to know my humour quite well.

(You can try this test at home folks, which would be a much nicer place to try it. You might discover how narcissistic you are).

'Do you suffer from headaches? Migraines? (No, but I know a man who does). Any occupational impairments? (high shelving at Little's). Prescribed medications? Abdominal pain? Nausea? Vomiting? Bloating? (yes, in here) Diarrhoea? (ditto). Intolerance of some foodstuffs? (I know a man who can't eat cucumbers). Back pain? Joint pain? Pain in the genitals? (actually, yes, a shooting pain right at the base of my penis, does that count?). Shortness of breath? (only in the dock). Chest pain? Loss of voice? (yes, but only because that's the human condition). Double vision? Palpitations? Dizziness? Difficulty swallowing? (steady!). Deafness? Blurred vision? Blindness? Loss of consciousness? (sometimes I have these blackout things when I'm angry, do they count?). Difficulty urinating? Seizures? Trouble walking? Long periods of no sexual desire? (absolutely not). Impotence? (Does one occasion count?).

We pause a moment while she makes a note. Very disconcerting.

I can't remember all the questions but I seemed to answer a lot with a "yes". Ever experienced heavy depression? (yes, when I was 18). Ever been prescribed anti-depressants? (ditto). Suffered from amnesia or fugue? (I like the word fugue and I do forget some things which is more than just forgetfulness). ECT? (no). Weight loss? (yes). Eating disorders? (I had mild bulimia when I was a teenager). Lack of sleep? (yes). Recent thoughts of death or suicide? (yes to both). Hear voices? (yes, but this is natural isn't it?). Do the voices come from inside you? (yes, otherwise they would be other people's voices). Do these voices argue in your head?

(sometimes). Do you ever speak about yourself as "Me" or "We" or "Us"? (did Queen Victoria have a personality disorder? '*We* are not amused...'). Do you ever feel that there is another person inside you? (I hope there is). Do you see the future while you are awake? (yes, and it's not very good). Do you see the future in your dreams? (unsure). Do you move objects with your mind? (I move objects *in* my mind, does that count?). Have you ever been possessed by a demon or spirit, a living or a dead person? (did you say possessed or obsessed?). Possessed (no). Do you make contact with ghosts or poltergeists? (no. Unsure. Yes). Difficulty concentrating? (Yes). Imaginary playmates as a child? (Yes. There was a Mrs Peacock and she was always telling me off for things. Joking. But yes, I did and he was called Frank). How old were you when the friendship stopped? (unsure). Do people come up to you as if they know you but you don't know them? (doesn't everybody?). Are there large parts of your childhood that you can't remember? (yes).

Dr Sparkes turns onto a new sheet, and I'm really enjoying it. 'For the following nine questions please answer yes only if you have been this way much of the time for much of your life.'

'Fire away.'

Impulsive? (yes).

Unpredictable behaviour which is potentially self-damaging? e.g. binge-drinking or eating, spending, drug abuse or sex? (sex).

Unstable personal relationships characterised by your alternating between extremes of positive and negative feelings? (yes).

Unstable identity or self-image or sense of self? (yes, if I'm honest).

Mood swings, irritable, anxious, swinging from normal to depressed? (unsure).

Frantic efforts to avoid feelings of abandonment? (unsure).

Recent suicidal behaviour, self-mutilation or thoughts of suicide? (Yes. Thoughts).

Chronic feelings of emptiness? (Yes. No. Unsure).

Transient stress-related paranoia? (Yes).

'How am I doing?'

'Very well,' she says.

'And it's only been 35 minutes.'

There were some other questions, like would I say I had a preoccupation with fame or wealth or achievement? Do I crave admiration, attention or praise? How important is beauty to me? Am I empathetic? Do I frequently feel rage or envy or fear? Do I think I'm self-aggrandizing? Could I ever be haughty? (such an old-fashioned word). Do I have unrealistic ideals?

You can probably answer all these on my behalf. You know me well enough by now.

When Dr Sparkes had finished, I said, 'The problem with all this is that it won't hold any water.'

'Why not?'

'Because itchy-wig Cummings will just say, "People with personality disorders like NPD and BPD are compulsive liars. You can't trust the paper the answers are written on".'

'There are built-in adjustors,' she said. 'Tried and tested for over a decade.'

'Trick questions?'

'They offset the potential for dishonesty.'

'So have I caught myself out?'

She put her DSM4 papers away, the guard looked through the door at us, and she pulled a grey cashmere coat over her two piece. 'For what it's worth, I think you've been entirely honest.'

'Shit,' I said. 'Then I can't have a personality disorder, can I?'

I think she really liked me. She had a nice smile. I must have been better than some of the dumbnuts you get in here. Imagine Manston! Doesn't bear thinking about. Dr Sparkes was welcome to her job.

[Enter The Titanic]

I am woken in the night by a howling creature in one of the other cells. He must be having a nightmare; maybe imagining he is human. I too have had a dream, and it is not a good one: Alex and I are standing on the upper deck of a ship. Not just any ship, it is The Titanic. An eccentric billionaire has rebuilt it to the exact specifications of the original, only with better navigational equipment and more turbine power. We pass by a ballroom on board and everyone's glammed up to the eyeballs. Alex and I are in tuxedos. Alex has a full head of hair and actually looks like Noel Coward. A jazz band is playing. A singer is singing beside a piano. We get bored and head for the deck again.

It is the middle of the night. We watch the moon glittering on the waves as a terrible announcement comes over the tanoi: 'All passengers please return to their cabins. A storm is approaching.' We see no storm and ignore the warning.

The ship is gliding slowly through the mid-ocean. We are so high up we can't hear the water. Morning is just over the horizon and we drink it in like pink champagne. We calmly hold hands. That's when we see them coming. Shadows the shapes of funnels. Tornados reaching high into the sky. Not two or three, but five or six or seven or more. The numbers increase by the second.

'Perhaps it will be like the Wizard of Oz,' I say. 'We'll be picked up and carried to another place.'

'Maybe we'll avoid them altogether,' Alex says. But there is no avoiding them. They are the Fates stealing through the empty ocean looking for our ship. The sun peeks above the line, silhouetting the tornados, each one a whirling dervish. We don't move. We are strangely calm. Whatever will be, will be.

The first one eases past as if it's a ghostly Conradian ship. The second brushes the front of the Titanic rocking us in its crib. The third pushes us into the path of the largest tornado as if we are a bowling ball, only we cannot knock anything down.

Alex laughs hysterically. We could be on a fairground attraction, bumping this way and that. People less strong than ourselves are being thrown overboard, disappearing into the black swell beneath and far away.

The mother of all tornados takes hold, swings us into its swirling vortex. We have walls now, made of water, and they are higher and wider than the ship. We are being sucked into a well, but moving up, not down.

'We're too heavy to be carried very far,' Alex says, but up we go, higher and higher, turning in the funnel to the top. And when we get to the top, it is morning. The sea far below is yellow and orange and red. We are suspended, no longer spinning, and there is only us. We are so high up now we could be in the stratosphere. We can see the curvature of the earth, the deep blue of the oceans, the greens and browns of continents, the jagged outlines of mountain ranges splashed with white.

'What happens if we fall?' I say, panicking for the first time. 'Where do you think we will land? If it's on land we will be ashes and if we drop in the sea we will bang our heads on the bottom.'

Alex doesn't smile, doesn't say anything. For a moment we are Gods, like heroes, suspended in the air; Gods, heroes on the brink of extinction.

That was the exact dream I had the night before sentencing. It doesn't take a genius. You don't have to be Dr Freud or Dr Sparkes. You might be at the Dr Seuss stage and still be able to read this dream!

Twenty-six

I'm supposed to say nothing at sentencing but I have prepared a speech.

There was a reason for keeping the biography of E.E. Cummings in my cell; something he said about life. If I'm going to lose years of my life in another cell (the notion of which fills me with dread) I shall acquit myself in the best and only way possible. I shall go down in history as someone worth listening to.

I have written it down for good measure: *Portrait happens to be an art, and artists happen to be human beings. An artist doesn't live in some geographical abstraction on a part of this beautiful earth by the hoary imaginings of unanimals and dedicated to the proposition that massacre is a social virtue because murder is an individual vice. Nor does an artist live in some so-called universe, nor does he live in any number of worlds, or any number of universes. As for the trifling delusions like the past, the present and the future of quote "Mankind" unquote, they may be big enough for a couple of billion super-mechanised sub-morons, but they're much too small for one human being. Every artist's strictly inimitable country is himself. An artist who plays that country's faults has committed suicide and even a good lawyer cannot kill the dead. But a human being who is true to himself, whoever himself may be, is immortal. Of all the anti-artists in space, time will never civilise immortality.*

The court galleries are jam-packed with faces. Some are familiar. Elvis and Blonde Bob are tight beside the Belonogs. Mrs Belonog might have smelling salts in her handkerchief, given what happened to her last time. Journalists. What will their headlines be tomorrow? *The Book, The Cheat, His Lover and the Fire? Fake's Progress?* Plain *Lovers and Losers?* or the more tabloid *Wannabe Ain't Gonnabe?* or *Tippet Goes Down?* (ha-ha).

There is no jury. Probably waiting by their TVs or radios at home, whatever. Two of them had thought me not guilty of manslaughter, remember? Perhaps they will go to the press in a year's time and reveal the difficulties they had in the deliberation room, fighting over the Blackpool rock. Who knows? Who cares?

There's no Alex, but that sure ain't no surprise. Frightened little sparrow had dipped his feet in the birdbath of me and not liked the temperature of the water after all.

The biggest and best surprise is my family. Mother, Father *and* Uncle D (in very discreet trouser suit and pearls) all together in the relatives' gallery. I wave at them and they wave back. It's not meant to rub anyone's nose in it. They are my family after all. A lot of hard work has gone into their reunification. Every family is a foreign country. They do things differently there. I've sent letters, made phone calls to both sets of parties. Dad is the least happy about it, but he'll come around, I'm sure. In time, out of bad things good things come.

Before crusty old Cummings passes sentence like terrible wind, I ask him if I can make an apology, something like that. 'Most unusual,' he says, but agrees. I turn to face the Belonogs. I've planned all sorts from a public confession to self-flagellation but in the end decide upon a simple sorry. 'I want to say how sorry I am for your loss. I can't claim to understand how you feel, but my family once felt grief. Similar but worse for you, I guess.'

Not exactly delivered in the right tone because the Belonogs shoot poisoned darts with their eyes. They think I'm being insincere when really I'm being honest. I turn to face the judge again and take out my piece of paper. I straighten it out so I can read my scratchy handwriting.

'What's this?' Cummings says.

'A speech,' I say, and his old mouth drops open.

'A what?'

I clear my throat and start reading: 'Portrait happens to be an art and artists happen to be human beings.'

'Enough!' itchy-wig snaps. He doesn't get it, so I explain about the real E.E. Cummings. He looks down at my QC who surfaces from behind his hands, groaning.

'Cummings could be a relation of yours, your Honour,' I say, lowering my hands. A reporter is writing everything down, or as much as he can. It will be in the papers next to photographs of me and Alex.

'I have never heard anything so disrespectful in an English Court of Law,' Cummings says. 'Not in thirty years. You've come here for sentencing and you quote E.E. Cummings?'

'Well, I could have chosen a poem. Something shorter.'

'You simulate an apology?'

'I'm not simulating anything, your Honour.'

'Silence! Or I'll hold you in contempt of court!

'It was supposed to make people think.'

'Stay standing,' he says. 'I'll give you something to think about.'

My knees should be knocking, my palms should be ice. I should be frightened of him like he is an angry parent or a head teacher. But my feet are firmly planted, my hands are room temperature and my heart is not fast. I'm only confused. Let him throw the book at me.

'I have read with great care the clinical psychologist's examination which purports to explain your actions on the night of December the 19th of last year, Mr Tippet. I don't doubt there are aspects of your self, identity and personality which are confusing and contradictory. Today is just one example. I agree with Dr Sparkes's conclusions that you are a fabulist, a fantasist. That you are a compulsive liar. Neither does it take an eminent psychologist to convince me of your narcissistic tendencies. You have shown here today your inordinate self-pride and self-aggrandizement. Your selfishness.'

Maybe I should be pouting.

'The report suggests that you are a deeply insecure person, probably stemming from childhood which has developed into an adult façade which she calls your "self-fiction". It says you were possibly smothered with motherly love as a child, that you were probably given too high an expectation in life. Probably, possibly, probably.

'I have searched for guarantees, for empirical data, for reliability, and cannot find any. You come from a loving, supportive, relatively privileged background. Indeed, a private education. There is no social deprivation. There is no account here of why you should set fire to a building and in the process kill a man. This report says you were a bomb waiting to happen and that, quote unquote, "bombs have a tendency to go off only once". I don't doubt that everyone who commits a series of offences of this nature can be made the subject of the kind of report which has been devoted to this case, but the responsibility for the interests of the innocent members of the public who suffer is left to the court, to the jury, and to the judge.'

Here we go then. I told Sparkes this would happen. There's no built-in adjustors with Cummings.

He shakes his head, scratches his wig. 'The form in which the court dispenses that responsibility should be to discourage others tempted to indulge their fantasies, their delusions and anger to enact a similar course of conduct. You have inflicted immeasurable heartache and hardship on the Belonog family which cannot be repaid with a ten-second half-apology. You have caused millions of pounds worth of damage to a publishing house.

'Mr Tippet, you stand charged with arson and involuntary manslaughter. You have committed an invidious crime. Arson is the most cowardly of crimes. It can never be justified, only condemned. I believe your defence counsel was taken in by your fanciful lies. Perhaps you yourself believed your own fictions. Given your fondness for quotes, Mr Tippet, you should be familiar with Geoffrey Chaucer who said that, "Trouthe is the hyeste thynge that man may kepe"?'

Now he is showboating.

'Involuntary manslaughter I'm bound to tell you comes at a heavy price; anything from a non-custodial sentence to life imprisonment…these days all too easily a sliding scale. I don't doubt your crime happened in a moment of red-hot temper and frustration, but losing a competition does not warrant an act of such recklessness. I note that you have committed no previous crimes before this one. I note too that you are not what we might call "ordinary" in terms of your mental state, but there is nothing to suggest diminished responsibility.

'Taking all of these things into account, I sentence you to ten years in prison, six months for aggravated arson to run concurrently…' Cheers and gasps from the galleries, so loud I can hardly hear the rest. 'I recommend most strongly that you serve the full term of ten years, and may you spend this time wisely, in contemplation of the damage you have caused both to the Belonog family who shall always feel a personal loss, and to your own family, and to Acorn publishing house too. Take him down.'

This is his swansong. But it is not quite mine.

Twenty-seven

It's cuffs and down to the cells then straight back to Pensbury Prison.

They move me out of my isolation cell and into prison proper. By that I mean I'm still in the same prison, only in the beating heart of it, with the true convicts. They can't put me back on remand and they need my segregation cell for a paedophile. I hate the idea of a kiddy-fiddler lying in my bed and using my toilet but you just got to leave some things behind.

Red helps me with my books, tells me there ain't no room in the other prisons. His attitude hasn't changed towards me despite me being a proper convict. A proper killer. Maybe he's just doing his job, being professional, but I think he likes me. He has a stack of my books and I have some prison-issue clothes to change into. Regulation dark blue nylon trousers and blue and white striped collarless shirt made of durable, chafing, cardboard cotton. You are what you wear, Tranny and Godzilla once said on TV. So true. You are just like anyone else now: a tiny cog in the machinations of State. You have a past which is as unique as your thumbprint, though like a thumbprint you are catalogued, databased, processed. You look in the mirror and don't even recognise yourself, like Mr Ben without the adventure. You are a lost child. No parents to help you. A bastard like all the other bastards alongside you. Maybe it was like this for Tom in the cub scouts. All that's left of his time in the cubs is his blue woggle, sitting like a fairy's hoola-hoop inside a box inside my wardrobe inside my flat inside the city walls.

'It's likely you'll go to London or the Isle of Wight,' Red says. 'Wormwood Scrubs. Pensbury's the town, Scrubs is the city.' A chilling way of putting it. 'This isn't a category 'A' prison. The system's in a squeeze.'

Anyway, it's okay staying at Pensbury. It is a familiar trip for my family and there's always Red. Reliable Red. My uncle in an alternative world, if that makes sense? I don't see him as a screw. He's too nice. I tell him this and he says I should see him when he's angry, like when his daughter got pregnant aged fifteen. 'Puts your pool cue into perspective,' he says.

Always with the jokes is Red. He's such a bad liar. The creases show around his eyes. You have to keep a straight face when you lie. The art of lying is to be cold, clinical and consistent with your story. You must tell the same lie to everyone or the people meet and discuss and you're screwed. The art of good lying is in the detail. The devil. Be consistent with the detail. No variations. Period. Believe your lie is the truth until you no longer recognise it as a lie. Follow the rules of fiction, which as Eudora Welty once said, is the lie which tells the truth.

A good lie, like a good story, is believable. But you must not forget the story you have told. You must be true to your story or the illusion is shattered. As with Red here. He told me two months ago that his eldest daughter, Frances, was the apple of his eye. He loved her more than his wife. So how was he ever going to knock her teeth out with a pool cue? He's just making friendly conversation and I'm grateful. I am grateful he doesn't only work on the remand wing. I am grateful he doesn't lie. I am terrified of the idea of Wormwood Scrubs.

I write a letter that night. I give it to Red the following morning. He is less likely to read it than the other officers whose duty it is to read letters at random, though I don't know why because you're not going to send drugs out from prison, but I suppose you could ask for them. It goes like this:

Dear Alex,

By the time you read this, you will know my fate. I don't blame you. I accept full responsibility. My QC says there will be an immediate appeal against the sentence, if not the verdict. By that he means at least three months and by then I'll probably be in Wormwood Scrubs or somewhere. The thought. It is a nightmare. It is a nightmare without you. I have written a dozen times telling you exactly how I feel. I have filled pages and pages trying not to be clichéd about love but still my heart genuinely bleeds. You won't write to me. Won't speak to me.

None of this is intended to make you feel guilty. You are the innocent one. I understand that. I have not stopped thinking about you the whole time in here. Not a single day or night. I keep imagining us together. I read your books over and over to be closer to you. I don't even have a photograph of you, just those inside the covers of your books. I looked for you in court but there was no Alex.

Have you deserted me? Am I really that bad? It is obvious to me now that I have made a complete fool of myself. The biggest fool in history to have believed you would wait for me. It is not against the law to visit someone in prison. I think I get the message loud and clear. Another sad little cliché to add to the list. Which is why this is my last letter to you, Alex. I won't write again. I can't bear your aloofness anymore.

I once played a song for you in your plane, do you remember? That awful day when they came for me? "Heroes". There's irony for you. I play the song over and over in my head. I thought it was my song, but actually it is more about you. You are my hero. And I hope that one day I can make you proud of me too. It might still be in your player. Listen to it. It says everything. It means everything. It will always be everything.

Take care. Goodbye, Alex.

I'll always love you.

Ben

xxx

I give Red the letter in the morning and he takes it away for stamping and posting. The letter is hopefully not going to be my last. It is a clever letter doing what it says it is not doing; namely, encouraging guilt. It could also be misconstrued as a suicide note, in which case he'll come in to see me. Apart from these things, it is an honest letter. It is emotionally true. I've thought of him constantly and I've occasionally, depressingly, thought of suicide. I still think of the young shoplifter who swallowed toilet paper which is probably the worst ever way to go back in the box.

My parents come that afternoon. There are no tears, only anger. What they had privately feared has come true. They've lost their only son. My dad is practical. He's spoken to Dearing who will head up my appeal. I'm worried he's burning up his personal savings and tell him I don't even like Dearing, and any QC will do. 'No,' he says, 'Dearing is a good man, it's the flaming judge. Dearing's going to get him for making an unfair example of you and leading the jury in his last ever trial. Then there's inadmissible evidence. The whole thing was compromised, prejudiced pre-trial. The punishment is meant to fit the crime,' correcting himself. 'When no crime was committed in the first place.'

Why am I bothering to lie about this still? Because it would crack their hearts open, that's why.

They leave me and I'm back in my cell, thinking about my letter. It's burning a hole in my head, even though I've worked out that it takes four days to even get through the prison security system and out the front gate.

Twenty-eight

[Enter Tom]
Don't be too surprised. I told you every good lie is based on a half-truth. Tom, my half-brother, is not dead. He sits across from me in the visitor's room. He's been coming in to see me now and then. He did not die in a motorcycle accident. I was never told anything by my Uncle D. Tom doesn't get on with the rest of my family, that's all. He has his own family now, living in Dagenham. He runs his own motorbike business. Not cheap things; Harley-Davidsons. He has three children; one is called Ziggy. He has a secret life no one knows about except me. He married Amy, his childhood sweetheart. Yes, he had the accident but he did not die. He has grown used to his face, the burns. He has had surgery but his face is still unnatural, disfigured. One eye is out of place, his lip a little drooping. He drivels sometimes when he speaks.

What do I care about how he looks? He is my only brother. Tom = devoted brother. He doesn't like to write. He's bad with words, though great with his hands; fixing up motorbikes etc. He goes on Harley weekends. I ask him if he wants his records back, but he shakes his head. He's moved on. What use is vinyl these days? He doesn't listen to Bowie anymore. He's moved on. He's thinking of moving to New Zealand where his natural (Reed) father still lives. There are more open roads to steer his Harley through. British roads are no good anymore. They're stuffed up. He is a gentle man. People look at him as if he's a freak, half-melted, a deformed human being, but he's not. His heart is in the right place, and everything's in working order. I love him very much. I love him like the hunch-backed brother loves his older brother in *Merry Christmas, Mr Lawrence*.

And, of course, it is me who conjures him up all of the time. A whole past, a future for him. These are the imaginings I sometimes have; seeing him, talking to him, painting a picture of him. Sometimes he is so real I actually shake his hand, hold him in an embrace and tell him all the things I have struggled to tell anyone other than Alex Fortune.

I go to sleep. I don't dream. I wake and Red is standing by my bed. I don't know if it's even the same day. He's holding a letter. I recognise the handwriting on the envelope. It's mine. 'What's wrong with it?' I say, about to get up.

'Stay where you are,' he says, puffing and perspiring. His shoulders are up near his ears. He scratches his woolly red hair, so much of it you could make a cardigan or a fleece. For a moment I think the whole thing is a dream; that I have never set a building alight and nobody has died; that I am fifteen and have woken up at home like Dorothy in *The Wizard of Oz*, and Red is my farmer uncle wringing a hat in his humble hands, not a prison officer wringing his keys; and that somewhere is my brother, Tom, still alive.

'Ben,' he says, 'I wanted -'

'Money for a stamp?'

He isn't in the mood. Such a miserable face. 'I wanted the opportunity to be the first to say -'

'You wanted the opportunity to say what a pleasure it's been before they cart me off to Scrubs in the morning?' This is what he has come to tell me, of course. But he doesn't want to tell me.

'I'm sorry about the Scrubs joke,' he says, shoulders relaxing a little.

'Forget about it. It was a joke. I can take a joke. *But where am I going?*'

'I've come to tell you...come to tell you...oh I don't know how to tell you exactly...that your man...the writer novelist?'

'Coming in to see me?'

'Dead, Ben.'

I snort or something. I look for the tell-tale signs of a lie, a joke in the creases of his eyes. But there are no reasons to lie, no creases. Just a cast-iron face. 'What's that?'

'I'm sorry. I got here as quickly as...I ran all the way so I could...it was on the...they said at first it might be a terrorist flying into the cliffs...they said his plane got-'

'Plane?' I look at my wrist. 'But what time is it?'

'Time?'

'Red, it's dark outside isn't it?'

He pulls up his sleeve, making his keys jangle. 'It's six-twenty, but...'

'In the morning?'

'At night, Ben. Did you hear what I just said?'

'Alex isn't dead. He never flies in the dark; only in daylight. He's not a fly by night. It's someone else, Red. Maybe it is a terrorist.'

He steps closer. I look into his shadow cast from the corridor light, and I know. A cold numbness creeps outwards from the core of me to my hands which begin to shake a little, I think. I can't remember. I hold them still on my lap so Red won't see. Some laughing men walk by, shadows joining. This large shadow whistles a tune. A lamentation. Nothing I recognise, nothing to latch on to. Everything goes quite dark, as if I am being eclipsed and left out in the cold.

'I know how much he meant.'

'*Alex's* plane?' I look up from my bed.

He nods, miserably. 'He didn't come back to the airfield at dusk.'

A sickness rises. 'He didn't get my letter.'

Red steps closer, so close I can't stand it. He places a hand on my shoulder, confirming everything, crushing me under the weight of it. 'I'm sorry. Really.'

'It's too late, isn't it?'

He places my letter on the bed. I look down. Alex's name stares back at me, though it's hard seeing him, my version of him, because a rock has lodged in my throat and my eyes are already melting.

'Will you be alright? I mean…do you need someone?'

'Need someone?'

'I'll be back,' he says, pulling at his chin. Everything blurs, even sound. I don't hear or see him leave. It's just me and my letter. It's odd, the sound that comes to me right then, filling my head. These angels, a little bit like monsters creeping out of the silence, out of the cracks in the ceiling and the walls. These dark angels descending all around me, singing in my emptiness. In my darkness.

Alex?

Enough really, enough to make you want to cry and never stop.

Twenty-nine

[Enter Pentonville]

Apologies for the hiatus. Not that you'd have noticed because if you're reading this the publishers won't have wasted paper on the physical notion of time passing and vacuous space which December, January and Early February became. They passed in a blur.

We are in a new year, a new prison, and all systems change. A new prison? A new system? (very old actually). And a new me. Well, not exactly new; quite spent and used up in fact. Changed in many ways. As Bowie used to say: *still don't know what I was waiting for and my time was running wild, a million dead-end streets, so I turned myself to face me but I'd never have caught a glimpse...of how the others must see a faker, I'm much too fast to take that test. Ch-ch-ch-ch-changes, turn to face the strange ch-ch-changes, don't want to be a richer man...ch-ch-ch-ch-changes, turn and face the strange, ch-ch-changes, just gonna have to be a different man. Time may change me, but I can't trace time.*

There's one common denominator in the deaths of Tom, Stepan and Alex, and it isn't the Tippet Curse. I was responsible for the raging infernos engulfing all three; none of them being accidents. Without me they'd be alive. Certainly, two dead bodies could be laid at my door; and who's to say an evil molecule of me hadn't rubbed off onto poor Tom's hands all those years ago through my swaddling clothes when he'd held me as a baby? Made him lose his grip on his motorcycle and skid into an oil tanker? (the fact, dear Ben, is not in the stars, but in yourself, that you are an underling).

'I, Ben Tippet, am the curse.'

That's what I told the shrink in here. He's not as good as Dr Sparkes in terms of probing questions, or looks, but he did encourage me to write again. To finish what I started; for catharsis if nothing else (oh, how the irony stings me). I couldn't write, you see; couldn't even sleep at Pensbury Prison and was given carefully-supervised sleeping pills. I was put on suicide watch. I wanted to die to tell the truth. I swallowed toilet paper, nearly choking to death. Then I just stopped eating. I lost my appetite for life you could say. I can say it anyway. I'd only take food from Red's hands. Soup and a roll, and even then it would take me an hour supping and nibbling at the edges like a mouse in the corner of my cell. It was enough to keep going. To stay alive.

Time passed, as I say, in a melancholic blur. Tom's anniversary came around in December (Stepan's too, of course) but barely registered. Christmas stodge was served and Red wore a paper hat, pulling a cracker with me. He let me win a plastic key ring and read the joke out himself: 'Q. Why do anarchists only drink herbal tea? A. Because all proper tea is theft!' There was something on the other side of the joke and it said: *do not confuse what is valuable with that which is sought after.* Some proverb I could have done without. I put it in my notebook and have used it here.

It's hard explaining how low I was. *Low* like the album. Low in spirit and in health. A kind of disembodiment. I couldn't pick myself up off the floor. The floor seemed part of my feet. Made of concrete. But my head was a balloon. I couldn't get Alex out of the hot air balloon of my head.

No one could ever accuse me of subtlety or of telling a story straight, but that's alright. Imogen once told me in class that there is a formula for a successful story and it goes something like this: a story is a shaped like a reverse tick. The reverse tick is how a story builds from the beginning (conflict), rises to a climax (crisis) and then dips away to a conclusion (resolution). This can be represented in the letters A, B, D, C, E where A=Action, B=Background, D=Development, C=Climax and E= Ending.

I've fucked that up anyway, haven't I? But Imogen also said that a good story doesn't conform, doesn't stick to any old formula or pattern; it does exactly what it wants to, and in no apparent order, only an order in which it happens, as long as the characters are changed by the end. Life is never finally resolved so why should a story be any different?

I'll finish *Fakers* if it kills me, though I might call it *The Art of Decomposing* or *Losing A Fortune*, in honour of Alex and because that's exactly how I feel. It is the truth of my life to date; the whole truth and nothing but. What are the chances of having it published anyway? Though I suppose miracles do happen for some people. Sometimes it can feel as if you're always swimming against the tide, but every now and then the waves break kindly.

No. I didn't write a single word after Red walked into my cell at six-twenty that night to tell me about the news on TV. It blew me to pieces. It was as if I'd been on that plane beside Alex. Not a word written since (except a letter to the Belonogs who don't want to know). I have spoken to Uncle D, who is looking after my parents. Pentonville is closer for them to visit and I see them each week. Uncle D picked up the broken Tippet pieces. My dad was the most shattered. Uncle D has redeemed himself finally, it seems. He's a good woman. It's difficult for my mother who cannot slip things so easily under the carpet anymore because her broom has worn too thin, but we are still the family we were, maybe closer. I don't know. I am their only living son after all. She has forgiven me. The church have forgiven me. But I'm sure it can't be easy for her.

I have given a full and frank confession to a Catholic priest. Not Father Mackie. Another man of the cloth who lives in Tottenham and visits the prison once a month. He told me that a soul burns in hell if you take your own life, yet doesn't go to hell if you take someone else's and are fully repentant to God. That's religion for you, and I'm grateful for it.

I've settled into things again. Same routine as Pensbury but scaled-up procedures. The queues are much longer for the phone and the showers, which are very dirty. Someone found a cockroach in their bed! I haven't got my own cell. That's fine, I don't like to be left long alone. Terrible thoughts. Terrible terrible thoughts. That's why I'm seeing the shrink every fortnight. That's why they put me in a cell with another man called Simon Patterson. He once worked as a bank clerk. A white-collar criminal. He swindled his employer out of £137,000 over the course of two years. He's okay. We get on. You have to or you'd kill each other. Pentonville was built in 1842, was meant to hold 900 prisoners, but there are close to 1,200. They get a hundred new inmates arriving each day, so it can only get worse. Sometimes the kitchens run out of food. Some evenings it's just fish fingers. The queue for the anti-depressants is longer than the dinner queue.

Patterson said he'd heard of me. Fortunately, it wasn't for cracking Manston's teeth into domino pieces. I don't want to fight anymore. The men in here make Manston pickle look like pureed gherkin (officers and inmates); or they would purée him if he ever came here. You keep your head down and your hands in your pockets.

Simon Patterson said he saw me on TV, rather my photograph which was plastered across the screen, the tabloids and the broadsheets for a long time. Alex's death was a big story from late November until January when the Coroner's report was concluded. You don't get famous writers crashing their planes into national geographical monuments every day. They called me his lover all the time; another reason never to be caught alone by myself in this place. I stick to Simon like "No Nails". He's served a year of his three-year sentence and knows the way of things. Who to avoid, who to butter-up etc. It was Simon who got me a job working in the library instead of doing the laundry.

The good news (there has to be some when you come close to finishing a story) is that my right to appeal has been won, thanks to Dearing. It will be in the spring. Just a couple of months' time. I am appealing against my ten-year sentence, but not the guilty verdict. Dearing says I should be set free to receive continuous and proper psychiatric help. They say I'm borderline narcissistic, borderline autistic, borderline personality disorder, borderline borderline. But either you are or you are not something, aren't you?

I have confessed everything in writing to the Belonogs. The only writing I have done this year, until now. The Belonogs don't want to know, even though I got books ordered in specially and translated the words myself into Ukrainian (only Stepan had good English). It's the truth. I'd like to apologise in person but they don't want to know.

The enquiry into Alex's death concluded with "death by misadventure", saving his two daughters any embarrassment. He was ill with a cluster of migraines, Willow and Summer were quoted as saying in the papers. He was under a lot of stress from the press, they said, but never enough to kill himself. He liked to take risks and this one hadn't come off. Something like that. *A novel way to go*, one paper said.

There was no suicide note, though this hasn't scotched rumours or defied common sense. There was nothing faulty with the plane and it had plenty of fuel. There was so much petrol in the tank that on impact a large chunk came out of the White Cliffs of Dover. I have seen the crash-site on TV. Black on White. I have been in the plane he flew, as you know, and I have seen how controlled he is, how in control he was about most things. He wanted to be a daredevil like his father. He missed his parents more than I can say.

Officially, it was death by misadventure because a man walking his golden retriever high up on Shakespeare's Cliff heard engines roaring, saw a rolling plane manoeuvring just as the sun was setting over the Channel. The sun was very low, he said, and the pilot was probably blinded so he didn't know what was sea and what was sky and ended up in a hard place. Almost like Icarus, just like Gloucester in King Lear, only there was no one to stop Alex. No one to take him home.

The irony of Alex's death was blinding. It has taken me quite a while to see that fiction is an accident by design and death is a fact of life. The collision of memory and imagination. And out of the collision comes the truth; the harsh reality of the truth. What would I know?

My application to attend the funeral was turned down by Alex's daughters. They hadn't enjoyed their father's company before his death but could enjoy his wealth now; the poisonous girls who hadn't been to the funeral of Alex's own father not that long ago. Who can explain families? Who can explain greed? Family and invited friends only. I'm not sure I can blame them. They had every right to do so. I can't help thinking I should have been there for him. He would have liked me there, maybe. He lies buried beside his parents at St. James's Church in Sussex, in the grave he said was waiting for him (in his autobiography).

I have a letter from Alex and I read it often.

Correction. I have a *photocopy* of a letter from Alex and I read it often. The original formed part of the Coroner's report and is filed away. Maybe the original is now with his daughters? It must be worth something after all, though it can never be worth as much to them as it is to me. It is dated the day after my sentence was handed out, shortly before I wrote my letter to him (the one he never got, if it's not stating the obvious).

Immediately following the news of his crash, a keen-eyed screw plucked his last ever letter from the prison mail and handed it over to the police who passed it on to accident investigators, then on to the Coroner, like Chinese whispers. Anyhow, I didn't even know about this letter until I was transferred to Pentonville. It landed on my pillow like a breath on my face. It's very long (nearly fifteen pages) and very personal, so I'll only reveal selected bits:

Dear Ben,

November is a cruel month. When I heard about the verdict, I waited for your sentence and hoped it wouldn't be harsh. You are not the person they say you are. Beneath the veneer, there lies a lovely young man. Forgive me for not coming to see you, forgive me for not replying to your letters. Each one is safely tucked up in my studio. I think of you now, looking out of your cell, waiting to be free, and it fills me with shame because I am sitting in my studio looking out at orchards. The boughs and branches were once full of fruit, weighted down to the ground, but now the apples and leaves are gone, the branches clipped back for next season' growth. The first frost has been, the ground not so yielding now....

...I saw the last wasp this morning, dying on my window sill. I know how much you hate wasps; have every right to hate them. They take but they don't appear to give. They are selfish creatures, this is true...To a stranger, it might look as if he is dancing in an elaborate circle, buzzing a too-late eight, thinking it is a bee. Then suddenly, he is quite normal and healthy, clear-sighted and cleaning his hairy legs and eyes and the tips of his tired old wings. There is hope, but sadly he is out of time, out of step in every way. He falls onto his side, stripy thorax heaving, breathing hard. And what are his last thoughts? "Why wasn't I a honeybee? People would have got closer to me, would have liked me, if I'd been a bee. Instead I am hated, alone, not mourned by anyone except a writer!"

It is ridiculous the thoughts we writers give to animals, insects, plants and inanimate objects. A sign of old age, maybe? Of desperation?

You see how he rambles? How he wants to be a honeybee, not a wasp. He was never a wasp to me. Perhaps the sweetest man I've ever known. *Sadly out of time*, he says. It's just like Emily Dickinson.

...It is a cruel joke, the way life allows you time to get used to it (what life is, who one might live to be) only to run dry before you have time to make use of the knowledge...I came home to Smuggler's from my solicitor's in London today. I put the key in the door, opened it and caught a smell which upset me. I walked right into this canker, and do you know what it was?

It was the future. The future was cold and clammy and empty. The future was cold-calling me. I built a fire but it would not light, as if the house was damp and saying: 'This is not your house, Alex. Not your house at all.' There is no place to be...

How can they say he did not kill himself? It is not between the lines so much as *in* the lines. I recall conversations where death was his main subject, his theme. It is what Alex revolved around, gravitated towards. What was it Alex said that time? Even over a leisurely Athenaeum dinner he could suddenly turn inwards on himself: 'Death is to life what a full stop is to a sentence, so you'd better make your last sentence a bloody good one.' And I'd replied: 'What's wrong with a semicolon, exclamation mark, question mark or ellipses?' Perhaps I planted an idea. 'They call semicolons "screamers" in the States,' he said. 'That and a dog's cock.' 'Then finish on a dog's cock,' I said. 'There must be worse ways to go.'

...I hope you can forgive me, Ben. I hope you continue to write as much as possible, because you are a good writer. My agent told me so. The future is full of opportunities. Grasp them, seize them, believe in them while you are young. Do you remember I once told you about getting old? It wasn't meant to frighten you. Now I've forgotten what I said...

What he'd actually said was: 'The weakness of youth is its desire of maturity; the weakness of maturity is its desire of youth.' I have remembered it for him now, haven't I?

I have only given you snippets. His letter is the longest letter I've ever read, and re-read. Long and full of happy things we did. It is not all morbid. It is full of "we" and "us" which fills me to the brim. It is pages and pages as if he is going to write forever; as if written in the anxiety of reaching the final last sentence; a bit like my Carver dream way back when, when I dreamed of being famous and dead at the same time.

And then it comes. Goes. Ends: *Do as I say, Ben, not as I do. Sorry to end on a cliché; I know how they irk you. I can see you turning your perfect Roman nose up now and that makes me smile; sometimes they are impossible to escape;*

Escape? Escape from cliché, or escape from smiling? Alex is ambiguous to the end. Other than a dog's cock (a private joke for me?) and his name (underscored) with three large kisses, this is the last written thing of his life. Alex being true to his last word writes about escapology which is tantamount to fiction. You set the ground rules - build the structure of your "lie" or "trick" - and when you have your audience right where you want them (holding their breath or shaking their heads or stroking their beards) you break free from the straightjacket of your own invention, and theirs. From the artifice of life to the truth of fiction. Isn't that what Alex believed?

Speaking of letters; they are turning up in their hundreds. Same as usual: freakoes and geekoes, wackoes and jackoes. I could have been married twenty times over. I don't mind the sympathy, it's the photographs that spook me. I look out for family's and friends' handwriting. I've told them to use bright purple envelopes which is my favourite colour. That way I know which ones to read first. I have written to Maurice and he has written back. There's some distance between us now, and not just in miles. He has permanently replaced me at Little's. Jenny has been elevated to the position of assistant manager. Paul has left for a job at Waterstone's. Sales are good, readings are full, but Maurice has changed his mind about calling the reading room "Tippet's".

He can't visit, he says, because of how busy he is. Really, it's his wife, Louise. I don't blame her. An arsonist murderer could never make a good role-model or godfather for a child. I think the papers have told horrible stories about me and the stories have scared the Littles off. I understand. It doesn't take a genius. Though it's a great pity (is this too neat? Too much summary towards the end, Ben? Whatever.)

Imogen is more conciliatory. She's not too bothered that I am responsible for so much devastation in the world. We all do bad things, she says. Good comes of bad, or so it seems. She thought of me the other day, in the zoo! Not *me* in the zoo, though I am in one. No, she is working for six months in London Zoo, doing research for her latest novel in which the central character is a gorilla called Chow. Not just any gorilla, Chow is a genius, brainier than the humans. He understands and uses syntax. Chow was brutalised as a baby, his family annihilated by trophy-hunters in the African jungle. The only survivor, Chow is brought up by a scientist family, and through copying this family he acts like a human and thinks like humans. But when the scientists are killed in a rebel bomb attack, Chow is the only survivor (again) and is brought to London for breeding purposes.

As the premise for her next novel, what did I think? she says. Well, Chow isn't even an African word, and well, monkeys have been done a million times with *Gorillas in the Mist* and *Planet of the Apes* and *King Kong* etc. She's reversing the Tarzan myth, she says. Great, I say, but don't get Charlton Heston to play any part in the movie. If he's still alive, I don't even know. She says Channel 9 have optioned a screenplay on the back of a three-page synopsis!

Imogen's fallen in love with primates, like she's living in Kubrick's *2001 A.D.* The silverbacks are awesome, she says. They could beat her brains out but they pass straws through the bars of their cages. She's been told to hand them right back to restore the gorillas' faith in humankind. *I'm a blonde chasing apes*, she writes, to cheer me up. She remembers my King Kong poster, asking if I want to sell it. I say she can have it. I've had it with King Kong, full stop. My flat is on the market too. I don't ever want to go back there either. Pensbury's over for me. I'm not sure I could really be happy anywhere now.

Thirty

Irony of ironies, I attended a couple of writing classes last week, to use up some time and find my writing feet again.

The wet-behind-the-ears tutor was called Ulysses Shaw. Don't think he came from a council estate like Imogen. He's a terrible teacher. So nervous, so nervous. Maybe he's expecting to be murdered any minute, and who can blame him? A leaflet found its way into my cell and it said that 33% of prisoners can't read, 50% can't write and 52% have dyslexia; so the odds are stacked against Ulysses.

Ulysses asked us to write an opening line to a short story using two words volunteered from his captive audience: "Chicken" and "Murder". Not much of a return from the multifaceted English language but Ulysses was determined to see the exercise through (now you bring chickens into the final equation, Ben?). He wrote the words shakily on a whiteboard and set us off on our fictional journeys and we returned from our imaginative travels with grand stories to tell: *I could murder a Kentucky Fried Chicken* was one, repeated about six times by inmates who didn't know what else to write. *A chicken murdered me* (which wasn't mine but wished was). *Once upon a time there was a chicken and it wanted to murder another chicken.*

'You've used TWO chickens!' an inmate balled. Honestly, it's *One Flew Over the Cuckoo's Nest* in here. 'There was only ONE chicken!'

'There's no rule about numbers of chickens is there?'

Ulysses Shaw didn't seem sure. 'It's not about chickens or numbers,' he said. 'It's about words, and the best words will be published in a pamphlet.'

Pamphlets-schmamphlets. I stopped going. I got on with my own words (everything's about letters in the end.) I wrote a letter to Red saying thanks for the memory. Thanks anyway for looking after me at Pensbury. They could do with a few more Reds in Pentonville, I said, to make him feel good. The officers here are abusive. They make Pensbury officers look like kindergarten children. I asked about alkie Rogers and Noses Moses. Red replied quite quickly. I wouldn't say it was friendly. Cordial. Something like that. Rogers was sent down for six months. He's in Durham. Moses is walking the streets of London because his case was thrown out for lack of evidence. He breathes free air, even with sinusitis and metropolitan smog. And Manston Pickle? Scrubs, fifteen years recommended. *We're still finding bits of his teeth in the TV room*, Red writes. This all makes me feel much better.

I got a letter from Cyprus and a postcard from Adelaide (you know who from of course). People from my past reaching out to me. People seem to like me. I am not alone, even if I think I am.

Uncle D gets wolf-whistled in the visiting room but we laugh it off. Nobody wants to take me on, it seems. I don't have to keep my head down too much and be someone I don't like to be. I can be funny sometimes and that smoothes over any misunderstandings with the resident psychos. I'm learning more about the human condition in here than I ever did outside. In prison, it's better not to rise above ordinariness in any way.

[Enter the theatre]
I am on the stage. The lip of a grand stage. The lights are just below "house". I can make out the faces of the audience because they're lit from the sidelines by torches. Huddled together on the left are Alex, Tom and Stepan. Stepan is two-dimensional like the photograph shown on TV. Tom has the same photographic quality. But Alex is three-dimensional. On the right side of the auditorium are everyone I have ever known: teachers like Miss Harkness and Miss Stone; school friends like Peter Klutz and his spying sister; writers like Imogen and the publicist Hilary pillory; there's Maurice, Jenny, Paul; the buxom Mrs Heaton; itchy-wig Cummings; David Bowie; my parents; Uncle D; Red Buchanan; Dearing daring do and Middle in the middle; the attractive forewoman of the jury; all my ex-lovers including Georgi and Megan Lake; Lea, the Princess Lea look-alike; even my old Labrador, Tyson, is sitting there; and the girl who sold me a bottle of champagne from the corner-shop the day I found out about the

Acorn longlist. The man with the umbrella I called Mr K. West is there too. The phonetic quest. He's wearing a bowler hat and has a Magrittian orange for a nose. I mean everybody is crammed in here from my life no matter how insignificant. Flotsam and jetsam and everything in between.

They are waiting for me to do something. It becomes clear exactly what when three people step out from the stage curtains holding things in their hands. A heavily-bearded individual (quite solemn but handsome with it) and two gorgeous women in long silk dresses and flowing hair. I say gorgeous, I say handsome, but they exceed natural beauty. They are divine. Is he God? Are they angels? Am I dead? (let's call him God, let's call them angels, let's call me dead for the purposes of this dream).

The angels move - more like glide - to the front of the stage and place things here and there. The faces in the seats stare. The objects are representations of historical figures and events. I'm panicking because I know very little about history. I have a closer look and discover that they have been placed in chronological order.

God comes to me. He places an object in my hands and tells me to put it where I think it should go. 'Where it should go? What is it?' The object turns into a heavy book in my hands. So weighty, each leaf could be spun of gold. It says *21st Century* on the cover. You don't get more downright obvious in a dream than this.

I walk the line of history. Thinking I'm really clever, I stand in the centre of the stage, in the middle of time and space, holding the 21st Century up in the air, high above my head. It is more important than all the other centuries because I am living in it. The audience clap loudly but God charges over, shaking his bearded face. He snaps the book out of my hand and the audience are silenced. The angels laugh, the audience are laughing at me, and it isn't a dream anymore. It is Malvolio's vain, cross-gartered, public humiliation. A fool's wasted Shakespearian journey. I say to God, 'You tell me where it goes then.' He hasn't got time to answer because it is the end of the nightmare and I wake up holding Simon Patterson's top-bunk bedsprings.

'Doesn't take a genius,' I tell the shrink. 'I was handed a responsibility.'

He gives me some gumpf about symbolism. The significance of the past, present and future. My role in them. Being judged by the past etc. You can't take a step in any direction unless you know where you came from and where you're going. Not total gumpf. Common sense. I needn't stumble along a tightrope anymore. I can give up writing. Full stop. Do something more humanitarian perhaps.

'It's about time,' he says.

'About time I what?' I say, making light of the darkness.

'Time itself. You are anxious about time.'

A truer word has never been spoken. The most obvious thing in the world and yet the most ungraspable, most impregnable. It is all around me. Blocks of time. All around you too. Invisible clocks ticking in our cells. The time is in my sentence and the sentence is in my time. All that.

I thought about the dream for days. The fact that Manston wasn't in it. Where was he? I've come to understand that the theatre is where (nearly) all of us end up when we go. We are seated together in one place, waiting to be entertained by new arrivals. We have to do a turn before we can take our seats in the stalls. Everyone has second chances. You can fail to make an impression the first time around, in life, and you might fall flat on your face as I have proved, but you can have a stab at it again later, in the theatre of your dreams (how far can one's fingers slip down one's throat?). How Alex would laugh at my fake religion, my corny imaginings. But you have to believe in something or you become Alex in the end.

Thirty-one

We are getting close to the end.

I smell it like the sea, can feel it in my fountain pen (actually, a plain old Bic has turned the tricks of this tale). The barrel is emptying, drying up, just as Tom's did in his old diary. Remember? The nib's blood is coagulating. I race it along the final pages of my last notebook. The mind outstrips the pen always. It does not know when to finally stop, and what with: comma, full stop. Question mark? Exclamation! Ellipses…? Three black dots can mean a lot, I guess: D.O.B. V.I.P. N.P.D. S.O.S. R.I.P. Dot. Dot. Dot. Life. Goes. On. Doesn't. It. Though? There seems nothing appropriate to end on. Nothing will do; only nothing will *not* do.

[Enter a mystery]
An ordinary and extraordinary day.
'Get up!' an officer barks. 'There's a visitor.'
This doesn't usually happen. You are normally notified a day or two in advance. Depends on the visitor. I know who it is. He's been coming all this time. Someone from the Belonog family has read my letters and finally braved the journey, wants a face-to-face with the man who killed his son. I have taken such an interest in the Belonogs, their country, culture, food and wine and language, everything. I have read a Ukrainian tractor novel. Sometimes I dream in Ukrainian. Of Stepan that is. He is the real innocent in this story, and he barely gets a page to himself. I am ashamed to have made anagrams of a dead man's name while his parents looked on in court. *Ben Gloo.* Stepan, I'm stuck on you.

I am led into the visitors' room and stand at the back of a long queue of inmates. I no longer feel the urge to be the first to everything. The screw points to a table in the corner which makes me shudder because I want the man at the table to be Alex. You can't bring the dead back. Only in your memory. I walk around the perimeter of the room unable to take my eyes off of the back of this stranger's head, salt and pepper hair, broad shoulders. Part of me wants to continue around the room and back out again before he sees me. That might be what the old Ben Tippet would do, avoiding trouble where and when it looms.

What am I to say? Will Mr Belonog break my nose in pieces? Will he try to strangle me? He has every right. If he can't speak English, what's the point? Will we just wave our hands about? Has he come just to look, and not to forgive? To continue hating me? To put a restless ghost to bed? Am I one of the six people he would most like to kill with a bullet from his vengeful gun?

I see Mr Belonog in profile. Older, much older than I remember from the court gallery. Pale around the gills, he swallows his Adam's apple. He has a prominent nose. Full in the face, he appears jowly, and weighty around the neck; an unhealthy lifestyle exacerbated by stress and drinking cheap Russian vodka, eating rock-hard bread and potato dumplings?

I am in front of him. He is holding leaves of paper, tapping them straight on the table. A speech written in English. He has no wedding ring. No jewellery. So the death of his son has broken his marriage? He registers my presence with a glance upwards. Large, dark eyes under a creased brow. No attempt to shake my hand, but what do I expect? I pull my chair from under the table, sit across from him, fold my arms, and there is a moment of complete unsettlement.

We stare at each other. This is the moment I've been waiting for; an opportunity to clear the air and make good my conscience. He coolly takes in every detail of my face: my Burton eyes, the small bump on the bridge of my nose, finishing between my eyes again after his scenic tour. It is an examination.

I have learnt some key phrases in anticipation of this moment but cannot open my mouth. The words clog my windpipe. He's still staring, though now it's with a measure of knowledge as if the tour of my face has given him more confidence. As if he is more familiar with the territory.

'I - am - very - sorry,' I say in slow, well-prepared Ukrainian; then again, slowly, in English.

Nothing. Maybe a sneer. And he is welcome to it.

Then it becomes quite obvious; I've never seen this man before. Not in a court of law. Not on TV. Not in real life. Only ever in my imagination, and on the telephone. The crumpled suit I'd thought was cheap-looking turns casual, lived-in and expensive. The teeth I'd expected to be uneven and uncared for from years of neglect are quite perfect and gleaming in a long, sardonic smile.

BB Crum no B is eyeballing me. Disdain or disrespect, I'm not quite sure. He parts his teeth and the accent is pure New York: 'I've come to see the man who killed my best friend.'

Hearing it makes my hair stand up. 'Too late,' I say. 'He flew into the White Cliffs of Dover.' Alex's longest-suffering friend and editor-in-chief at Friedman and Friedman is stumped for words. 'Look, Mr Crum, whatever. Why are you even here? I thought you were going to be someone else, someone important.'

'Oh, I am important,' he says, so arrogant it's untrue. There's a long pause, filled with question marks on both sides. 'I've done my research on you, Mr Tippet. I know all about you, but you're not what I expected.'

'Which was...?'

'Oh, I can see you're Alex's type, Alex's style even, but you're a bit more than that I think.'

Our conversation goes on like this. Cagily, point-scoringly. Not exactly going anywhere. Then he draws my attention to the real reason he's in a room full of convicts. He's carrying out his duty for his best friend, acting in his role as executor. I'd be lying if I said I wasn't excited. For some people deaths can change lives, in a good and in a bad way.

The house, Alex's car, everything in the grounds is mine.

'What?' he scoffs. 'You didn't know?' As if his research has thrown up a gravedigger, a goldminer. 'Did you want his plane too?' His thick eyebrows climb up his fifty-something forehead.

'I didn't want anything. That's the truth.'

'You can't have them anyway,' he says. 'Not yet in any case. Because you're serving a sentence and the will is being contested.' He leans on the table, self-satisfied, points to the sheets of paper. 'It's all in here.' He pushes them across and one of the screws shoots his eyes over us. 'It explains the current state of play.'

I read the gobbledygook, focusing on the highlighted sections. 'Alex's daughters?'

'They've got a handsome apartment in Greenwich village, copyrights to most things but not his autobiography, though they want it. Alex left it to me, but they want it. That's about the measure of it, and when you're released the things listed there should be yours, if you win.'

'His studio?'

'The whole of Smuggler's.'

It is hard to explain the excitement now it has properly sunk in. 'I don't get it, Mr Crum.'

'Oh, you'll get it if you have a good attorney. They'll be held in a trust and managed by yours truly. We can do it through attorneys. Do you have one?'

I nod.

'Good. Well, I've done what I've come to do, so…' He stands up and I follow suit, the legs of our chairs screeching '…I won't say it has been a pleasure but I'm glad to have honoured my part of the bargain.' He puts out a hand and I shake it. The frost between us is not as cold as I thought it would be.

'Listen…about Alex's book…'

'What about it?' he says, turning.

'He said if he didn't finish it, I could.'

'Alex said that?'

'I want to finish it.'

'Alex, Alex, Alex, always making damn promises. We wanted to publish it ourselves of course, but Evelyn wants the rights.'

'Will it be published?'

'You're so naive. They'll publish it. They'll publish it with someone else, not with Friedman and Friedman. It will be butchered or mothballed. It might never be seen. I've not even seen it myself.' He turns his back, starts walking.

'I read it, Mr Crum. I read it.'

He stops in his tracks, comes back to me. He gives me a long, lingering look, then retakes his seat. 'Please. Please. No one calls me Mr Crum except my attorney. It's BB.'

'No B?'

He cracks a smile; maybe a frown. Not dissimilar to Alex in that way. 'I took things from his studio, BB. I mean, in my head. I have a good memory. I wrote things down in my notebook. I put them into my own words. It was going to be my story but now it's as much his, isn't it?'

His eyebrows arch, meeting in the middle like an M. 'Is that right? Is that so?' He makes a pyramid of his hands on the table, searches me with his big brown eyes. 'Alex said you were a writer.'

'Not much of one,' I say, glowing because it feels as if Alex is saying it.

'Well…how much have you written?'

'Files and files in longhand. Writing was supposed to keep me sane but it's sent me in the other direction.'

'Oh, that's the way of it,' he snorts. 'I've never met a sane author yet.'

'I can't find the right title. First it's *Fakers*, then it's *Exhibit C*, then it's *Portrait of a Dog in Motion*, and I never got around to explaining that one; then it's *Ashes to Ashes* which is too painful, then *The Art of Decomposing* which was Alex's.'

He lets out a guttural sound, air jetting through flared nostrils. 'Should I stick my neck out?'

I wait for him.

'*Exhibit C* would be good.'

'But it's about fakers and dogs, not exhibits.'

'Dogs?' He looks at me quizzically. 'You really don't know, do you? Of course, I read your stories in the newspapers. Exhibit A and Exhibit B? You really don't know, do you? Well…' he laughs to himself. 'They were sold by a juror after the crash. Kicked up a stink. The public have an insatiable appetite for getting inside the head of a murderer.'

The irony strikes me. Millions reading a story that lost a competition and would have been read by a couple of thousand people, even if it had won. 'They all want a piece of me,' I say, recalling something Alex said way back. 'Those stories are a lifetime ago.' They are a life's time ago, of course.

He runs an index finger across his lower lip, thinking. 'The title will come to you. One day you will wake up and it will be staring you straight in the face. So, we'll be in touch then, Mr Tippet?'

'Ben,' I say. 'Only the police call me Tippet.'

'I remember,' he says, rising. 'Two Ps, two Ts. Well, you just keep writing your story, Ben Tippet.' We shake hands, only this time our hands are warmer, the grip is tighter.

I'm a nearly-millionaire in fifteen minutes. What was it Andy Warhol said? I don't walk so much as fly back to my cell. I'm as light as the time I floated from the taxi rank to my flat with Alex

Fortune's personal card in my pocket. Almost a year ago now. Of course, it's not the same; can never be the same. His card is confetti.

I am torn between Alex's memory and seeing myself alone in his house: throwing logs on his fire, playing his mother's Beckstein, lying in his raggedy Jacobean four-poster bed, scoffing soft-boiled eggs, writing in his studio with views of the orchard, driving his Aston Martin! Opening his gates. Swimming in his pool. I had forgotten about the exact details of Smuggler's Cottage but now they stream back to me as if I am their source. I am the only one in my mental pictures until I'm floored by the absence of Alex, no longer seeing myself in his writing studio.

He's the writer, was the writer, not me. Must keep telling myself that. The best writer of his generation. He is the reason I write anything in the first place. He is the reason for this, what you have in your hands. I want to be a writer and I don't want to be a writer. Being Ben Tippet is plenty to be getting on with. Besides, I've nearly written myself out. I have tried to get beyond him in my life, with only partial success. Ben Tippet, I think I mean.

Thirty-two

There are things and there are memories of things; which would you rather have?

I ask because two nights after BB's visit I had a vivid memory of something. A simple memory and Alex was not even in it. I'm not sure what stirred it up. I remember, it was after a creative writing class at Pensbury; way before meeting Alex at Little's Bookshop; way before the Acorn shortlist was announced; way before the fire; way before I slept with Imogen. It might have been where everything started for all I know.

I was standing in the university car park, next to a music practice room, near the English department. My Saab wouldn't start. It had only just been serviced. It was like Fawlty Towers, refusing to turn over. It was chilly and windy. Autumn was passing into winter. Maybe the car was cold, or had a cold, I don't know. I got out and clapped my hand off the bonnet in a temper. My hand was stinging. I deserved a better car than this. I deserved a better life than this. I deserved to be somebody, not just me. I needed to rise above ordinariness.

My RAC coverage had lapsed. I hate buses, so I called a cab. They said they'd be twenty minutes; a euphemism for more like forty. I could hear it in the bloke's voice. He was lying to me. He was a total faker. I had a choice; wait or walk. I'm sometimes lazy. I waited, and as each minute passed I felt an anger building up inside. An explosives wire shortening. The sun was passing down the hill to the cathedral. The sky was engraved pink and purple plane-trails. Black birds were heading deep south for breeding in an imperfect arrow. Beech leaves were blowing, getting caught by the wind and thrown into the nooks and crooks of concrete steps.

Beech leaves? There are no beech trees on campus.

It should have been a beautiful mystery but I was so angry, so wrapped up in myself and I didn't know what for. I had good health, good looks, good family etc, so why so bitter? Was it my class? My writing? My age? My car? My job? Or was it just me? Very bourgeois anxieties, Imogen would have said.

Students and lecturers poured from the English department, so many I thought there was a fire, but there wasn't. They disappeared into cars and dispersed until there was just me again. It was dusk then. The lights in the buildings went on one-by-one in no particular order.

These are the things you're supposed to remember, Imogen once told us; notice the minutiae that non-writers are blind to. 'Grow bowl-sized eyes and satellite-dish ears to capture the moment and write it down.' I'd hated hearing that because I'm a natural born voyeur (get on with it, Ben. You're near the end of your story. Where's the forward-thrusting narrative? How much forward-thrust can you fit inside a cell, so close to the end?).

That's when I heard a soft note fluttering from a high-up open window. A beautiful, beguiling note. Strings. Hairy. High but deep at the same time. A violin. The nets had the wind in their sails. I looked through the glass but couldn't see anyone inside. Only the music was visible. I didn't even like classical music back then, but this was something else. It trickled over my drums like heavenly water. I thought a siren of the sea was singing, but there was no sense of danger. No crashing rocks. It had me thinking of T.S. Eliot's *Love Song*. No mermaid ever sang for J. Alfred Prufrock.

A light came on inside and I had another peek. I blocked out the world, shielded myself from it with both hands against the glass. And what did I see? I saw only me; a clear reflection of my face; an angular, good-looking but rather empty young man. Then I saw a shadow move behind the veil. Not a human form. Just a shape. A muse? A ghost? The music kept coming, reaching a crescendo, then stopping abruptly, going right back to the beginning. After a while, the sound grew hoarse like a voice over-straining, the bow dragging along the strings slowly, mournfully, like a letter or a word catching in the throat. Finally, there was a tired exhalation. Someone or something was practising a difficult piece.

It was not the end, only a new beginning. There came the voice again, brighter and more siren-like than ever, only smoother, clearer and more pronounced. It lifted me up and put me down as if I was on a wave. It picked me up and put me down close to shore and I forgot all about my anger.

The music was constructed like a poem, in stanzas; a poem left unfinished or the poet had forgotten how to finish. It wasn't perfect, only trying to be is what I'm saying. He or she played their tune, each time building towards a resolution, a conclusion which wouldn't come. All foreplay, no orgasm. A crude way to think of it, but true. A light fingering. Elbows and thumbs. My heart spread out with the sound. It was the blind conviction of the playing; and still I couldn't see anybody, as if this was all a dream. But it couldn't be.

I sat on the kerb near the window and listened, my head cocked like a dog's. My mind ran free, just as the dog had in Tom's old diary. The leaves gushed under the tunnel of my knees like a family, brown and russet and rustling and dead. They were doing a danse macabre; a circle, a loop, just as the music was circling through and around me. It should have been beautiful, yet I was filled with an awful dread: what if I am a leaf? One of these leaves. For a second I was being blown along the ring-road of life. I was an outsider. I was actually quite dead.

But he or she or it was not going to give up their trial by notes. He or she or it would keep going until they reached the end, and I admired that. I had to keep going too. I had to stretch myself further than ever before. I had to get inside this room, come alive, metaphorically speaking. It was a metaphor for life in general (I hope I haven't over-dramatized the situation by saying that). The music stopped and the light went out, but I have never stopped thinking about it. More importantly, I have remembered it now.

This memory started a snowball rolling in my cell. Memories sticking to other memories; infinite riches in a small room. I couldn't stop the finer details emerging. Memories with not just me in them. I was Albert Camus' main character in *The Outsider*. The book Imogen said she would lend me. The novel that Maurice said I could keep. A man called Mersault is in prison for murder and keeps sane by remembering things in minute detail. He writes: *The more I think about it the more things I dig out of my memory that I hadn't noticed or that I'd forgotten about. I realized then that a man who'd only lived one day could easily live for a hundred years in a prison. He'd have enough memories...*

I should be able to conjure a million memories, a billion details from the few months I spent with Alex. Some of them I've shared with you. I don't have any decent pictures of him, except the ones stored in my head. The ones in my head are fine. They are how I remember him. The physical things I cannot touch but am touched by: an appendectomy scar milky-white across his tanned stomach; the innuendo of his eyes, the colour of wintry English clouds; long fingers like his mother, the pianist; his laugh and insinuation of a smile so orchid-rare they mean something still; the downy bumps of his bellybutton, soft segments of a plush chrysalis; his not-quite-perfect cupid's bow, very kissable; his *physiognomie*, scented cedar, rose and honey; the shape of his dome in my hands, so much pain and promise inside; the fact he sneezed whenever the sunlight caught him directly in the eyes, sneezing repeatedly as if he had an allergy to life. No photograph can hold these sorts of memories. Even if published, Alex's autobiography won't contain these things. Memories are an invisible body of work, though not invisible to me. As Saul Bellow once said, everybody needs his memories. They keep the wolf of insignificance from the door. For the one remembering, but also for the one remembered.

I could go on, but this dog has stopped running. Everything has come to an end, everything must come to an end (is this how it ends, Ben? With only you, right back at the beginning again? Too symmetrical, too neatly wrapped. What about the thready ends? They're here and there and might unravel. Is the moral to your story that crime pays? It should be the other way around).

No moral is intended. I never claimed to understand how the world works. I just hazarded a guess at it. Some people are born great, some acquire greatness, and others have greatness thrust upon them. Whatever. As Shakespeare said.

(This really is the end, Ben. Let it go).

Like in the letter?

(Like in the letter).

No more Tom? No more Bowie?

(No more Bowie).

No more Alex or Elvis?

(No more Elvis).

Just one more sentence?

(If you must. Just one. But please don't finish with "escape").

Some people never discover who they really are, they are pretending their whole lives; they are fakers and cardboards and I am not one of those; (this is cheating, Ben, you cannot end on a lie and a semicolon; a dog's cock of all things...no, you must finish on a...what exactly?...how should one end?...can one end?...on a question mark?...to myself?...)...that's not what I meant...that is not it at all...these are not my words at all...

Exhibit A:

Big Raisins
by Ben Tippet

'Are you ready?' comes the bodiless question. Miss Stone is standing behind a makeshift screen; a board on wheels which holds historical figures and scenes: Hadrian's Wall, a centurion on guard dressed in a leather skirt and helmet; Alfred the Great seated beside a fire, eating cakes; William the Conqueror, crown crooked; Harold The One Eye (I named him this and drew his eyeball on the point of a Norman arrow with dangling nerve-endings for dramatic effect); Churchill, fat cigar and v-sign.

There's movement behind the history. Miss Stone's shiny maroon shoes and smooth ankles are now in the sitting down position.

'Ready,' the kids shout.

They're up for the guessing game. They've been talking about it for days. What will we have to do? Who'll be first? Is it possible to get it wrong? Are there any prizes for guessing right? This dummo game we get in dummo class. If we're not acting something out for a stupid play like *Billy Liar* we're being acted upon. I shouldn't even be here. It's all a mistake. I should be in Latin class, but I was sick at the beginning of term and missed too much, and now I'm in with the dummos twice a week. Monday and Thursday. It's like primary school. Maybe I should tell my parents.

I'm third in line behind Ryan and Nadia. Oates is fourth, squeezing my shoulders. He pants mysteries down my neck. 'She's doing what?' I say. He gives me his mischievous grin, ear-to-ear and gummy. The teachers call it dirty but it's just Oates's way.

Ryan steps forward, disappearing behind the screen, emerging a moment later, wide-eyed and rolling his tongue inside a flushed cheek. He has a wisdom needs taking out he said, but he's too young for a wisdom. 'What d'you get?' Oates asks and Ryan shrugs his shoulders, unreadable expression, retaking his seat.

'Next!'

Nadia rushes forward, disappearing, and the guessing line shuffles forward. She strides out seconds later, smacking her lips deliberately loud. Some of the boys want to kiss those lips. They talk about it all of the time. Oates nudges me into pole position. 'Go on,' he says. 'Get in there.' It's like going to confession at St. Mark's only not so dark and scary, and there's nothing to confess and there's no priest or holy grid. It's just the feeling's the same. Almost fear. The unknown.

Miss Stone is sitting in her usual high-backed chair, tanned legs crossed. She's got decent legs for an older woman though no one knows how old her legs are. She's unmarried. Maybe thirty. Quite old. They reach right up to her bum which is quite holdable. There's a bowl of secret things under a tea towel on the table beside her. I've never seen the table before. Maybe it's hers. She gestures to take the stool next to her and slips a blindfold over my eyes making my lashes curl. The elastic pinches the hairs on the back of my neck.

'Open wide,' she says. I tilt my head back, parting my teeth. 'I want you to taste, go back to your desk and describe.' I nod, sweaty palms on my lap. 'Tongue,' she says in her sing-song voice. I stretch it into the air. There's morning fur on it and the thought makes my face beam. I touch her finger first and playful sniggers rise over the screen as if we are actually visible. Something rustles. A wrapper? A packet? I sense the presence of nothing just before something touches the tips of my teeth, then my searching tongue.

'A tiny taste,' she whispers.

It's not hard. Not soft. A mystery. I bite down but it's gone and there's soft rustling again. 'That's it,' she says, pulling the blindfold free. The lights are blinding. 'Done. Fini. Over,' she says, smiling.

'Aren't we supposed to eat something, Miss?'

'Next!' she balls, so loud it drums my ears. I re-emerge, walk the line of eyes. Oates tugs my shirt so hard a button pings right off, rolling under a desk. 'Did you get a banana?'

'A banana?' It's all a mystery. I sit at my desk and try to remember what the taste was. What it felt like. It's nothing easy. I look down at my exercise book, the title at the top of the page:

My Senses.

Nothing. Senseless. Empty. Done. Fini. Over. Before I've even started.

Ten minutes on, everyone's had their taste-buds challenged. They're chewing their conclusions over, licking them off their lips. Miss Stone drags the screen to the far wall where it belongs, and the class natters. The kids scrawl with inky pens. Everyone's scribbling except me and Oates. I look at my empty page, then down at his. 'What did you get?'

He's staring point-blank at Miss Stone, trance-like. 'You first,' he says, turning his face, eyes darting left-right-left, scanning mine. He's thinking something important. That crooked smile.

'Dunno,' I say. 'A sultana?'

His grin splits in two, showing chipped teeth. His knees knock, thighs locking around the leg of the desk. Miss Stone glares. Her hair seems very red today. 'You two,' she says, 'you're worse than Laurel and Hardy. Now concentrate, Philip. I'm going to ask you first.'

'Me?' Blood pumps my face. 'I don't know what it was.'

'Just describe it in words. Someone else can do the guessing. Think taste, smell, texture.'

'Smell? Texture? I'm not sure it had any of those.'

Oates whispers in my ear, 'Fanny.' I shrug his hand from my shoulder. 'I could see over the blindfold,' he says.

'Liar.'

'I could see everything in the bowl. There was a packet or Revels, grapes, slices of banana, oranges, apples, tomatoes. There was even an onion.'

'An onion?'

'Some sod got an onion. Imagine that? Raw onion. But you know an onion when you taste it, don't you?'

'Were there any raisins?'

He shakes his head.

'You didn't see nothing.'

Oates plants an elbow on my desk, rests his chin in the heel of his hand tapping his bony head with his grubby fingers. 'She pulled the blindfold down too far. I could move it with my eyebrows.'

'You saw everything in a millisecond?'

'Two minutes!' Miss Stone shouts.

It spreads down my legs, up my spine and down again. Fear? Excitement? Electricity? 'Tell me. What did you get?'

'Banana,' Oates says. He's watching Miss Stone's every move. 'A boring bloody banana. I could describe that with my friggin eyes shut.' He rattles his desk. 'Get it? Eyes shut? Blindfold?'

He lurches forward suddenly, snatching up his pen. Miss Stone bounds towards us and I stretch an arm across my desk, hiding my empty page. She wags a finger, then returns to the front of the class. Oates watches her religiously; that lost expression he gets in her lesson, the only lesson he never misses. 'Did you smell her perfume?' he says, taking a full breath and holding it in. All I can smell is Oates's chip-fag breath and his older brother's aftershave. It's not such a bad smell. Freshly- sawn pine and soapy lemons.

Miss Stone pulls open a drawer, takes out a box of chalk, rattles it twice, opens the lid and shakes multi-coloured fingernails into her hand. Oates gets animated, pointing to the wooden shelf attached to the board. 'New chalk over there, Miss!'

'Thank you, Paul,' she says. 'What eagle-eyes.' The class look at him, amazed, as if they hadn't known he was called Paul.

She bends down to pick up a stick, tweed knee-length skirt no longer knee-length, parting at the top of her rear zipper. Oates's thighs clamp the table-leg. 'Thank you, Miss,' he mumbles, more like groans. She scratches purple lines across the board which make my hairs stand up. She forms a perfect grid and in big bold capital letters writes: SMELL, TEXTURE, FLAVOUR.

Oates laughs into his sleeve.

'Ssshhh!' She taps her watch and I scan the room. Wall-to-wall smiling faces and folded arms. Everyone's finished; even Oates. What a speller. *Mushey Bannarna* he's written. Thick as a proverbial brick, but he's the wise-guy today.

'Were there any prunes?'

Oates's eyeballs swell. 'Prunes? There weren't any friggin prunes.'

The chalk squeals on the board. Miss Stone's drawing large question marks. The metal strap of her watch slaps against her wrist. Oates tucks his face right inside mine, mouth gaping, taunting me. He rubs his hands in anticipation. 'Hurry up, Philip. She's gonna ask you first.'

'Right,' shrills Miss Stone.

Something squirts from my stomach to my fingers to my bits. I don't want to look stupid. 'Oatesy,' I hiss through my teeth, 'what was in the bowl?'

'Nuh,' he says, as if he's paying me back for a lifetime's humiliation.

'Some friend you are.'

Miss Stone folds her arms. 'Philip?'

I drop my head, scribbling on my bare page: W*rinkly, rubbery. Not hard. Not soft. Big Raisin.* Oates leans over, reading it. He rocks back and forth in his seat holding his sides together because they're splitting.

'What have you got, Philip?'

I look around the classroom for help.

'Not hard, not soft,' I say.

Oates yelps.

'More detail,' she says.

I'm thinking how stupid I am, how inadequate my words are, how ugly Oatesy can be at times, when it breaks. A long, rattling ring vibrating on the wall above the board; more ringing down the corridor outside. Oates jolts upright in his seat as if plugged into the mains. Neck rigid, fingers clenched. 'Fire drill, Miss.' She stares at the alarm as if it might dance off the wall.

'All stand!'

Chairs screech across the floor. She forces the emergency doors open. 'Hurry up. Out you go.' She sweeps us onto the tennis courts, motions us like a lollypop lady guiding toddlers to pre-school.

'But your nice coat, Miss,' Nadia says, teasing her well-brushed hair. 'It'll go up in flames.'

'Is there a real fire, Miss?'

'Hooray!' Ryan screams. 'The school's burning down.'

'This isn't a dress rehearsal. Out you go!'

We file up in alphabetical order, teeth jaddering, eyes watering in the wind, ears buzzing with bells. Above our heads, pouring from the kitchen roof, is a pall of grey-black smoke which smells of spoiled gravy. 'Humans cooking,' Oates says. 'The staff barbecue.' The thought makes my spine tingle. A week ago, at the council bonfire, I saw a family of hedgehogs burning. There were four of them. Two big ones and two small ones. They hadn't even tried to escape. They hadn't run or crawled or whatever hedgehogs do. They just huddled together as if ignoring the flames would make them disappear, and I remember thinking, do hedgehogs make wishes?

Miss Stone brushes along the line, tapping the tops of our heads with her fingertips. She whispers our names, ticks us off on her clipboard, then rejoins the teachers at the side of the court. Head Teacher, Mr Poole, tells everyone to be quiet but Oates leans forward and whispers hot words in my ear, 'See that?' He's following the smoke with his eyes; smoke trailing across the sky towards the estate where we both live. At least, I think he is.

'See what?' I feel the needle-point of his elbow digging into the small of my back.

'Miss Stone,' he hisses.

I look at her. She's rubbing her bare arms which have goose-bumps running up and down like hills. 'What about her?'

'Look,' he says. 'Look. Look.'

She makes little jumps, stamps her feet on the tarmac. She blows into the balls of her hands, breathing out freezing speech bubbles.

'Look!' he says, standing on tip-toe. I stare where Oates stares but I don't know what at. He shakes his head in exasperation. 'Look, you blind lummox.'

'Where?'

'Do I have to spell it out?'

A straightened finger emerges from his holey jumper, bolting like an arrow towards Miss Stone's nipples. I follow the trajectory, coming across them for the first time, or so it seems, from a distance.

'Big raisins,' Oates sniggers, and I join him.

Exhibit B:

Me and You
by Ben Tippet

I was going to the shops. I was going to the shops *alone* until Joe
showed up. I tried to hide by leaning into the doorway.
    "Where you going?"
    Shit. "Taking my coat back to the shop," I said.
    "That's strange. So am I," he said.
    I was taken by the coat Joe was wearing. It looked so much like
mine. Long, black and shiny. He looked at my coat and then he
looked at his. Then he opened my coat to look at the lining and I
opened his, to look at his. It was the same.
    "Lets the rain in."
    "It does," I said.
    "Taking it back."
    "Me too," I said.
    "We can kill two birds with one stone."
    We walked up Gladstone Road past Victorian terraces and
detached modern homes where ancient orchards used to be. The
rain started to pour. "Fucking coat!" Joe snapped, flipping his
collar up to protect his swan-like neck.
    "Fucking rain. Fucking coat," I snapped back.
    "It cost me a fortune," he said. "And it won't resist a fucking
drop."
    "Mine's the same," I said. "Not a fucking drop."
    "What's the point of having a raincoat that doesn't stop the
rain?"
    "My point exactly," I replied. "Look, it's on my jumper already."
    "Nice jumper."

"Thank you," I said. "It's a present from Nena." I looked closely at his jumper. It was the same as mine.

We reached the railway bridge and ran up the steps to watch a train pass underneath. It shook the metal rail we were holding.

"Going places," Joe said.

"It is."

At that moment, Joe turned and ran back to the steps. A large woman was struggling with her pram. The toddler inside looked like he'd been sleeping but the lifting motion woke him. Under the woman's coat was another baby, still inside her belly. I'd seen her before, but she had a name I couldn't get hold of.

"Thank you for helping," she said. She gave me a funny look. "You alright?"

"No, all left," I said and Joe laughed.

"Where are you going?" she said.

"That's easy," said Joe. "We're going to return our coats to the shop that sold us them."

"What shop?"

"I don't know its name," Joe said. "It's the one by McDonald's, next to the clock tower."

"Oh," she said. "And what's wrong with your coat?"

"It's the fucking rain, Mrs Bloggs."

She frowned. The toddler's fingers emerged from his blanket like a pink spider, pointing up to the sky. She followed the fingers with her eyes, sighing, "It never rains but it pours."

"The rain in Spain falls mainly on the brain," I said.

She gave me the funny look, then she pulled an umbrella from the back of the pram and opened it. Some of the spokes refused to straighten. They looked like buckled legs, barely holding onto their flowery fabric.

"That's a shitty umbrella," I said. "Did you get it from the coat shop?"

"Everything shuts early on a Sunday," she said. "We're in a hurry."

We helped lift the pram down the steps at the far end of the bridge and she rushed towards Dane John Gardens, toddler howling like a siren.

"She's not Mrs Bloggs," I said.

"I know," Joe said, "but I call the people whose names I've forgotten, Mrs Bloggs or Mr Bloggs."

I stared at him.

"I nearly called you Mr Bloggs a few minutes ago, until I remembered your name."

"Bloody good job," I huffed. "I've known you for years."

"Twenty-one, " he said.

"Come on," I said. "Let's get to the shop before I drown in my own coat."

"He-he," he said. "Drown in our own coat."

We stood at the kerb of the ring road beside a busy roundabout, at the edge of the city. Drivers tooted their horns and shook their fists each time we stepped out. They were screaming obscenities out of their windows. But what can you do, I said to Joe, when it's so busy?

"Use the fuckin' underpass, arse!" yelled a man in a white van.

"Fuck off!" shouted Joe. He jumped into the middle of the traffic. Cars screeched to a halt. He could have been Clint Eastwood in *A Fistful of Dollars*, coat flapping like a poncho, hands hovering at his holster.

The man in the van unlocked his seatbelt. Joe pulled out his gun and drew, left palm cocking the hammer, right index squeezing the trigger: "Pow! Pow! Pe-Pow Pow!" The bullets rained, spraying the bastard dead. He blew smoke from the barrel and strolled with a swagger to the opposite kerb. I heard a heavy clunk and then a gravelly shout:

"Come 'ere!"

"But I shot you dead!" shouted Joe.

"Zombie!" I shouted back. "Leg it!"

Joe raced across the grass verge and into the bus station. I chased, heart banging, not slowing until we reached the safety of the high city walls. We looked down onto the road. The Zombie was getting back into his white van. We cheered and he looked up, giving us the big V.

"You're nuts," I puffed, leaning on the flint wall.

"Yep," Joe said. "Nutty as a fruit cake don't you know."

"A fruit cake does not by definition have nuts in, does it?"

"It might," he said. "My mum has nuts in her fruit cakes."

"Joe," I said, "you haven't got a mum, remember?"

"You're right," he said, "we should get to the shop before we drown in our coats."

We kicked our way through discarded McDonald's cartons, passing the clock tower. We stood shoulder to shoulder outside Coats 'R' Us. The lights were on but nobody was in. The double-doors rattled in our hands. We peered through the window at the raincoats. Hundreds, hanging on rails, all the bloody same as ours. Joe got on his hands and knees and shouted through the letterbox: "Your coats are no fucking good!" He got up and peered in again.

I got down on my hands and knees and shouted: "I'll second that!"

"Can I help you?"

A policeman was standing behind us, rain bouncing off his nipple hat.

"PC Bloggs," Joe said, "we're pissed off with this shop."

"Oh, we are, are we?"

"We are," I said. "And if you had a coat from this shop, you'd be on your hands and knees blowing some air through the letterbox."

The policeman's radio crackled. A policewoman must have been connected by a piece of string at the other end, mouth inside a tin can; the way it sounded: "Suspected...*crackle*...shop...*crackle*...seen leaving...*crackle*...Street."

Joe's eyes bulged. "Suspected shop seen leaving the street," he squeaked through his fingers.

PC Bloggs tilted his head forwards. Water rolled around the rim of his hat, down his nose and into his radio set, which might explain all the crackling. "Repeat street. Over."

"Castle...*crackle*...Street. Over," the stringy lady said.

"Crackle Street. Over the rainbow. Over," I said.

"Go home," said PC Bloggs. "Bring your gripe back tomorrow."

Joe spluttered. I saw what he saw, like telepathy. Us walking through the swinging doors, shop manager rustling his hands through the raincoats, Joe wading in, hands full of tripe.

"That's funny, is it?" the policeman said, tipping back his sodden hat.

"Yeah," sniffed Joe.

"If you are here when I get back, I'll have you in the cells. Now hop it!"

We did exactly that, up the cobbled High Street, looking back over our shoulders now and then. PC Bloggs was doing his version of Clint Eastwood, hands at hips, steely stare. *A Fistful of Collars.*

Joe grinned. "Should of socked him."

"Who? Me?"

"Me and you," he said. "We're so identical he'd never know which one did it."

"We're like telepathic twins," I said. "We could feel the same things but be on different sides of the world."

Joe turned. For a second, it was like looking at my reflection in a shop window, but I understood that his left was my right and my right was his left. Sinister and dexter, depending on where you stood. We couldn't be exactly the same.

"I can tell how you are feeling right now," he said.

I waited.

"Fucking wet," he said.

We trudged through town, socks like sponges, fingers rigid as icicles in the caves of our pockets. We had no money but it didn't matter, the shops had closed. And anyway, we were tired of the funny looks from retiring city workers and stragglers. The don't care in the communities. We sat in Dane John Gardens, not a soul around. I wondered about the pregnant woman. Darkness was falling. The lime trees creaked against the wind like arthritic giants. The base of the water fountain looked like a carefully carved grapefruit, juice spouting from its core, pushing up through the gravy rain. Georgian buildings loomed behind it like long faces. Sparrows were fighting over a half-eaten sandwich left on top of an over-loaded bin, and my belly rumbled.

"Home?" said Joe.

"The home," I said.

We raced each other, scrambling up steep muddy banks to the top of the medieval walls. Joe nodded his signal and we climbed up from the path to the battlements, arms outstretched, feet scraping and slipping along the curves of the stones, glare of the city lights in our eyes. Motorists bibbed and flashed, as if that would stop us.

At an impassable turret, we jumped down and crossed the Off-The-Wall bridge close to Pensbury station. Passengers were streaming out of the entrance like leaks from a cracked dam. They were looking at their watches and gathering their heavy bags and flashing open their umbrellas and turning up their collars and tipping their heads down. We were leaves going backwards in the flood until Joe broke free and I followed him down to Wincheap.

The rain fell in sheets. Cars filed along the street, headlights blinding, wipers swishing. Water slipped down the slatted gutters like brown glue. We took shelter under a railway bridge and a train vibrated overhead. Recycled whisky hung in the stale, pissy air. Two drunkies had their backs against the wall, purple heads bowed.

"Ahm alright," groaned one. "Just bin mixin' wi' the wrong sort of drinks."

"Don't worry ole fella," his shadow replied, holding onto the bricks. "There's light at the end o' the tumbler."

"At the end of the tunnel, you loser," Joe said.

"Not ready to go back yet," I said. "Don't want to go back."

"We could go to Martyrs' Field?"

"Tomatoes' Field?"

Joe forced a smile. We bent our heads and leaned into each other, merging as we walked.

Martyrs' Field was not much of a park, but we had it to ourselves. The junkies and drunkies didn't like the rain. Hard frosts and freezing gales couldn't shake them, but for people who were never dry, they sure hated getting wet.

We sat on a slippery bench. Joe lit a cigarette and looked up at the monument to burnt Protestants. Then he looked down at the dog shit and the broken glass scattered at its foot. "What do you think it's like to burn?" he said.

I took a drag from the cigarette and handed it back. "Hot."

"Yeah hot, but what kind of hot?"

"The kind of hot you can only imagine."

He shook his head, spraying rain onto my shoulder. "Like a fagburn?"

"A hundred times worse, Joe. All over your skin. Your hair would crackle. Your eyes would melt like balls of wax."

Joe stroked his eyelids.

I got up from the bench and walked around the cold, grey monolith. There was enough light to read the names of Bland, Sole, Waterer, Fishcock, Albright and Final. *Lest We Forget*, it said.

The hallway light was blazing.

"You can come in," I said. "No one's gonna bite your head off."

Joe shrugged and looked up and down the street as if in two minds. I put the key in the lock, but the door seemed to open by itself.

"Joe!"

It was Nena. She was standing in the doorway, in her prettiest dress. She was munching an apple. Her silky dark hair was pulled tight around pink rollers. "You're in big trouble," she said. "Mrs Watts found some stuff in the bottom of your wardrobe."

My heart stopped. My stomach dropped. My diary. My letters. My thoughts. They were all in there. All in a box. All in a box in my wardrobe. Were. *Mrs Watts is a cunt. Jimmy is a fucking drunk. Joan's a skinny runt who puked herself to death. Robert is a junkie fuck. Mr Watts is a buggering paedophile.* All the things I said about everyone in the home, including Nena. A sheet for each freak.

I searched her eyes for clues. I sloped inside and stood with my back against the banisters. Rainwater pooled around my shoes. Nena closed the door. The stairs creaked, and I looked up. Mrs Watts was standing on the top stair, my note paper in her hand, my empty bottle of red Smarties in the other. She took a step down.

In slow-motion, I saw her falling, down each step rolling. She lay at my feet in a viscous pool of red, my sheets of paper flapping in the air like a halo of doves. In my head she was, but in my eyes she wasn't, and they weren't, and I was as small as a mouse.

She said nothing at first. Nothing to add to her raw expression. She reached the bottom step. My head was hanging down like it weighed too much. "You haven't taken your prescription today, Joe." It was cold and clinical, just like my decision to flush the pills down the bog.

I was happy enough as two or three people. They came in and out of my life like friends through a door. Sometimes too angry, sometimes too friendly, but they kept me alive. Sometimes, we'd walk into the city, if we could all sneak past Mrs Watts. You see, these friends of mine, they never shut up. It's like they have too much going on up top. Too much to say. When we're all together, it's like a noisy party. I have to shout to be heard. And that's when I get the funny looks. But anything is better than being a Comalone. My name for it; what the pills did to me. They made me a sleepy Joe. A dry-mouthed Joe. A too frightened to go out in the bright sun Joe. Alone Joe. Lone. Joe. I was just an ordinary-looking man, twenty-one, and I was wondering where the key was and where the door was.

"There's a cake for you," said Nena. "It's in the kitchen."

Mrs Watts brushed by, cardigan swinging, smell of tobacco from her husband's pipe swirling around her fat shoulders.

I looked at Nena and she smiled. "I made it specially," she said.

Nena, the fruit in my nutty cake. She was the only thing in the house I wanted to taste but could not bring myself to. Everything I thought about her, all the deep and scary, dark and beautiful things were trapped inside my head, and on a page. She was watching me, waiting for me to go into the kitchen, big brown eyes open wide. I searched them for knowledge, for a change, but it wasn't there.

The cake was a circle of white, twenty-one candles dotted around the edge like the markings on a clock face. In the centre, pink icing curls made three letters: **Joe**. Mrs Watts sat down, sighing. She placed the paper on the table in front of her, fingers resting on it. She stared out of the window into the backyard. The washing on the line was slapping itself in the wind. Tea towels, jeans, shirts, and Nena's knickers. Mr Watts's Mondeo was parked underneath. Then I saw him. His red face staring out from behind the rain-splattered windscreen.

"I'm going to burn these," said Mrs Watts. "I'm going to burn these like they were never written."

Nena's hand hovered over her mouth as if she was going to laugh.

"I'm not even going to ask why," said Mrs Watts. It was almost a whisper. "Because there can't be a good enough reason."

"Cut the cake," said Nena, rushing to the table. "No, wait, I've got to light the candles first." She ran out. I heard her feet thumping up the stairs.

"Mr Watts will never forgive you," she said. "You couldn't be crueller if you tried."

I knew then that I'd be moving on. Not for the first time. If only I'd taken the bloody pills. If I just said sorry.

"Fuck it," Joe blurted. "Fuck, fuck, fuck, fuck, fuck, FUCK!"

Mrs Watts dragged a hand across her eyes. I saw her husband opening the door of his car, a boot treading in a puddle. Nena bounced in, flicking a lighter on and off. She leaned into the cake and sparked all the candles to life. She stood next to me, eyes sparkling. "Hurry up, Joe. Wait! Wait! Make a wish!"

I did. I was tearing the paper up with Mrs Watts's hands.

I bent over and blew so hard there was no air left in me. Nena clapped, then squeezed my arm. The smoke from the wicks hung like a cloud over the table. A beautiful, beautiful smell. Sweet, beautiful smell. Next to Nena's skin, it was the best smell in the world.

"Twenty-one," said Nena. "I'm sorry they're not all the same colour. I had to mix and match." She pecked my cheek like a bird, a bird from paradise. The back door creaked, and Mrs Watts frowned at me.

"Fuck."

"Be quiet, Joe," I said.

Mr Watts came in. He turned his back on me at first, throwing his flat cap next to the mugs on the drainer. He opened a tap and rinsed his hands. Mrs Watts looked over her shoulder at him.

"You've been cheating," he said to me, wiping his hands dry. "You've been lying." His voice grew louder each time he spoke.

"Fuck you!"

"Joe!" I said. "Keep out!"

Mr Watts snatched the paper out of his wife's hands. Bash, strangle, cut, burn him, Joe was saying. Shoot him, shoot him dead! My heart was pumping and I lunged. If I'd had a knife it would have pierced his heart and nailed it to the wall.

"No, no," he said, pulling away. "We've got to hear this masterpiece."

"Gordon!" Mrs Watts pleaded. "Not with Nena in the room."

Nena stared at me.

Mr Watts licked his finger and thumbed through the sheets, reading lines one by one. Each word punched and pushed the emptiness around inside me. He was coming to Nena.

"None of it is real," I said, but she clapped her hands over her ears.

He read and read. Words from another planet. Words from an alien nation. A male alien nation for all I knew. My ears buzzed. Nena started to hum, louder and louder, then she stopped. It was over and there was silence.

Mr Watts placed the paper on the table and patted his wife's shoulder. Her face was ashen, her bottom lip lightly trembling. Nena slumped against the wall, staring at her feet. She looked up and caught my eye briefly, then turned her face away. Her face. It looked like something had been stripped from it.

So weighted with water was I, so much water waiting, I could barely see my way to the table. I collected up my thoughts, my written feelings, turned my back and trudged the stairs three floors to my room; my symptom-attic. I peeled off my useless coat and let it fall to the floor. I sat on the edge of the newly-made old bed, staring at the circles I'd worn into the carpet. I folded up my thoughts carefully and placed them in my box. I lay the box inside the wardrobe and closed it.

He was waiting for me inside the mirror on the door. Distorted, fragmented. An image of a man through rain-swept glass.

"Freak," he said.

"Freak," I said.

"Freak," we said.

The air was heavy.

I crossed the carpet to the dormer window and opened it as wide as it would go. The winter air poured in. It smelt different. The birds were singing as if they sensed a change. Leading away from the house in blurred lines, the amber street lamps seemed to beat a path from the city into the dark, like a runway.

"We're leaving," I said.

"What?" said Joe.

"Me and you, Joe Bloggs."

I waited for a reply, but Joe didn't say a word. He didn't have to. I already knew what he was thinking.

Acknowledgements

A huge debt of gratitude goes to my wife, Janice, without whom this journey would not have been possible, nor as worthwhile. She read countless drafts without once complaining. Her input is incalculable.

Many thanks to my sister, Angela, for advice regarding legal lexicon and criminal court procedures; any apparent lapses or exaggerations remaining are for fictional purposes and entirely of my own making.

Gratitude is extended to Patricia Debney who offered me so much encouragement when I first started writing fiction, and still does.

The same goes to my good friend, Craig Dadds, who in many ways has travelled along the road with me.

Thanks to my brother, Eamon, who introduced me to David Bowie's music when I was an impressionable child.

Thanks to Henry Wrenn-Meleck at RZO/Tintoretto Music, New York, for his assistance regarding David Bowie's lyrics.

Finally, thanks to Anthony at bluechrome, for taking Ben Tippet on.

AFM